D0971538

REVOLVER

ALSO BY DUANE SWIERCZYNSKI

Canary

Secret Dead Men

The Wheelman

The Blonde

Severance Package

Expiration Date

THE CHARLIE HARDIE TRILOGY

Fun and Games

Hell and Gone

Point and Shoot

THE LEVEL 26 TRILOGY (WITH ANTHONY E. ZUIKER)

Dark Origins

Dark Prophecy

Dark Revelations

REVOLVER

DUANE SWIERCZYNSKI

MULHOLLAND BOOKS

Little, Brown and Company
New York Boston London

Copyright © 2016 by Duane Swierczynski

All rights reserved. In accordance with the U.S. Copyright Act of 1976, the scanning, uploading, and electronic sharing of any part of this book without the permission of the publisher constitute unlawful piracy and theft of the author's intellectual property. If you would like to use material from the book (other than for review purposes), prior written permission must be obtained by contacting the publisher at permissions@hbgusa.com. Thank you for your support of the author's rights.

Mulholland Books/Little, Brown and Company
Hachette Book Group
1290 Avenue of the Americas
New York, NY 10104
mulhollandbooks.com

First Edition: July 2016

Mulholland Books is an imprint of Little, Brown and Company, a division of Hachette Book Group, Inc. The Mulholland Books name and logo are trademarks of Hachette Book Group, Inc.

The publisher is not responsible for websites (or their content) that are not owned by the publisher.

The Hachette Speakers Bureau provides a wide range of authors for speaking events. To find out more, go to hachettespeakersbureau.com or call (866) 376-6591.

Map by Mark Adams and Jason Killinger of Eyes Habit (eyeshabit.com)

Library of Congress Cataloging-in-Publication Data
Names: Swierczynski, Duane, author.
Title: Revolver / Duane Swierczynski.
Description: First edition. | New York: Mulholland Books / Little, Brown and Company, 2016.
Identifiers: LCCN 2016010145 | ISBN 978-0-316-40323-8 (hardcover)
Subjects: LCSH: Police—Pennsylvania—Philadelphia—Fiction. | Cold cases (Criminal investigation)—Fiction. | Police—Crimes against—Fiction. | Murder—Investigation—Fiction. | BISAC: FICTION / Suspense. | FICTION / Mystery & Detective / General. | GSAFD: Suspense fiction. | Mystery fiction.
Classification: LCC PS3619.W53 R49 2016 | DDC 813/.6—dc23 LC record available at https://lccn.loc.gov/2016010145

10 9 8 7 6 5 4 3 2 1

RRD-C

Printed in the United States of America

*In memory of
Philadelphia police officer
Joseph T. Swierczynski
1892–1919*

CONTENTS

CONTENTS

CONTENTS

AUDREY'S
PHILADELPHIA

Locations from
Duane Swierczynski's REVOLVER

Center City, Fairmount, Queen Village, Kensington, Fishtown,
Southwark, North Philly, The Midway/Gayborhood

Frankford, Mayfair, Rhawnhurst, Pennypack Park

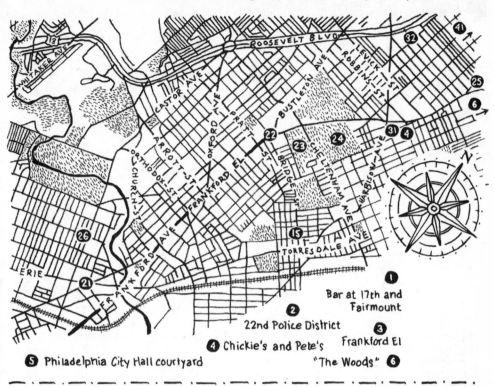

1. Bar at 17th and Fairmount
2. 22nd Police District
3. Frankford El
4. Chickie's and Pete's
5. Philadelphia City Hall courtyard
6. "The Woods"

1965

7. 22nd and Columbia: flashpoint of the Columbia Ave Riots
8. Girard College
9. 13th and Berks: riot staging area
10. Divine Lorraine Hotel
11. Cadillac Club
12. Columbia Avenue, between Broad and 18th, "The Gold Coast"
13. Connie Mack Stadium
14. Drug Deal Apartment
15. Stan's House (1965 and 1995)
16. 226 Queen Street

1995

17. The Palm
18. Pen and Pencil Club
19. Circa
20. Locust Room
21. Erie Torresdale Station
22. Bridge Street Terminal
23. Cedar Hill Cemetery
24. Wissonoming Park
25. The Walczak House (1995 and 2015)
26. Stanton's Halfway House
27. The Jogger's Apartment
28. The Murder Scene
29. Metropolitan Magazine
30. DeHaven's Apartment
31. Mugsy's Tavern

2015

32. Acme
33. McGillin's Olde Ale House
34. The Roundhouse
35. 30th Street Station
36. Memorial Buffet
37. Will's Apt
38. Free Library of Philadelphia, Central Branch
39. Pennsylvania Hospital
40. The Kaminski House
41. St. Matthew's Church
31. The Grey Lodge Pub

Who stole the keeshka?
Someone call a cop

—*The Matys Brothers*

REVOLVER

STAN WALCZAK

May 7, 1965

Officer Stanisław "Stan" Walczak usually takes his beer by the gallon, but he's taking it easy this hot spring afternoon. He uses the backs of his thick fingers to wipe away the sweat beading up on his forehead. It's seventy-two degrees and very humid. His Polish blood can't stand the humidity.

He looks over at his partner, George W. Wildey. Unlike Stan, Wildey rarely breaks a sweat. He also hardly ever drinks. But after the week they've had, George said a cold one was most definitely in order. Stan couldn't agree more.

They're in plain clothes, but anybody setting foot in the bar would immediately tag them as cops. No white guy ever hangs out with a black guy in North Philly unless they're undercover fuzz.

Technically, both are shirking duty.

A dozen blocks away, protestors are surrounding Girard College, and Stan and George are supposed to be there to help keep order. Over 130 years ago the richest man in Philadelphia willed most of his considerable fortune to establish a school for "poor, white, male" orphans on the outskirts of the city. Over the next 100 years, neighborhoods rose up around the campus. The neighborhood changed from German to Irish to Jewish and finally to black, even as the students of Girard College remained poor, white, and male.

After *Brown v. Board of Education,* however, blacks began to fight for their seats in the classroom. Picketing by the NAACP began seven days ago, and the commissioner dispatched a thousand police to the scene to make sure nothing got out of hand. The last thing the city wants is another riot like that clusterfuck on Columbia Avenue last August.

Stan and George were assigned to the protests from the very first day. Punishment detail, best they can figure. They must have pissed off someone high up. But despite fears of another riot, nothing has really happened. A few jokers trying to scale the twenty-foot wall onto the campus, but that's been it. Otherwise, just a lot of standing around and waiting. Stan is pretty sure nobody will miss them.

"Still taking Jimmy to the game tonight?" George asks.

"That's the plan," Stan replies.

"I don't know about the Phils," George says. "It's the Cards. World Champs. Phillies are gonna have to figure out something new this time around."

"They'll do all right."

"You forget the Cards still have Simmons and Sadecki?"

"And we got Dick Allen and Tony Taylor, who's the best second baseman in the game," Stan says, thick finger bouncing on the bar top to emphasize each syllable. "You wanna talk lefties, look at Covington."

"Sure, but you're talking about the same team that made twenty-two errors over the last twelve games. That ain't good."

"They've been on the road. We got ten home games ahead of us."

"Dreamer."

Stan has nothing to say to that. He just wants his boy Jimmy to see a good game, recapture some of that feeling from last August when the Phils were unbeatable and the whole city felt like it mattered. Something to look forward to, instead of another summer of dread. He half-drains his beer, reminding himself to take it slow. After all, he has all day to drink.

"Lemme put something on the box," George says after a while.

Stan nods. "Sure, whatever."

The taproom is dead quiet. It's just the two of them, plus two winos in the back, each at his own table. The ancient barkeep wipes down the top of the bar, lifts their beers for a swipe, places them back down, never once making eye contact. The rag smells like industrial bleach.

A thought occurs to Stan. He half-spins on his stool, calls out, "Hey, none of that soul shit."

"Come on," George says with a big smile. "You love the soul shit."

Secretly, Stan thinks some of that soul shit isn't half bad. But he wouldn't tell anyone that. Least of all his partner.

George drops the quarter, presses a button. Metal panels, three records on each, a loud metallic *flap* with every push. There's a shockingly diverse mix on this machine, George thinks, as if this juke can't make up its mind if it's in a black bar or a white bar. George makes his selection with a three-number button punch. After a few sips Stan hears Solomon Burke over the tinny speakers. "Got to Get You Off My Mind."

Stan shakes his head and smiles. Taps his fingers on the bar top like it's a piano.

"Don't worry, Stanny boy," George says, searching for his final selection, "I've got something special for you coming up next."

"Yeah, I'm sure."

Flap. Flap. Flap.

"So what's Jimmy listening to these days? He's the only one with taste in the family."

Stan's boy Jimmy wants to be a professional musician when he grows up. He's twelve and already pretty good with the guitar, even though he walks around the house playing the same riffs over, and over, and over again. Just like all the bands he listens to.

"He's also listening to some other British group now. The Clinks?"

"Heh heh. The Kinks, man."

5

Stan knows that George's son Junior wants to be a musician, too. But he hasn't gotten around to settling on an instrument yet. That's this whole next generation, George said a few weeks back. They all want to be in bands, don't want to put in the work.

I know, Solomon Burke croons, *it's just a matter of time.*

George walks back across the tiled floor, then eases his frame back onto his stool, takes a sip of his beer. "Don't know how you drink this shit all the time."

"Only way I can put up with you," Stan says.

Their snitch is running late. Terrill Lee asked them to meet him here, at this taproom on the corner of Seventeenth and Fairmount.

Stan and George have worked this general neighborhood for the past nine months but have never set foot in this place. They aren't the kind of partners who drink on the job. And the Twenty-Second keeps them plenty busy; it isn't Whitetown.

This taproom has no name. It's a shotgun bar, long and narrow, with a front entrance on Fairmount and a side entrance that most likely used to be marked FOR LADIES. A working-class bar that straddles two neighborhoods, white and black. Maybe that's why their snitch picked it. Make both Stan and George feel comfortable.

Stan wishes they'd arranged to meet someplace else.

"Say our man tells us something," George says. "He tells us something, what are we gonna do about it? And who do we tell?"

"This is going to bring a shitstorm down on our heads, you know that."

"That's what I'm saying, we cross that line, and—"

George stops speaking as the front door opens. A burst of harsh sunlight blasts the bar, hot air funnels in. Could be their man.

Nope. Not their man.

This man is a tall and doughy guy in dirty jeans, carrying a hard hat. He pulls the door closed behind him. He hesitates in the vestibule, doing his own reconnaissance. He looks at Stan and George—white guy, black guy—then turns around and leaves. More bright sun, more hot air. The door slams shut.

"Guess he doesn't want to drink with an ugly Polack."

"Or an ugly *murzyn*."

"I am a black Adonis, my friend."

Stan laughs but not for real. Been hard to really laugh these days.

"So what are we gonna do, George?"

"Well, we gotta do *something*. We can agree on that much, right? Can't just pretend none of this shit is happening We gotta take it all the way."

"Yeah," Stan says quietly.

They sip their beers. Even George has to admit there's a certain comfort in an ice-cold beer on a hot August day. His daddy would do a 360 in his grave if he saw his son drinking a cold beer. The bartender, nothing else to do, cleans off some of the bottles of rail liquor.

You've found somebody new, and our romance is through.

"Is this supposed to be my surprise?"

"Naw, man, you get three songs for a quarter. Yours is up next. I promise, you're gonna like it."

"Yeah, yeah."

Yesterday, at the end of their shift, they decided they'd had enough of the mindless protest duty. So instead of reporting for duty today they drove a few blocks away to go visit an inmate at Eastern State. They convinced him that talking could help him. They were both lying, but it seemed to work. The inmate talked. Now Stan and George almost wish he hadn't.

"You want another one?" Stan asks, gesturing to his empty mug.

"No, but you go ahead. I ain't showing up at home drunk. Carla would have my ass served up with mint jelly."

"Geez, I'd need a few dozen of these things to get drunk."

"That ain't what Rosie tells me."

Stan is about to warn George about talking to his beautiful wife when the third song comes on—a pair of sharp cowbell strikes, a zippy accordion riff, and then a descending bass line into a polka rave-up. George belly-laughs—he can't hold it in any longer. A goofy smile breaks out over Stan's face, against his own will.

Someone stole the keeshka
Someone stole the keeshka
Someone stole the keeshka
From the butcher's shop

First time Stan played it for George, his partner couldn't stop laughing. It was simply the most absurd song George had ever heard. Oompa, oompa, kishka kishka. What made it even funnier was when Stan told them the performers were local boys from Chester, the Matys Brothers, and they'd recorded the song at Broad and Columbia, the fringes of the Jungle in the heart of North Philly. Stan said it with such pride, which just made George laugh even harder.

"Hey, barkeep," George calls out over the song, "get my Polish boy here another Schmidt's. Who stole the kishka, man. Heh heh."

Round and firm and fully packed
It was hanging on the rack
Someone stole the keeshka
When I turned my back

The world-weary bartender looks up as if wondering why a black cop would play a silly polka on the jukebox, then shuffles over to the taps.

At that moment sunlight blasts into the bar, along with another gust of hot air wafting off Fairmount Avenue. Both Stan and George turn to look, half-expecting to see the construction worker again. Maybe changed his mind, decided a cold one here was better than a cold one nowhere.

But it's not the construction worker.

It's a man with a gun.

A revolver.

JIM WALCZAK

May 7, 1995

Homicide Detective Jim Walczak stands on the corner of Seventeenth and Fairmount holding a bunch of flowers and a cold bottle of Schmidt's. His boy, Cary, fifteen, kicks the sidewalk, looks up at the shuttered bar.

"I thought you said it'd be open, Dad."

"I said I *hoped* it would be open."

Jim crouches down, flowers in hand, props them up against the front door. Or where the front door would have been, had it not been covered and nailed shut with wooden boards. A warm breeze flutters the petals, the wrapping.

Then Jim removes the Schmidt's from its brown paper bag. Twists off the cap. Drops it into the bag.

"Here's to you, Pop."

Takes a sip. It's not good beer, but it's what his father drank.

Cary watches him. Jim waits a second, as if thinking it over, then hands the bottle to Cary. But Cary shakes his head, mumbles, "No thanks." Good kid. When he offered the bottle to his older boy, Staś, he'd pretty much downed half the fucking thing before Jim could pry it out of his fingers.

The bar closed five years ago. Sure, it was a sad little dive on its last legs, holding on to what little trade could be drummed up in this neighborhood. All the action is downtown; nobody wants to hang on the fringes.

"So this is where it happened, Dad?"

Jim nods, lips pursed. "Yeah. This is it."

He brought Staś here the last couple of years, but this is Cary's first time. Jim also wanted to bring Audrey, but Claire put her foot down. No way. Not a five-year-old, not in this neighborhood. Jim reminded his wife that he was a cop, carried a big-boy gun and everything. But it was no use. She told him he was lucky she let Cary go.

Shame the bar was still shuttered. Each year, on the anniversary of his father's murder, Jim liked to go inside, sit on the same barstool in the same place (best he could figure), soak in the warmth and the dark, order a Schmidt's. If someone was already occupying that barstool, Jim would wait until the patron left, then take his place and drink his beer in silence. He'd have just the one, then leave a very generous tip.

This tradition changed with the loss of Schmidt's on tap back in '89, and then the closing of the bar in '90. Jim hoped someone would open it up again. It wasn't the same thing, standing outside in the heat, with a bottle of not-so-great beer and a bunch of flowers. No wonder the older boy took a pass this time.

But it is important that they remember. Important they hear the story. They might tear this corner down, but what happened here needs to be remembered.

Jim stands there, staring at the shuttered door as if he can will it to pop open. He wonders what the place looks like inside now, after five years of decay.

"What happened?" Cary asks.

Jim hesitates, but in truth he's already made up his mind. Cary's old enough to hear this. Hell, he was younger than Cary when it happened. He'll be able to handle it.

"Thirty years ago today," Jim says, "right around this time, your grandpop Stan and his partner, Officer George W. Wildey, were inside this bar when an armed man walked in and tried to rob it."

"He tried to rob it with two cops inside?"

"It was a Friday. Maybe this robber thought the till would be full."

Cary nods slowly. It's clear he doesn't know what a till is but quickly figures out it's the same thing as the cash register. *Till.* Jim watches him commit the word to memory. Once he learns it, the boy never forgets anything.

"Apparently the robber held your grandfather and his partner at gunpoint, then made them take off their uniforms."

Cary blinks. "Why'd he do that?"

"No one knows for sure, but probably so they wouldn't run after him right away. Their uniforms were found in the trash about a dozen blocks away, along with their belts and guns. Unfired."

"But he didn't just run away."

"No, he didn't."

Cary processes this, but clearly something bothers him about it.

"How did one robber manage to hold up two cops? Didn't they have their guns on them?"

Jim smiles. His boy knows to ask questions. Look for evidence. Be smart. He drums this into both his boys, and will do the same with Audrey when she's old enough.

"Well, that's a great question, Care. One I've been asking myself ever since I was your age. And the answer is simple. They knew their killer. It was most likely someone they trusted."

"Jesus," Cary says. "Who was it?"

Jim shakes his head. "No one was ever officially charged with the murder."

"But you know who did it."

Jim nods. "Yeah, I have a pretty good idea."

There's not much to do except hang around here on the corner with a bottle of beer that's beading sweat and flowers that are already wilting. The May sun is punishing and hot. God help him the day they knock this place down to build condos or some such shit. Jim realizes that yeah, cities need to change and evolve, but this corner should stay the way it is, as a reminder. But nobody remembers. Nobody cares. Jim is lost in a reverie when he feels a tug on his coat sleeve and hears an urgent plea from Cary.

"*Dad.*"

"Hey, man," a weary voice calls out.

Jim turns around to see some homeless guy wearing a green army jacket, cautiously ambling up Seventeenth Street toward them. He's scuffed, dirty, and shivering despite the heat.

Jim puts his hand on his son's shoulder and squeezes it. "It's okay, Care."

The mayor has spent the last four years chasing the homeless out of Center City, so they've started drifting up here, to the outskirts, in increasing numbers. This guy probably sees Jim in his jacket and tie and thinks he can hit him up for a few bucks. Or maybe whatever's left of the Schmidt's in his hand.

"Sorry, can't help you, buddy."

Jim turns his attention back to the flowers on the ground. He's not in the mood to deal with this shit right now. But it looks like his visit is going to be shorter than usual. He squeezes his son's shoulder again.

"You ready to go?"

"Hey, man," the guy says again, pleading now. Jim senses Cary tensing up. He's a fragile kid, easily spooked, just like his mother. Jim's deciding whether it's worth flashing his badge or not, tell the guy to go bother someone else, when the guys says,

"Jimmy . . . it's *me.*"

Jim gives the guy a closer look. Red eyes, trembling lips. High on something. But his features *are* familiar, even if Jim can't place them. Somebody he busted? No, somebody he busted wouldn't call him Jimmy.

"It's *George,* man," the guy says, and then it all clicks so hard Jim's head spins a little.

Jesus.

The last time Jim saw George Wildey, Jr., it was more than ten years ago, in an interrogation room, back when Jim was working narcotics. *Guy says he knows you.* Yeah, Jim knew the guy. He did what he could for him, which wasn't much. He had a few felony arrests for burglary, dope dealing, auto theft. There are two paths you can follow. Even as a kid, Jim knew George Junior here was headed down the wrong one, despite what his father did for a living.

"Hey, George," Jim says. "I'm sorry, it's been a while."

"Yes it has, yes it has. Is that your oldest?" George asks, looking at Cary.

"No, no. This is Cary, my second-born," Jim says. "Care, this is my friend George. His daddy was—"

"Grandpop's partner," Cary says, getting it.

George Junior gestures to the bunch of flowers leaning up against the wall.

"Shoulda thought of that."

Jim shakes his head. "They're for both of them. My pop and yours."

George Junior nods at the beer in Jim's hand. "Heh heh. That for them, too?"

"Yeah, I guess so. You want a pull?"

"Nah, man, I don't drink anymore."

They're roughly the same age. In the short time their fathers were partners, they socialized twice—and both were very awkward experiences. Jim actually liked Officer Wildey quite a bit. His big bear laugh, his cool taste in soul, jazz, and even rock. Wildey was the guy who pointed out that the Stones pretty much ripped off "The Last Time" from the Staple Singers, and this always came to mind when the song came on the radio. Or when he played it at home, late at night.

His son Junior, though, is another story. Always has this look in his eye that's part accusation, part confrontation.

"You still working narco?" Junior asks now.

"Nah. Moved over to homicide about ten years back."

"Hom-i-cide," George Junior says, drawing out the syllables as if holding the word up to the light to inspect it. "That's good, real good."

George Junior stands there shivering in the heat. He seems to want to lean against the wall but doesn't want to appear weak. Jim wants to ask a lot of questions—where are you living, what are you doing, how's your mom—but decides he really doesn't want to hear the answers. Jim just wants to go home to his family and hope the visit next year is a little better. Maybe someone will finally decide to reopen the bar.

Jim pulls out his wallet, flips it open, reaches inside.

"Here."

"No, man, I don't need nothing like that."

Jim shakes his head as he pulls out a white business card, emblazoned with a golden badge and his beeper number. Your basic get-out-of-a-gentle-scrape card. It wouldn't help you with, say, possession with intent to sell. Or homicide. But it could make a traffic stop a little easier.

"Just in case," Jim says.

George Junior takes the card, blinks. "In case of what?"

Every time Jim pulls up in front of his house he can't help but feel disappointed. They bought their row on Unruh Avenue as their starter home in the late seventies when Mayfair was still solid—lots of guys on the force lived in the Northeast—and they had one kid. The loose plan was to stick around for five, six years, then bolt for someplace bigger. Maybe even out in the near burbs.

But those five years passed in a blink, and in the meantime came their second boy (Cary), and before long it was 1990, and they realized they'd been there a dozen years and now with a new baby girl in the house. Instead of moving they doubled down, building a deck off the back of the house to make up for the lack of a yard. According to conventional wisdom in Northeast Philly, once you put on a deck you were there for life. But who cares. In the warm weather, the deck is pretty much where they live.

Jim holds the door open for his widowed mom, Rose, whom they picked up after their visit to the shuttered bar. Rose Walczak still lives in the house she bought with her husband almost fifty years ago, but sooner or later she's going to have to move. Not necessarily to an old-age home—she's a bit too young for that—but to a small apartment, maybe, in a better neighborhood. This was a decent slice of Frankford for a long while, but lately it's joined the rest of the city in becoming one sprawling high-crime area. Jim dreads taking the call someday that someone's attacked her.

Rose will refuse, of course. This is her world, and all she knows. Part of Jim can't blame her—and if he's honest, that same part of him will be gutted to put the house up for sale. The ghost of his father still looms large there.

"DADDEEEEEEEEEE!"

Audrey comes thundering across the wooden floor. She's five years old and crazy and strong as a bull.

BAM—a wrecking ball right to Jim's upper thighs. He scoops her up and blows raspberries into the side of her neck, causing her to wail and squirm around in his arms.

Rose hands Claire her homemade potato salad (which the kids love) and beet salad (which they loathe). She kisses Staś on his forehead, then pats his girlfriend, Bethanne, on her cheek. "Such a pretty girl," she says. Bethanne blushes.

Cary walks behind Rose, in her wake, and winks at Bethanne, his gaze lingering. He has a public crush on his brother's girlfriend that sometimes borders on the inappropriate.

"Fuck off, Care," Staś says.

Jim wanted to name their firstborn after his father. But Claire didn't want him going through life saddled with a name like Stanisław, or even the shorter version, Stan. ("Stan's the guy who fixes your plumbing," she said.) So they settled on the alternate form Staś, pronounced "Stosh." People mishear it all the time, call him Josh, which drives him nuts.

Claire wraps her arms around Jim's burly torso and tucks herself in.

"Time to get your disgusting Polish meat out of my fridge onto the grill," she says.

Jim whispers:

"I can think of someplace more fun than the grill."

She pokes him again, harder this time, laughing despite herself. But she really does hate the smell of the kielbasa. Despite this, she already has the links cut and butterflied so all he has to do is char them a little. Jim buys kielbasa from Czerw's, a small shop in Port Richmond that's been grinding and smoking the stuff since the Great Depression. Pop used to shop there.

Claire doesn't eat red meat—and even if she did, she wouldn't eat pork—so this is something she only tolerates on special occasions. To Jim there's nothing better than the aroma of the smoked stuff wafting out of the fridge whenever you open it. Claire more or less gags every time.

As Jim turns the links, Audrey is spinning around lip-syncing to her new favorite song, which is pumping from a CD boom box:

An older version of me, is she perverted like me?

Jim doesn't know whether to laugh or burn the goddamned CD. Then again, his parents never stopped him from listening to whatever he wanted. Songs about how sweet brown sugar tasted probably went over Ma's head anyway.

He twists the cap off another Yuengling, flips the kielbasa, tries to slow down time enough to enjoy the moment, because in this life moments like this are all too rare. His boys fighting, Audrey running around the deck like a spaz. All of them together, kielbasa on the grill, cold beer in his hand, Claire surprising him, slipping her hand around his chest, kissing him on the side of his neck. She's happiest when everybody's home. Jim has to admit—he is, too.

AUDREY KORNBLUTH

May 7, 2015

Audrey Kornbluth, twenty-five, hasn't set foot in Philadelphia for close to two years.

She also hasn't seen her father, aka the Captain, in over three. Word is, he's shaved his beard because it went gray. Which must be weird—she's never seen him without facial hair. Whatever. Either way, he's no doubt the same old grim asshole.

The flight from Houston to Philly took four hours and change. She's essentially trading one oppressively humid city (the fourth largest) for another oppressively humid city (the fifth largest—or is it sixth or seventh now? Audrey's lost track). A wasted morning flying from one armpit to the next. All in an ill-fitting black dress with long sleeves that hug her arms a bit too much.

"Your grandmother asked me to remind you about the sleeves," her mom texted her, although she speaks her texts so it came out *Your grand mopper asked me to rewind you about the Steves.*

That is, Steves/sleeves to cover her beautiful fully inked arm sleeves. God forbid a young lady should show off her tats in mixed company. But she complies, because Audrey loves her Grandma Rose. Or maybe she loves the idea of Grandma Rose more. Because in real life, she's kind of a pain in the ass.

Outside the terminal the hot humid air smacks her in the face. Her long black hair goes whipping around like Medusa's snakes. Her eyes tear up. She clutches her overnight bag—oh yes, this is going to be a short visit, guilt only buys you twenty-four hours, people— and looks for the limo. For all this hassle, she was promised a limo.

No limo.

Instead what she gets is a minivan. Cyanotic blue Honda What-ever, a few years old, dinged up here and there.

She gets a sister-in-law, the only one who talks to her, waving and yelling at her, hurry up, hurry up, we're running late. Cheering kids in the back. Wait; they're not cheering. They're yelling.

This is going to be a nightmare.

She was promised a limo, goddammit.

So Audrey Kornbluth, grown-ass woman, wedges herself between two toddlers in the third row of a six-year-old minivan. A dirty finger violates the personal space around her face.

"Who are *you?*"

Patience; he's an innocent.

"I'm your aunt Audrey."

"No you're not! Our aunt Audrey lives in Texas."

"Psst, kid. See those buildings?" She points at the squat ugly gray terminals of concrete and glass that they are currently speeding past. "Behind them are these magical devices that transport you from one location to another. One of them brought me here from Texas!"

"Aunt Audrey is pretty."

"You're not pretty," says the other toddler with the certainty of a judge delivering a verdict.

Audrey twists up her face and leans in close to her nephew.

"Yeah, and you've got peanut butter on your lip."

Audrey pulls the seat belt across her torso. It locks up. She pulls again. It locks up. Yanks it hard. Locks up. Oh fuck it. If they crash she'll be well protected by all the human meat around her.

"Who are you two firecrackers, anyway?"

Audrey is not being funny. She can barely keep her nieces and nephews straight. She hasn't been home in close to two years, and her two brothers keep multiplying, as if they're making a hedge against Armageddon. In the second row in front of her are three boys who she knows belong to either Staś or Cary, but she'll be damned if she knows which is which.

One of her sisters-in-law turns around, placing her hand on the back of the driver's seat. "You okay back there, Audrey?"

"I'm fine."

"You look like Houston's agreeing with you."

"Yeah, it's a cool city."

"How's CSI school?"

"Just great," she lies.

CSI school is going very, very badly. In fact, the University of Houston is about seven days away from saying *fuck you very much, pleasure taking your tuition money, good luck out there in the world of the desperate and unemployed.*

It seemed like a fun idea at the time. Audrey grew up watching *CSI* — way before she was officially allowed to watch such gruesome things. Mom would have been mortified. Dad just smiled and looked the other way while his ten-year-old daughter was treated to the image of a human head being pulverized by a golf club or a rib-spreader going to work on a hooker's torso. Audrey reveled in it.

And she continues to revel in it. The problem isn't the science; the problem is the whirling chaos of her life that prevents her from doing the science. And universities tend not to care about whirling chaos. They want you to show up and just do the science.

The ride from the airport to the city proper takes you through an industrial wasteland of smoke and oil and machines and fire, then sports stadiums and a thousand billboards. Apparently there's a mayoral primary this month, because the ads are full of names that Audrey dimly remembers. ABRAHAM. WILLIAMS. DE-HAVEN. KENNEY.

Predictably, there's a traffic slowdown near the stadiums.

"We're going to be late," says the sister-in-law who is driving. She's not speaking to anyone in particular, but she's especially not speaking to Audrey.

Her name is Bethanne, which, of course, Audrey mentally auto-corrects to *Bitchanne*. She's never done a thing to Bitchanne, except maybe breathe. But Bitchanne is married to Staś, her older sibling, and since Staś doesn't talk to Audrey anymore, his wife follows suit. It's kind of a shame because Audrey remembers when she was just a kid and used to look forward to Bethanne coming over. She'd play all the silly girly board games that Staś and Cary refused to play. Now she doesn't talk to Audrey at all.

The sister-in-law whose skinny ass occupies the passenger seat *does* speak to Audrey, but delights in telling backstabbing whore lies. Which is far, far worse—Audrey would prefer the stony silence. The backstabber's name is Jean and she is the reason her brother Cary drinks so much.

Speaking of...

"Uh, I thought there was supposed to be a limo?"

Jean turns, puts on a faux pout and says,

"The city only arranged for two per family, honey. There's one for your dad, Grandma Rose, and Staś, the other for your mom, Will, Cary, and Gene."

Audrey seethes as she does the family calculus in her head: okay, so the Walczak sons (Staś, Cary) get a limo ride, and mean-while, Audrey's stuck in a cluttered minivan with the peanut butter gang. But lo! It's not just siblings in the limo. There's Will, Mom's newish boyfriend. And Gene, who is Cary's son.

Gene—*the grandkid?*—gets in the limo before fat ugly Aunt Audrey from Texas?

Then again, it makes sense, she guesses. She's the adopted one. The only member of the family who doesn't have almighty Walczak blood running through her veins.

"Don't worry," Jean says. "We're going to meet up with them near Spring Garden Street before driving up to the corner."

"Wunderbar," Audrey says.

The corner is where, precisely fifty years ago, on May 7, 1965, Audrey's grandfather was murdered.

Growing up, Audrey Kornbluth heard a lot about her grandpop Stan. Hero cop. Family man, only forty-one when he died, far too young, and so on.

She only saw Grandpop Stan when she was visiting her grandmother's house and had to pee.

See, the only bathroom was upstairs, and Grandpop Stan's black-and-white picture hung slightly askew on the wall by the staircase—one of three photos arranged in a triptych on the wood paneling along the shag-carpeted staircase. In order of ascension:

Her older brother Staś, who is pretty much a dick. Photo taken the day he graduated from the Academy. Audrey remembers that day clearly, which ended with Staś and Cary in a fistfight. (Is there a Walczak family gathering that doesn't end in a fistfight?)

Next in line: her father, the Captain, taken the day *he* graduated from the Academy back in 1971. Young Audrey used to laugh at his longish blond hair, which is now long gone. A Study of Her Father as Early-1970s Hipster.

And finally: Grandpop Stan, taken the day *he* graduated from the police academy (you might be sensing a theme here) in May 1951. He had close-cropped blond hair, deep-set eyes, an uneasy smile.

Staring at you, whenever you needed to go pee.

She has to admit, it used to creep her out, the way his eyes seemed to *follow you*.

That's Audrey's memory of her grandfather.

The limos pull up to the corner under police escort, followed by the motley assortment of civilian vehicles. Uniformed cops salute stiff and precise as the vehicles pass. One whole block of Fairmount Avenue, from Seventeenth to Eighteenth, has been cordoned off to accommodate rows of folding chairs facing the pizza joint. A police flag covers the memorial plaques, with four roses anchoring each corner. Bagpipers wail in the background.

Audrey climbs out of the back of the minivan and steels herself for the painful and awkward hours to come.

Her father, the Captain, climbs out of the back of the first limo. And as rumored, he is indeed beardless. His big pink cheeks are freshly shaved and raw. He's also about thirty pounds heavier. Blond hair so light it's almost gray, cropped close to the skull. The man is a mountain, considerably heavier than the last time she saw him. Which was painful, awkward, shitty.

And wouldn't you know it—the first person he locks eyes with is Audrey.

Even as he puts his sunglasses on, he continues to stare at her. No discernible emotion on his face.

Audrey flinches first and looks away. Oh god, this is going to be awful.

One by one, her siblings and Mom and boyfriend Will—and yes, even little Gene—climb out of their limos and gawk at Audrey. Wow. She actually showed up. Wonder what the over/under is on her appearance.

Mom is the first to break ranks to come over to give her a hug.

"You look good, daughter," she says.

"The phrase you're searching for is *pleasingly plump*," Audrey says.

"I didn't say that."

"Ah, but you *were* thinking it, Claire."

She always calls her mother Claire, while Claire refers to Audrey as daughter. It's a thing they do.

As the bagpipers continue to wail and asses begin to fill seats, Audrey nervously scans the crowd for other familiar faces. It's not difficult to tell the Walczaks from the Wildeys (duh), though the Wildey side is much more sparse. There will be empty chairs. Audrey considers sitting on the Wildey side, just for the hell of it. *Why yes, I'm the white sheep of the family.*

The police commissioner shakes hands with her father. The mayor, she notices, must be running late.

And then, without warning, it's time to get started.

A local oldies radio DJ is the MC. Boy, what a depressing gig, Audrey thinks. At no point will he be able to lighten the mood by playing "Let's Twist Again" or "Hanky Panky."

Audrey chooses a seat in the second row, figuring the front row is Reserved for Limo Riders Only. Cary, though, surprises her by making his way down her row and plopping his lean body down into the seat next to hers. He's wearing his police uniform even though he's just a paper-pusher.

"You're looking rather bosomy these days," he says, nodding at her torso.

"Eat me," she whispers.

"You're a regular Chesty McChesterton."

"Seriously—suck it, Care."

Cary chuckles under his breath.

The Captain—she can tell—is *this* close to turning around and telling them to shut the fuck up already. Ah, some things never change.

A monsignor from Sts. Peter and Paul gives the opening invocation.

"May the almighty God grant us peace now and forever. O God, by whose mercy your faithful find rest, bless this plaque with which we mark the place where our brothers, Officers Stanisław Walczak and George Wildey, were taken from us, as they sought to protect their fellow citizens, your people, from the certain harm that faced them. May they have everlasting life in your peaceful presence forever. Amen."

"Psst. Here."

Cary knocks a silver flask against the knuckles of Audrey's right hand. She pivots her wrist, grabs it.

So this is how it's going to be. Getting drunk at her grandfather's memorial. Not the classiest move ever, but oh so necessary.

Of course Audrey, being no dummy, front-loaded on the plane: two mini-bottles of Stoli, a can of tomato juice, and teensy pepper packets were the ingredients for her MacGyver-ish in-flight Bloody Mary (she told the flight attendant "My grandfather died, okay?" when he raised an eyebrow) and another fully loaded one at the Chickie's & Pete's in the terminal. So these hits from Cary's flask are just maintenance. Hell, he's just as buzzed.

The Walczak siblings have allegiances and wars going back decades. Audrey and Cary got along the best, even if they were born a decade apart and could lash out at each other with precision-strike cruelty when needed. Their mother, Claire, named them after the stars in her favorite movie, *Charade*.

Meanwhile, Jim named his firstborn after his father. Staś may have inherited the family legacy, but Audrey and Cary agree they got the cooler names. (Also, Audrey called him Josh whenever possible because it pissed him off.)

Now an honor guard is posting the colors. Rifleman, American flag bearer, state flag bearer, police flag bearer, rifleman. Everyone says the Pledge of Allegiance, during which Audrey realizes she's slurring a little. She'd better slow down, unless she plans on passing out at the banquet later.

The police commissioner takes the podium.

"It doesn't matter how long ago the murders took place," he says. "When a member of our family loses his life in the performance of duty, we never, ever forget. Not only don't we forget them, we don't forget their family as well."

These two plaques are the fifty-seventh and fifty-eighth in the program, which was founded by the Fraternal Order of Police. Their goal: honor all 258 Philadelphia police officers killed in the line of duty with plaques. Stan's and George's turns came on the fiftieth anniversary of their deaths.

Cary knocks the flask against her knuckles again.

Audrey stares dead ahead as her fingers blindly screw open the top of the flask. As the commissioner finishes his speech, she leans forward, as if stretching her back, hair tumbling over her face. She takes a gulp. The bourbon is a sweet burn past her tongue, down her throat. She sits up. Screws the top back on. Nudges the flask against the back of Cary's hand. He takes it, notes the weight, looks at Audrey, eyebrows raised. Chug much?

Audrey shrugs. It's a Walczak gathering. Aren't we supposed to get wasted?

The commissioner introduces a woman named Sonya Kaminski, daughter of longtime political fixer "Sonny Jim" Kaminski, who is notably absent. Audrey's father and Sonya are longtime friends; Audrey can only assume they were fucking at some point. For all she knows they still are—though Sonya here looks like she pursues a higher pedigree of cock.

"It's a unique pleasure to welcome the Walczak and Wildey

families," says Sonya Kaminski. "This is now hallowed ground. This will be never be disturbed, defaced, or displaced."

Yeah, Audrey thinks, until someone vomits pepperoni all over the corner late one night.

And then it comes time for Audrey's father to speak. She sits up in her chair once she realizes she's been slouching. Captain Jim takes the podium, sunglasses still on his face. She hasn't heard her father's voice in close to three years.

"Good morning," he says. "My name is James Walczak. Officer Stanisław Walczak was my father. As I stand here today, I'm humbled. I've never been more proud to be a member of the Philadelphia Police Department. I'd like to thank Commissioner..."

From there, Captain Jim goes off on a litany of thanks, from the commissioner up to the mayor and back down again, hitting pretty much everybody who needs to be name-checked. It doesn't sound like her father at all. Even when he's in total asshole mode, there's still a weird, dark humor to him. His speech isn't him. It could have been delivered by a robot.

Captain Jim sits back down.

Lieutenant Ben Wildey's speech is much more animated. He's George Wildey's grandson—and surprise surprise, another cop.

"I never met my grandpop George," he says, "but I've heard a lot about him over the years. And from what I understand, I think he'd be upset that we weren't spinning some soul tunes up in this j—corner."

Murmurs of polite laughter. Audrey giggles. She could have sworn he was about to say "...*jawn*." Good on you, Lieutenant Ben.

And then it's finally time to unveil the plaques. A lone bugler plays "Nearer My God to Thee" as the roses are removed, and finally the flag, revealing the two bronze memorials set into the concrete.

It would be super-classy, if not for the red, green and white sign tacked directly above:

PHILLY CHEESE STEAK

HOT ITALIAN SAUSAGE

HOAGIE

FRIES * WINGS

ORDER INSIDE

Order inside, Audrey thinks, *and pray you make it out alive.* She's tipsy, but grateful that she's not so drunk she's saying this shit out loud.

The commissioner hands the Captain a pillow. Audrey wonders if he'll press it down over his own face just to get out of this memorial service.

The head of the police union takes the podium.

"To the relatives of Stan and George, please know that you will always be a member of the Philadelphia police family. This plaque joins the memories, recollections, written history, and the Walczak and Wildey families as further evidence that heroes protecting the citizens of Philadelphia were killed here in the line of duty. May God bless you."

The bugle plays taps.

Bagpipes crank out some "Amazing Grace."

Audrey's with Lieutenant Ben: she'd much prefer some soul tunes up in this jawn.

The oldies DJ—who presumably could arrange such a thing— takes the mike to close things out.

"See you next time," he says.

Audrey runs her fingers along the countertop, which is slightly greasy, even though the place has just opened for the day. Outside, the chairs are being folded up and put on a truck. The crowd is dispersing.

She's inside the pizza joint because she had to pee. But on the way back she stopped to look at the place. Tried to imagine it as it was fifty years ago, when it was a bar. She takes a step back and looks at the dimensions of the room, and then back down at the counter, and how long it is, and realizes, with a shock:

They just covered up the actual bar. It's *still under there.*

Probably riddled with bullet holes.

The Memorial Fund springs for a small buffet at a restaurant a few blocks away, on the corner of Twenty-First and Green. Cash bar, though, which is disappointing. She doesn't think she has enough cash on hand for a Bloody.

There are assigned seats, but once Audrey sees the other names on the cards (Bitchanne, Jean, brood) she opts for a stool at the bar in the next room, orders a Yuengling. When's her plane out of here?

The room, then, is segregated by design, just like the seating arrangement out on Fairmount Avenue. Philadelphia, don't ever change.

Everyone scarfs down roast beef sandwiches, ziti, and coleslaw. Most of the kids run around like maniacs, knocking over chairs and screaming so piercingly that it cuts through Audrey's fine, strong buzz.

Audrey doesn't know what to do with herself, so she gravitates to Grandma Rose, who sits with some of her cousins. Audrey can remember none of their names; she prays they don't talk to her.

"Hey, Grandma."

Rose's eyes take a second or two to focus on Audrey. Every sensory organ seems to be failing her these days. But soon she zeroes in.

"Oh, Audrey. You got fat."

Audrey wonders if any court of law would convict her for punching her grandmother in the side of the head right now.

"Are you coming back home now?" Grandma Rose asks. "I don't know why you had to move to Texas in the first place."

"It's a good school," Audrey lies, not wanting to speak truth: *Because I had to get away from all you people.*

"Aren't there good schools here?"

In a family of cops it's not difficult to feel like the local criminal. Audrey is the youngest sibling by a good stretch of years—and the only adopted child. They refer to her as Hot Mess Express. Don't think she doesn't hear them.

It was a mistake to mix among the civilians, Audrey thinks. Truth is, she'd feel more comfortable mixing with the Wildeys. Though they'd probably look at her and gently suggest she return to her own crazy-ass family.

Nowhere else to go, Audrey walks up to the portraits of the fallen cops, which are printed on cardboard and mounted on two easels positioned next to each other, as if they're having an eternal gab session in the afterlife.

The photos are their police identification photos, stark black-and-white, blown up to poster size.

Grandpop Stan was a wide-jawed Polish-American guy with deep-set eyes. There's a lot of hurt in those eyes. He's a WWII vet, orphan, cop. He's seen some shit.

His partner Wildey, meanwhile, is a round-cheeked African-American with the faintest glimmer of a smile on his face, as if the camera clicked just as he heard a very funny joke and he was about to explode into a laugh.

"Freaky, huh?" a voice says.

Audrey glances over at the black cop standing next to her, looking at the portraits, too. Ah—it's funny Lieutenant Ben from the ceremony. Mr. Jawn up in here. Turns out he's a dead ringer (excuse the expression) for his grandfather.

"You look just like him," Audrey says.

"I keep hearing that," the cop says. "Not sure I see it, aside from the uniform and skin color. I've got a lot of my mama in me."

"Why did you say this was weird, then?"

Ben Wildey smiles.

"The two of us here, you know. Couple of grandkids who never met their grandfathers. I know I look like an old man, but my grand-pop George was already gone sixteen years before I showed up. Just weird, all this to-do"—Ben waves his hand around—"for guys we never met."

He extends a hand, introduces himself. "You're the baby daughter, right? I hear you're on the job, too."

"No, I'm not police. I'm still in school."

"But forensics, right?"

"Yeah. Hopefully."

"Cool."

They stand there, looking at their dead grandfathers.

"Well," Ben says, "maybe when you get your degree, you can come back home and finally solve this thing."

Audrey turns to look at Ben Wildey.

"Wait...what?"

STAN MEETS GEORGE

August 28-30, 1964

The whole thing started because a car at Twenty-Second and Columbia refused to move.

Husband is standing outside the car, pleading with his wife to pull the damn car over already. But wife is behind the wheel and she is not budging. Gunning the accelerator and the brake at the same time. *Come on,* the husband yells. Wife says *Uh-uh, you go and fuck yourself.* They've both had more than a few.

Soon drivers are lined up behind them pounding fists into horns. *BLAAAAARP.*

It's a hot summer Friday night in late August and folks just want to go home. Even if it's just to a sweltering hot box of a home, drinking beer and watching *Make That Spare.* Would sure beat sitting here on Columbia Avenue behind a car that won't fuckin' move.

Eventually, somebody calls the cops.

Word gets to the Twenty-Second. Two patrolmen show up—a salt-and-pepper set. You see a lot of black-and-white duos around the Jungle these days. The idea is that the civilians, no matter their skin color, will have someone to relate to at all times.

But the truth is, blacks trust white cops more. And conventional wisdom around the department is that you never send two black cops out in a squad car—because it would be like sending out no car at all.

White cop tries to talk to the couple. The couple ignore him, keep on fighting. The wife has her feet locked on those damn pedals. No way is she moving. Uh-uh.

Cars honk. The sound echoes off the two- and three-story buildings like in a canyon.

Come on!

Black cop finally says, hell with this. He reaches in and pulls the woman out from behind the wheel. It's a hot summer evening; people need to get home.

But this is the Jungle, and it is the summer of 1964, and the fury has been simmering all summer. It's gonna reach full boil at some point—everybody can feel it.

White cop hops in, steers the car off the road so people can finally pass. He steps out of the car, slams the door shut, prepares to haul the couple in so that *he* can go home and drink beer and put on some TV when—

WHAM.

A black guy comes bounding out of the crowd and socks the white cop in the jaw, snapping his head around, popping the helmet off his head.

The assailant runs off before the white cop can recover from that sucker punch or his black partner can catch him. And the assailant is quick.

Black cop calls in an "assist officer."

A block away, the same assailant proceeds to spread the word around town. Yo, some white cop just snuffed a black lady! She was all pregnant, too! No, man, for real, I saw it happen, right at Twenty-Second and Columbia!

Lots of bodies in the streets now, moving down Columbia Avenue.

A dozen cops arrive in response to that "assist officer."

Even more bodies in the streets now, milling around, wondering what's going to happen next. These pigs gonna kill another pregnant black woman? Maybe even a kid?

A red squad car turns onto Columbia from Twentieth Street and—

BAM BAM BAM BAM BAM

—a barrage of rocks pelt the windshield and hood.

Later, they'll say this was a setup, and salt-and-pepper team here drew the unlucky straw that struck flint and WHOOOSH, up goes the whole Jungle.

Right around the time the Columbia Avenue Riots kick into high gear, Patrolman Stan Walczak is passed out cold on his recliner, having downed a six-pack of Schmidt's while reading the *Bulletin*. He has the night off. In fact, he has the whole weekend off. Just the way he likes it.

Somewhere, a phone rings.

He prays it's a dream. Or a neighbor's phone. Or a dream about his neighbor's phone.

But no—there's another goddamned ring. Stan forces his eyes open. It is just past 11 p.m., and this has been a long week. All Stan wants to do is go back to sleep. Who the hell's calling him at this hour?

All at once he realizes there's only one person who could be calling this late at night, and dammit, Rosie had better not answer the phone.

As Stan rises from his recliner the noise in his house blends together in an uneasy background rumble. Rosie has soft opera on the radio in the kitchen. Jimmy is upstairs with his record player, listening to either the Beatles or the Rolling Stones or some other loud whining group. Which is all the boy listens to these days—on his record player, on the radio, humming out loud. Every song sounds like the same song, too. *Because I told you before, oh you can't do that.*

Yeah, well, I know what you *can* do, Stan thinks. Turn off the goddamned record player.

He turns around and sees that Rosie has beaten him to the phone.

"No, Rosie, wait—"

"It's for you," she says, holding the receiver out, a worried look in her eyes.

The feeling has gone out of his feet. It hurts to walk. Finally he makes it to the phone, takes the phone from Rosie.

"Yeah?"

"Yo, Stoshie, I need you to pick me up." It's his partner, Billy Taney.

"What do you mean pick you up?"

"Don't you have the TV on? Fucking Democrats have set the Jungle on fire!"

No, Stan doesn't have the TV on. He spent the evening reading the *Bulletin* and talking to Rosie, who's worried about her sister-in-law, who's having trouble with her husband. And then he drank a lot of beer and fell asleep.

"Fire? Where?"

"They're setting everything on fire up in the Gold Coast, and they say it's getting real ugly. So come pick me up already."

"Okay, okay."

Stan hangs up the phone. His undershirt is finally almost dry from the sweat of the day's shift, but now he'll have to put himself back together and head back to the streets.

Rosie is already in the kitchen, fixing him food for the road. She doesn't allow Stan to leave the house without food—maybe a liverwurst and onion on white, cold meatballs on an Italian roll—packed in a brown paper bag. His wife's secret fear is that Stan will eat a meal that wasn't prepared in their home and it'll be the end of the world.

"I'll be right back down," Stan says.

Up in the bathroom he washes his hands and face with hot water, towels himself dry. Jimmy's room is right next door and now Stan can hear that folk singer, Bob Dylan. That's the other one the boy listens to all the time. One sings "Like a Rolling Stone." Then you have the other ones that *call* themselves the Rolling Stones. None of it makes any sense. But Jimmy saves up and buys the albums himself, at a shop on Torresdale Avenue, so Stan can't say anything. Maybe he'll grow out of it. Or maybe Stan will buy him a set of headphones for his birthday.

As if beckoned, Jimmy appears in the doorway. "You going back in, Pop?"

"Yeah, they called us."

"You're going to the riot, aren't you?"

Stan raises an eyebrow. "How did you hear about that?"

"The radio. They said people are starting fires, smashing windows. Why are they doing that? What's going on?"

"I don't know, Jimmy. Guess I'm going to go find out."

Stan goes to his bedroom to find a clean shirt. Jimmy follows him.

"Sounds pretty bad out there."

"I'll be fine. We just gotta calm everyone down."

Jimmy considers this for a moment. "The radio said it all started around Twenty-Second and Columbia," he says. "That's near the stadium, isn't it?"

"Ballpark's up on Lehigh. Blocks and blocks away."

"I looked at a map. It's not that far."

Stan looks at his boy, knows what he's getting at. "Don't worry, they're not gonna cancel the Phillies over this."

They're supposed to be headed to the game next Tuesday night. Stan bought tickets back when the Phillies were still on a losing streak. But now they're heating up, and everybody in the city is getting excited, talking about the World Series, and those tickets were the smartest buy he ever made. Jimmy is out of his mind with excitement.

"I hope not," Jimmy says.

37

"Off to the scene of the crime," Stan says, then tousles Jimmy's hair. Jimmy pretends to hate it but smiles.

On their way in Stan sees a skinny *murzyn* kid hurl a Molotov cocktail at a red patrol car, shattering the back window. Three uniformed officers scramble out of the back door, brushing the glass from their shirts, looking for the kid, but he's long gone, having zipped down a dark alley.

You'd think the three would chase the little bastard down the alley, but they don't even try. They just stand there, looking around at each other.

Once they reach the staging area at Thirteenth and Berks, near Temple University, Stan learns why. They're handing out white domed riot helmets. They're handing out street assignments. And they're handing out strict orders from up on high:

Avoid physical confrontations.
Keep violence and casualties as low as possible.
No nightsticks.
No drawn pistols.
No dogs.
No horses.
No fire hoses.

What, Stan wonders, are they supposed to use? Mean looks? Guess the scuttlebutt around the department is true. The commissioner isn't a real street cop; he's a goddamned egghead.

"Your main instrument of control," he tells his deputies," is making an arrest."

Stan is within earshot of the deputy commissioner—Frank Rizzo.

"That gutless son of a bitch," Rizzo says. "He doesn't know a goddamned thing."

Much as he might agree with Rizzo, Stan doesn't like the deputy commissioner very much and the feeling is mutual. They worked together back ten years ago, policing the club district for a while, back when Stan felt like a real cop, invested in the job. That is, until things went very wrong and Stan found himself in exile in Whitetown.

Anyway, Rizzo's idea of a conversation with a suspect was a slap across the forehead, no further questions, Your Honor. To Stan's mind he was worse than a thug. He was a thug with ambition.

So of course this *no-rough-stuff* decree from the commissioner has Rizzo fuming, practically jumping out of his skin, wishing his cock were a nightstick that he could use to club all of North Philly into submission.

Stan walks out of earshot. Somebody hands him a helmet. He tries to put it on, but it won't fit. He hands it over to Taney.

"Fucking Democrats," Taney says, plopping the dome on his head. "I knew this was coming. All summer long I've been tellin' ya, this is coming. Haven't I?"

Democrats: Taney's new favorite word for blacks. He insists he's not racist. Instead, he says, it's political. Because all Democrats are nigger-lovers.

"Yeah, you been telling me," Stan says.

"The way they challenge ya. Daring ya to do something."

"Uh-huh."

"Guess they're gonna find out what happens when you dare a cop."

Billy Taney is an okay guy and a decent cop but a blowhard, especially when he's been drinking. The more he drinks, the angrier he gets, the more his eyes disappear. Clearly he's been drinking a lot tonight.

"They let us crack some skulls," Taney says, "this would be over in an hour."

It's past midnight now and Stan can see the glow of the fires from a dozen blocks away. This whole thing is nuts. He should be home asleep instead of here in the Jungle.

Lieutenants continue handing out helmets and assignments. They are also handing out rookies. Three-man teams, two veterans and a rook, sent out to keep the peace. Weird, but orders are orders. Like everything else, it's done alphabetically.

"Wildey!"

"Uh, that's *Will-dee,* Lieutenant," says a voice.

"Don't give a shit. You're with Walczak and Taney. Walczak, where are you?"

Stan reluctantly raises a hand in the air, trying to find the face that matches the voice. *Will-dee.* The crowd of cops parts to reveal Wildey. He's a *murzyn.* Should have figured. Wildey can't find him, so Stan raises his hand again, shouts,

"Over here, Wildey."

Wildey finally locks eyes with him—but only for a second. Wildey doesn't smile. Stan takes a wild guess about Wildey's spot assessment: big blond Polish boy. Head too big for a helmet. Yeah, well, Stan's not too happy to see him, either.

"How's it going?" Wildey says.

Stan nods. This neighborhood is tearing itself apart. How does he think it's going?

"I'm Walczak, and that's Taney."

Taney grunts and fiddles with the straps on his riot helmet.

"Looks like we're in for a long fucking night," Wildey says.

"Yeah. Looks like it, rook."

Wildey recoils as if he's been slapped. "Rook? I ain't no rook."

"Then why are you with us?" Taney asks.

"You heard the lieutenant, same as I did. Thought maybe one of you guys was new."

Stan looks at the dozens and dozens of uniforms out here. Maybe if they just hang back they can stay out of the worst of it. Some dumb bastard comes running out of the riot zone, then they can lock him up. Maybe there's even a bar around here. They could hole up, have a few. Keep the internal peace.

"Well," Wildey says, "shall we get in there?"

Stan and Taney look at each other, then sigh. This guy, *Will-dee,* seems to be one of those overeager types.

They used to call this part of Columbia Avenue the Gold Coast. Back in the 1930s, when Stan was just a kid, the gangsters would stash their molls up here, in apartments from Broad all the way to Eighteenth Street. There were so many store awnings you could walk from Broad to the park during a rainstorm without getting a single drop of water on your head. Now it's all Jewish-owned stores desperately hanging on in a *murzyn* neighborhood. And tonight the *murzyns* are trying to burn it all down.

But first: they want to pick it clean.

Stan spies a kid, maybe seven years old, toddling out of a grocery store with at least a dozen cartons of cigarettes in his arms.

"Hey! Put those back!"

Kid stares at him with no expression. He's not dumb, or frozen with fear. He just doesn't care. His pops probably told him to go out there and bring home some smokes. Doesn't even occur to him he has to pay.

"You hear me?"

Wildey approaches him.

"Boy, get your ass back home right now."

The kid takes a step back, unsure of what to do. After all, he was headed home. With the cigarettes. For his pops.

This exchange catches the attention of some older kids, teenagers, a few storefronts away. They've got bottles in their hands. They watch Wildey try to grab the kid—why is he trying to grab the kid, for Christ's sake—and they saunter forward, feeling strong. Maybe word has reached them. Cops aren't allowed to use their weapons. You can do whatever you want tonight. Take whatever you want. You're owed it. They ain't gonna do shit except growl at you.

"C'mere, you little son of a gun," Wildey says, but the kid's too lithe, too wiry. And by that time the older kids have already decided to throw their bottles at Wildey.

"Black pig!"

A bottle shatters at Wildey's shoes, but he barely has time to react before he swats another out of the air and then a third clonks his forehead. "Motherfucker!" Wildey forgets the kid and charges toward the teens, who are already reloading—with rocks.

Stan looks at Taney and says, "Come on."

They pull their nightsticks out—they're not going to use them, except to scare these bastards off. But Wildey's already on the kids, yelling, which has them turning tail and scrambling back down the street. By the time he comes back, Taney is fuming.

"The hell you doing, rook? Trying to get us killed?"

"Told you, I'm no rook."

"Why were you going for the kid?" Stan asks. "Trying to arrest him?"

"No," Wildey says. "I was trying to get him out of the way before someone stomped his ass."

The three of them move down Columbia Avenue, broken glass crunching underfoot. Stan looks inside the ruins of stores. Pharmacies, their shelves cleaned out. Shoe stores. Butcher shops. No doubt there's some kid right now running up Twenty-Second Street with a side of beef.

Stan's seen the stories in the paper about the riots in Rochester and Harlem and Brooklyn. He can't figure out the rationale. If you're pissed off at someone, why burn down your own neighborhood? Why not go off to where all the rich people live and set their houses on fire? Makes no sense whatsoever.

There isn't much glass left in any of the windows on this block. Stan looks up and down the block to see if there's even a single window left intact. There is—right across the street. A women's shoe store. Somebody will get to it sooner or later, he's sure.

But it's a good thing Stan looks at that window at that exact moment, because he can see their own reflections as they move down the avenue.

And two stories above them—a huge, flaming mass that is just beginning its descent. He can practically feel the heat on the top of his head as he looks up.

Later Stan will think about his impulse in that moment. He barely has time to see the fireball and yell the word *shit,* let alone push both of his partners out of the way. So why does he pick the new guy?

Stan throws his shoulder at Wildey, knocking him off his feet. The fireball—or whatever the hell it is, a meteor maybe—slams into the pavement behind him so close Stan thinks it's burned off the backs of his shoes. Forward momentum carries him over Wildey's body and Stan throws his hands out. His palms scrape roadway, then his elbows take most of the impact of his fall, followed by the rest of his body. It's an ungraceful landing. But at least he isn't pummeled by the flaming object that dropped down from the heavens.

Which is when he realizes—oh no, Taney.

"Mother-*fucker,*" Wildey mumbles, still clearly dazed. He's looking at his bleeding palms as Stan climbs to his feet to look for his partner. Finally he recognizes the object that almost took all of them out.

It's a couch. A couch that someone set ablaze and heaved off the roof. Had to take at least two of them, probably more, to lift that thing over the edge.

Partially pinned under that couch is Officer Billy Taney.

"Come on, help me!" Stan is shouting, pulling Wildey all the way to his feet. Wildey looking at the burning couch as if he doesn't exactly know what he is seeing.

"Is that a couch?"

"Taney's under there!"

Being cooked alive. All Stan can see are two arms. Hands splayed, fingers trembling. Stan and Wildey exchange quick glances, unsure of what to do. They're going to have to touch this burning couch to pull it off Taney. There's no question that they're going to do it— Taney's under there. But they need it noted for the mutual record.

"Shit," Wildey says.

"Let's do it. One, two..."

"Wait!"

"Wait for what?"

"Kick it over!"

Stan understands immediately. Much, much better idea. Both men nudge the toes of their right shoes under the burning furniture and *lift*.

The couch rolls backward, revealing a moaning and charred Taney. Moaning is good. Moaning means Taney is still alive.

"Get an ambulance," Stan says, kneeling down.

Wildey nods twice, eyes still fixed on Taney, who looks like an action figure belonging to a pair of sadistic children. Limbs all akimbo, uniform ripped, skin smoking.

"Wildey, go!"

But by now other officers are swarming to the scene. Word travels through the ranks at synapse speed. *Niggers dropped a couch on Billy Taney!* Somebody says an ambulance is on its way.

Stan touches the back of Taney's head. He can feel the sharp edges of the man's recent haircut. His skin is hot. He's still moaning.

"Hang on there, Billy," Stan says, not daring to move him. All he can do is pat the back of Taney's head until help arrives. What city has this city become? After a time Stan hears a sharp voice, cutting through the din.

"Officer Walczak."

"What's that, Wildey."

"How about we go catch the sons a bitches who did this?"

This is stupid, this is stupid, this is stupid, Stan thinks as he runs along the rooftops above Columbia Avenue, looking for the people who would be crazy enough to toss a burning couch on top of three cops.

But there is no stopping Wildey. The only thing Stan could do was follow him—through the broken door, up the two flights of stairs to the fire escape and then the roof.

As they run, tar sticks to the bottoms of their shoes. Stan can hardly see where the roofs end and the gaping holes between buildings begin.

"I think I see them!" Wildey says.

Stan can't see a damn thing. North Philadelphia looks very different from up here. Maybe that's because everything seems to be on fire.

But they reach the end of the block and see nothing. Maybe the couch-tossers went downstairs again. Broke into another place.

A voice comes cutting through the noise. Stan doesn't know who it is. Did one of these *murzyns* steal a bullhorn?

"Huh," Wildey says. "That's Georgie Woods."

The bewildered look on Stan's face leads Wildey to explain.

"Georgie Woods, man—WDAS? The DJ?"

Stan has no idea who he's talking about. He stands on the roof, fists on his hips, and listens to the man plead.

"Please get off the streets," the voice bellows. "If you have problems, this is no way to solve them!"

That's for goddamn sure, Stan thinks.

"The woman you heard about is fine," the voice says. "No one was killed tonight! Please get *off* the streets!"

They continue to search the rooftops for another half hour but there are no signs of the sofa-tossers, nor any proof of their existence. If they had rags and cans of fuel, they must have taken it with them.

"Really wanted to slap the cuffs on those bastards," Wildey mutters.

Stan will bet Taney does, too.

By dawn people have grown tired of smashing windows and looting and setting fires and wander back to their homes. Like a tide receding off the shores. Cops are still wired with adrenaline, but there's no one to chase, no one to yell at. Just emptied, hollowed-out stores. When the owners return and see what's happened here, they're going to weep.

Stan tells Wildey he'll see him later. Wildey nods, does a half-wave.

"Get some sleep while you can. This ain't over. We're gonna hunt down and catch these guys. Throwing a goddamn couch on us!"

We, huh, Stan thinks.

Stan feels like hell the next afternoon. He's at the age where messing with sleep patterns throws his body into total chaos. His deepest bones ache. His stomach is leery about processing anything, and reminds him with belches and other alarming sounds. The world appears to have been draped in gauze, yet sounds and sensations are sharper than ever. Like his headache, for instance. Or Jimmy's records, which are loud, even though they're being played on the other side of the house.

Yet he's up, getting dressed, preparing himself to head back into the burning Jungle. Jimmy pokes his head into the bedroom just as Stan is pulling on a fresh white T-shirt.

"You were out pretty late, Pop. Was it bad?"

"Well, it wasn't good. But I think the worst is over."

"Think we're still going to the game on Tuesday?"

Stan looks at his boy. "We're *going*," he assures him. But he doesn't want to admit that he's not really sure, because he's got this sneaking suspicion the whole thing may boil up again. And again. And again. Until the *murzyns* have destroyed everything in North Philly.

Downstairs Stan pours tomato and clam juice over some ice and throws a shot of vodka in there, too. Drinks it down and makes another. Rosie pretends not to see, offers to make him some eggs and pork roll. Stan shakes his head. He doesn't want anything to eat right now.

He also doesn't want to tell Rosie and the boy about the fireball couch. But Rosie will talk to Taney's wife at some point today and then she'll be pissed at him for not telling her.

But of course Rosie gets pissed anyway, because two sentences into his story—which downplays the danger as much as he can—she's off on a tear, slapping him on the shoulder for not telling her earlier. Earlier? How much earlier did she want to know? *Good morning, Rosie, some* murzyns *dropped a burning couch on Billy Taney, hey, you feel like making me some eggs?*

Rosie makes a beeline to the phone just as Jimmy enters the kitchen, having heard enough of the story.

"They dropped a couch on you?"

"No, not me or Wildey—just Billy."

"Who's Wildey?"

"Some guy they partnered up with us last night."

Jimmy takes a seat across from his dad. Their rectangular table takes up most of the floor space in the kitchen. You have to shimmy around the table to do anything else in there, like open the fridge or check something in the oven. Stan never could understand why they need a table in the kitchen, because they have a perfectly good one in the dining room. But Rosie is stubborn. The dining room table is for holidays and entertaining; otherwise, they take their meals in the kitchen.

"Did you see who did it?" young Jimmy asks.

"No."

"You'll catch 'em, Dad."

"Yeah, you think?"

"Hey, partner. Welcome back to Hell."

Stan grunts.

While daylight seemed to send the worst of the looters into hiding, the fast-approaching evening has fired them up again. Even more cops were brought in for tonight's shifts, yet somehow, in all the chaos, Wildey found him again.

Wildey is waiting for him at the rendezvous point. "Hey, Stan. How's Taney?"

Stan shakes his head. He honestly doesn't know—he's a little ashamed that he hasn't thought of Taney much today. But that Irish bastard is tough. What's a flaming couch to a man like that?

"My wife talked to his wife," Stan says. "I think he'll be okay."

"You ready to do some hunting?"

"What do you mean?"

Wildey smirks. "Don't tell me you're gonna let some guys throw a motherfuckin' couch on us and just get away with it."

"Jesus, you sound like Jimmy."

"Who?"

"Never mind."

A few hours after dark the riot is in full swing again. Rioters: throwing bottles, bricks, launching more furniture off the roofs. Scrambling to start fires. Smashing any remaining windows that by some miracle weren't smashed the night before. Stan swears the word must have gotten out to neighboring areas. *Free shit on Columbia Avenue! Bring your own bricks and bats, take whatever you want.*

Tonight, though, their marching orders are different.

Tonight Deputy Commissioner Rizzo spreads word through the ranks: *Take no prisoners. The club is trump.* Meaning: Use your baton to stop any and all looting. "Beat 'em and leave 'em." No arrests. And if some bastard has the stone to take a shot at you, then you shoot back. He doesn't care what Leary said.

Wildey glances over at Stan.

"Tonight's gonna be interesting."

Stan's about to ask what he means when a police inspector walks up to him and taps his nameplate.

"Walczak. Stick your badge and your name in your pocket. Tell your partner to do the same."

"What for?"

The inspector stops and turns on his heel. A hairy fireplug of a man, he's clearly used to snapping orders without anyone questioning him.

"Just do it."

All the other uniforms in the area have apparently gotten the same word, because they're shoving all pieces of ID into their pants pockets.

"No," Stan says.

"What the fuck do you mean, no? Take 'em off! Orders from the deputy commissioner."

"I'm not taking my name off."

The inspector's face goes red. But he's apparently all hair and no backbone. He stalks away without another word. Stan catches Wildey staring at him.

"What? You want me to take it off?"

"Not at all," Wildey says, smiling. "C'mon. We'd better get in there."

"Yeah. Just don't do anything stupid like last night."

"I say we hit the roof again. See what we see."

"Yeah, that's what I'm talking about."

Tonight's assignment: search the rooftops to look for bottle-throwers—or worse, guys with guns. Wildey gestures to Stan: *Follow me.* Wildey tries to kick in a door next to Hollywood Shoes. The door won't yield. He tries again, putting more body weight into it, but Wildey's a lean, wiry guy. He could shoot himself out of a cannon pointed at that door and nothing would happen.

"Move out of the way."

Stan is not the swiftest cop on the force. He is not the smartest. He is nowhere near the most agile. Nor the most athletic. But at six two and 277 pounds, he's a force of nature. He's kicked in doors before.

One stomp of his black oxford and the door splinters and pops open. Wildey gives Stan an appreciative glance. Whatever. There's a moment of indecision before Stan sweeps his arms toward the door.

"After you."

Wildey shakes his head. "Okay, boss."

By the time they make it all the way up to the roof, Stan huffing and puffing, there's a loud shattering of glass and a terrified scream coming from street level. Wildey is already headed back down the rickety and dusty stairs they just climbed. What the hell. What choice does Stan have but to follow?

There, on the corner, a crowd armed with bats and rocks surrounds a man in a suit inside a glass telephone booth that's been shattered and knocked over on its side. The man has his forearms up to shield his face from the blows. The crowd seems intent on smashing the booth until there is nothing left—except the cowering white man inside.

Wildey is already running across the street with his nightstick out, yelling at them.

"The fuck's wrong with you? Get away from that man!"

The mob turns. They lift their bats. A few break off to greet Wildey with colorful language of their own.

Goddammit—Stan refuses to lose two partners in the same weekend.

Stan picks up his pace, pulling out his nightstick. By the time he reaches the crowd some of them are already pushing back on Wildey. Stan grips the stick at both ends, leaving two inches poking out on either side, just like he was taught at the Academy. When it's time to hit, you use controlled movements, firmly gripping the butt of the baton and keeping your feet balanced. Stan's going by the book for this—he's not going to start swinging wildly. Someone doesn't move, you go for the fleshy areas first—buttocks, meat of the arms and legs. Still won't move? Then you go for the joints—elbows, knees, wrists.

A few strikes and the crowd knows Stan is serious and starts backing away. They call him all kinds of names—devil, cracker, whitey—he's heard it all before and doesn't care.

Wildey pulls the man out of all that broken glass, wrapping his arm around the man's torso, helping him to a clear piece of sidewalk. He continues to yell at the crowd. "What the hell's wrong with you?" Stan keeps guard, ready to strike if need be.

The guy's cut up and knocked around pretty bad, but he'll be okay. Wildey talks to him for a while in a low, quiet voice until the fire department medics show up.

"They didn't know what that was," Wildey mutters. "Unbelievable."

Stan squints. "Who was that?"

"Radio reporter for DAS. He was calling in what he was seeing. They saw the suit, thought he was a white guy, then started throwing rocks at the booth. He barricaded himself up, so they knocked the fucking booth over on its side."

"What do you mean, thought he was a white guy? Isn't he?"

Wildey stares at him. "Would it matter?"

JIM CATCHES A CASE

November 2, 1995

Jim wakes up with no idea where he is. He tries to roll over. Claire's unconscious grip on his arm tightens.

Oh, that's right. I'm home.

He'd made it a late one, and he can only remember pieces of it. It all started when he decided he could use a drink or three at the Palm, but that wasn't enough, so he headed over to…gahhh. Some other bar. Come on, think…wait wait. The Pen & Pencil, over on Latimer Street. He barged his way in for an impromptu game of darts with the newspaper boys. Ron Patel was there. Clark DeLeon, too. Danny tending bar, talking him into a fat juicy cheeseburger he really shouldn't be eating, considering he's gone up two full pant sizes since spring. Lots of young kids—aspiring reporters, making stupid jokes and killing brain cells by the bucketload. But it was a much-needed break from the job.

Jim frees his arm and glides out of bed and steps on something hard yet pliable in places. Turns out to be his watch. He swallows a yelp. Claire stirs but doesn't wake up. Some lizard part of her brain knows she doesn't have to rise until the first child awakens, so she doesn't.

And now there's an urgent beeping sound. Shit, where are his pants? His beeper is in his pants.

Shit.

The beeper goes off again. Jim finally locates his pants (great detective work, Detective). His beeper inside the right pocket. The 215 number on the display belongs to Jim's partner, Aisha, which means somebody has died.

Jim slips on his pants, makes his way downstairs and around Staś on the pullout couch and finally over to the kitchen phone, stepping around Audrey's dolls and trucks and Fisher-Price doctor gear. He loves the girl, but damn if she isn't like a locust, spreading a wide swath of destruction and ruin everywhere she goes.

He dials his partner without even thinking about the number. Of course she's up, most likely freshly showered, dressed, highly caffeinated.

"What's up, Aisha?"

"We've got a dead girl near Twenty-First and Pine. How fast can you get there?"

"We're up again?"

"Apparently. So how soon?"

"I'll be there in fifteen."

And he can. The joy of being awake in Mayfair at this time of the morning is that he can zoom down I-95 in ten minutes flat, merge right, dart up the Vine Street Expressway, and boom, he's in Center City. If this were an hour later, though, he'd be screwed, and better off crawling down Aramingo Avenue. Or huffing his way down there on foot.

Jim hangs up, take a deep cleansing breath. There's no time for a shower, just breakfast. He dresses in whatever's available and makes his way down to the kitchen, where he pours a glass of orange juice, spiked with a little Absolut — perfect hangover cure.

Pants on, shirt buttoned, tucked in, tie tied, jacket on, shoes on, wallet check (check), watch on, badge check (check), gun (check), and downstairs Jim goes, as quietly as possible.

That's because his oldest, Staś, is sprawled out on the sleeper sofa, one gangly foot sticking out from under an afghan his grandma made. This past school year Staś, a senior, announced he was sick and tired of sharing a bedroom with his brother. So until (a) they moved into a bigger house, or (b) Dad surrendered the basement and finished it into a spare bedroom, Staś informed the family he would be taking over the living room couch at 11 p.m. every night.

Jim really couldn't say much to that. Kid was right.

So now he edges around the sofa bed, which takes up a fair chunk of living room real estate. Staś snores with his mouth open. Just like he did when he was a baby.

Jim is almost home free.

Almost...

Because standing there, in the kitchen doorway, is baby girl Audrey.

Swear to God—the girl never, *ever* sleeps.

"Honey, what are you doing up?"

"Good morning, Daddy!" she says, knuckling her eyeball to dislodge the sleepies and crusties. "I'm hungry."

Jim kneels down next to her, even though dipping down like this makes him a little dizzy.

"Shhh or you'll wake Staś."

"I'm hungry!"

"Look, I've got to go to work, sweetie. Your mommy will be up soon. She'll fix you breakfast."

"But I want pork roll!"

"I wish I could stay and make you pork roll. Believe me, sweetie. But I really have to go and be a policeman."

She pouts. Jim hugs her. She still pouts. Jim picks her up, twirls her around once (even though it roils his stomach in an extremely disturbing way), sets her back down, kisses her forehead, then sends her back up to Claire. Let her deal with the pork roll situation.

Outside, Jim blinks as the harsh early-November wind whips down the street and flash-freezes his sweat. It's raining, too, which adds more moisture to the sweat. He's got his own weather system going on, in addition to the hurricane in his guts.

And it's not going to get any better once he sees what's waiting for him downtown.

Two squad cars are blocking off Twentieth and Pine, yellow tape already up. The uniforms' faces are familiar but Jim can't recall their names. He fakes it with a nod.

They lead him to a stairwell a dozen yards away from the corner, along the side of a building. A black wrought-iron fence prevents passersby from taking a tumble down the stairwell, which leads to the basement level.

And there she is.

Her neck is twisted as if someone called her name and she whipped her head around to see who. Mouth slightly open, registering surprise. Eyes closed.

Top half of her is on the concrete landing, the rest of her curled up on the last two steps from the bottom. She's athletic, good body, wearing nothing but a pair of sneakers, socks, and a sports bra. A ripped black tank top is in the corner of the landing. No sign of her pants.

A set of keys, a few steps down.

Jim takes a step back, takes in the context. This is a beautiful block, one of the nicest Philadelphia has to offer. Tree-lined, with immaculate turn-of-the-century rowhomes, with late-model cars parked in front of them. The kind of place Jim could afford if he didn't have three kids.

Jim's beeper goes off. The number: 215-744-5655. He doesn't recognize it. If it doesn't have anything to do with this particular job, he doesn't want to hear about it right now. He's no good at multitasking.

A few yards away, the passenger window of a Plymouth Acclaim is cracked.

"Does the car belong to the 5292?"

The number is slang for a dead body—and the last four digits of the old city morgue phone number.

"We're running the plates now."

"Call Tow Squad and make this car a guard for prints."

Between the Acclaim and the stairwell is a Walkman, headphones still attached. Jim bags it—maybe it belonged to the vic. If so, robbery was not a motive. Though he knew that from the missing pants.

"Any ID on the 5292?"

Nope.

He asks a uniform who called it in.

At about 7:40 a.m., guy walking his dog happened to look down, see the body. At first he thought it was a department store dummy. Then he realized she was real. He threw up, then went to a pay phone to dial 911.

Guy checks out, at first glance—he's an attorney, gay, young, rich. Worth a follow-up, but he's probably not *the* guy.

"Who can tell me about that door?"

A patrolman tells Jim the landlord says it can only be opened from the inside. No knob on the outside.

Aisha's not here yet—she's coming all the way from Mount Airy and Lincoln Drive is probably a nightmare.

Jim has the stairwell photographed like crazy. He doesn't want a single detail to disappear.

Jim tells the uniforms to watch for any lookiloos. The kind of creep who would snuff a girl, then hang around to watch the aftermath. There's always a decent chance the doer is there watching them process the scene.

The TV news trucks arrive, one after the other. Word spreads fast. Jim has the patrolmen keep them back. This story is going to blow up; he knows that already. Pretty dead white girl killed in a nice neighborhood—the nicest neighborhood in the city, in fact.

Aisha arrives just after the first news van. She's a few years younger than Jim, pretty new to homicide, married with two kids, unhappily from what you gather. But works hard to keep both sides of her life going at full tilt.

"Hey."

"Detective. What do you have?"

Jim tells her, jack shit, then brings her up to speed. The girl is probably in her early twenties. The coroner will tell you more.

But a narrative is already forming. Part fact, part questions, part possibilities.

Girl out for a morning run, some scumbag grabs her, maybe with the idea that he's going to pull her into a car and take her somewhere. She's strong and fit; she fights back. Scumbag doesn't like that. Scumbag slams her into the Acclaim. Punches her once or twice to let her know he means it for real. She drops her cassette player. Why doesn't she scream? Even at 7 a.m., this block is full of joggers, dog-walkers, people headed into work early. Up and down this block, people were waking up, squeezing their eyes open, knocking back their first cup of Folgers. If she screamed, someone would have heard it, called it in. This isn't the sixties; this isn't a Kitty Genovese situation.

No, scumbag cut off her air supply, most likely. And when he couldn't get her into the car, maybe he dragged her down into the stairwell to do his thing. He got as far as pulling off her pants—jogging pants, had to be—before realizing that his forced "date" was dead.

Then, presumably, scumbag flees.

But nobody sees him? This time of morning, in a busy neighborhood just waking up for the Thursday workday?

What—did he vanish into the early-morning rain?

Doesn't make sense.

People ask Jim all the time, how do you stay professional and dispassionate at a murder scene? Jim usually smiles, says it's not about that.

Homicide, he tells them, is a story.

That story begins with someone's death. Homicide detectives simply ask the who, the what, the why, the where, the how.

But seeing someone all dead, just laying there, I don't know how you handle it.

At which point Jim just says something about it being part of the job. Most people don't want to dwell on the topic. They're usually looking for a lurid detail or two, maybe a grisly story they can share with their friends.

Which is why Jim doesn't tell them the whole story.

Truth is, if you are killed in Philadelphia, and the police don't solve it within a week, then chances are your killer will get away with it. This is thanks to sheer volume—in a city the size of Philadelphia, with bodies dropping on a daily basis, the homicide department will have other dead bodies demanding their attention.

The other truth is, it depends what kind of person you were.

Every homicide cop says the same thing in private. When they see your body on the ground, they ask themselves: Are you a good guy, or a bad guy?

Do you have a record? You just get out of prison? You steal from your dealer? You beat your wife, your kids? You kill other people?

In which case, yeah, homicide cops will do their jobs. But that's just going through the motions. It's not about you, scumbag, it's about clearing jobs.

But if you're a good guy, then nothing gets the adrenaline pumping quicker. You deserve the full-court press.

Jim's at his best when there's an innocent victim whose story demands to be told.

Just like this woman, who was out minding her own business, jogging in Center City early in the morning, because everyone told her it was safe to do so.

Jim imagines Audrey twenty years from now, living downtown, going for a run, then some scumbag lunges at her...

By noon the 5292 is identified.

The staff at a local magazine called *Metropolitan* heard about the dead girl, said one of their employees matching her description (blond, pretty) hadn't shown up for work.

Her name is Kelly Anne Farrace. Twenty-five years old, fact-checker, new to the city, moved here in the spring from Ohio.

Jim and Aisha head over to 1919 Market Street, thirty-sixth floor, to look at her employment records, the company head shot. Yeah, it's definitely her.

Jim's familiar with the magazine, though not a fan. It's allegedly a city magazine, but more concerned with rich people out in the suburbs. What to wear, where to eat. When they write about cops, they're usually condescending and focusing on the bad, never the good. As usual.

Jim gathers the staff in a conference room to get a general sense of Kelly Anne. At this point he's not worried about one-on-ones with close friends. That will come next. What Jim's looking for now is a quick overview—learn as much as possible, then plot their next moves.

Aisha, meanwhile, volunteers to call Kelly Anne's parents. They usually take turns, unless they get the idea that the awful news would be better coming from a white man or a black woman. In this case, they're meeting with an all-white magazine staff, so they don't bother having the conversation. Aisha will call the parents, Jim will get the ball rolling here.

Outwardly, Jim aims to be friendly, patient, calm, and easygoing. He's your priest. He's your rabbi. He's here to set things right.

"Tell me about Kelly Anne," Jim says, then leans back to listen.

"She was a sweetheart," the editor-in-chief says, "with a tremendous future ahead of her."

"Funny, sweet"—the same words are repeated over and over. "Clearly, she's not from around here," one copy editor says, trying to lighten the mood. But Jim knows what they mean. Philadelphians have this protective shell you have to work to get past. (If you ever get past it.) Apparently Kelly Anne didn't have the same kind of armor.

Jim gives a polite laugh. "So her job here was...?"

"Research editor. She goes through every article and makes sure they're factually accurate."

Jim nods, writes this down. He's surprised the mag has such a thing, considering the amount of bullshit it publishes.

"Was she working on any stories of her own?"

The editor-in-chief's eyes fall to the man on his right. Blow-dried hair, handsome, roughly Jim's age, maybe a little younger, a lot more slender.

"Uh, yeah. Kelly Anne was part of the reporting team for our next 'Thirty Under Thirty' package," Blow-Dry Guy says.

"And what's that?"

"You know, where we profile thirty up-and-coming Philadelphians under the age of thirty."

Jim nods as if he's familiar with the feature. He's never heard of it. *Metropolitan* is not really his choice of reading material.

Jim continues to pick away at them. The entire staff seems to be in shock; some cry. But some of the editors and writers fire back questions. They can't help it. It's in their blood. This is a tragedy, but it's also potentially the biggest story in the magazine's history. Why would someone assault and strangle their fact-checker? Or was it just coincidence?

Jim asks the coworkers about boyfriends, and the younger staffers tell him Kelly was single and dated around a little, no one specific. He hates talking to journalists because they read into everything, come up with stories on their own with little regard to fact.

What is Kelly Farrace's story going to be? Random attack, or someone she knew? Those are the only two options.

Jim's beeper goes off again. Same unknown number. 215-744-5655. Who the hell is this? Who cares. Not now.

Aisha returns, her eyes puffy. Parents are never an easy call to make. Looks like it didn't go too well.

"You okay?" Jim asks when they're alone in the lobby.

"Yeah, I'll be fine. They're going to come out here late tonight. I scheduled a time for us to meet with them tomorrow morning."

"Sounds good. Okay, let's wrap up here and get to her place."

Now that Aisha is back they divide and conquer: she talks to the women, Jim handles the men. But in the end they have very little that's new. Kelly Anne Farrace was a very sweet girl from out of state who worked long hours as a fact-checker, dated around a little, nothing serious, and kept to herself a lot.

Nobody even knew she jogged.

Now that they know her name, it's time to visit her place. The magazine's human resources person gives them the address. Luckily, it's not far—close enough to walk, in fact. They drive anyway.

Kelly Anne's apartment is small, expensive, and cluttered. The price is thanks to the location, Sixteenth and Spruce, just a few blocks away from *Metropolitan*'s office. Jim guesses she preferred to stay within a certain radius of her new magazine job. That meant taking a claustrophobic studio apartment that cost her $500 a month when she was bringing home no more than $650 every two weeks.

The rest of her paycheck apparently went to clothes, which are scattered everywhere. It reminds him of Audrey's disaster area of a bedroom. Kelly Anne probably treated this studio apartment as one big walk-in closet, and the rest of Center City as her living room.

Maybe that's why she felt comfortable jogging at 5 a.m. She considered the streets outside *her* streets.

Jim scans the apartment, trying to run the narrative, visualizing her final few hours in this place. Aisha follows behind. She's only been with homicide for a year; Jim is her senior by far. She's also the only black woman in the department.

"So she wakes up early, decides to go for a run," Jim says.

"But there's no bed," Aisha says.

Turns out Kelly Anne has a pullout sleeper sofa, one of the early-1980s variety, probably a hand-me-down from her parents. Jim thinks about his boy Staś, crashing out in their living room on the pullout every night. All over this couch are a bunch of multicolored clothes—skirts, bras, blouses. As if her closet got drunk one night and threw up all over the place.

"Looks like she was trying things on and not liking anything," Aisha says.

"You don't get up in the morning, push your bed back into a couch, and then scatter your clothes all over it, do you?"

"I don't. So maybe she slept somewhere else. Like a boyfriend's place."

"I don't know," Jim says. "Her coworkers don't seem to think she was seeing anyone steady."

"Maybe someone new."

"Maybe."

Jim moves through the apartment, careful not to step on anything or touch anything that would taint the scene. He's been to thousands of crime scenes over the past twenty years and his careful movements are hardwired into his body. Aisha, meanwhile, hangs back. The crime-scene unit tore her a new one a few months ago, and the scolding is still fresh in her head.

Was Kelly Anne this messy? Jim wonders. Or is this staged? Was someone else in this tiny apartment?

Over on a dresser drawer that doubles as a desk, Jim spots a weekly minder book, open to the current week. There are initials penciled in for last night: *MS* next to the 9 p.m. line, and then *JDH* at the 11 p.m. line.

There are more initials set for today, and tomorrow, but clearly Kelly Anne won't be making those appointments.

Jim taps yesterday's space. Aisha looks over his shoulder.

"We need to put some names to these initials," he says.

Back at the Roundhouse, Jim has a visitor making herself at home in his cubicle.

"Hello, handsome," she says.

Aisha shoots him a look: *This somebody I need to know about?* She's been in the department long enough to know you cover up a partner's infidelities. But Jim gives a quick shake of his head to tell her *no*, then narrows his eyes to follow up with *You're an asshole for even thinking it.*

"Aisha, this is Sonya Kaminski. Sonya, this is my partner, Aisha Mothers."

Sonya seems to float out of her chair and extends a hand. "Pleasure to meet you. I'm with the mayor's office."

Aisha's eyebrows levitate. Mayor's office. Well, la-dee-dah.

Sonya is probably close to Jim's age, though he'd never say such a thing out loud. When guessing a woman's age, always shave off at least a decade. Or better yet—shut the fuck up entirely.

Jim should have known the mayor would send someone. After all, a pretty white girl in her twenties has been raped and murdered in Center City.

What surprises Jim is that he sent Sonya Kaminski.

Jim met her two years ago when he caught her smoking pot with a bunch of journalists on a Green Street rooftop. She charmed him into forgetting about it (not that he was going to bust the fifth estate over a few joints), said they should have drinks sometime soon, she'd heard a lot of great things about him, practically sitting in his lap. ("She's fresh off a divorce and holding open auditions for the next one," police pals said.) She saw Jim's nameplate and made a Polish joke. *Sto lat!* Hundred years. Polish Mafia, in da house.

Later, he realized who she was—and was doubly glad he hadn't busted her. Sonya's father is wheelchair-bound union boss Sonny Kaminski, the King of Queen Village, who reportedly made millions when they razed whole blocks to build I-95. Never make enemies who can bury you in cash.

"How are the boys?" she asks now.

"Crazy as ever."

"And your little girl, Audrey?"

"Great, just great," he says, making it a point to smile. "What's up, Sonya?"

"I'm thrilled you caught this one, Jimmy," she says. "If anyone's going to catch this monster, it's you. Along with Detective Mothers, of course. We need this resolved as soon as possible."

"Resolved."

"You know what I mean."

Any crime that happens to people in the imaginary safe zone that is Center City Philadelphia needs to be *resolved* as quickly as possible. Philadelphia has spent a lot of time and effort convincing people there is at least one neighborhood within the city limits where you probably won't be beaten, raped, and strangled to death. Part of Sonya's job, best as Jim can figure, is maintaining this illusion.

"I understand the parents are flying in first thing tomorrow," Sonya says. "The mayor would like to meet with them personally."

"That's a good idea. After we talk to them, of course."

Sonya smiles. "Of course. So I want to be able to tell the mayor something. Whatcha got so far?"

Jim spreads his hands. "We're doing everything we can to catch this guy."

"So you think it's one guy?"

"I don't think anything yet, Sonya. What do you want me to say? You know how this works."

"I want something specific that I can give the mayor. I want to be able to tell him that a rapist-killer isn't stalking the streets right now, prowling for his next victim."

"You'll be the first to know when I have something, I promise."

Jim remembers: next Tuesday is Election Day. The mayor, running for his second term, doesn't want this lingering in people's minds. Never mind that the challenger is no threat whatsoever—this town hasn't put a Republican in room 215 for nearly fifty years. But the mayor wants to be America's mayor. There's already talk about a run for the governor's office, maybe even the White House in 2000.

So that's what this is about. A pretty blonde turns up dead in the worst possible way, in what is allegedly the safest part of the city.

Sonya turns to appraise Aisha. "You're new to the homicide unit, aren't you?"

"New enough, I guess."

"You're in good hands with Detective Walczak here."

Aisha just stares at her.

What Sonya means to say, Jim thinks, is you're the perfect partner for our white male detective here. Black female. Balances it out perfectly. Especially if it's the worst-case scenario and it turns out that a black male had something to do with Kelly Anne Farrace's death. Considering all that racial shit in the Thirty-Ninth this past summer.

Sonya reaches out and lays her hand on Jim's tie. "Drinks soon?"

"Sure, Sonya. Drinks soon. On the mayor's office, right?"

She pulls his tie once—a playful little snap that loosens the knot a bit.

The drinks will never happen, he thinks. But she'll be riding his ass right up until Election Day, that's for sure.

They work into the late hours. Jim calls home to update Claire. Thankfully, she doesn't mention last night. She knows what a case like this means for his hours and mental state. Jim asks about the boys. No surprise, Staś and Cary almost came to blows during dinner. Over what? Who knows.

"Audrey says she misses you."

"Tell the little animal I miss her, too."

"Someone called the house looking for you. Wouldn't leave his name."

"Oh yeah? What was the number?"

Claire checks the caller ID, tells him it was 215-744-5655. Right. Same number that's been beeping him all day. Calling his home now, too, huh? Cops' homes are supposed to be sacred, but people have all kinds of ways of glomming numbers and addresses. Jim should call the guy back, but he's pissed at the intrusion. Let him wait. There's real work to be done.

Jim begins assembling the murder book while Aisha puts together an interview list. Close to eleven, Aisha decides she's had it—she needs to go home, freshen up, tackle this one with clear eyes first thing in the morning. This is the cue for Jim to go home, too. But he's too wired. "Gonna stay and work at this a little while longer," he says.

"Whatever, man, you're the mayor's best friend."

"Very funny."

But after a while it all becomes a blur. He needs rest but heads over to the Palm for a nightcap—Stoli martini, dry. The bartender slides it across the wood and says, "You ever leave last night?" Jim nods and smiles, takes the drink, downs half of it in a single go. Pulls the green olives from the toothpick with his teeth, one by one. Chews them, thinking about Kelly Anne. Imagining her down in the concrete stairwell, neck twisted up like that. Jim orders another martini. The bartender nods, sets about pouring the ingredients into the silver shaker. Just two. A respectable nightcap. Any more and we start getting into *should I really be driving* territory. But twenty minutes later, Jim orders one more anyway. Thinking about all those clothes on Kelly Anne Farrace's couch.

Jim arrives home at Unruh Avenue well after midnight to find a black man sitting on his stoop.

A second later he's going to hate himself for reaching for his gun. The guy must see the tension in the moment because he immediately throws up his hands and says,

"Hey, man—it's me!"

Jim pauses.

Jesus Christ, it's George Wildey, Jr.

Jim hasn't seen him since this past May, outside that bar at Seventeenth and Fairmount, looking all shivery and cracked out.

"George," Jim finally says. "Sorry. You kind of startled me there. How's it going? You been out here long?"

Jim looks up to see if the front bedroom light is still on, but no. Claire's gone to sleep. Good thing Junior here had the good sense not to knock.

"You got a minute?" George Junior asks. "I didn't mean to scare you, but I've been trying you on that beeper all day."

Ah, so *this* is 215-744-5655. Jim remembers slipping George Junior here his professional courtesy card back in May. So maybe the guy is in real trouble. Again. Why else would he be sitting out here on a front stoop on a cold November night?

"You want to come inside?" Jim asks.

George Junior blinks. "Naw, I know it's late. I just wanted to make sure you saw this." He reaches under his jacket and for a strange moment Jim thinks, He's got a piece under there.

Turns out, it's just a newspaper. Today's *Daily News,* folded in half. "What's this?"

Jim figures George Junior's in some kind of jam and he's reaching out for help. Back when their dads worked together they would be forced to play with each other, but it was clear neither boy liked the other. Jim remembered the Wildeys coming over sometime around the holidays, and he was pretty sure George Junior broke some of his new toys out of spite. And Jim absolutely hated being in the Wildeys' neighborhood. Lots of eyes, staring you down.

"They're letting him out," George Junior says.

"Who?" Jim asks, taking the paper.

"Page five," George Junior says.

Jim squints in the dim light and scans the page until his eyes find the name buried in the six-inch piece. There it is. The name. That *horrible* name. It hurts him even to look at it. He hasn't seen that name in print for a long, long time.

Terrill Lee Stanton, fifty-two years old, sprung early from his supposed life sentence through some kind of new amnesty program based on his hard work and good behavior while behind bars.

"Can't fucking believe it," Jim mutters.

"See what I'm saying? This is why I've been calling you, man. There ain't no statute of limitation or whatever on murder, right?"

The reporter—who's either a veteran or has done some righteous digging in the newspaper's morgue—mentions Stanton was a notorious North Philly "agitator" who got under the skin of both police officers and civil rights leaders. Some even claimed he was one of the men who helped fan the flames of the '64 riots on Columbia Avenue. He led a life of petty crime until 1970, when he was tried and convicted of killing a shopkeeper during a liquor store robbery gone wrong.

"You can reopen the case, can't you? Nail his ass proper this time?"

There is no quote from Stanton himself, but his caseworker told the paper that "Mr. Stanton is eager to make a positive contribution to the city of Philadelphia, and he's grateful for the support he's received." Family of the shopkeeper could not be reached.

"Jimmy, man, you hearing what I'm saying?"

"Yeah, I hear you, George." Jim folds the paper and hands it back. He has to be careful here. Inner Jim is screaming, but George Junior doesn't need to meet him. So it's Outer Jim who tells him,

"It's been thirty years—no physical evidence, no witnesses. I don't think there's much I could do."

(Yes there is. You promised.)

George Junior takes the paper, sighs, smacks it on his leg, lowers his head.

"Fuck, man."

"I know that's not what you want to hear."

"Damn sure isn't," he says before lifting his head and locking eyes with Jim. "This motherfucker shot our daddies point-blank in the head—and he gets to walk away? Why does he get a free pass? Shit, I know people been locked up for longer than this and they ain't murderers!"

He's right, Jim. You going to let this monster score a free pass?

"George, buddy, it's late."

Junior takes this as his cue, but he's not happy about it. He grunts as he pulls himself up from the concrete stoop, then pats Jim on the shoulder.

"I know, man. I just wish..."

"Look, let me see what I can do. I'm not going to promise anything, but let me see."

"Yeah, yeah, okay."

Junior makes like he's going to leave but then stops in his tracks.

"Oh—and look, I never scratched your record."

Jim stares at him, truly perplexed. "What?"

"When we were kids, I was over with my old man on New Year's Day, you thought I scratched one of your new records. It wasn't me, man. It was one of those other kids. What's his name, Taney. One of Taney's kids."

"It's okay, George. I'm over the record. You take care."

Jim waits until George Junior has walked back down the block and turned the corner before reaching into his pocket to pull out his keys. His hand is shaking so violently it's as if the keys have been electrified.

Jim opens the front door as quietly as he can. Which is a real trick, considering the damned thing has a deep-set creak that more or less alerts the whole house to anyone's arrival. He can't see anyone tonight. He just can't.

Put the Stanton stuff out of your head for now, Jim, there's nothing you can do.

(But then again, you did promise.)

The living room is dark. Staś is dead asleep. Jim starts creeping up the stairs toward the bathroom, where he can finally peel off his clothes. He remembers something. He sniffs his shirt. Any telltale signs?

"Hi, Daddy," a voice whispers from the darkness.

Audrey sits patiently at the top of the staircase, elbows on her knees, little feet poking out from under her nightshirt.

Shit.

"Hi, sugar," Jim whispers back. "You should be in bed."

She's light but squirmy. Jim puts her down.

"What did you do today, Daddy?"

All Jim can see is Kelly Anne Farrace's head twisted at an unnatural angle. His father in his coffin, thick hands folded, waxen eyes shut. I dealt with dead people, Audrey, he wants to say. But of course he can't.

"Tried to catch some bad guys. And now I'm going to put a drunk and disorderly female to bed."

She giggles. He carries her to her room. She insists, of course, on being carried, even though she's getting a little too big for that. The stairs creak under his shoes as he carries their collective weight up, up, up. He's still drunk and feels the house do a tiny spin around him.

"Good night, sweetheart."

"Read me a story."

"Honey, it's way too late for a story."

"I'm not tired."

"Admit it, kid. We're both exhausted."

He lays her down in bed and reaches out to touch her cheek, but stops when he realizes his hand is still trembling. *Fuck.* He drops it. Audrey senses him pulling away and reaches out to grab the sleeve of his shirt.

"Daddy, please?"

"Audrey, *please,* go to sleep. Daddy's had a really long day."

AUDREY SAVES HER ASS

May 8, 2015

Audrey rolls over and her knuckles bang hard on hard wood. Even in its half-awake state, her brain informs her: *Wow, that kinda fucking hurt.* She forces her eyes to open.

For a brief moment she has no idea where she is. Then it all comes back: the flight home, the memorial, the drinking, the drinking, the drinking, and then this...yes, this glorious hangover.

She's in her mother's apartment. Technically, her mother's boyfriend Will's apartment. Audrey is in the guest bedroom, but don't let that fool you. There's no bed in here.

She rolls off the inflatable bed and comes down hard on a knee, reminded once again that it's all hardwood floors up in this mother. Fancy Center City living at its finest. Audrey recalls with delight the words tumbling out of Will's mouth ("Sure, uh, make yourself at home") with his eyes saying quite the opposite (*You're a tattooed trainwreck—I don't want you anywhere near my home*).

Well, sorry, Will. I'm going to be hanging around for a little longer than you thought.

Oh yes I. Am.

She sent the email last night. She was drunk enough to be heartfelt, yet sober enough to make a convincing proposition.

And lo! Within an hour, her advisor responded. A cautious yes, and a request for a formal proposal by first thing Monday, but still a yes. A life preserver, tossed into the churning waters.

Audrey celebrating by going drinking with Cary in a series of bars in the vicinity of Thirteenth and Sansom. The logic: if things got ugly, they could literally crawl home to Will's apartment building. In retrospect, both should have stayed home. Nobody guessed they were brother and sister out on a sibling bender. With Cary still in his police dress uniform and Audrey in her...well, her usual duds... everybody was thinking *cop and suspect*.

Now she shuffles zombielike through the kitchen. A cat (Audrey can't remember its stupid name) tumbles out of its litter box, shaking, as if it's just taken an epic shit and has to recover its senses.

Audrey needs a Bloody Mary, stat.

She gathers the ingredients from Will's well-stocked kitchen. Four ounces of tomato juice, one (okay, two) ounces of Tito's Handmade Vodka, a teaspoon of lemon juice, an ounce of Worcestershire sauce, generous dashes of Tabasco sauce, then freshly ground salt, pepper, and a quarter teaspoon of celery salt. She rocks it back and forth between a Boston shaker and a pint glass, then dumps it into an ice-filled pint glass. Garnishes it with black olives—very important— pickle, lemon, and, of course, a celery stalk, which she psychologically associates with a life jacket.

Then she settles down to read the paper. Which always depresses her, even though she can't help herself.

The first story that catches Audrey's eye: a twenty-six-year-old mother, eight months pregnant, shot in the face by a stray bullet. Late on a Sunday morning. The girl was sitting outside, watching a neighbor's kid for a little while. Friends say she often sat outside to read. A block away, some monster saw a car he recognized and opened fire. The bullets missed the car. They hit the girl. She died at the hospital. They tried to save the baby. The baby died early this morning.

She wishes the Captain were still on the job. This is the kind of case he'd love. He'd track down the shooters in no time.

Then there's an update on what happened on Chancellor Street last September 11, of all days. A gang of clean-cut white people, dressed up for a night on the town, approached a gay couple, asked one of them, What are you, his boyfriend? Then proceeded to beat the shit out of them, fracturing skulls, before running away. Reportedly, police have some footage and will be posting a video soon.

What is wrong with this stupid city? Audrey sips her Bloody just as something out in the living room groans.

It's Cary, who crashed out on the couch, still in his dress uniform. And shoes.

And ooh, look, a can of beer in his hand.

"Uhhhhhhhhhhhhh," he says.

"Yeah, brother. Exactly."

Cary got into a fight with Jean via text last night. At first, she demanded he come home. Then, later, she told him he'd better not dare show up at home all drunk. She told her husband she was done. It's over. He can't keep doing this. Apparently, Jean says this all the time. Cary, meanwhile, still complains about being on restricted duty, as he has been for the past six years. He hurt his back (so he says) jumping out of a police van and his doctor says he can't handle the street yet. If ever. Nice work if you can get it, Audrey thinks.

"Time's your plane," Cary asks. Not out of curiosity. He promised to drive her, and he's wondering how he's possibly going to sober up in time.

"I changed my flight. I'm staying for a few more days."

Cary sits up and shakes his head. The question he's trying to formulate is hampered by endless fields of dead brain cells. His brain needs to reroute. *Rerouting. Rerouting. Rerouting...* Ah. There we go.

"Wait... why?"

Give me a slice and a double homicide,

Audrey wants to say.

But instead she asks for an iced tea. Her stomach can't handle pizza right now. She's still sweating from the walk up here, which was farther than she thought. She needs to replenish fluids, stat.

"That all?" the guy at the counter asks.

Audrey smiles at him. It's going to be important to lay on the charm, extra chunky style, with this guy.

"That's all."

She brings her drink to a Formica-topped table situated on the other side of the room, pulls out the wooden chair, which scrapes along the tiled floor, then sits down and takes in the whole place.

You can totally tell it used to be a bar, which is a relief to Audrey. If the owner had totally gutted the joint, she wouldn't have much to work with, and her advisor would sadly shake her head before pulling the chain that would flush Audrey's academic career down the toilet.

But no . . . this *totally* used to be a bar.

For one thing, the bar is still here.

The mammoth wooden bar itself, on which rest the register, the takeout menus, and the warming case holding slices of plain, mushroom, pepperoni, vegetarian, and so on. Instead of removing the bar, they just slapped some panels on the front to cover up the wood.

Then there's the floor, a mosaic of tiles that extends throughout the entire room. That's pretty amazing, too.

As a pizza place, it's no great shakes, even though it claims to be THE BEST IN PHILADELPHIA. There are a few tables, of course, but mostly they want you to stop in, order your slices and sodas, then get the fuck out. The owner has mounted a TV in the corner; right now CNN is live-updating the situation in Ferguson. They also cut the former tavern in half and put the ovens in the middle; in the other half of the joint, out of customers' view, is most likely the prep kitchen, employee restrooms, all that.

She can work with this.

Audrey takes a sip of her iced tea, then walks over to the counter, feeling the wooden top with her fingers. They've painted it to match the paneling. Shame, covering up good wood like this.

She peers up and down the counter, like a carpenter making mental measurements.

Pizza Counter Guy gives her a quizzical look.

"You want something else, miss?"

"No," Audrey says as cheerily as possible.

"Let me know if you do."

"Oh, I will."

Flash that smile. Work that charm, honey.

Audrey crouches down and touches the cool tile with her fingertips. Fifty years ago her grandfather bled out on these tiles. Once, a very stoned friend told Audrey that we exchange atoms with everything we ever touch. If that's true, then she's touching some infinitesimal part of her grandfather. Then again, Audrey also learned in some physics class that we never actually touch anything—that it's all a sensory illusion courtesy of our brain, and that in reality, existence is merely an ever-growing ball of quantum energy.

Pizza Counter Guy peeks over the top. "You okay?"

"Yeah," she says.

She looks at the paneling. Some of it will have to come off. If she's lucky, the holes will still be there.

"No, Aud, just... *no*. Real bad frickin' idea"

is what Cary said after Audrey told her brother she planned on solving their grandfather's murder, thereby putting a family mystery to rest—and saving her academic bacon at the same time.

"Why not?"

"Oh, I don't know. Because maybe Dad will go ballistic."

"Interesting choice of words," Audrey says.

"It's a stupid idea, Aud."

"Come on, Care. You're a cop. Sort of. Don't you want to find out who did it?"

"What are you talking about? Everybody knows who did it."

"What do you mean?"

Cary makes exasperated bug eyes. "Dad *knows* who did it."

Which is the exact moment that Claire emerges from her bedroom.

"Dad knows who did what?"

"Killed Grandpop Stan."

"Oh, Audrey," Claire says. "Don't go poking that wound, please, for all our sakes."

Audrey opens her purse and looks at the tools she scrounged from Will's apartment. It's one of those turnkey, maintenance-free deals, but Will likes to pretend he has testicles and keeps a small, pristine box of tools under the kitchen sink. He'll never miss the stuff. She finds the tool she's looking for: a crowbar so petite it should have the words FISHER-PRICE stamped on its side.

Crouching down, she looks for a weak spot, fingertips gliding along the paneling.

Finds one.

She shoves the end of her baby crowbar into the gap, then pulls.

KEEEERAACK.

Tiny nails jiggle in the holes. This was slapped up in a hurry. This joint may have THE BEST PIZZA IN PHILADELPHIA, but they employed a shoddy-ass remodeling crew.

Counter Guy can't exactly ignore the noise, of course. He comes out from around his counter to look at what the crazy white girl with the tattoos is doing.

"Uh, miss?"

"Just a second," Audrey says.

KEEERAACK.

There. Panel off.

She gingerly lays it up against the next panel, then turns her attention back to the exposed bar.

"If you didn't like the iced tea, I would have given you something different."

"Shit," Audrey says.

"Maybe a Diet Coke?"

The naked bar reveals... nothing obvious. Burn marks from countless cigarettes. Nicks and chips from decades of shoe tips and knees and bar stools. Audrey runs her palms along the exposed surface. Maybe the former owners patched up the holes? Or she's looking in the wrong spot.

"I don't mean to pry into my customer's business," Pizza Counter Guy says, "but what are you doing?"

Audrey knows this is where she's going to have to (a) come clean and (b) pour on the maximum charm. But now that she's sizing up Pizza Counter Guy, she's betting it won't be about making pouty kissy-faces. There's a light on behind his eyes. The Diet Coke line *was* pretty funny.

She stands up to face him, petite crowbar in her hands. Pizza Counter Guy eyes the crowbar.

"Before it was a fine Italian-themed dining establishment," Audrey says, "this place was a bar. A taproom, if you will."

Pizza Counter Guy nods. "Yeah, there's a lot of crazy old stuff in the basement. Lots of sports memorabilia, neon signs."

"Well, in this very taproom, exactly fifty years ago," Audrey continues, "my grandfather was shot to death."

"What? You serious?"

Audrey was hoping he'd say something like that. When your prey is stunned, you go in for the kill.

She crooks her finger twice: *Follow me*. Counter Guy looks around, wondering if he's being led to an ambush or a practical joke, then follows anyway.

Outside, the early-May morning sun is high and hot in the sky. Audrey looks down at the memorial plaques. A day later, the caulk has completely dried. Someone's already flicked a cigarette butt on it, and ashes spray out over Officer Wildey's name.

Audrey crouches down, picks up the butt, flicks it into the street. Goddamned savages in this town.

"Ahhh," Counter Guy says. "The service yesterday, I get it. That was for your grandfather?"

Audrey nods solemnly.

"Which one is he?"

Audrey taps her boot on Stanisław Walczak's name.

"The Polish one."

"Walczak," he says, blurring the *cz* into a long *z*.

"Uh-uh. Pronounced wall-CHAK. Nobody ever says it right."

"Walczak," he says again, getting it right.

"There you go."

Pizza Counter Guy looks down at the fresh plaques for a while.

"So what happened?"

They're back inside now. Audrey's giving him the tour—as if she didn't set foot in this place for the first time yesterday. But she's been reading all morning and boning up on the essentials.

"Here's what I know. It happened around three in the afternoon. All those mirrors weren't here back then. Just plain old wood paneling. Grandpop Stan and his partner were at the bar, talking, having beers, their backs to the side door behind us."

"Drinking on the job?"

"They were supposed to be on picket detail."

"Wait—did you say this was back in sixty-five? By picket detail, do you mean the Girard College protests?"

"Yeah. And if I had a crap detail like that, I think I'd go drinking, too."

"That wasn't crap. That was historic."

"So is my thirst some nights. Anyway, stop interrupting me. You're supposed to be my sounding board."

"Oh, am I?" Smile on his face now.

But Pizza Counter Guy barely has the last syllable out before Audrey puts an index finger to his lips. She smiles sweetly, but her eyes say *Shut the fuck up*. Pizza Counter Guy purses his lips reflexively, which makes it look like he's kissing her finger.

"Yes, you are."

Audrey removes her finger. There's an uncomfortable moment where they're forced to acknowledge that yes, he just sort of kissed her finger. But then she moves on.

"Anyway, there are only three witnesses. The bartender and two old drunks at a couple of tables in the back—I'm guessing right where your kitchen is."

Audrey turns and points to the door on the Seventeenth Street side. "The shooter enters here, pistol in his hand. Bartender sees him first, said 'shit' or something. Which got Grandpop's attention."

Audrey points to the mirror behind the bar.

"Now, remember—those mirrors weren't there. So Grandpop had to turn around to see what was going on. So did his partner. I'm guessing this is the moment this dickbag saw that he was about to stick up a bar with two cops sitting about ten feet away."

"Were they in uniform?"

"Two sources say yes, one doesn't say. Either way, I've gotta think my grandpop tells the idiot he's a cop. And at that point, the smart thing would have been to drop the gun and run, right? Not this asshole. He opens fire."

Audrey stands up, walks to the side door. She turns to Pizza Counter Guy, fingers on her right hand making a gun.

"The shooter empties his gun into my grandpop, Wildey, and the bartender. Six bullets. Pshew. Pshew. Pshew."

She clears the distance between them, then drives her index and middle fingers into the flesh directly above Pizza Counter Guy's left nipple.

"Ow."

"First shot, right to the heart."

Her fingers hover in front of Pizza Counter Guy's lower belly.

"Second shot, to a few inches lower, in the gut."

She pokes. *Hard.* He cringes, a little self-conscious about the flab there.

"So then Wildey pulls his gun and is lifting it to return fire when the killer hits him with the third bullet, right in the throat. Wildey squeezes off a shot..."

Audrey walks back across the bar to the Seventeenth Street door, points to the wood frame.

"...that misses the shooter's head only by a few inches, according to the two drunks in the back."

Audrey slowly spins with her finger-gun, and now the other customers are really giving her worried looks.

"Hey, it's okay. Just telling my pal here about how my grandfather died."

Pizza Counter Guy doesn't react at all, as if people are always coming in here saying that. Audrey likes his cool, calm eyes.

"I would not lie about something that totally ruined my family."

Pizza Counter Guy nods like, *Okay, okay.*

"So we're up to what, four bullets? Grandpop was struck twice, according to the newspapers. But he still managed to draw his weapon and point it at the shooter. By then the shooter had locked on him again, and the best we can tell, they fired almost simultaneously, with the shooter beating him by a second."

Audrey leans in close, pointing her finger-gun again.

"Grandpop was shot in the jaw. The shooter caught a slug in the arm before firing one last time, at Wildey's chest. Shot to the heart. Then the shooter turned and stumbled out of the bar."

Audrey crouches down, touches the tile floor.

"Right here. This is where he bled out and died. This same tile floor."

The floor has been swept and mopped and covered in dirt and beer and ice and whiskey and slush and rock salt and everything else you'd track in from either Fairmount or Seventeenth Street. There is no trace of her grandfather left; Audrey knows this. But the tiles seem haunted anyway. Her grandfather touched them in his worst and final moments.

Pizza Counter Guy says, "They never caught the guy."

"They never caught the guy."

"That really sucks."

"My dad has a theory. He thinks it was a drug dealer named Terrill Lee Stanton. But officially, in the eyes of the law, nobody was arrested or even brought in for questioning."

"Terrill Lee Stanton still around?"

"Nope. Died about twenty years ago, according to my mother."

Audrey and Pizza Counter Guy stand across from each other, soaking it all in. The customers drift back to their conversations now that the crazy white girl seems to have finished shooting up the place.

"So... tomorrow morning, can you open early for me?"

"You want me to get up early on a Saturday to open a place that I don't even own just so you can tear apart our front counter to do some magical CSI stuff? You haven't even asked my name."

"Pretty much it. And I know your name."

"You do?"

"Sure I do. You're Sexy Pizza Counter Guy."

That gets a big silly smile out of him.

"Why are you doing this?"

Audrey says, "I have seven days to solve this murder."

"You have a week to solve a fifty-year-old murder?"

She explains that she's a graduate student, studying forensic science. (It's the only thing her dad would agree to bankroll.) Anyway, she's five months late on her winter independent project. In what amounts to an academic Hail Mary pass, she wants to see if the evidence trail points to a new suspect. There have been a lot of forensic advances since 1965.

"All due respect to your grandfather, but it sounds like this was just a robbery gone wrong. How can you possibly solve this?"

"The magic of forensic science, my friend."

"Are you hoping to exonerate Terrill Lee Stanton? Or confirm he actually did it?"

"I'm just trying to get my degree, man."

Pizza Counter Guy can't help it—he breaks out into a wide grin. Which makes him look all the more handsome.

"See?" Audrey says. "You're so fucking in."

After the pizza shop Audrey heads to the central branch of the Free Library up on the Parkway. They still have the same microfilm/newspaper room she hated visiting back in high school for class projects—it always felt like the reading room in a prison. Duh, there's this thing called the Internet, people, she used to say. But now she has to admit: the Internet doesn't have everything. So much of the past is tucked away on tiny strips of film.

She spends all day and countless quarters (pilfered from a cup in Will's place) traveling back in time, checking out May 1965.

There were five Philadelphia newspapers back then and all of them ran pieces about the Walczak-Wildey murders. A lot of them goofed up the details about the shooting. The cops fought back, the cops were on their knees, there was a shootout, there were only execution-style shots fired, blah blah blah. The details are sketchy, and contradictory. Some claim there were witnesses; others report no one saw what happened.

And none of them can seem to get her grandfather's last name right. Come on, people. There are worse Polish names out there.

Audrey knows she's going to need more than clips.

Last semester a professor of hers back in Houston passed out a *New York Times Magazine* essay about historical research by novelist Susan Cheever—daughter of the legendary novelist (and power-drinker!) John Cheever. She talks about four kinds of sources:

Primary: original historical documents, such as police files, the murder book, death certificates, autopsy report, and so on. No idea how tough that would be to dig up in this case. Philly police records, especially going back fifty years, might be a little spotty. Maybe the Captain could help, but she's not ready to make that painful and sure-to-be-awkward call quite yet.

Secondary: the work of other writers and researchers. (The contradictory newspaper clips, for instance.) Kind of useless at this point, as Audrey is discovering.

Tertiary: interviews with experts, other writers and researchers, or "people whose memories are useful." Audrey loves that one. *Hey there, hot stuff. That's one hell of a useful memory you've got on you.* But who was left who knew about May 1965? Grandma Rose and Audrey's father. Other cops, she guesses, who aren't dead or in the grip of dementia. We're talking about guys in their eighties by now.

Finally there's the fourth kind, a more nebulous and haunting category.

"It doesn't have a fancy name," Cheever wrote. "It is just going to the places where the story happened."

If Audrey is going to solve the murders of her grandfather and his partner, she's going to need all four. She's going to need to walk the streets they walked. And she's going to have to interview people with useful memories. Who knew her grandfather and his partner back in the 1960s? And are their minds still intact?

But most importantly, she's going to have to tear apart that pizza joint to find out what really happened to them.

STAN PUNCHES

September-October 1964

"That's his dick."

"Say what?"

"Swear to God," Wildey says, with the conviction of a man testifying under oath, "that guy on the corner is waving his dick around."

Stan tries to keep one eye on the road while using his other to look for this guy Wildey's talking about. Somehow, Wildey sees everything. To Stan, North Philly is nothing but a chaotic blur of people doing questionable shit all the time. This is their sector. This is what he deals with every night.

"You're crazy," Stan says. "Where?"

Right there, on Broad Street, in front of the mammoth Divine Lorraine Hotel. Black folks give the white perv a wide berth as he struts like a mummer, baton in hand. Teenagers yelling and pointing at the stupid honky with his peeper out. Unbelievable.

Stan pulls their big red machine to a halt but before the springs can finish rocking Wildey is up and out the door. They've been partners for exactly ten minutes and this is the job they catch. If Stan believed in omens, this would be a perfect one.

"Hey, man, what's going on?" Wildey says, looking around to make sure Weenie-Waggler here doesn't have any friends nearby. Sometimes holdup crews will bait you. Or in this case, masturbate you.

"Get away from me, you black pig!"

Furious strokes now, like he's trying to start a fire. His entire body quivers with pure rage.

"Why don't you put that thing away?"

"Why don't you suck on it for a while!"

"Thanks, man, but I've already had supper."

Stan's out of the car by this point, nervously scoping the scene. He hates uptown. Back before the war, the Lorraine Hotel used to be a fancy joint. But in 1948 it was sold to Father Divine and his Universal Peace Mission Movement. From what Stan understands, anybody could stay here—whites, blacks, men, women, whoever. A fully integrated hotel. You just couldn't drink, smoke, screw, or curse. And you had to dress modestly.

Maybe that's why they kicked this guy out.

"You don't want to say things like that, man," Wildey tells the guy. "Not in front of my partner."

"Fuck your partner!" the guy screams, stroking his cock and pointing it in Stan's general direction. Almost as if he's being literal.

Stan pulls his baton, thinking, Yeah, well, mine's bigger. One tap on the ol' *wacek* and this will be over.

"Hold on, hold on," Wildey says, as if reading his mind. He looks over at Stan, motions with his hand. *Easy.* "There's no need for that, Father."

Father? Did his new partner just call him Father? How old does he think he is, anyway?

Wildey turns his attention back to the perv.

"I'm telling you, man, you shouldn't curse around my partner. He's new on the force."

Weenie-Waggler is confused. He doesn't cease his stroking, but it most definitely slows down a little.

"And you know what he did before joining the force? He was an ordained minister. Isn't that right, Father Walczak?"

Stan blinks. Has Wildey lost his mind along with this guy? What the hell is he talking about, ordained minister?

But as Weenie-Waggler's face drops and goes ashen, Stan gets it.

"You really should put that away, my son," Stan says in a low, calm tone.

"Oh god, I'm sorry, Father! I didn't know, I didn't know," Weenie-Waggler stammers as he tries to tuck his cock back into his trousers. It's still too stiff to go in. All that blood refuses to dissipate, despite the presence of a man of the cloth.

"Father, you've gotta help me."

Stan looks at Wildey. Wildey nods at Stan's baton.

"Help him out."

Stan sighs, then raises the baton over the perv's head.

"Yeah, go in peace to love and serve the Lord."

The guy drops to his knees, and finally his fervor appears to flag.

As they're pulling away, Stan tells his partner, "Nice one." Wildey belly-laughs. "We ever in a tight spot with a black guy, you do the same for me, okay?"

This is the kind of shit they deal with at first.

And when Stan gets home the next morning and tells Jimmy the story about the guy with his *wacek* out, Rosie gets mad. He can't win.

Their bailiwick is the Jungle. Last-out shift, 11 p.m. to 7 a.m.

Stan Walczak knows this is his punishment, and he's just going to have to deal with it. He should have expected that his low-key tour of Whitetown couldn't go on forever. Hauling in boozehounds and busting up small-time numbers rackets is the cushiest assignment you can get in Philadelphia, outside of the Far Northeast or Chestnut Hill. Stan and Taney had their routine down, no surprises, no hassles. They took the expected payoffs—not too much, not too little.

Now Stan has to learn everything all over again in a neighborhood that is actively trying to burn itself down. How are you supposed to help people like that?

They sell it to him as a promotion, of course. Since Stan and

Wildey showed "extreme bravery" in pursuit of the rioters who dumped a flaming couch on top of poor Billy Taney, they were named part of a special "riot area detail," which is essentially the 420 worst blocks in North Philly. If there were any embers of the riot left, the detail was to stomp 'em out immediately. There would be zero tolerance for shit from now on.

The reaction at home to his "promotion" is mixed. Jimmy thinks the new assignment is exciting—but then again, he labors under the delusion that his father's some kind of cop like on *Dragnet*. The kid's devoured everything he could about the riots and asked Stan endless questions. Jimmy thinks his cop dad is famous, single-handedly stopping the looting and burning before it engulfed the entire city. He also likes the fact that his dad now wears a leather jacket to work, because technically the riot squad is a part of the highway patrol.

Rosie, on the other hand, is mortified. She grew up in a South Philly neighborhood that butted up against a black neighborhood, and her family would regale Stan with stories of how awful it was with all those moolies around. Now Rosie listens to her suburban cousins who think black people are going to bring about the end of the world. Get out now, they say. Move to Montgomery County, they say.

"We can move, Stanisław."

"Where, Rosie?" he asks, full well knowing the answer.

"Up in Telford," she says. "We can have a real backyard for Jimmy. And be closer to my sisters."

"What the hell would I do up in Telford? And how would we afford it?"

She hugs him around his chest. He feels her large, heavy breasts press into his stomach. This is calculated, but he doesn't mind.

And to be honest, Stan concedes she has a point. He wonders how much longer he can go on. Stan's been on the force since '51, and it's another seven years until he can think about retirement. Can he survive that long without his new *murzyn* partner getting him killed?

This is what he wonders about every morning in September when he drags his exhausted body home just in time for breakfast and to see Jimmy for a few minutes before he walks over to St. Bart's.

Sleep doesn't come easy. But when it does, it's time to wake up and shower and pull on the shirt and the Sam Browne belt and the shoes and go out and do it all over again.

"We gonna catch another game, Pop?"

"I don't know, Jimmy."

Doesn't know if he wants to bother.

On top of everything else, the Phils have completely fallen apart, as if the riot jinxed things. Sometimes Stan thinks he fell asleep in late August and woke up in an alternate universe. And in this version of Philadelphia, nothing is allowed to go right.

One night they're driving their big red machine by Twenty-Third and Lehigh, near Connie Mack. George tells Stan to stop, look at that. Stan hits the brakes, but before he can look, Wildey's out of the car and running across the street to where three white guys are beating an elderly Negro.

Stan scrambles out of the car to follow. Wildey yells for them to stop. Before Wildey can reach them, however, all three muggers turn their attention back to Wildey.

Now, Wildey expected the sight of a squad car and a couple of badges to stop these assholes from putting the beatdown on an old man.

These assholes, however, don't seem to care about badges. They do the math. They like their odds. One of them shouts,

"Kick his black ass!"

As Stan tries to clear the distance between them, he can see his new partner's split-second decision-making. Wildey's right hand, briefly reaching for the gun strapped to his hip. But what's he going to do—shoot one? These guys are jacked up on rage. If a badge won't stop them, the sight of a gun won't do it, either. And you never draw unless you're prepared to put them all down. Does he really want to kill three assholes?

Instead Wildey reaches for his baton.

Stan, still breathing heavy and running, reaches for his, too.

Wildey's stick has barely cleared leather when one of the punks launches a lucky shot across the side of his head. He staggers for a second before another tackles him, knocking him to the ground. Now comes the part where they'll try to kick him unconscious.

But they've forgotten about his partner.

Stan whips his stick around and cracks the nearest punk across his shoulders. That drops him. He whimpers like a whipped dog. A shot across the sternum brings the second mugger to his knees. Guy looks around for the car that just hit him. The third thinks Stan is distracted and serves up a haymaker that would knock most men off their feet. But Stan is not most men. He may not be fast, he may not be smart, he may be a terrible piano player, but he has one skill that sets him apart from the rest of the force: he's a tough-ass Pole who can take a punch. And he can give just as good as he gets.

So when Stan absorbs the blow, he straightens back up and releases the same amount of kinetic energy at his attacker, concentrated in his fist, which obliterates the cartilage in the mugger's nose with a loud and messy *pop*.

Mugger snuffs blood, staggers backward, drops.

Stan attends to his fallen partner, helps him to his feet.

"You're pretty slow, partner," Wildey says, "but you one strong Polack."

"And you've got a glass jaw."

Wildey taps his chin, blood running down his lips. "Still intact. Heh heh heh."

"Come on, let's bring these *schnudaks* in."

"What's *schnudak* mean?"

"Probably what you think it means," Stan tells him.

There's downtime, of course. Any cop will tell you—a lot of the time you're just sitting around waiting for shit to blow up. Even the Jungle has its long stretches of nothing, when the hot night seems to just broil and residents are too exhausted to fight, fuck, or steal.

So they are compelled to talk. Or rather, Wildey is compelled to talk, with Stan trying to figure out the magic answer that will shut him up for just a few minutes. Three weeks in and he's still not adjusted to the last-out shift. Instead of sleeping next to Rosie, arm curled around her, he's shacked up with this guy.

Who won't shut up, even while they're eating their lunch at 3 a.m.

"What is that?" Wildey asks, pointing at Stan's sandwich.

"Liverwurst."

"Shit looks like cat food, man. Doesn't smell much better, either."

What is Stan supposed to say to that? Hey, do you want a bite? Stan continues eating. Wildey, meanwhile, is chowing down on two sloppy peanut butter and jelly sandwiches he most likely made himself.

"Been asking around," Wildey says. "Didn't know you worked in the Wild West."

The Wild West, or the Midway, or whatever the nickname is these days, meant the club district in midtown. Jazz clubs, strip joints, betting parlors, all in a tight little pocket. Celebrity magnets like Frankie Bradley's, backroom wheeler-dealer joints like Lew Tendler's, and a dozen other sin dens.

"Yeah, for a while," Stan says.

He spent his best years in the Midway district and it almost ruined him and his marriage. He doesn't like to think about it much. The transfer to Whitetown was a godsend. He thought life had finally calmed down... until this.

"What about you? Where were you before this?"

Wildey chuckles. "Heh heh. Nowhere fun, that's for sure. I think they bounced me around to whatever out-of-the-way district needed a black guy."

Stan nods his head like he understands, but of course he doesn't. Was Wildey exiled? Or just rootless?

"Glad we ended up here, though," Wildey says.

"You're glad? How the hell are you glad about this?"

"What d'you mean?"

"I mean this is the worst kind of punishment I can imagine. This is pretty much the last place I wanna be."

Wildey throws his hands up as if directing traffic. "Wait a minute. You think we're being punished? I *asked* for you, man. You and me, in the Double-Deuce. A plum assignment. A few weeks ago you were walking the beat in Kensington. Now you're in a leather jacket and a car!"

"You got us a plum assignment in the middle of Hell!"

"Don't you want to catch the guys who tried to drop a couch on us?"

Stan is flabbergasted. This is all about the *murzyns* with the couch. He can't believe it. Why would Wildey do this to him?

"Look," Wildey says. "I'm seeing this as a way to a promotion. Everybody's paying attention to the Twenty-Second. We hustle out here, we can have our picks of spots."

But Stan is not looking for a promotion. He was fine where he was.

The trick to being a cop, a veteran detective once told him, is to go home after every shift.

That old-timer was old Rod Wiethop, a member of Smedley Butler's famed soup-and-fish squad, raiding ballrooms during Prohibition. Stan thought Wiethop was pulling his leg—the equivalent of telling a rook to not get shot—but as time went on, he saw the simple wisdom in it. Coming home every night, or morning, or whenever your shift ends, makes all the difference. You remember why you're working so hard. You avoid stupid mistakes or losing yourself to the job, as Stan once did.

So every morning, Stan goes home. Some of the other guys in the Twenty-Two go out for beers at a cop bar near the Boulevard and Erie, but not Stan, who prefers to do his drinking at home. And Wildey, who says he rarely touches the stuff, heads home to Germantown. They wave goodbye and go off to opposite corners of the city.

By the time Stan reaches Bridge Street, Rosie has already been up for hours—she doesn't sleep much—and Jimmy is scrambling to get ready for school. Stan usually pours himself a tomato and clam juice and Rosie pretends not to see him dump some Smirnoff into the glass. The drink helps him sleep. Sometimes. He tries to get Rosie to join him, joking about the house being empty and all. She pretends to be cross with him, calling him a dirty old man, but just lets him sleep. For which Stan is grateful, because he's usually exhausted. He'll never get used to last-out shift.

"Wildey wants us all to go out sometime," Stan tells Rosie one night as she prepares supper. Jimmy works on his math problems at the kitchen table.

"Who's that?"

"You know, Rosie. George Wildey. My partner?"

Rosie knows exactly who he's talking about.

"Anyway, he wants us to come over some night."

"Where does he live?"

"Germantown. He also keeps talking about this club over near Broad and Erie, supposed to be good music."

"Well, we'll see about that."

"Is he talking about the Cadillac Club?" Jimmy asks.

Stan shoots his boy the side-eye. "How do you know about the Cadillac Club?"

"Supposed to be great music," Jimmy says, ducking the question. "You should definitely go."

Rosie dishes some hot sausage and peppers onto Stan's plate. "Well, we'll see about that," she says.

That last week of September the city seems to lose its goddamned mind. The relative lull after the storm of the riots has faded away. The Phils are done, their winning summer tarnished by an embarrassing collapse over the past few weeks. THE GREAT PHOLD, one newspaper says. And all at once, Philadelphia remembers it wants to destroy itself. Break-ins. Muggings. Assaults. Armed robberies.

And in the Jungle, lots of Negroes killing Negroes.

The homicide dicks, with their wrinkled suits and potbellies, have a code name for it—NHI.

No Humans Involved.

Stan and Wildey don't investigate any of them, of course. But as members of the mobile squad, they're often the first responders that fall.

"Goddammit," Wildey says each time they roll up on another body.

Their job is to secure the scene, grab any witnesses, and make them stay put until the homicide dicks arrive. Usually, these homicide guys are the bottom of the barrel—drunks, career burnouts, incompetents. Why throw good men at blacks killing blacks up here?

They catch their first dead body on the first day of October.

Just some nappy-haired kid, barely out of his teens, one bullet in the side of his head and another through his skinny guts. It's a messy kill, right outside a crumbling pool hall with a tilting roof near Broad Street. Already a crowd has gathered.

Bad news travels through the Jungle like telepathy. Seems like seconds after someone is shot, everybody within a three-block radius is out of their rowhomes and making their way to the scene to see for themselves. The police never have to alert next of kin; the Jungle does it for them.

A woman, presumably the mother, touches the side of the pool hall repeatedly, like she needs to make sure it's real, as she moves up the sidewalk toward the vic. Then she wails and falls to her knees next to the body. Stan and Wildey catch her before she can throw herself on the corpse.

"We're gonna take care of him, honey," Wildey coos. "I promise, we'll take care of him."

But she's not calmed. She sees big Stan there, looming over the body, and she starts screaming at him, calling him a blue-eyed devil. As if Stan pulled the trigger on this poor kid.

"Hey, it's all right," Stan says, trying his best to imitate Wildey's soothing voice. But it comes out all wrong and infuriates the woman all the more. She doesn't want some honky bastard telling her everything is going to be all right. What on God's holy earth could be *all right* about this?

Wildey gives him a look and holds up a hand, like *Let me handle this.*

Eventually the detectives show up—white guys, of course. Potential witnesses scatter. The dicks aren't too concerned; they don't see any great mystery to be solved here. Wildey passes along what the mother told him, but they listen with only half an ear. Thanks, buddy.

Back in the car, Stan is still sulking.

"Hey, you all right?" Wildey asks.

"I've never done anything to these people."

"It's not you. It's the uniform. They hate me just as much."

"Kind of doubt that."

"You know what? You're absolutely right. They hate me even more. I'm a traitor. A brother who put on a badge and is fighting for the other team."

Stan says nothing.

"Look, man," George says, "you talk to anybody in the Jungle. I'm talkin' anybody, from a street tough to a minister to a gospel singer to a smiling grandma sitting on her front stoop. They've all got one thing in common."

"What's that?"

"At some point—and I guarantee this to be one hundred percent true—some cop has treated them like shit."

"Come on, everybody's been hassled by the police at some point."

"Uh-uh. I'm not talking about hassling somebody because they ran a light. I'm talking about cops fucking with them just because of the color of their skin. Man, it happens to me. So you've got to cut them a break, give 'em time. There's good people in this neighborhood. We just have to earn their trust."

Stan doesn't know what to say to that. He slips and mutters that he "never wanted to be assigned to this goddamn *murzyn* neighborhood."

"What was that?" Wildey asks. "You callin' them Muslims?"

"No, forget it."

"What are you sayin', then? Come on, man, it's a word I've never heard before. What was that, *mooshin?*"

"*Murzyn.*"

"That's what I thought you said. *Mooshin.* That Polish?"

"Yeah."

"What's it mean?"

"I think you probably know what it means."

Wildey blinks as if he's been slapped. "I'm really hoping that's not true."

Stan sighs. "It's Polish for black, somebody with a dark tan. That's it."

"Huh. So do you call me a *mooshin?*"

"No, I call you a pain in the goddamned ass, that's what I call you."

For a long couple of seconds Stan is not sure how it's going to go. Will his new partner take a swing at him?

Instead he belly-laughs.

"That's more like it," Wildey says. "Finally the truth comes out. My partner here thinks I'm a goddamned pain in the ass! Now we're getting somewhere."

Stan forces a smile.

"You a goddamned pain in the ass, too, you know," Wildey says.

Stan doesn't want to tell him that among Poles, *murzyn* has another connotation. Like *slave*—someone who toils for another. Stan's father used to complain about all the *murzyns* stealing good jobs, that they should go back down to the South where they belong. He's embarrassed to say that he heard it growing up so much, it just became part of his language. They *were murzyns,* weren't they? It'd be like retraining yourself to call an apple something else. But he also knows it's wrong, and he needs to cut this shit out. Especially around Wildey.

By late October they've already got a reputation as the toughest cop duo in the Jungle. Relentless, tough, fair. Somehow word reaches the *Bulletin* and they send one of their best reporters, Joe Daughen, to interview them. He writes a good, tough, fair piece.

Wildey is especially happy that they sent Daughen. Apparently he's known in Negro circles for his fair reporting and straight shooting. A rare quality in white reporters, or so Wildey says.

Stan, for his part, doesn't like how the photograph turned out. His head looks three sizes too big, and he's squinting nervously, making him look like he has two blackened eyes. All the attention, too, worries him.

"This could backfire on us, you know," Stan says the night the story appears, during their 3 a.m. lunch break. Stan, with his liverwurst on white. Wildey, with his peanut butter and jelly on wheat with the crusts cut off. Like he's still in grade school.

"How's that, Hondo?" Wildey asks.

"We become so well known, all the damn crooks are gonna see us coming."

"No," Wildey says. "They're gonna *fear us*. Which is the point. Now c'mon and finish your cat food sandwich. I'm not going to let you ruin one of the best days of my life. You know who called me after the papers hit the racks this afternoon? Carla."

Carla is Wildey's on-again, off-again ex. Mother of his boy, George Junior.

"She said I was looking all handsome and shit."

Jimmy is also over the moon about the article. He uses his allowance to buy a dozen copies from the newsstand at Bridge and Pratt. (The corner store had already sold out.) He sacrifices one to clip the article so that he can Scotch-tape it to the paneling in his bedroom, joining his rock band posters. And each night as he does his homework, Jimmy has Dylan and Jagger and Lennon and Walczak and Wildey looking down on him. For the first time, Jimmy tells his pop:

"When I grow up, I think I want to be a cop."

JIM INVESTIGATES

November 3, 1995

Surprise, surprise, Jim is having a hard time focusing this morning. Could it be the fact that he was up drinking and brooding until at least three, maybe even four in the morning? He doesn't remember going to bed.

But now he and Aisha are standing around in the chilly medical examiner's office, he's got a five-alarm hangover, and the coroner is telling them he found *two* different types of semen inside Kelly Anne Farrace: one type in the vaginal cavity, the other in the rectum.

"Now it's just a matter of figuring out who came first," he says, lifting an eyebrow, waiting for a reaction.

"Jesus, Lew," Jim says wearily when the fog clears and he finally gets it.

Aisha shakes her head, disgusted.

"What?" says the coroner. "Homicide cops don't make jokes anymore?"

"You're not a parent, are you, Lew?" Jim says.

Aisha forces the conversation back to the subject at hand. "Any signs of trauma?"

"None that I can see. I think this was consensual."

"How long before she died, Baxter?"

The coroner rubs his stubbly chin and considers this. "I'd have to say up to a day before."

So Kelly Anne was sleeping with somebody. Or a couple of somebodies. One of whom liked it traditional, Jim thinks, and one of whom liked it Greek.

"You get me a DNA sample and I can try to match it against either," Baxter says.

The parents are due here any minute. Jesus. Do you tell the Farraces that? That her daughter was one of those "do-me feminists"? Jim recalls some drunk idiot journalist kid at the Pen & Pencil Club the other night joking/whining, *How come all these do-me feminists aren't doin' me?*

What's now clear is that they need to build a complete picture of Kelly Anne's social circles. There's the magazine staff. There are friends outside the magazine. And there are (potentially) the dozens of people she talks to on a daily basis. Any life bumps up against hundreds of lives, once you start looking.

But most importantly, there are *MS* and *JDH*.

To Jim, this is looking less like a random attack and more like someone who knew her. *(They said Terrill Lee Stanton randomly chose that bar, but of course that wasn't true—he knew Jim's father and his partner.)* Maybe the killer even told her he loved her, then changed his mind. Please let it be someone overconfident, Jim thinks, so that they can find him and fry his ass, posthaste. To do that, they need to construct a complete timeline of her last twenty-four hours. From work that morning, to her movements that day throughout Center City, right up until the moment she ends up in a stairwell on Pine Street.

Kelly, no matter what you did in your life, you didn't deserve this. I'm going to find the monster who ended your life. Your case isn't going to go unsolved.

Now help me fact-check your last day.

Wednesday, November 1, you report to work just before 8 a.m.

You're always one of the first ones in the office, according to Marie, the sweet older woman who runs the front desk. You like to get an early jump on your fact-checking calls. People are sharper, less harried, first thing in the morning. Lots of restaurants and shops aren't open quite yet. You take your job seriously. You like to sip coffee as you make your to-do lists. You're sharp, focused, determined.

You remain in the office at 1919 Market until twelve thirty, when you and the editorial assistant, Lauren Feldman, take the elevator down to Market Street and walk two blocks to Berri Blues deli on the corner of Nineteenth and Chestnut, where you both hit the salad bar and pick up Snapples and return to work. Deadline week; can't spend too much time away. Production needs facts so they can finalize the text and send around full galleys for corrections. Even though you're gone only a short while, there will be four galleys waiting on your desk by the time you return.

You work steadily all afternoon.

You make little bracket marks in pencil around each individual fact in a manuscript.

You make phone calls, and as you confirm each fact, you make a little pencil check mark in the middle of the bracket.

You make corrections in pencil, too.

For larger corrections, you attach a yellow Post-it note to the side of the manuscript for later review with the editor.

Do I have all this right, Kelly Anne?

The magazine is preparing the December issue, and you work late—until almost 7 p.m. This is confirmed by the managing editor, Marcy Lombardi, who cracks the whip on deadline week.

Then finally you go home to change. We know this because the clothes you were wearing to work that day—black skirt, maroon turtleneck sweater, flats—were in your apartment, on the couch.

Have you had time to have sex so far? Unlikely. Lew Baxter says the window is only twenty-four hours, so unless you had an early-morning session, you meet up with someone after work.

Do you eat something? Or do you head right out?

Help me out. Give me some clues as to where you're headed...

The weekly minder Jim found at her desk only gives two cryptic suggestions about the rest of her evening. There are the initials *MS* for 9 p.m., and then *JDH* at 11.

Who are they?

Meanwhile the local media are busy following their own leads. The story is on the front pages and at the top of every radio and TV news hour. Jim will keep an eye on this—once in a while the media digs up something new. People will always talk to some reporter more freely than to someone with a badge. On the downside, all the attention will mean that the mayor—and Sonya Kaminski—will be further up his ass with every column inch published.

The Farraces are not what Jim expected.

For starters, they're not even Farraces.

The father is tall and doughy and, as a result, almost boyish, which he tries to offset with a long blond beard. Is he old enough to have a daughter Kelly Anne's age? The wife, meanwhile, looks at least a decade older, with gray streaking her long dark hair, and her clothes pulled on like an afterthought—oh, I should wear something in public. Understandable, given the circumstances. But to Jim's eye, her soul wasn't just broken in the last twelve hours. It's been broken for a while.

Aisha takes the lead.

"Detective Walczak and I are very sorry for your loss," Aisha says, "and please know that we're doing everything in our power to find the man who did this to your daughter."

The father extends a hand. "George Linden."

Aisha blinks. "You're not Mr. Farrace?"

The wife shakes her head. "I remarried."

"Does Kelly Anne's father know what happened?"

"I don't think he knows much about anything," Mrs. Linden says.

"Kelly Anne's father hasn't been in the picture for quite a while," Mr. Linden says quickly, not so much stepping on his wife's last syllable as merely continuing her sentence.

Jim thinks about Kelly, her prematurely aged mother, her pompous stepfather, her deadbeat dad. Yeah, I'd leave Beerfart, Ohio, too.

"When's the last time you heard from Kelly Anne?"

"She calls home every week."

"And the last time was..."

"Last week," Mrs. Linden says, as if it's the most obvious answer in the world.

Aisha's asking the questions, but the Lindens keep looking at Jim when they answer.

"What I'm getting at is," Aisha says, "did she mention anything strange to you the last time you spoke? Maybe trouble with a boyfriend, or at work? Anything like that?"

No, there was nothing like that. Round and round they go and the deeper they get the clearer it becomes that the Lindens had very little idea what was going on with Kelly Anne once she moved to Philadelphia. Out of sight out of mind. Apparently there are three other daughters, all younger, to deal with. Kelly Anne is the only Farrace; the other three have a different father. Who is not Mr. Linden here. Seems this college professor stepped into their lives to bat cleanup.

Jim wonders, Did you flee Ohio to get away from beardo here? Was he lingering in your doorway? Married the mom but wanted the oldest daughter?

"What do you teach?" Jim asks Linden.

"Nineteenth-century literature. Why?"

"College?"

"Community. Look, is this important? What does this have to do with finding Kelly Anne's killer?"

College guys. Jim doesn't understand people who pay all that money and spend all that time to dick around. Sure, he wants Staś to go to college, but for something useful.

Jim shakes his head. "Nothing."

The mayor's office wanted to put them up at the Four Seasons on the Parkway, but they insist on returning home to make funeral arrangements and see to their other daughters.

"Any idea where we can find Kelly Anne's father?" Aisha asks.

Mrs. Linden blinks. "You would know better than us."

Jim sits up. "What do you mean?"

"He's here," Mr. Linden says. "Here in Philadelphia, somewhere."

Jim and Aisha exchange glances. After the Lindens leave, he asks her to check out the father.

"What are you going to do?"

"I need to follow up on something," he says, and doesn't elaborate. Aisha knows better than to press him on it.

Come on, Terrill Lee Stanton, rise and shine, you scumbag.

According to your record you've got a job at a soup kitchen all the way over in West Philly. If you're going to make it on time, you're going to have to be leaving this halfway house near Erie and Castor in a few minutes to catch the El.

Jim sits across the street in his car, waiting, feeling vaguely guilty about lying to Aisha, knowing she's left alone to handle the press and everything else. But this can't wait. Jim's already waited thirty years for this moment.

At the small reception after Stan's funeral, Jim was approached by Officer Billy Taney, his dad's former partner. He needed a cane to walk and steadied himself on Jimmy's shoulder as he leaned down.

"Your father saved my life," he said solemnly, his eyes buttery and unfocused, his breath like cold whiskey. "Anything you need, you come find me."

Over the next five years, Jim did just that on a regular basis. They met once a month for breakfast at the Aramingo Diner, not far from where Taney lived. Jim always ordered oatmeal—the cheapest breakfast item on the menu. Taney stuck with black coffee, augmented by some "syrup" he kept in a silver flask.

At first Taney just spun "Stan Walczak stories" from their days on the force. They both became cops the same year, 1951. Bounced around various districts—including a wild tour of the Tenderloin 1950s—until they joined the vice squad in the mid-1950s, mostly working the clubs and bordellos around Juniper Street. Frank Rizzo's turf, Taney would add with pride. Taney loved to talk about rousting drunks, hookers, and "slick boys"—ethnic gangsters who would run numbers, pimp, and embroil themselves in stupid little dramas.

As a kid, Jim listened politely. The stories *were* interesting; his father had never told him much about those days. But what Jim really wanted to hear about was his father's murder investigation.

"I can't tell you about that, Jimmy," Taney would say at first. "Just know that we're going to catch the son of a bitch who did this. Your father saved my life."

But gradually, as the months wore on, Taney's tongue loosened slightly. "I heard that homicide is looking at a guy."

And then: "I didn't tell you this, but I think homicide found the gun."

And by the summer of 1968: "Pretty sure they know who did it."

"So why aren't they arresting him?" a fifteen-year-old Jimmy asked.

"They don't know that it's enough. Look, we're going to catch this black son of a bitch. Your father, he saved my life."

"Tell me his name."

"Jimmy, come on."

"I deserve to know his name!"

But Taney held back.

For a few years, at least.

One morning in early 1972, not long after Jimmy himself joined the force, a drunk Billy Taney slipped and gave him the name of the "person of interest" in the murder of Stanisław Walczak and George W. Wildey.

The name was Terrill Lee Stanton.

Which filled Patrolman Jimmy Walczak with a cold kind of energy. Immediately he wanted to know where this Terrill Lee Stanton lived, what he'd been doing for the past seven years.

"Thing is," Taney said, "he's already in prison."

Doing thirty to life for another murder.

"He's paying for it, believe me," Taney added.

Not enough, Jim thought.

So for the next few decades he'd dream of the day they let Stanton out of prison, so that he could look him in the eye and ask why why *why* . . .

And there he is, bold as day.

His father's killer steps out of the halfway house, fists shoved into the pockets of a fleece jacket. The weird thing is, he looks nothing like the mug shot Jim knows in vivid detail *(obsesses over)*. The guy in the mug shot looks feral, ready to punch you in the gut as soon as say hello. But this later, postprison version is just a skinny old man, walking down Erie Avenue with his head hung like there are invisible weights attached to his forehead, presumably headed for the El so he can ladle out chicken noodle to the less fortunate.

Don't let him fool you, Jim. This is the man who pointed a revolver at your father and pulled the trigger, repeatedly.

Probably liked it.

Probably still gets off on it...

Stop it.

Jim watches Terrill Lee Stanton shuffle down Erie. Pathetic old man. It's a shame for someone his age to be walking out here in the cold like that. Maybe Jim should scoop him up, give him a ride, save him the token money.

Outer Jim commands: *No. Don't be an idiot. There are a million reasons you shouldn't do this. You shouldn't even be out here this morning.*

And in the end, Outer Jim wins. He has a murder case to solve. This sorry old man? He's not going anywhere.

While he's been gone, Aisha's been busy.

Robert Raymond Farrace, turns out, has priors. B&E guy, picked up a bunch of times over the last ten years.

And as it turns out, he's still behind bars, so there goes that idea.

Jim and Aisha split the next jobs at hand. Aisha goes through Kelly Anne's friends and/or possible boyfriends, while Jim works on a timeline of her movements the last day of her life. He scrawls out times and puts them on a dry-erase board. This part of the job always reminds him of high school. The paper's already way late, and all you're doing is racing to catch up.

And then sometimes, you get a free pass from the teacher.

Aisha rushes into their cubicle all excited.

"Think I've got something good here."

AUDREY PRIES

May 9, 2015

Audrey arrives at the pizza joint bright and early and relatively hangover-free, fully prepared to tear it the hell apart.

Hey, it's not her fault she has to do a little remodeling. The new owners should have kept it a bar.

She's relieved she didn't have to sleep with Pizza Counter Guy to get him to open up extra early. Not that he isn't handsome—he is. Warm smile and soft eyes. But Audrey's got too much crazy in her life to invite more. What exactly is she supposed to do with a Pizza Counter Guy here in Philadelphia when she has ongoing drama back in Houston?

Audrey crouches down, mini-crowbar in hand. She tucks one end under a lip of paneling and begins to pry. Hard, fast, quick, move move move. She needs this bar naked and quick.

KEEERRRAAAAAAK.

She can tell Pizza Counter Guy is normally a very chill dude, but you can see him getting all worked up.

"Whoa! Take it easy!"

"Sorry, man, but I told you we had a deadline."

"Yeah, but you're denting the hell out of that stuff."

"Look, I'm going to put everything back the way it was. I've got a hammer and everything. Coolio?"

Pizza Counter Guy blinks.

"Did you just use the word *coolio* in terms of asking me if I agree?"

Audrey doesn't reply.

KEEEERRAAAAAAAK.

This, appropriately enough, used to be a shotgun bar.

Main entrance off Fairmount, side entrance off Seventeenth. Long skinny place. Bar running down one side, almost all the way to the back. Rows of bottles in front of the mirror. A couple of tables in the back. But the main business was done at the bar, on stools. Tile floor. Little off-white square tiles, interrupted by a small burst of blue and green tiles in a geometric pattern.

The bar, though. It's beautiful. What a crime to cover it up with these cheap panels.

Legend has it that this place was the preferred watering hole of poet and writer Charles Bukowski back in the mid-1940s when he worked at the Fairmount Motor Works. Bukowski supposedly used it as the basis for the Golden Horn in his original screenplay for *Barfly,* which would star Mickey Rourke. (Audrey has a friend who insists the movie is pronounced *Barf-lee.*) The name of the bar back in Bukowski's day has been lost to time. Nor did it have a name back when her grandfather was shot to death here.

Pizza Counter Guy watches her work. What else does he have to do? It's 7 a.m. and he doesn't have to start slinging dough for another two hours.

"What's with the string?"

What's with the string is that Audrey is approximately 2,500 miles from her college campus and is unable to use the university's fancy-pants 3-D laser scanner that would map this entire pizza joint in a couple of hours. Audrey loves it. The thing spins around, making millions of ridiculously accurate measurements. The end result: 360 degrees of cold hard data. The entire crime scene on your laptop.

So instead, she has to go old-school.

"It's highly technical," she says. "You wouldn't understand."

Pizza Counter Guy says uh-huh.

She might be a lousy student, but Audrey remembers quite a lot from her forensic science classes. Her favorite six words, courtesy of her favorite professor: "We're basically a bag of water."

In terms of a bullet striking a human being.

(He made this awesome *SPOFFFF* sound effect while slowly bringing his splayed hands apart.)

Audrey truly enjoys shooting guns into ballistic gelatin, which is the closest you can get to human tissue. She loves ballistic gelatin so much she wants to slice it up and grill it, put it on a bun.

But back to the double murder at hand.

"In a bullet murder, there is no area of evidence more important than the autopsy," said the same professor. "With the wounds, you can infer the trajectory of the bullet."

Well, as the song goes, *she ain't got no body*. Unless she goes for a double unearthing. Which would please exactly nobody.

"Examination of the victim's clothing is a very important part of that autopsy."

No clothes, either.

Nor fingerprints... nor prime-time TV's favorite, blood splatter.

Which is fine, because all that bullshit is "more art than science," according to one of her profs. The fingerprint lecture was particularly eye-opening. Everyone grows up thinking that no two sets of fingerprints are alike. Well, guess what, chief: that all depends on the methods of taking said fingerprints. With the most commonly used methods, parts of fingerprints can be so similar that two different chumps can be linked to the same latent print. No cop wants to admit it, but it's true.

Just talk to the sorry asshole who was almost convicted of the Madrid train bombing back in 2004. Whose fingerprints kinda sorta matched the ones found at the scene. Only... he had nothing do with it.

As another professor put it: "There's just not enough science in forensic science."

The same professor: "Folks, it's all about angles and distances."

That, Audrey can do.

Hence the string, scissors, and tape. All pilfered from Will's apartment.

She's going to retrace the path of each bullet fired in this joint over fifty years ago. And while the bar isn't made of ballistic gelatin (and if it were, for the record, it would quickly become Audrey's favorite bar *ever*), a huge slab of heavy wood can hold a bullet trail almost as well. Sure, there are decades' worth of nicks and bumps and cracks. But they're easy to distinguish from bullet holes.

"The essence of good forensic science?" her favorite professor once asked. "Look at the competing explanations of an event. Like Sherlock Holmes once said, if you can rule out the impossible, whatever remains—however seemingly improbable—must be the truth."

Audrey kneels down, scissors and string in hand, and begins to work.

"Back up, kid," she says. "I need to work."

Pizza Counter Guy raises his hands in surrender, takes a few long and slow steps backward.

As Audrey works, Pizza Counter Guy, leaning against a table, arms folded, fires questions at her anyway. He probably should be in the back, hurling a circle of dough into the air or whatever, but he seems fascinated by what she's doing.

"So your last name is Kornbluth. Does this mean you have a husband?"

Snip snip.

"No, it means I have an asshole father. I was born a Walczak, but I took my mother's maiden name a few years ago."

"Wow that's fairly…hard-core."

"Well, Dad's a pretty hard-core asshole. He's a cop, by the way. Retired, but knows a guy who knows a guy, if you know what I mean."

"I'm not sure I know what you mean."

"I'm sure you know exactly what I mean, Pizza Counter Guy."

"I have a name, you know."

"That's nice. Everybody does. But please. Shut the fuck up."

Snip snip.

Tape tape.

She's basically working in reverse, starting with the bullet hole and tracing its path backward. It's not as simple as a straight line, of course. There's air resistance, wind, good ol' gravity. And that's assuming the bullet was in pristine condition. Imperfect bullets can tumble and yaw. Or maybe the shooter loaded the wrong caliber, which can really screw with your spin rate and velocity.

But she can get into the weird physics shit later. You have to start with the bare bones—how many bullets were fired, and where did they come from?

Right away, Audrey realizes there are issues with the stories in the newspaper.

"No way."

"What?"

She doesn't need fancy physics. After all, she can count.

When Audrey returns to the apartment from an honest day's labor of snipping and taping and conjecturing, she's surprised to learn she has a guest. There he is. On the couch, ankle resting on his knee, arm sprawled over the back, *Mad Men* style.

"We need to talk," her older brother Staś says.

Fucking Cary, Audrey thinks. Can never, ever, keep his mouth shut. Then again, she's as much to blame for telling him in the first place.

Audrey doesn't reply. Instead, she ticks off an invisible count on her fingers. *One two three four.*

"Audrey, are you listening to me?"

She continues the count. *Five six seven eight nine ten,* while nodding her head and pursing her lips in mock astonishment.

"What the hell are you doing?" Staś finally asks, exasperated.

"Counting words," Audrey says. "You know what? That's the most you've spoken to me in five years. Impressive, really. You're practically gushing, Stoshie."

Claire, meanwhile, hovers around in the kitchen, silently bearing yet another round of sibling arguments. Will quickly spirits himself off to another room—possibly the bathroom, to hang himself.

"Let's go," Staś says.

"I just got home."

"This isn't your home. Come on, I need a cup of coffee."

"There's a cozy little Starbucks a couple of blocks away, I believe. Try the Mocha Fucka Offa!"

They have the ability to go on like this for hours, it seems. So it's fortunate that Claire interrupts with a sharp "Audrey!" Both kids stop speaking and turn and look at her with sheepish expressions on their faces. Yes, even the badass Philly cop.

"For Christ's sake, go have coffee with your brother."

You know it's serious when a Jewish lady invokes the name of Jesus to get her kids to stop fighting.

Audrey talks him into drinks at McGillin's Olde Ale House, right around the corner and one of the places she and Cary hit last night. If she's not mistaken, there's a corner where he may have puked. Audrey suggests the bar. Staś says no, a table. Oh boy. He's serious about this conversation.

Staś asks for a club soda and lime. Audrey calls him a pussy. Staś changes his order to a Jack on the rocks, Yuengling back. Audrey asks for a Bloody Mary, Yuengling back. The bartender doesn't bat an eye—a Bloody Mary at 7 p.m., sure, why not. This is the same place that serves pickle martinis every January twenty-first in honor of Ben Franklin's birthday. (Long story, don't ask.) So a Bloody Mary is nothing.

Staś blinks. "You do know it's not Sunday morning, right?"

"If it were Sunday morning," Audrey says, "I'd be drinking the vodka straight."

"Fair enough," he says. There might even be a smile there.

She mentally racks up the score against Bitchanne, who probably hasn't tasted alcohol since the last time she had a slight cough. But before the drinks arrive, her brother gets serious again—down to business.

"Look, I'm going to tell you how it's going to be, and you're going to sit there and listen. This project of yours is *over*. I know you're claiming this is for school, and if that's the case, I've got access to a dozen other cold cases that are far more interesting. I'll let you see everything. Access nobody else has. You hearing me?"

"So this isn't really a conversation," Audrey says, nodding her head. "More of an edict."

"Call it whatever you want."

"Well, yeah, see, I don't respond very well to edicts. Especially from you."

Their drinks arrive. Service is lightning quick at McGillin's. The waitress asks Staś if he and his daughter would like to see menus. Audrey giggles. *You old buzzard,* she whispers. Staś says no thanks. Audrey sips her Bloody like a grade-schooler with her first Shirley Temple. My, how that refreshes!

Once the waitress is out of earshot, Staś continues. "There's something you don't know. About Dad's heart."

The straw flicks out of her mouth. "What about Dad's heart?"

Staś: dead earnest look. "You've really got to stop this shit."

"You asshole. What about Dad's heart?"

Oh, he's enjoying this. The man with the scoop. Staś tells her only the basics: congestive heart failure. Brought to the hospital four times over the past three years—minor heart attacks. Audrey's about to scream at him: Why didn't any of you pricks think to pick up the phone and tell me? But then she remembers she hasn't picked up the phone, either.

"So you start digging into this stuff? Now? It's going to push him over the edge. Is that what you want? To put him in an early grave?"

Audrey's still thinking about her father. Sure, he's an asshole, but she also doesn't want to have to fly back to Philly to bury him in a few weeks.

Staś leans back, takes a big swallow of his Jack. He sees her reaction and now he's all smug and satisfied—conversation over. Audrey mimics him, draining half her Bloody in a single go.

"Well," she says, "there's something you don't know."

"What's that?"

Audrey doesn't answer. Instead she digs into her purse for her notebook. She opens up to her crude diagram from earlier today, pressing the pages down with her palms.

"I went to the murder scene today. Took apart the counter. Spent all day tracing the ballistic trajectories."

But Staś is already looking through her fingers at the diagram. He reaches out with both sets of fingers, pressing them down on the notebook, then spins them around so he can take a better look.

Staś is a jerk. But he's also supposed to be a really good cop. Methodical, slow, but ultimately right. He knows what he's looking at. He realizes the implications right away.

"There were *two* shooters?"

Audrey lifts her Bloody, clinks Staś's glass on the table, then takes a long swallow. Bet you don't have a cold case like this, Stoshie.

By the time Audrey returns to the apartment she's had two more Bloodies, two Yuengling backs. But Claire is up waiting for her, plush robe wrapped around her body, cigarette between her middle and ring finger. There are a half dozen dead ones in the ashtray. She's Philadelphia's last unrepentant smoker, and clearly she's been up for a while now.

"So you talked to Staś," Claire says. She doesn't bother to phrase it as a question, because she knows the answer. Knows what Staś *told her* would happen.

Audrey nods as she fishes a beer from Will's fridge. Oooh, a Blue Point Toasted Lager. Probably buys his beer by the six-pack so he can enjoy the variety.

Claire nods in return. Good, good. "So I'll be driving you to the airport tomorrow."

"Not exactly," Audrey says, cracking the cap off the top.

"What do you mean?"

Now it's time for the hard sell.

Audrey explains her independent study project, how important the project is to her academic future, what she's discovered, and how she needs to stay here for at least a few more days to do some more fact-finding. Maybe a little more, certainly no more than a week, and hopefully you guys would be cool with that . . . ?

"Actually, Audrey . . ." Claire says, letting the thought finish itself.

"Seriously? I can't stay here?"

"It's not my apartment."

"Okay. So fucking *Will* won't let me stay here?"

"You're putting me in a very awkward position."

Awkward? How about being in no position? She doesn't have the money or credit for a hotel. If the Captain hadn't sprung for her plane ticket, she would be back in Houston right now. What is she supposed to do?

"Mom...come on."

"Oh, when you want something I'm Mom. Otherwise, I'm just dumb old Claire."

"What did he say? I want your bitch adopted daughter out now? Do I have time to collect my things, or should I report to the sidewalk immediately?"

Claire takes a final drag on her cigarette before mashing it out in the ashtray. Will's probably trying to get her to stop smoking, too. Keep up the good fight, Mom. Don't let the bastards change everything.

"I'm sure you'll figure out something, Audrey," she says. "You always do."

And with that, Claire rises and makes her way to the bedroom. Will's bedroom, that is, which is situated next to Will's guest room, which currently contains Audrey's things...at least for the next 120 seconds. Because she's getting the fuck out of here *immediately*.

Audrey wanders toward Broad Street, then walks around City Hall and its giant off-white boner tower with the jaundiced-yellow clock in the center. As she rounds the other side, Audrey waves at the ten-foot-tall statue of former mayor Frank Rizzo, who is stuck waving back for all eternity. "Yo, Frank."

She tries her grandma again on the phone. Gets the answering machine with the voice message that hasn't changed since 1990 or so, as far as Audrey can tell. Come on, Grandma Rose, answer. It's not *that* late.

As she's cutting through the City Hall courtyard, something catches her eye: the two memorial tablets devoted to Philly's fallen officers.

She stares at the police memorial, which is off to the right, near the East Market Street portal. So many dead cops, they needed to build a second memorial to keep going.

Audrey runs her fingers down the names and finds STANISŁAW WALCZAK.

And GEORGE W. WILDEY.

Audrey runs her numb fingertips over the stubby brass letters of her grandfather's name.

Don't know if you're out there, or up there, or whatever, Grandpop. This is your granddaughter speaking. I'm not using your death to get ahead, I swear. If anything, I'm using your death to avoid drowning.

So help me out here.

Let me figure this out.

If he's up there listening, Audrey has no idea. Because there is no reply. No soft whispers. No lightning claps. No acknowledgment whatsoever.

She fishes two bucks and a quarter out of her bag and rides the El all the way to the end of the line, Bridge and Pratt. Not a great neighborhood. A thriving drug corner just up Bridge Street. She doesn't want to stand around all night waiting for a bus, so she decides to blow five more bucks on a cab out to Ditman Street. It's going to suck staying out here in Frankford for the week.

Then again, Audrey thinks, maybe this will bring her closer to her grandfather. You know, that fourth source that Susan Cheever was talking about. He was living at 2046 Bridge when he was killed. He ate here, slept here, dreamed here. Maybe staying in his house will reveal some kind of new dimension.

But when Grandma Rose opens the door, smiles nervously, and says, "Your mother called," Audrey realizes she's screwed.

STAN GOES TO CHURCH

November 4, 1964

Rosie nudges Stan. "Honey, wake up. Someone's here to see you." Stan groans. It's still afternoon. Hours before his shift at least. He can tell by the bright sunlight stabbing him in the eyes. When he sits up he's dizzy. He reaches over on the floor for his pants. The belt buckle bangs against the metal frame of the bed. He's about to ask Rosie who it is, but she's already left the room.

There's no rock music playing, so Jimmy isn't even home from school yet. What the hell's going on?

Pants on, belt buckled lazily, Stan shuffles out of the room and ambles downstairs.

Turns out, it's Wildey, fully dressed for work, standing in his doorway. "Hey, partner." Stan with no socks or shoes, no shirt, and self-conscious about the way his lower gut hangs over his belt buckle.

"Hey, Wildey. What's going on?"

"How about LBJ, huh? No real surprise there, I guess. Though I didn't think he'd bury Goldwater like that."

Yesterday was Election Day. The president won by a landslide. Not that it matters to Stan. Who the hell cares about which person sits behind that big desk in the Oval Office? They're all the same, the politicians. But Stan knows better than to get into it with his partner, who has yet to meet a topic he doesn't love to expound upon.

Rosie eyes his partner suspiciously. She's waiting to hear what this is all about, too.

"I was just telling your wife here how great it's been working with you these past few months," Wildey finally says. "I'm even getting used to the liverwurst sandwiches."

"Uh-huh," Stan says. Then after a pause, "So what's going on?"

"Let's talk about it in the car."

"It's a little early, isn't it?"

Wildey's eyes widen slightly. He doesn't want to raise his voice in front of the missus here, but...

"This, uh, *can't* wait."

The door opens behind Wildey. It's Jimmy, home from school, backpack slung over his shoulder. He looks at his pop, then at the stranger in the police uniform.

"You're Officer Wildey, aren't you?"

Wildey looks at Stan and beams with pride. "Boy even pronounces it correctly." He turns his attention back to Jimmy and extends a hand. "How are you doing, young man?"

Jimmy reaches up and shakes his hand, a little bit of awe in his expression. He has this man's photo up on his wall, but seeing him in real life is something else. While Stan goes back upstairs to dress, Rosie does the best she can, offering Wildey a cup of tea while he waits. Stan can hear the conversation through the floorboards.

"Do you take sugar and milk?"

"Yeah, honey, lots of both, thank you."

"My pop said you go to the Cadillac Club. What's that like?"

"Two teaspoons, Mr. Wildey?"

"Call me George, please. And that would be fine. Young James, how do you know about the Cadillac Club?"

"I hear about it on WDAS. The Cadillac, the Zanzibar, all those places."

"Your daddy didn't tell me you had such fine taste in music."

"How much milk...er, George?"

"I'll take care of it, Mizz Walczak. Unless I can call you Rose?"

"Well, the Beatles and the Stones were influenced by soul music so I figured I'd go straight to the source and listen to what they're listening to."

"Of course . . . Rose is fine."

"Smart man. So who are you digging?"

Stan doesn't hear the rest of the conversation because he splashes cold water on his face in an attempt to shock himself back to full consciousness. He brushes his teeth, then combs and parts his thinning blond hair. By the time he gets downstairs Jimmy is showing Wildey the LP collection by the stereo console. Stan sees his Sinatra, Crosby, Como, Mathis records out. Wildey sips his tea, then points, looking at Stan.

"Johnny Mathis? For real? You make your family listen to this stuff?"

"Come on, let's go," Stan says.

"To be continued, young man," Wildey says, putting his hand on Jimmy's shoulder. "You've got some education coming your way."

Spray-painted messages on the side of a Baptist church up on the northern edge of the Jungle, where it borders Frog Hollow, one of the last Irish-German strongholds in North Philly:

GET THE FUK OUT
HATE NIGERS

"I hate racist motherfuckers who can't spell," Wildey says.

"This what we were called about? A property crime?"

"No, there's more to it. Come on, Pastor's waiting on us inside."

Stan feels strange being inside the church of a different faith. Sure, the basics are the same—the cross, the pews, Jesus—but it's the little differences that make him feel like he's stepped onto foreign soil.

He was raised Polish Catholic, still hits mass when he feels guilty enough. When he was a teenager, he even attended mass on his own, when nobody was forcing him. He'd duck into an Italian parish, Mater Dolorosa, and listen to the Latin words and hymns and just enjoy the peace of it all.

The pastor, a tall and reedy black man named Jeremiah Stebbens, shakes hands with Wildey and greets Stan warmly, then leads them toward the back of the church. There's a battered upright piano off to the side.

"If you wouldn't mind waiting here for a moment, Officers. Just want to make sure he's ready."

Stan doesn't mind. He's still half asleep. After Stebbens leaves he turns to Wildey and asks, "So who are we waiting for?"

"Patience, my man. We're finally about to get some answers."

Wildey paces a little as Stan takes a seat on the piano bench. He swings his knees around, lifts the lid, starts noodling around on the keys. A chord first, then another, and another, until it blossoms into an almost unconscious progression, a song hard-wired into his hands even though he hasn't touched a keyboard in almost a decade.

Da-dum, da-da-da-da da dum da-dum

Stan is pleasantly surprised to see his fingers moving on their own, remembering the chord changes of the song he and Rosie danced to on their wedding day. The song he's played a thousand times since he was a teenager.

But he's even more surprised when Wildey starts singing along, his voice strong and clear and tender.

"I don't want to set the world...on...fi-*ure*..."

They continue for the rest of the chorus, until Wildey sings about his *one desiiiiiire* and Stan, embarrassed, drops his fingers from the keyboard.

"Hey, why'd you stop, man?"

"Didn't know you were a singer," Stan says to Wildey.

Wildey waves his hand. "Naw, just something I mess around with now and again. But you're quite the piano man. You and Jimmy do a little jamming now and again?"

Stan shakes his head. He shouldn't have sat down here. Why did he play just now? He blames the misjudgment on a lack of sleep. Jimmy probably doesn't even know he plays. They don't keep a piano in the house. For Stan music is the past, and belongs there. A reminder of a life he's left behind to have a family. A family man shouldn't be out nights, playing Tin Pan Alley tunes for drunks.

Soon the pastor returns and leads them down a long, cramped corridor to a kitchen in the back with an old table where a short, squat black man is hunkered over a cup of coffee. He looks up as they enter, terror in his eyes. He's about to face some kind of music.

"Officers, this young man's got something important to tell," the pastor says, "and would like your promise that this conversation will be kept confidential. His name is Terrill Lee Stanton."

JIM KICKS IN A DOOR

November 3, 1995

One busted garage door yields one extremely nervous scumbag.

Scumbag tries blasting past Jim. Almost makes it, too, the speedy little fucker. But Jim has girth on his side, and the garage doorway isn't very wide. He blocks the kid's path, grabs up a bunch of his shirt, and hurls him against the cinder-block wall, knocking the air out of him.

"You in a hurry to get somewhere, Timmy?" Jim asks.

Aisha fielded the anonymous tip—a twenty-two-year-old kid was supposedly in a Fishtown bar last night bragging about the pretty blond jogger he'd banged early yesterday morning. "She fucked him but wouldn't give him her phone number, so he choked her out and left her on the street." *What's his name?* Timmy Hoober, that's H-double-O-B-E-R. *What's your name?* "Eh, I don't want to get involved in this." *Sir, it's very important that we—* "Look, I ain't giving you my name. But you can find Timmy..." and then he rattled off this address quick and hung up.

One Miranda reading later Timmy Hoober is cuffed in the back of their car. Aisha keeps an eye on him while Jim snaps on some gloves and does a quick check of the rest of the garage. Forensics is on its way, but sometimes a quick scan can give him something he can use in the interrogation room. Something like this...little leather ditty bag, the kind you'd find in a traveling businessman's luggage. Jim zips it open. Needle, spoon, baggie—he's a junkie. Good to know. He'll be twitchy soon enough.

Jim dumps the kit in a Ziploc, then steps back outside, looks around. Across from the garage, an older man peeks out from behind the curtains. Jim waves. The guy ducks back behind the curtains, not curious at all about the pair of detectives who just yanked a skinny punk out of his garage. Yeah, hello, anonymous caller.

"What do you think?" Aisha asks as they wait for a couple of uniforms to guard the garage until forensics can arrive.

"I think he's a skinny little knucklehead," Jim says.

"I mean about him being our guy."

"I'm not sure that knucklehead there could have overpowered our girl."

"He could have surprised her. Knocked her on the head before she even knew he was coming. Dragged her down the steps, did his thing..."

"Let's talk to him before we jump to any conclusions."

Jim will say one thing—Timmy *is* awfully quiet back there. The whole ride down to the Roundhouse he doesn't ask a single question. Not even *what am I being charged with*. Almost always the sign of a guilty mind.

DNA won't be the home run in this case.

They've got the two semen samples from Kelly Anne, and Timmy let them swab the inside of his cheek for a sample. But processing it for any kind of hit will take weeks. And that's only if it's a five-alarm rush job, with the mayor's office begging the state police (who have the best labs—even better than the Feds) to hurry with the samples. Same goes for anything the forensics guys will find in the garage. Whatever they find on this front will be useful to the DA's office in a trial somewhere down the line.

Right now, though, it does jack shit for Jim.

Now it's all about Jim in a room with this guy. Reading him. Working on him.

(You wish you had Terrill Lee Stanton in this room so you could work on him, don't ya, Jim?)

He sends in Aisha first, for the basics, get him comfortable. They don't have one of those fancy fish tanks you see on TV cop shows with the one-way glass. All they have is a square conference room they all share. There's no recording gear, either. Aisha picks up the receiver of a phone, rests it on the table with the line open while Jim sits in his cubicle and listens in. When it's Jim's turn, they'll switch.

Timmy Hoober claims to be a "delivery guy," only he won't say for who.

"You live in that garage?" Aisha asks.

"My friend Bobby lets me stay there."

"Tell me about Bobby."

Robert Haas, twenty-five or twenty-six—Timmy doesn't know for sure. He's also a delivery guy, handyman. Jim makes notes as Aisha digs more details out of him. Hoober, it seems, squats in the detached garage out behind his friend Bobby's place, where Bobby lives with his alcoholic divorced father. Most likely the man Jim saw at the window and the source of their "anonymous" tip.

Jim makes a call. Both Hoober and Haas have jackets. Car theft mostly, some B&E, a few assaults. *(Pretty much Terrill Lee Stantons in training, Jimbo. Ask them about the bars they case.)* He sends a car out to pick up Haas. Meanwhile, Aisha pops out of the conference room. "He's all yours."

"Wish I had a bunny suit for this one," Jim says.

"What?" Aisha says.

"Nothing," he says. "Some story my pop once told me."

The movie and TV cliché is that a good cop can *crawl into the mind* of a killer. That's not the case with Jim. The last thing he wants to do is step inside some scumbag killer's head. No, his preferred method is to lock eyes with the monster and wear him down until the truth finally comes tumbling out.

He doesn't mean beatings. That doesn't help anything. People will lie to avoid pain just as easily as tell the truth. But when you look someone in the eye, you've got some kind of tractor beam going. You're letting him know *you know*. And you're not going to stop gnawing on this particular bone until the marrow of truth is exposed.

(Maybe you should flash your badge, talk your way into his room, be there, sitting on the edge of his ratty-ass bed, when he comes home from the soup kitchen.)

"So why did you pick her?"

Timmy breaks eye contact after 1.2 seconds.

"I didn't pick anybody. You gotta let me out of here, man. What the fuck is this about?"

"No, you saw her and liked her. What was it about her, though? Maybe her hair. You like blondes?"

Timmy shakes his head. "What are you talking about?"

"I know, I know," Jim says. "I'm just messin' with ya. Because you're an ass man, aren't you?"

"Aren't you narco?"

A few more back-and-forths like that and it becomes clear that either Hoober here is a gifted liar or he doesn't know anything about Kelly Anne Farrace. We'll see soon enough, Jim thinks. The old man called in the tip for a reason. Maybe it was a cover for his own boy, Bobby. Feed the cops this clueless scumbag, keep the attention away from his own kid.

They let Timmy cool in the conference room for a while. They can hold him for up to forty-eight hours before charging him, and the mook hasn't asked for a lawyer yet.

Jim is at his desk, replaying the mental footage of Terrill Lee Stanton walking down Erie Avenue, when his desk phone rings. But it's not the call from the CSU that he's been expecting.

"Give me some good news, my Polish brother," Sonya says.

Jesus. Jim knows word travels fast around the department, but he didn't know it extended to the halls of the mayor's office as well. He supposes Sonya has more than one friend in the Roundhouse. Makes sense; her power broker father got to where he is by making plenty of friends around town.

"Come on, Sonya, you know how this works," Jim says, more than a little exasperated. "Let me do my job."

"I hear you've got two very good suspects."

"Two? Where did you hear that?"

She ignores the question. "Just keep me updated. And this goes without saying, but whatever resources you need, you got it. You need the state police forensics lab, I'll get them to roll out the red carpet."

"Believe me, Sonya, you'll be my first call."

Not, as the kids say.

The rest of the afternoon is full of conflicting evidence. Robert Haas turns out to be just as goofy and clueless as his young pal, assuming he's being hauled in on a drug charge. But at least he's heard of Kelly Anne Farrace. His father kept talking about it yesterday — "such a waste of a fine piece of ass," his son quoted him as saying. Jim's beginning to think that Haas's father called in that tip about Hoober because he wanted the little bastard out of his detached garage.

But just before Jim can talk to Aisha about shaking them loose, forensics comes back with not only hair samples that seem to match Kelly Anne's hair type and color, but her missing jogging pants — black, ripped, and stuffed into the bottom of a wastebasket. This changes everything. Haas and Hoober, in a rare moment of clarity, decide to clam up and lawyer up. Jim and Aisha plot a new strategy: connecting the dots between the Idiot Twins' movements on the night of the first into the morning of the second. It might be tedious, but it'll get them there.

Which is good, because around 4:30 p.m. Jim excuses himself, tells Aisha he has to take care of something. Aisha, who's too good a detective not to realize that this is the second day in a row her partner has been pulling this shit, simply nods and says she'll update him with any news.

She probably thinks I'm banging that woman from the mayor's office, Jim thinks.

Good. It's better than the truth.

Hello, motherfucker.

Jim watches as Terrill Lee Stanton emerges from the Erie-Torresdale El station, hands in his pockets, head down. For a moment the old man seems to consider stepping into a nearby Dunkin' Donuts, but seems to think better of it, then crosses Kensington Avenue toward Erie. Headed home after a long day of ladling or whatever the fuck it is they do in soup kitchens.

(*You should be inside his place already. Let him know that you know everything about him. That there's no escape for him. That he's not going to have a moment's peace until he answers for what he did.*)

Jim watches the man's every movement, looking for a tell or a tremor. You skipped that coffee. Maybe you're hoping for a quiet drink somewhere, get your nerve up. You haven't had a real drink in a long time, have you, killer? Maybe some of that pruno shit they brew up in toilets and plastic bags inside the Big House. But not a real drink, at a real bar. You're probably dying for one of those.

But no. Terrill Lee Stanton climbs the stairs to his halfway home and disappears behind the door.

So what now?

Jim sits in his car for the longest time, and with every minute that ticks by, he feels more like a fool. What would his father think about this? He can almost—*almost*—hear the old man's voice in his head. *Go the hell home to your family. Don't go picking fights for me.*

And you know what? This is stupid. He should go home. The Kelly Anne Farrace murder is looking like it will come together sooner than later, so he should enjoy some quiet time with Claire and the kids before he's caught up in something else. You want this motherfucker to keep you out here like a fool? He's not going anywhere.

Jim's hand is on the gearshift and he's just about to put the sedan into reverse when . . .

The front door of the halfway house opens again.

And Terrill Lee Stanton steps outside, making a beeline for the El.

Jim hasn't trailed anyone on foot for a while—it's not exactly part of your daily duties as a homicide dick. But he was a beat cop long enough for it to all come back. Staying out of your target's line of sight. Using reflections to track his movements without laying eyeballs on him (because targets can always, *always* feel the eyes). Using a piece of his clothing as a handy visual marker. For Terrill Lee Stanton, it's the white tag of his Goodwill fleece, sticking up out of his collar. Hard to miss that, once you've decided to focus on it.

So Jim locks his car and follows his quarry up to the El tracks. Surprisingly, he's not headed toward the Badlands (where he could score some drugs) or Center City beyond (where he could mug rich people). Instead, Terrill Lee Stanton chooses the eastbound platform, headed toward Northeast Philly.

It's still rush hour, so it's easy for Jim to stay in the background as he rides along with his quarry all the way to the Bridge Street Terminal, the end of the line. Terrill Lee Stanton could catch any number of buses, but he doesn't. Instead he proceeds north on Frankford Avenue, walking along the edge of the Cedar Hill Cemetery. He crosses Cheltenham, then walks along the fringes of Wissinoming Park. Stanton didn't hop a bus, which means his destination is somewhere nearby, but what? What's up here?

The longer Terrill Lee Stanton marches up Frankford Avenue, the more worried Jim gets. Because eventually, they're going to be pretty fucking close to his own house on Unruh Avenue.

(What if he knows you've been trailing him, Jimbo? What if somebody slipped him your home address, and he's going to pay your family a little visit? Would Claire like that? Would Audrey?)

By the time Terrill Lee Stanton is crossing Harbison Avenue, Jim is all but convinced that this motherfucker is headed straight for Unruh Avenue—which is not too many blocks away. How the fuck did he get Jim's home address? *(George Wildey, Jr., got it; you have to assume everybody can get it.)* Well, if this *is* the plan, then Terrill Lee here is in for a rude surprise when he walks up those steps and the next thing he sees is his own brains splattered over the white front door.

A block later—at Robbins Street—Jim is already fantasizing about reporting the incident to his superiors. *I had every reason to believe, Deputy Commissioner, that Terrill Lee Stanton intended to inflict serious harm on my family...*

But then Terrill Lee changes it up. Before he can cross the light at Robbins, he turns around and goes marching back up the block. Toward Jim. Right *for* Jim, as a matter of fact.

(He went back to the halfway house for the gun he'd stashed there. He led you here so he could shoot you on the street before laughing at you, then going up to Unruh Avenue to finish off your fucking family—every last one of them, the whole bloodline...)

Terrill Lee's head is down, and stays down, as they approach each other. Jim saw no evidence of him packing heat before, but maybe it's somewhere in that fleece jacket of his. Doesn't matter. Jim's right hand is wrapped around his own service revolver. If there's going to be a shootout, Jim's not going to stop firing until he's sure this son of a bitch is dead and hurtling like a comet toward the flaming center of Hell.

Come on, look up. Let me see your eyes.

They're ten feet apart.

Come on.

Five feet now.

Just one look.

As they pass each other, Terrill Lee does look up, and there's a moment of instant recognition on his face.

But there is no gun, there is no shootout, there is no bloody climax to thirty years of hate.

There is only Terrill Lee Stanton ducking his head back down because a burly white man is looking at him funny, and he doesn't want to start any trouble, not up in this neighborhood.

Jim eventually figures it out.

He's casing the bars.

On the long, downward-sloping block of Frankford Avenue between Harbison and Robbins, there are three lower-middle-class drinking establishments. Havens for the hardworking folks of Mayfair, Wissinoming, and nearby Frankford to order up a Bud and watch the Eagles game.

You have the venerable Chickie's & Pete's tucked away on Robbins Street, just a quarter of a block east of Frankford Avenue. Middle of the block, you have Mugsy's Tavern, a watering hole with a piano. And finally, near the top of the block, Lou's Bar, a shot-and-beer dive. All of them working-class joints that do most (if not all) of their business in cash. This is Friday, after all. Best time of the week to go rob a bar. Like he told Cary a few months back—this is when the tills are full.

135

Jim has tucked himself into the doorway of the apartment complex across the street, which affords him a view of the entire block. He watches Terrill Lee Stanton walk up and down, up and down, as if trying to make up his mind about which bar to rob. The sun's already set; night is when the predators come out. Terrill Lee Stanton: not such a pathetic old man after all.

But he is possibly senile, because he'll go up to the front of Mugsy's, pause, then shake his head and walk back down toward Chickie's & Pete's, where again he'll hesitate before walking the length of the block up to Lou's, again hesitating. Does he not remember which bar he intended to rob?

Just go ahead and pick one so I can arrest you and we can all move along with our lives, Jim thinks.

(Go ahead, stick a gun in a bartender's face so that I can justifiably blow your head off.)

After a solid twenty minutes of hithering and dithering, however, Terrill Lee Stanton walks toward Harbison Avenue and continues south down Frankford. He's changed his mind, apparently. Perhaps he needs another few days of hauling trash and cleaning toilets before he has the courage to fall back into his old line of work.

Jim follows him back to the El, back to Erie Avenue, back to the halfway house, with the ex-con having no idea he's had a police escort all this time.

For the longest time, Jim stands across the street, staring up at the fourth floor of the house.

You're working up the courage, that's all.

Well, that's fair.

So am I.

After dinner Jim is out digging around in the garage, which is actually just a piece of his basement sectioned off by cinder blocks.

Theoretically there's room to squeeze a car in here, but they use it for family storage. One half of the garage is Halloween decorations, Thanksgiving place settings, Christmas gear (including a giant fake blue spruce in its original box), Valentine's Day crap, all of it in plastic bins and carefully labeled by Claire. The other half is more or less Jim's stuff—books, papers, and everything else he doesn't know what to do with.

The search is driving him nuts. He *knows* the file is here somewhere. He wouldn't get rid of it. No way. Did Claire move it?

As if responding to his thought, the back screen door slams shut. Jim turns to see Claire there, backlit by the security spotlight behind their house.

"You scared the shit out of me," she says. "I didn't even know you were home."

"Did you or the kids move any of my files?"

"What are you talking about?"

Jim snaps at her without intending to. "My old files!" But he catches himself immediately. "I'm sorry. It's been a long day."

"The girl on Pine Street," she says.

"Yeah," Jim lies.

"Any luck?"

"Some, but not the kind I was hoping for."

Claire steps into the garage, despite the fact that she's barefoot with her thin silk robe wrapped tight around her skinny body. She knows not to press any further. He's never been one to talk about his work. Doesn't want that shit in the house, he'd explain. But when your life is your work, what else do you have to bring home?

"Let me help you find it."

Claire—who's been up all day, too, chasing after three kids by herself while trying to squeeze in tutoring hours. Offering to help him dig through old boxes at one in the morning.

Christ, I'm such a dick, he thinks.

Jim steps over the array of boxes and crates he's pulled out and goes to his wife, wraps his burly arms around her.

"They let him out yesterday, Claire. The guy who shot my father."

The look on Claire's face confirms what Jim already knows: she wasn't expecting this. "Oh Jesus, Jim. I'm sorry. How did that happen?"

"I don't know. It was in the paper. Time off his parole for something."

"You told me they don't know who shot your father."

"Yeah, well, *I* do."

They hold each other in the open garage. Claire shivers.

"You should go back up," Jim says. "I'll be there soon, I promise."

Jim can tell she knows he means it, but also knows he's lying.

He needs to find a binder.

The binder he spent years assembling—the one with the spine marked STANISŁAW WALCZAK.

AUDREY KNOCKS BACK A BEER

May 9, 2015

So apparently Claire issued a BOLO to the entire goddamned family because her sweet grandma Rose is now telling her that her father is on his way. Yes, at 11 p.m. Why? She won't say. Audrey guesses that apparently it's his turn to "deal with her." Oh blessed joy.

CLAIRE: 1

FAT AUDREY: ZIP.

"Do you want something to drink?" Grandma Rose asks.

Oh yes, a drink would be splendiferous right about now. Audrey follows her grandmother into the kitchen and starts opening cabinets. One thing becomes clear: Grandma's house has an alarming lack of Bloody Mary ingredients. Most alarmingly: zero vodka. Come to think of it, Audrey can't remember her grandmother ever enjoying an alcoholic beverage. It's probably a safe bet that Rose Walczak hasn't had a bottle of booze in this house since May 1965.

"I'll make some coffee," Grandma Rose says.

Audrey nods, not because she wants coffee (she never touches the stuff) but because she wants to seem totally agreeable before she pleads her case. She slides into a kitchen chair, one of the same Grandma's had since forever. When she was a kid she'd rock the wheels back and forth, spin around on the rotating seat, much to the annoyance of anyone who happened to be sitting nearby. She likes to think of them as AUDREY STOP IT RIGHT NOW™ chairs.

Grandma Rose asks if she wants sugar or milk.

"You know me, Grandma. I like my coffee like my men—strong, hot, and black."

Grandma Rose should be used to this sort of sass from her only grand-daughter. This time, however, it only seems to piss her off. Her face hardens into a petite scowl. Without responding, Rose sits down across from her granddaughter and waits until she catches her attention.

"What?" Audrey asks. "Are you all out of coffee? That's okay, I didn't really want any."

Grandma Rose doesn't make eye contact with Audrey as she quietly says, "Your mother told me what you were doing for your school project."

"I'm glad she told you. This is why I thought it might be a good idea for me to stay here for a couple of days. I would completely stay out of your way, but help out when you needed me."

Grandma shakes her head. "Oh no, that wouldn't work."

"But you'd hardly know I was here."

"No, no. I understand, but I don't think it's a good idea."

"But I could help you out, you know? You shouldn't be living alone anyway. Maybe this is a blessing in disguise!"

"Audrey, I'm telling you no."

"Apparently," she mutters. And yes, there is some eye-rolling here, too.

"Young *lady!*"

The stern tone in Grandma's voice catches Audrey off guard. She's never heard her use it before. Never. Even when Staś and Cary used to bloody each other's noses in the backyard and threaten to set each on fire for an encore. Not even when Audrey accidentally flipped a freshly cooked pot roast upside down and onto the kitchen floor.

"You will *not* do this," Grandma Rose says. "It's profane and wrong and I will *not* have it. Do you understand me?"

All Audrey can do is nod, stunned. How can she possibly defend her profane and wrongheaded quest for the truth?

But Grandma's anger fades away as quickly as it appeared, and what's left in Rose Walczak's eyes is a weary sadness.

As much as it pained Audrey to hear those words, it pains her more that her grandmother was forced to spit them out.

The women sit in silence. Audrey too embarrassed to drink the coffee her grandma made (not that she wanted it in the first place). Rose, looking like she'd like to be anywhere but here.

Audrey is almost happy to hear the Captain's voice call out, "Ma?"

"Going back to Unruh Avenue" is right up there with "lemon juice and Sriracha douches" on Audrey's list of Least Favorite Things. The very idea of returning to her childhood home makes her twitch. She still doesn't know why her father lingers there, after all these years. Big swinging police captain, he could afford to live anywhere. Yet he chooses to remain in that dumpy three-bedroom place in Mayfair. The place can't exactly be swimming in happy memories. Least of all for Audrey.

But as painful as it might be, she has no other option. Unless she wants to tuck her fat tail between her legs and slink back home to Houston, where she can flunk out of grad school in person. Or stay here in Philadelphia and investigate the fifty-year-old homicides as a homeless person. Call it *CSI: Skid Row*.

Her other family options are not options. Her older brother? Please. Staś and Bitchanne would sooner welcome a bucket of body lice into their Jenkintown home. Cary's place up in Somerton wouldn't be a good idea, either. Even though he's fun, his near-suburban house is a circus of full-on crazy. Jean would spend most of the time smiling at her while searching for the ideal location on Audrey's back to insert a steak knife. *Ooops, I'm sorry, did I do that?* And their kids wouldn't want their Ugly Aunt Audrey from Texas around.

God forbid one of their parents should give a moment's attention to another sentient life-form in their presence.

So it's down to the one family member who has two bedrooms to spare.

The Captain arrives, hugs his mother, barely looking at Audrey when he says, "You got everything?"

She shrugs. "Pretty much got nothing."

"Let's go, then. Bye, Ma. I'll call you in the morning."

The drive home takes barely five minutes, especially this time of night. You just drive down Bridge Street, hang a right, drive past four cemeteries—oh yeah, the dead rule this part of town—and a few minutes later you're in Mayfair.

Audrey's pals in Houston don't believe such a neighborhood exists. It just sounds so made-up. Which it is. Thank the local chamber of commerce during the Great Depression for giving it such an uplifting name, as in "May you be given a fair deal."

Her father says nothing the whole five minutes. Audrey can smell his aftershave, which means he cleaned himself up before coming over to retrieve her. She wonders if he's drunk and is covering up.

When her parents split, Audrey moved with her mom to a rented house over in Rhawnhurst to be closer to Claire's family. To Audrey, the 'Hurst was the Wurst. She couldn't wait to leave. Visits back to Mayfair were limited and awkward and usually weekend deals; Audrey realizes she hasn't slept in this house *since the last century,* when she was nine years old.

The Captain hasn't done much with the place.

There's a newish couch in the living room, and of course, his beloved turntable, tuner, and speakers, along with a dozen crates of vinyl. An IKEA bookshelf stuffed with hardcovers—all history. But that's about it, as far as the living room goes. The dining room contains the same table the Walczaks have used since before Audrey was born.

"You hungry?" he asks.

"Sure."

She isn't, but it feels rude to refuse food.

Late dining on Unruh Avenue means cold cuts on rolls and macaroni salad of questionable vintage, all of which the Captain no doubt picked up from Acme up on Harbison and the Boulevard. He pulls out the plastic bags of rolls, lunchmeat, and cheese and puts them on the table. Audrey hangs her bag over the high back of one of the surviving chairs. (Half of the original six have seemingly bit the dust.)

"Mind if I use the ladies'?"

"You know where it is."

She doesn't have to go. She just wants to scope out the old place a little.

Dad's bedroom has a California king that appears not to have been made since Claire moved out. The door to the second bedroom, the boys' old room, is shut. This, of course, is merely an enticement for Audrey. Growing up, she had a fascination with drawers, closets, boxes, doors, and anything else hidden from public view, much to the dismay of her older brothers. She found shit in their dresser drawers that still gives her nightmares.

Audrey tries the knob; it turns. She pushes the door open a few inches—no squeak. Beyond the edge of the door she can see stacks of cardboard boxes, black-and-white photos stuck on corkboards, a laptop on the floor, with its extension cord snaking its way to the wall outlet. Covering the walls are mug shots and news clippings. This is the way a five-year-old or a serial killer might decorate a room.

"What are you doing?"

Shit.

Audrey turns to face the Captain, whose frame fills the hallway. She puts on a look of confusion.

"Um, this room full of files and stuff clearly isn't the bathroom. Sorry!"

He takes a moment, one of those lingering *cop* moments, then says, "Just close it."

Shit shit shit. Audrey pulls the door shut, then continues to the bathroom, where she pretends to pee. The bathroom smells like Old Dude. Not entirely a bad thing, but slightly overwhelming. There is nothing feminine here to balance things out. This relieves yet depresses Audrey.

Back in the dining room, Audrey and the Captain spend the next twenty minutes pretending that second bedroom full of files, clearly *police shit,* doesn't exist. She makes an imported-ham sandwich slathered with enough spicy mustard to choke a horse. The Captain sticks with turkey and pickles on a kaiser, dry.

With dining formalities out of the way, the Captain gives her the eyes that say, *To what do I owe this pleasure?*

"You know I just started my second year," Audrey says.

"Yeah, I just got the bill a few days ago. Glad you're sticking with it."

"Well, it's a two-year intensive program, but they make you do an independent research project over the winter break."

"Huh. So what'd you end up doing?"

Audrey exhales. "I didn't do it. I mean, I worked on some of it, but it's late. Don't worry, though. I have an extension."

"Until when?"

"The end of next week."

"That's one hell of an extension."

Audrey smiles. "I can be very convincing."

But the Captain is unconvinced. Audrey's smile evaporates. She takes a bite of her sandwich. The Captain eases his burly frame against the seat back. And in that moment, she realizes that Claire has no doubt told him, too. He's just drawing her out, like a cop with a suspect.

"So what's the project?" he asks.

"I've already completed the proposal and experimental design. All approved. Which just leaves the data collection and analysis."

The Captain lifts his right eyebrow a fraction of an inch. *And...?*

"I want to investigate Grandpop Stan's murder."

The Captain just stares at her. His eyes lock onto his daughter's, and she's treated to the strangest transformation. Usually his eyes throw up a force field to repel anyone attempting to read them. But slowly, with each blink, the defenses fade away. And for a moment, Audrey isn't staring at her sixty-two-year-old father anymore. For an instant, he looks like a big kid.

Then he stands up and the spell is broken. "You want a beer?"

"Sure."

As the Captain fetches two cold bottles of Yuengling from the fridge, Audrey tries to divine any kind of reaction from his movements. Is he upset? Is he interested? Is he feeling any glimmer of an emotion?

The Captain twists the top off one Yuengling, hands it to his daughter. She takes it, brings it to her lips, tips the end up. Her father does the same, still standing there.

"I was reading this travel article about France, sightseeing the old World War Two battlefields where American soldiers died," he says.

"Oh, you planning a trip?" Audrey asks. "You, bunch of old guys, doing the history thing?"

He ignores her. Takes a long swallow of his beer, then places the bottle back on the table. "If you head into the woods in Lorraine, Champagne, or Picardy," he says, "you can still find shrapnel and bullets in newly plowed fields. You can even find live shells. And every year, people are still getting maimed or killed by these things. Can you imagine that? A hundred years later?"

Audrey sees where this is going. "Well, that's subtle, Dad."

She presses on as she makes her pitch—the same one she gave her professor.

"Look, you know better than anybody—forensic science has improved a great deal in the past five years, let alone fifty," she says. "I want to enter as much data as possible to come up with a computer model of the shooting and see where it all leads."

"Where it leads," the Captain repeats.

"Yeah," Audrey says. "So... will you help?"

The Captain stares at her for a while, then says,

"Good night, Audrey."

Audrey's bedroom is still painted pink—which she still hates—and just as claustrophobic as ever. Both of the bedrooms are empty, hers and the boys', and the boys had the bigger room. But she prefers to stick to known territory, at least for a few days.

She hadn't planned on staying in Philly for longer than a day and night, so her wardrobe is pretty much limited to three T-shirts and one pair of jeans. Oh, and that long-sleeved black dress. She's even going to have to sink-wash her panties in the man-bathroom, hang them on the shower curtain rod to dry. Boy, Dad will love that.

She gets the eerie feeling that this is it—that Philadelphia has lured her back home to trap her, like one of those fly-eating plants. She sleeps inside this pink nightmare, she may never wake up.

But she's too pissed off to sleep. She turns and fidgets and sticks her bare leg out from under the dusty old comforter, then sticks it back under again. The more people who tell her no, the more she wants to solve this goddamned thing.

STAN AND THE PLAN

November 4, 1964

Terrill Lee Stanton looks as if he's been scrounging around on the streets for days on end. Stan's been in the Jungle long enough to know his type. Shifty look on his face, like he's just broken a window or lifted a TV or boosted a machine and is waiting to see if you're smart enough to catch him. They can tell just by looking at you.

"My mama always told me I'm like the boy who cried wolf," says Terrill Lee. "And Pastor knows that yeah, maybe I do sometimes. But not now. I'm telling you, the wolves is real. I've seen 'em."

Stan chokes back a sigh, struggling to maintain his calm demeanor. Wolves? Yeah, sure, wolves. This punk is probably hooked on something and seeing wolves in his drugged-out nightmares. What the hell are they doing here, anyway?

"Slow down now," Wildey says, almost cooing. "You're all right here. Pastor Stebbens wasn't lying to you. You can talk to us."

The kid turns and points at Stan. "What about him? Huh? I don't know him. Shit, I don't know either of you. Just a couple of fucking pigs for all I know!"

Oh boy. Pigs, wolves, we got the whole barnyard here. Stan gives Wildey a hard look. Can we get on with this?

Pastor Stebbens *tut-tut*s. "Terrill, we talked about language in the house of the Lord."

"Easy, brother," Wildey says, pulling up a wooden chair next to Stanton and easing into it. "The good pastor told me you might know something about a couple of ruffians down on Columbia Avenue. You know, the kind who might set a couch on fire, heave it off a roof?"

The pastor nods, puts a hand on Terrill Lee's shoulder, as if channeling courage from the Lord Almighty into this boy's scrawny frame.

Jesus Christ, Stan thinks. So this is what this is about. Woke him up from his nap for the goddamned sofa-tossers. He's gotta hand it to Wildey. Once something crosses the man's path, he don't forget about it. Stan's partner really wants to see these little bastards fry.

Terrill Lee's mouth pops open, but it's like his throat is changing gears.

"Look," Wildey says. "This is just between you and me. Nobody's gonna hang a snitch jacket on you. That's why you reached out to Pastor Stebbens, right? Well, we go way back. He can vouch for me. And I can vouch for my partner here. Whatever you tell me, I didn't hear it from you."

"Well..."

"Go on, son," Pastor Stebbens says.

"I don't know nothing about no couch," Stanton says. "I just said that so you'd listen to me. But I'm telling you, we've got wolves out there. And things are about to get *real* scary."

"What are you talking about?"

"They've started *the Plan,* man."

For a moment, Wildey keeps his cool. Looks at young Terrill Lee, smiling and nodding.

And then he goes into overdrive. Terrill Lee is lifted off his feet and out of the chair and the next time he blinks he's pressed up against the kitchen wall, his back spasming with 210 pounds of Officer George Wildey in his face.

"Why are you wasting my time with this bullshit?"

"George!" the pastor admonishes. "Language!"

Wildey isn't concerned with his language, though. He's about to explode all over this skinny punk—who's now got this dead earnest look on his face.

"Guess we had too much fun," Terrill Lee says.

"What fun?" Wildey says through clenched teeth.

"Columbia Avenue. You have to admit, *brother,* you never seen anything like that before. All those fires! They didn't think we'd do it like they did up in New York. But we forced their hand. They're coming after all of us now."

Stan shakes his head. "Come on, Wildey, let him go."

Which only attracts Terrill Lee's wild eyes. "*MMMMMM,* is that roast pig I smell? You're part of the Plan, you blue-eyed motherfucker! We're not gonna let you win! Your whole family's gonna burn!"

"Shut the fuck up," Wildey says.

"George Wildey!"

"And you, my brother," Stanton says, "will be the first swinging by your neck when the Revolution comes."

Wildey can do one of two things in this moment. He can either pop this stupid prick's head off the kitchen wall. Or he can let him go. Wildey chooses the latter and releases his grip on Terrill Lee. After all, they're still in the Lord's house. The pastor takes a deep breath and tries to bring logic and reason back into the conversation. "Terrill Lee, you sit down and tell these policemen what you told me."

"I ain't telling them shit. They're agents of the devil, Preacher—don't you know that? They're sizing me up for a body bag. Especially that blond one."

"Terrill Lee!"

The young punk sighs, then opens his mouth and lets the words pour out a mile a minute.

"Look, they're startin' the Plan, man. They've been gearing it up for years now but the riots gave them an excuse to do it. I'm seeing the white wolves all over. You ask around. They're everywhere, selling the poison—shit, they're even giving it away. You want it, they got it, and brothers are lining up for it. Not me, though, man, I don't trust anything on the street no more."

"The Plan," Wildey says.

"Come on, man, don't be pretending you haven't heard about it before. You know they've been dying to do it!"

"No, I've heard of it." Wildey stands up and shakes Stebbens's hand. "Thanks for your hospitality, Pastor."

The man of the cloth, however, is confused. "Can't you stay a little longer and hear what this boy has to say?"

"All due respect, Pastor, I've heard enough."

When Stan was working the vice district back in the fifties, they had a favorite interrogation technique for crazy punks like Stanton here. They kept it in a cardboard box in a supply closet and only broke it out on rare occasions. They built it up, too, talking between themselves, ignoring the suspect. *Should we?* Absolutely. *I don't know, Loot. You think he deserves it?* Yeah, this guy's a real cutie-pie—go ahead into the closet and bring it out. *Aw, Loot, you can't do that. Remember what happened the last time?*

Building it up, and meanwhile the suspect starts sweating bullets.

Eventually they send one guy out "to the closet." And then they leave the suspect alone for a while. Maybe a half hour, forty-five minutes, with his mind running wild. What could possibly be in that closet?

Finally the door opens, and in walks...

A giant bunny.

Specifically, a cop in a bunny suit. White and pink, with big sad eyes and floppy ears. The fur is old and full of dust and matted and worn in places. They take turns wearing it, but honestly, it only fits a couple of them comfortably. Not that it's comfortable. The head smells like onions and beer, and the interior is scratchy. But perhaps the toughest thing about wearing the suit is not sneezing during the interrogation.

At this point the suspect is looking at the giant bunny and thinking, What the hell is this all about?

And then maybe he'll laugh a little, because, you know—it's a giant bunny.

The bunny will bounce a little, closing the distance between him and the perp.

The suspect's laugh at this point dies away quick, because he sees something in the bunny's body language he doesn't like.

Which is smart, because

POW.

The bunny gives the suspect a right cross that makes the suspect's eyes tear up.

Then

BAM.

A left hook.

And

POP POP POP.

Hammerlike punches to the ribs.

Sure, the fluffy gloves pad the hits a little, but they still hurt like hell. The suspect is cuffed to a chair, wrists behind his back, unable to protect himself.

The trick, though, is to keep the beating swift and strong. Then get the hell out of there while he's still dazed and all teared up.

The detectives then return and ask, "You ready to talk now?"

"The f-f-fuck's with that bunny?"

Bunny? What bunny. Kid, you must be goofy in the head.

Of course, if the suspect still won't talk, you ask the bunny to make a return appearance. But usually, once is enough. Because even the dumbest skell knows that he's never going to tell anyone—not his friend, not a judge, *nobody*—that a giant white-and-pink bunny beat the shit out of him down at the station house.

On their way out, Wildey apologies to Stan for waking him up early and for the wasted trip. He should have known better. They climb into their car, Stan behind the wheel as usual. Wildey sinks into the passenger seat, sulking.

"Pastor Stebbens told me the crazy asshole was scared to come to the police directly," Wildey says. "So he arranged this meeting. I thought he was gonna offer up the assholes with the sofa."

"You're really stuck on that whole thing."

"Aren't you?"

Stan shakes his head. No, he's not. Somebody ought to be stuck on it, it should be Taney. Let him climb out of bed early to go to a Baptist church and be called a blue-eyed devil. Told he's gonna see his family burn.

"Your friend back there sure hates police," Stan says.

"Yeah, well, he's not going to like them any better after I'm through with him."

"What's this stuff about the Plan?"

Wildey sighs. "You really want to hear this?"

Stan spreads his hands as if to say, *Would I ask if I didn't?*

"Remember I was telling you most black folk have had some kind of run-in with the police?" Wildey says. "I was no different. And I was the son of a cop! Sure, it pissed me off, and it was easy to get bitter. But soon I learned that life goes on. You can't hold on to grudges, otherwise one day you're a seventy-year-old angry man with a lot of hate in your heart and wasted years behind you. What the hell good is that? Instead I became a cop, trying to help everybody, white, black, or whatever."

"So what's the Plan?"

"The Plan is paranoid talk from bitter people who aren't happy unless they're frightening other people. The Plan is that the US government is trying to kill off the entire black race. That they're poisoning black kids with vaccines. Putting drugs in free lunches in black schools. Passing out heroin and pot and coke and guns like it's Halloween and everybody in the Jungle is trick-or-treating. The Plan means don't trust any white man. Especially don't trust a white man with a badge. Or a black man with a badge, for that matter. 'Cause, see, to their way of thinking, we're all part of the Plan. We're the ones who are gonna set it in motion."

Stan doesn't know what to say in response, so he lets the words just hang there in the quiet space of the car. It's up to Wildey to wave them away.

"Come on, let's go get something to eat before our shift."

Stan says sure, but he's not hungry. Because he's thinking about the Plan, and thinking about his father. Rosie and her family, too. They all think black people have a Plan of their own.

JIM AND HIS VOW

November 4, 1995

Jim doesn't manage to put his hands on the binder until long after everyone else has gone to sleep. Go figure, it's in the very last box in the stack. Jim takes it back to his office in the basement and stays up until after three leafing through its pages, sipping on a vodka rocks as he reabsorbs the case. He hasn't looked at this book in ten, fifteen years. But the details are surprisingly fresh in his mind, just waiting for someone to blow the dust off a little.

When he does manage a little snatch of sleep the gory details tumble around in his brain. The past and present collide with no concern for dates, logic, or reason. The murder of Kelly Anne Farrace. The murder of Stan Walczak. The murder of George Wildey. They're all part of the same conspiracy. In the wee hours his mind is like a fevered bloodhound, racing from scent to scent. Around 4 a.m. the two cases merge and he starts confusing details, one for the other. The same guy who raped and strangled Kelly Anne Farrace and threw her down a cement staircase knows something about the guy who killed Jim's father and his partner.

He rises before the rest of the house and manages to slip out even before Audrey can catch him leaving.

Imagine that.

Jim drives to the national cemetery in Beverly, New Jersey, a drive he's made a thousand times. Jim didn't understand why his dad was buried all the way over here in another state until his mother explained it. *Your father was a veteran*, she said, *and this is a national cemetery for soldiers.* His younger self asked: Isn't there a soldier cemetery near us? His mother nodded. *There is, but it's all full up. So they put him over here.*

The gates are not open yet, so he parks on the street, hops the fence, and makes his way to his father's grave.

STANISŁAW WALCZAK, PFC, WORLD WAR II

The marble slab is set into the grass at the base of a tree on the edge of the grounds. Jim has watched that tree grow over the past thirty years. He's also watched the sharp lettering of his father's name fade.

The air is humid, and the overcast skies could burst at any moment. His shoes sink into the grass and mud as he walks up to the headstone.

"Hey, Pop," Jim whispers.

His father, of course, does not reply.

Over the years Jim has left flowers, toys, cigarettes, booze. Even a few polka records, which have always disappeared by his next visit. You'd think the polka, of all things, would be safe. But the groundskeepers must be serious about keeping this place pristine. You look in any direction and you see a row of perfectly symmetrical white tablets, lined up in formation like they're still fighting a war even after death.

When he was younger, Jim would imagine his father waiting until he left the cemetery before reaching up out of the grave with bony fingers to snatch a smoke, or maybe a bottle he left behind. Jim wasn't a dummy; he knew cemetery employees cleared away the flowers, downed the booze, and smoked the cigarettes themselves. And apparently, enjoyed the polka.

Eventually Jim stopped bringing things—what was the point, really—and started having one-way conversations. *What would you do, Dad? I've got this really tough case, Dad. You won't believe it. Yeah, I'm finally getting married, Dad. And Mom even likes her, so there's that.*

And he'd remember the promise he made.

His father's wake is an event Jim still remembers in astonishing detail, from the suit worn by the undertaker (shiny, pegged pants, skinny tie) to the fragrance of the flowers arrayed around the coffin to the selection of organ music being played on a perpetual loop by the ancient woman who smelled like wet paper.

The casket had been gray and streamlined like a new car. Fancier than his father's car, or any piece of furniture in the house, for that matter. The padding on the inside looked plush and comfortable. You've had a tough life, Stan. But look, we saved all the luxury for the end.

At wakes you were supposed to kneel down and say a prayer for the deceased. But all twelve-year-old Jim could think about was how unnatural his father looked. As if they'd replaced him with a wax dummy. Jim's young mind ran with the fantasy for a few moments. Somewhere out there a gang was keeping his real dad hostage, waiting for his son to save him...

But no. This was his father. Someone had shot him, repeatedly. Now that Jim was close, you could see the damage the mortician had struggled to repair.

So as Jim touched the sleeve of his father's dress blues, he said a quick prayer. He made a promise.

I'm going to find the man who did this to you.

And I'm going to make him pay.

The drive back down the Boulevard is hazy. Jim is operating on practically zero sleep. Aisha's waiting for him at the Roundhouse practically bursting at the seams. Almost nobody's ever happy to be at work on a Saturday morning, but today is different.

Forensics says the blond hair in the garage is a definite match for Kelly Anne Farrace's; they're still working on the jogging pants. As a consequence, the ADA likes them for it. Aisha likes them for it. The mayor's office certainly likes them for it. Two white rapist dumbasses? This could be the best news they've had for months. They were probably doing cartwheels in City Hall once they heard the perps were white.

It's been a tough year for this (still) racially divided city. First the whole Thirty-Ninth District scandal blew up over the summer. The goddamned Four Horsemen of the Apocalypse, raiding drug houses on the sly and stealing whatever cash they found, hassling innocent people (mostly of color). Word had it that the Feds were going to start digging into over a thousand cases, most of them cases against black citizens.

Jim doesn't give a shit about the racial politics of it—that's Sonya's headache, the mayor's headache. He simply wants justice for Kelly Anne Farrace. And the sooner she gets it, the sooner he can get back to serving justice to Terrill Lee Stanton.

After waiting the appropriate length of time (or so he guesses), Jim excuses himself, telling Aisha he has a quick errand to run.

"Tell Son-ya I said hi," Aisha says, drawing out the name like she's a telephone sex worker or something.

"Hey," Jim says. "Cut that shit out."

"What?"

"That's not what this is about."

(But I don't honestly mind if that's what you're thinking, because it gives me an alibi, of sorts.)

"Hey, it's none of my affair."

No, it's not, Jim thinks. *Lucky you.*

Terrill Lee Stanton is not at the halfway house at Erie and Castor, best as Jim can tell. No movement in the fourth-floor window, no sign of him anywhere nearby.

A short drive to Mayfair, however, reveals that Terrill Lee *is* hanging out near Mugsy's Tavern at 9:45 a.m., trying to look all inconspicuous. Which to the trained eye of Jim Walczak makes the motherfucker look as conspicuous as hell.

What's the idea, dumb-ass? Catch the lone bartender first thing in the morning, so you can empty out his sure-to-be-already-empty till?

Or maybe it's not about the money at all. Maybe you've got a thing for shooting people in bars while they drink beer.

Jim honestly doesn't know what he wants more—to prevent Terrill Lee from carrying out another horrible crime, or to catch him in the act just so he can shoot the old bastard legally, justifiably.

It's 9:55 a.m. Guess he'll find out sooner than later.

A minute later and the presumed owner shows up—a white guy with dark, bushy hair, young, no more than twenty-five. From the looks of Mugsy's, Jim was expecting someone a little older, more grizzled. The owner doesn't pay Terrill Lee much mind as he digs a set of keys out of his jeans pocket, opens up, then steps inside.

Jim tenses, prepared to run across busy Frankford Avenue with his gun in hand. The very idea of it makes his blood jump.

Go ahead. Do it!

But Terrill Lee seems oddly disappointed. He looks up and down the block, then glances at the bar before shaking his head and walking back toward Harbison Avenue and, presumably, the El and the halfway house.

Chicken-ass motherfucker.

Jim breathes in deep, trying to get his hands to stop shaking. He should go home—after all, it's just a dozen or so blocks away—and take a nap before heading back downtown. Eat some breakfast, drink a gallon of water. Tell Aisha he's feeling sick, to beep him with any-thing urgent.

Which of course is when his beeper goes off.

Aisha's number pops up.

It must be important, since she probably thinks he's balls-deep in Sonya Kaminski by now.

AUDREY AND THE OLD BASTARD

May 10, 2015

Audrey awakens to the smell of death, of flesh burning, of acrid smoke. Soon it becomes clear: Dad is cooking breakfast.

She staggers downstairs, grease and salt heavy in the air, cutting through her head fog. Then she comes to the sad realization that Dad probably doesn't have the ingredients for a proper Bloody. Or a *passable* Bloody, for that matter. Or a drop of tomato juice. It's not as if she can toddle off to a hip brunch spot a few blocks away. This is Mayfair. The only bars open this time of morning will be serving the night shift, and their idea of a cocktail is a Coors Light with a shot of Jack. Horrors; she might be forced to make do with a Polish mimosa—vodka and orange juice.

"How did you sleep?"

"Not sure. I was unconscious for most of it."

The Captain shoots her a look: You're not as funny as you think.

Whatever.

Flesh-colored pork roll sizzles in a dinged-up frying pan. Dad's got the ingredients for a healthy Philly-style breakfast scattered all over the counter: the leftover rolls, dozen eggs, pound of American cheese. The Ween song "Pork Roll Egg and Cheese" starts playing in her head. She hasn't thought about that one since forever.

"Are you supposed to be eating that?" Audrey says, looking down into the pan as she steps behind her father and snoops over his shoulder.

Dad flips one of the meat discs. He's cut four notches on the edges of the circle, like a rifle scope, to prevent them from curling up. Audrey can't help but smile. Nothing ever changes.

"What's the matter with pork roll?" the Captain asks.

"Nothing, if you want *pork roll* listed as your cause of death."

"I'm fine."

Audrey opens the fridge, bends over to scan the inside. No tomato juice. No OJ. There are not many other liquid options.

And shit, even *she's* not a big enough alcoholic to mix vodka with half-and-half.

But lo! There *is* a six-pack of eight-ounce V8s hidden in the back. She plucks one from the plastic ring and carries it to the hutch in the living room, which doubles as Dad's bar. He's got some Stoli under there—she scoped it out last night. With a little pepper, she can fake it.

Dad plates the sandwiches and Audrey stirs her white-trash Bloody. She drinks it down in three swallows, then gets up to make another.

"You'd better eat this before it gets cold," Dad says. "And go easy on the booze. It's still morning."

The booze isn't going to kill me, Audrey thinks, *as fast as that hockey puck of processed meat.*

They chow down in silence, Audrey trying to find another way to convince the Captain to help her with her project. The Captain thinking about...well, hell. Who knows what the Captain is thinking about at any given moment? He is an emotionless golem.

Back in the kitchen, Audrey stealthily makes and chugs her second Bloody, then stirs a third, which Dad will think is her second. Not that she cares what he thinks. She carries it back to the table, the red up to the brim.

"I know that's your third," he says.

"What does it matter? I'm not going anywhere."

The Captain grunts. Chews. Then something seems to occur to him.

"What's the Houston number that keeps calling you?"

"Hmm?" she asks, mid-sip.

"The area code, 713, that's Houston. You got a bunch of calls from 713-524-8597."

Audrey puts down the Bloody. "You're seriously looking at my phone?"

The Captain shrugs. As if to say, Hey, it's in *my* house, plugged into *my* power supply, so I have the right to search your crappy cell phone.

"You can't do that," Audrey says. "You fascist."

"Shut up. Who is it?"

"A Catholic nun. First name—Of Your Business. Weird, I know. Speaking of calls, should I call your vascular surgeon this morning? Tell him you'll be in for an angioplasty after lunch?"

"Hey, lay off me and the food."

"Fine. Lay off my calls."

The Captain stares at her.

Audrey drains the rest of her Bloody, then rises from her chair to go mix a fourth. She's in it for as long as the V8 holds out.

"Come on, enough of that. You should go upstairs and get dressed."

"Why? What's the hurry?"

The Captain looks at her. "Don't you want to go off and play detective today?"

They leave Mayfair an hour later, heading up Frankford Avenue toward Holmesburg. It's a commercial strip, with plenty of bars and flower shops and delis and even a place to buy a gun. Back in the old days, you didn't drive to a mall, you just wandered down to the Avenue. If they didn't have it, you didn't need it.

The Captain drives. Which is a good thing, because Audrey is a little tipsy. She managed a fourth crap Bloody while the Captain wasn't looking.

"The man who killed your grandfather is dead," the Captain says. "He spent most of his life in prison for another charge, got out in late ninety-five. But within a few days he was gone."

"What happened to him?"

"They said it was an overdose. Heroin."

Audrey knew Terrill Lee Stanton died twenty years ago. But this new bit of information cuts through her boozy blur. "Well, geez, that's a little suspicious."

The Captain turns to look at her. "Why do you say that?"

"Why would he kill himself after spending so long in stir? Sounds like someone with an old score to settle bumped him off. Easy enough to fake an overdose."

"Says the forensics expert."

"Hey, you're paying for it. Just want you to know you're getting your money's worth."

"Well, take your face out of your books and take a look at the man. Some people can't adjust to life on the outside."

"How very *Shawshank*."

"What?"

"Never mind."

"Your brothers talked about it all the time after it happened. Don't you remember?"

"Uh...no?"

Sometimes Audrey thinks her childhood was an implanted memory that never fully took. And her parents, who know the script, will always bring up details or events that mean absolutely nothing to her.

"Jesus. So the patsy either killed himself, or it was made to look like he killed himself."

"Patsy? Aud, the guy did it. You say there was a second shooter, then fine, I'm not going to argue with your homework. In that case, maybe he had some help. But he's definitely responsible. I've looked in his eyes. He's a killer."

Audrey fishes her notebook out of her backpack. "Hold on," she says.

"What, are you quoting me?"

"If I'm going to write an independent study, I might, you know, need a stray detail or two."

The Captain grunts. "You'll get plenty of details in a few minutes. I called ahead, and he's awake and ready to talk to us."

"Who?"

"Your grandfather's former partner."

The residents call it the Woods, but to Audrey it looks like a bunch of Cracker Jack boxes lined up on dinky and depressing little cul-de-sacs.

Back in 1942, a few months after Pearl Harbor, the Philadelphia defense business was booming. You had the Frankford Arsenal, the Bendix Corporation, Budd Company, and five dozen other contractors—many of them slapped up in the wide-open spaces of Northeast Philly. Problem was, where do you house all the workers toiling in these plants? The Northeast was like...way out there.

That was when a local architect got the idea to slap up a $4-million development of clapboard houses on a giant patch of mud adjacent to Pennypack Park. The mud, they hoped (prayed), would eventually turn into lush green spaces. Instant Suburbia: Just Add White People. "Workers and their families will live among broad lawns in a suburban atmosphere within the city limits," gushed one press release. Who could say no? The rent was cheap: $27 a month, which most young families could swing. And work was plentiful. Even if the bus service was shitty and the mud got everywhere.

After the war, the residents decided they didn't want to let a good thing slip by. So they bought the entire development and established a cooperative. Hells no, it wasn't communism! Each resident owned 1/1,000th of the land and paid a small monthly upkeep fee. Houses could only be passed down to blood relatives. When free slots opened up, they were filled by people on a waiting list. By the 1980s, the average wait for a two-bedroom, one-bathroom box was ten years.

Officer Billy Taney waited fifteen years for his.

Finally got his chance back in '96, moving out of his row house in Kensington and hightailing it to the faux-burbs. He's sitting in the backyard now, grass freshly mown, working on his fourth (maybe fifth) Bud of the day.

"Hey, Bill," the Captain says.

"Hey, kid," Billy says. "And who's this? Your girlfriend? Hah hah hah."

Hah hah hah *pervo*.

Audrey doesn't like him. Not one bit. Reminds her of all the old men playing grab-ass at the Kelvin Arms. You can practically see his bulging liver sticking out of his white V-neck T-shirt, which is actually gray from countless cycles in the washing machine. There's no sign of a woman's touch in this place, which means his wife either passed away, split, or hanged herself on the second floor.

"This is my daughter, Audrey," the Captain says. "She's down in Houston, studying forensics."

Billy laughs. "You want my body for science, honey?"

Science wouldn't know where to begin with your body, Audrey thinks. *Honey.*

"How are you, Mr. Taney?"

Taney, he says, is pronounced to rhyme with "Manny."

"Because I'm all man."

The Captain smiles politely, declines the third and fourth offer of a Bud, then turns to the business at hand.

"Audrey's doing a report on Dad."

"Hell of a guy! Saved my white ass during the riots, I'll tell you what. You hear what those bastards did? They set a couch on fire and dropped it on top of me. Didn't want to fight me man to man, I guess. Still got the scars, if you want to see."

"I'm actually looking into his murder," Audrey says.

Billy Taney stops cold as if some invisible hand has reached down from Heaven and slapped him.

"You're what? Whaddya want to do that for?" He looks at the Captain for backup. "Jim, why are you letting her do this? We all know the cocksucker who did it, may he rest in pieces—"

The Captain interrupts. "Yeah, yeah, Billy, I told Audrey what you told me. But I thought she should hear it from the source."

"Source? Source for what. Excuse me for a sec, I gotta shake the dew off my lily."

Billy Taney toddles back into his cracker box to drain the contents of his bladder into the single bathroom on the second floor. Fifteen years he waited for the privilege of pissing in this part of town, Audrey thinks. Hope he enjoys it.

Audrey goes inside and takes a look around Taney's place. The Captain follows her, hands in his pockets, mouth zipped shut.

A set of marbled, mirrored glass panels, straight out of your favorite early-eighties porn film, covers the main living room wall. Audrey hates the sight of her own self in the mirror. God knows how Taney puts up with it. The shag carpet looks like it was last vacuumed on installation day. Everything else is covered by a visible film of nicotine.

"Charming fella," Audrey says.

"Taney and your grandfather were partners for a long time," the Captain says. "You want someone who knows what happened, he's your guy."

"But not for the last nine months of his life," Audrey says.

The Captain doesn't respond. The heavy creak of steps heralds Taney's return. Taney blinks, surprised that little Jimmy and his baby daughter are standing in his living room.

"Do you guys want a drink? Maybe something to eat?"

"Do you ever leave sausages around here and wait to see if they'll smoke themselves?"

Taney lights up. "What?"

"We're good, Billy," the Captain says.

"Your grandfather was a good man," Taney says. "I'm sorry you never had the chance to meet him."

"Me, too."

"But that *murzyn* partner of his got him killed, and I'll never forgive him for that."

Audrey really can't believe she's hearing this racist shit pour out of this man's fat mouth...right here...*live.* The worst part about being white around racists is that they automatically assume you're one of their kind. Don't even think twice about it. She thinks about Bryant, back home in Houston, and she's overcome with the urge to slap the shit out of this guy.

"Excuse me? Do you mean his African-American partner? The man who also was shot and killed in that bar?"

167

Taney snorts. "Bet you voted for Ho-bama, didn't you, honey?"

"What can I say? I thought we could use a Muslim in the White House."

Taney looks like he's about to have a stroke due to cognitive dissonance. Here is his partner's granddaughter—and he doesn't want to disrespect her or anything, but he also doesn't want some snotty little bitch sassing him in his own house.

The Captain lowers his eyes and shakes his head. At first, Audrey think he's mad. But then she catches it. That little hint of a smile he's trying to hide from Taney.

"Well, let me tell you a little something you probably don't know," Taney says. "Nobody knew, except just a few of us. Wildey was bad. News."

He separates the words for emphasis.

"He worked undercover back in the fifties, trying to run with some black heist gangs that were cropping up all over town. Got a little too friendly with the *brothers* he was supposed to bust. Suddenly, Wildey's flush. Living high on the hog, hitting the nightclubs, wearing silk suits. Gee, how did that happen? Oh, I don't know, maybe he's using police files to help his criminal buddies? But they could never prove it, so all they could do was bust him back down to patrol, bouncing him from district to district. But see, I didn't know this, back when we first met him. Thought he was an okay guy at first. He was slick, that one."

Audrey periodically glances over at her father, but his face is set in stone again as he listens. Guess he knows all this.

"We met him at the riots, your grandfather and me, and like I said, he seemed okay. But later, when I was in the hospital, I started hearing things. Like how Wildey was back with some of his old gang buddies. And this time they were pushing dope, all over the Jungle. You know what the Jungle is, don't you, honey?"

"I am indeed familiar with that racist term used to describe a certain section of North Philadelphia," Audrey says.

Taney's not sure how to take that. The Captain swallows another smile. Taney decides to ignore the remark, keeps going.

"Terrill Lee Stanton ran drugs all over the Jungle. Wanna know when heroin first started showing up? The fall of sixty-four and spring of sixty-five, right after the riots. You know who to thank? That scumbag Stanton. You know who gave him protection? Officer George Dubya Wildey."

"Are you saying my grandfather was involved in this, too?"

Taney holds up his liver-spotted hands. "No no. Not Stan. All this was behind his back. Wildey used your grandfather as his own protection. See, back then you'd never send two black guys out as partners. Shit, you might as well not send a car at all, in that case. But the white cops was supposed to keep an eye on their black cop partners, to prevent shit like this."

"So why didn't he?" Audrey asks.

"Look, I don't mean no offense. Jimmy, you know I loved your pop like a brother. But he wasn't that kind of cop. Stan was a bruiser. There's nobody else I'd want watching my back. As far as his detective skills go..."

Audrey watches her father tighten his fists. Taney'd better watch out, unless he wants another couch dropped on him.

"Jimmy, come on, no disrespect. I'm not that kind of cop, either. I mean, look at me."

"So why did Stanton turn on his own protector?"

Taney looks away for a moment. "Same story as always. Wildey got greedy. Stanton didn't like that. Stanton decided to kill him. Wildey had outlived his usefulness."

"Why in that bar? Why both of them? Stanton could have killed Wildey somewhere else."

Taney leans in closer to Audrey. She can't stand his whole smoky aura and foul breath and watery eyes but doesn't flinch.

"I think Wildey knew something was coming. And he talked Stan into going along with him for backup. That black bastard *got your grandfather killed.*"

HAPPY NEW YEAR, STAN

January 1, 1965

"Happy New Year," Stan says as he opens the door, cold air blasting his body.

Wildey and his kid have shown up early, which sends Rose into near fits. She likes to have food and drinks ready long before the first guests arrive.

"Happy New Year, partner," George says, big smile on his face, arms open wide, expecting a hug that is only halfheartedly returned.

It's New Year's Day, and in a Polish household this means a roast pork in the oven and the mummers on the television. Stan's favorite string band, the Polish American (naturally), took top honors last year with "Fantasy of Jungle Drums." He's hoping they'll be able to take top prize again this year.

George Junior is looking up at his father, waiting for an introduction. To Stan's eye, he's a sullen little boy, not at all happy to be here. He looks a year or two younger than Jimmy.

"Hey, little man, see Jimmy over there? I'm sure he'd love to play with you. Go on, let me talk to my partner here."

Jimmy smiles uneasily. He's kneeling down near the Christmas tree surrounded by this year's loot—a couple of new albums, new guitar strings, socks, a bottle of spicy cologne.

Wildey nudges Little George in his direction. "Go on." His boy toddles over to the Christmas tree and kneels down, mirroring Jimmy.

Rose comes out of the kitchen with a cup of tea. "Lots of milk, lots of sugar," she says, handing him the cup.

171

"Ah, you remembered. Happy New Year, sweetie."

Wildey goes to kiss her cheek and Rosie freezes, accepts the embrace, and pats him on the shoulder.

"Uh, Rosie, it's New Year's, for Christ's sake. I'm sure George would like something else. How about a beer?"

"No, no, tea's good."

Rose goes back to the kitchen. Wildey nods at the TV.

"Mummers, huh. I know a couple of guys who did some session work with some of the comics."

"You watch the parade?" Stan asks with some surprise.

"Eh, no, not a big fan of banjo music," Wildey says. Nor *white guys in blackface,* for that matter.

"Come on, you've never been to a parade?"

"You know how the mummers started out?" Wildey says. "Hear me out now, I read about this. First mummers were a bunch of guys in masks, shooting guns in the air, demanding free drinks from tavern owners. Finally got so bad that the city said screw it, let's organize this damned thing and keep it under control."

"There you go," Stan says. "Ruining everything. It's just music and laughs. Thought you'd appreciate that."

"Sure. Who doesn't like to hear an off-key rendition of 'Oh Dem Golden Slippers' by a bunch of drunk dockworkers."

"Pork's ready," Rosie says.

Billy Taney and his wife, Judith, arrive late, irritable and hung over. Their two boys come barreling into the living room, relieving the awkward stalemate between Jimmy and Little George. The look on Billy's face, as he sees Wildey, is one of amusement and surprise.

"My saviors," he finally says.

Taney's face and arms are still raw with burn scars, and he's using a cane, with additional support from his wife. She guides him to Stan's easy chair, which is cocked in front of the TV, and guides his big frame down into it. Which is where he'll remain for the rest of the evening, with Judith bringing him pork, sauerkraut, and rye bread on a plate and a steady supply of Stan's beer. Stan and Wildey end up standing around Taney, plates in hand, just so he's not left out. He doesn't say much, anyway. Most of his attention is focused on the parade.

After dinner the somewhat uncomfortable subject of George's wife comes up. Stan shoots Rosie a look but she ignores him. "Well, thanks for asking about her," George says, "but she's visiting her own family for a while. It's just me and Junior today."

Taney's kids go back to playing with Jimmy and Little George near the Christmas tree, but a fight breaks out. Jimmy holds up one of his new records—*Beatles '65*.

"Look what he did!"

"I ain't scratch nothing, you liar!"

"Dad!"

Stan shakes his head. "Enough, enough."

Wildey immediately goes to his boy, picks him up off the floor by his upper arm, asks him what the hell's going on here. Stan tells him, hey, it's okay. "Me and Junior are going to have a little talk," Wildey says, then marches him to the kitchen, Junior's feet struggling to keep pace with his father's.

Taney turns himself around in his easy chair and starts to laugh. "Oooh, hey hey, somebody's gonna get it."

Later, Stan is draining his sixth can of Schmidt's while Wildey continues to nip at the red wine Rosie insisted on pouring him, with little birdlike sips. That isn't going to get the job done, Stan thinks. Wildey says, "Hey, can we go out back or something?"

"It's freezing out."

"Somewhere a little more private, then."

Somewhere a little more private turns out to be the basement, where it's not much warmer than outside. Stan unfolds two metal chairs and they sit across from each other.

"Now, you know I came over here to see your family," Wildey says. "But I also wanted to talk to you away from the station house, off the streets. Something's bothering me about our friend Terrill Lee."

"A lot of things bother me about that guy."

"No, serious now. I think he was onto something."

"About what?"

Wildey stands up. "Let me get you another beer. Got a feeling you're gonna need it."

Stan shrugs. It's New Year's Day. Drinking is the order of the day, no matter what his partner has to say. Wildey walks over to the basement icebox, plucks a can of Schmidt's out of a row, tosses it to his partner. Stan hooks a finger around the tab and pulls it off, sticks the tab in his shirt pocket, where it joins the others.

"Listen, Stan. I'm gonna tell you what I haven't told anybody. And the only reason I'm telling you is because I think you've seen it, too. And buddy, I'm going to need you on my side for this one."

"Just spit it out already. I don't want to miss the Polish American."

Wildey twists his mouth into a slack smile and shakes his head slowly. "Dammit, when I want to kid around, you're all serious. When I'm serious, you're talking about a fucking string band."

"Who's kidding?"

Wildey sighs.

"I've been asking around, on my spare time. That shit Stanton was slinging about wolves? I think he's telling the truth. There's all kind of product in the Jungle now, and word is it's a bunch of white guys selling it to the gangs."

"Product?"

"Heroin, man. Horse. Junk."

Stan takes a long pull of his beer. "What white guys?"

"Yeah, well...that's the thing that's gonna make you spit your Schmidt's there."

Stan spreads his arms, beer in hand, waiting for it.

"Maybe this Plan he was talking about is real."

Wildey qualifies all this by saying his evidence is anecdotal— he doesn't have any hard evidence. But his sources are good people. Pastor Stebbens, some of his parishioners, other North Philly residents who've got nothing to gain by telling lies. "There have always been junkies in North Philly," Wildey says. "But the problem just went..." He spreads his hands and makes an explosion sound by pursing his lips and blowing them apart. "Haven't you noticed that we got a whole lot busier these past few months?"

"Yeah, but what's that prove?"

"Come on, man, I don't have to spell it out for you, do I? You got a need, you'll do anything to satisfy that need. You'll knock over stores, steal cars, smack somebody upside the head for their wallet, whatever. Exactly what we've been seeing."

"Okay, fine. But what's this about white guys being responsible?"

"All those good people I mentioned before? They've been seeing a lot of white faces round the Jungle. People they don't recognize. Sharp suits and sunglasses, looking like landlords."

"I don't know, George..."

"Look, I'm not saying I've got hard proof. But it's something I think we should be looking out for, you know? Anyway, I just want to know if you've got my back on this. That you'll keep your eyes open along with me."

"Yeah, okay, George."

Wildey smiles, claps Stan on his shoulder. "Good man." Stan smiles uneasily, drains the rest of his beer, crushes the can. He's not sure what to think. About a month ago, Wildey here thought this whole Plan thing was a crock. Now he thinks there's a conspiracy going on? Stan doesn't believe in them. You don't need conspiracies. There are plenty of bad men around doing things to make this city a worse place.

As they head back upstairs to join the party Wildey says, "Hey—what was that polka album you wanted to play me? The one Jimmy got you for Christmas? 'Who Stole the Krishna,' or something?"

LISTEN TO HER, JIM

November 4, 1995

"What's up, Aisha?"

"Sorry to, uh, bother you if you're in the middle of something."

"You're not bothering me."

Jim can imagine his partner rolling her eyes, not believing a word of it.

"Look," Aisha says, "I don't know where you are, but one of Kelly Anne's coworkers—Lauren Feldman, one of the editorial assistants, wants to talk to you right away."

"Can you handle it?"

"She insisted on you."

"Why?"

"Clearly you've got a way with the ladies."

"Bite me," Jim says, then hangs up.

Jim calls Ms. Feldman and suggests they meet at the food court at Liberty Place, since it's near the *Metropolitan* office. But it's Saturday, and she's not at work, so Feldman countersuggests the Locust Room—a notorious hookup joint near the Academy of Music. It's the kind of place where the money you save buying rail booze will come in handy later when you're paying for dialysis.

An hour later Feldman orders a double gin and tonic; Jim sticks with a Yuengling, as it's barely noon. He's still rattled from his early-morning detour to Juniata Park. He doesn't want to dump hard booze on top of all that.

"Kelly Anne was banging Mike," Lauren says, in a way that is probably intended to shock.

That would be Michael Sarkissian, the executive editor of the magazine. Otherwise known as Blow-Dry Guy. So why does Kelly's friend want to volunteer this information now, on a Saturday? Is she really trying to offer up her boss as a suspect? Or does she want to bury her friend Kelly Anne Farrace even deeper?

But all this conjecture is Inner Jim. Meanwhile, Outer Jim nods like he understands, sure, sure.

"Tell me what you know."

Lauren doesn't know everything; just what she saw around the office. The flirting, the grab-assing, the voice mails. Michael is older, married, four kids, big Main Line family. His wife is apparently some superstar attorney. The more Lauren gushes, the more Jim begins to realize that she was probably "banging" Sarkissian, too. If he had to guess, their affair ended right around the time Kelly Anne showed up to be the new fact-checker.

"Do you think Mr. Sarkissian had anything to do with Kelly Anne's death?"

"No! Of course not."

"So why are you telling me this?"

Seriously, lady — because we have this thing pretty much wrapped up.

Lauren looks at her drink. "Because his wife's a real psycho."

Jim blinks. "The superstar attorney? You think she did this?"

"Personally? No, not herself. But think about it."

"Think about what?"

Lauren seems exasperated that he's making her spell it out. "Maybe even a former client of his? I don't know. I'm just saying, it's something you'll want to look into. And nobody else wants to admit it — but we're all thinking it."

Jim takes a pull of his lager while he watches Feldman. Sure, it's easy to have someone killed. Just look up *hit man* in the phone book. Especially those rich Main Line types. They probably keep a few pro killers on their Rolodexes at all times because you never know.

So what are you hoping for, Lauren? That the wife did it, or paid someone to do it, and while she's sent upstate, you'll be there to console a grieving editor and his four children? Jim is annoyed she's wasting his time. He tells her he'll look into it, and that obviously, writing about any of this would be a mistake.

"They were together Wednesday night," she adds as he calls for the check.

Jim lowers his arm and stares at her for a moment. "Where? And what time?"

Turns out Lauren Feldman here has the receipts, because Sarkissian submitted them for reimbursement yesterday—Friday—and Feldman is in charge of filing expense reports with accounting. Well, this alone makes the conversation worth it. Another block of time, potentially filled in.

She tells him: Circa (obnoxiously pronouncing it *chair-KA*). "I don't know the time, but Michael signed for the tab at ten forty. And then he caught the train home to Narberth."

Jim hopes he hasn't visibly jolted in front of the editorial assistant because on Wednesday night, around ten forty, he was sipping martinis at Circa, too. Not only did he most likely see Kelly Anne during her last night alive—he may have seen her killer, too.

But more important, it explains the initials in her weekly minder. *MS.*

Michael Sarkissian.

During the short time he was nursing a beer at the Locust Room, Sonya Kaminski has left a half dozen messages. Little pink WHILE YOU WERE OUT slips litter his desk like confetti. Jim can't duck them forever.

"What's up, Sonya?"

"When are you going to announce your suspects?" she asks. "The mayor's real eager to see this thing wrapped up. And there's still time to make the Sunday paper."

"We're nowhere near ready for that. They've got a lawyer and we're fighting with him to give 'em poly tests."

"Please tell me you're not going to just let them walk. You need to make this case."

"Sonya—can I talk to you off the record for a minute? Pretend you're not here representing the mayor?"

"Of course. Haven't we been doing that all along?"

"This isn't as open-and-shut as it looks. I've got a lead on another suspect. And, respectfully, if you take your high heel off my neck for two minutes, maybe I can wrap this up before Election Day."

"You're such a tease, Detective. So who is it? Come on, between us."

"Let me do my job, Sonya."

"You free for drinks tonight?" she asks. "After work, I mean. I've got this Nicole Miller thing at eight, but think I'll be out of there and at the Palm by ten or so. You can update me then."

"Pretty sure I'm going to be busy."

"Your loss. But be sure to keep me posted, and I'll do everything in my power to help."

Jim wonders why he let that detail about a new suspect slip. He tells himself it was to shut Sonya up for a while, give him some space to work without worry about the need for constant updates. But the truth is, Sonya can be useful, and he doesn't want to alienate her. He has his future to consider, and it's always smart to have someone like Sonya Kaminski owe you a favor. Like the drink she suggested tonight. He knows it's not about anything beyond work. She just wants his full attention. She wants the inside dirt first. Let her have it.

Besides, he may need Sonya later, if things get a little ugly for him.

When Jim comes home dinner is almost over. It's just Claire, Cary, and Aud—Staś is out with Bethanne at the Neshaminy Mall, catching a movie. "Staś wanted to see *Fair Game*, but Bethanne talked him into *Home for the Holidays*," Claire explains. Which means it's relatively quiet in the house except for Audrey, who hums to herself constantly as she twirls spaghetti around on her fork. There's more sauce on her face than on her plate. But when she sees him—

"DADDY!"

"Hey, sauce face."

"Hey, Pop," Cary says.

"Didn't expect you home," Claire says. "Hold on, I'll nuke a plate for you."

But Jim can hardly stand to eat. Not with Terrill Lee Stanton on his mind. He's picked his bar. He's going to do something. But what? And when? The ex-con has got to be feeding his parole officer some kind of bullshit, but it won't last forever. Terrill Lee may be stupid, but he knows as much.

Jim glances at the clock built into the microwave oven. Five till seven. Terrill Lee might have already gone back to the bar by now, when it's more crowded. Mugsy's was probably busy on a Saturday night. That was it. He wanted to rob the place but got cold feet last night. He was casing the place again this morning, but the owner scared him off. Now, though, he's ready to do it.

(*Or he's already done it, and you're too late, Jimbo. Once again.*)

He wonders if he should call the place, just to see . . .

(*If what? There are any suspicious characters lurking about it? It's a Mayfair bar. The place will be full of them.*)

Jim is busy working up an excuse for Claire so he can head out again—after all, the bar is barely a two-minute drive away—when Staś arrives home. He's also surprised to find his father sitting at the kitchen table.

(Don't worry, son, I wouldn't ordinarily be here, but I suspect a crime is going to happen nearby, and I want to be there quick if it does.)

"STOSHIE!" Audrey screams. "Where's your girlfriend?"

"She had to go home. Hey, Dad."

"How was your movie?" Claire asks.

"Eh, it was okay. Look, Dad...you got a minute to talk?"

Jim realizes he's only half-paying attention. Some part of his brain screams at him: Hey. Asshole. Your older son wants to talk to you. Don't fuck this up by asking him to repeat himself.

"Sure, Staś," Jim says.

Then, after a moment's thought, adds almost casually,

"Hey—want to go for a short ride?"

They head south on Frankford Avenue. Jim plays it like it's random—just somewhere to drive. At first they don't say much to each other. Jim can tell Staś needs to unburden himself of something, but he's not going to force it. He'll talk when he's ready. And sure enough...

"I've been thinking about school," Staś says.

"You mean, where to apply? I guess it is that time of senior year."

"No. I'm not talking about college. I want to join the department."

Oh boy. Claire will not like this. Jim's not sure how he feels about it, either. To be honest, he didn't see this one coming. Staś is at that age when he's more interested in Bethanne than anything else in his life. Jim assumed his boy would follow his girlfriend to whichever college she chose and figure it all out later.

"Dad?"

"No, I heard you. I'm just processing it."

The boy sulks.

"Thought you'd be happy."

Jim, of course, is torn over the news. What man wouldn't be over-joyed by the news that his firstborn child wants to follow him into his chosen profession? But not when the profession is police work. Jim realizes now that he didn't ever really choose it. It was inevitable. Someone kills your father, you seek vengeance. You can do so through extralegal means, or you can do it within the boundaries of the law.

(Like you stalking Stanton last night and this morning, Jimbo? Was that within the boundaries of the law?)

Jim finds an empty space directly across the street from Mugsy's. He thinks about coming up with some excuse for being here—some kind of surveillance work tied in to the Kelly Anne Farrace murders. But no, this is his firstborn son here. Staś doesn't deserve a charade. The air is cold and crisp, dipping below freezing. He turns off the car.

"What are we doing here?"

"The man who killed your grandfather has been casing this bar."

"Are you for real? Where?" Staś peers out of the window, cupping his hands on the glass. It's night and too cold for anyone to be standing outside.

"He's not here now. But I have a feeling he could wander by at some point. I think he wants to rob it."

Staś considers this.

"If he killed Grandpop, how's he walking around free?"

"He was never convicted of the murders. He was put away for a drug-related murder back in 1972. He got out just a few months ago. I didn't know until just a few days ago."

"Terrill Lee Stanton," Staś says.

Jim turns to look at him. "How did you know that name?"

"I looked in your scrapbook a few years ago."

Jim should smack him upside the head for snooping through his private papers, but it's a relief to be honest. He doesn't have to explain it all to Staś the way he would the other kids.

"So you know the whole story, then."

"I think I do."

"I became a police officer because I felt I owed something to your grandfather. I swore I would avenge him. Find the guy who did it. By the time I found out who that was, it was too late."

"It's not too late! Can't you reopen the case? Nail his ass?"

Jim sighs. He meant it was too late to choose another profession— not too late to go after Stanton for murder.

"I know how you feel, but sadly, that's never gonna happen. This case is thirty years old. All the witnesses are dead, there's no physical evidence. When I was your age I thought I could do that, but I've worked enough homicides to know the truth. Best chance they had to nail this son of a bitch was back in sixty-five and that didn't happen."

Jim hears himself speaking the words while Inner Jim heckles him simultaneously.

(*If that's what you really think, then why are you out here?*)

"Anyway, what I'm trying to say is, *you* don't have to do this. Forget the police for now. Go to college, earn your degree. If police work is still something you want to do, then great. Department needs guys with college training. Especially forensics. Point is, I want you to have the chances I never did."

"But Dad, this is what I want to do right now. I don't want to waste time."

"The family debt is paid. I think the Walczaks have done plenty for the Philadelphia Police Department."

Staś squirms in the passenger seat. "It's not about that," he says finally.

"What's it about, then?"

"The Kelly Anne Farrace murder. When I saw the story, I knew this was what I wanted to do with my life."

"What do you mean?"

"I've been following the case in the newspapers. I follow *all* your cases, Dad. But this one . . . I don't know. It's horrible and all, but I'm also glad you're the one trying to find the asshole who did this. I don't even know if that makes any sense. I want to do what you do. Catch the guys who think they can get away with it."

Jim leans back in his seat, sort of stunned. The two of them sit there in silence on Frankford Avenue.

The heat in the car has disappeared and a chill has set in. For a moment, Jim feels the tiniest bit redeemed. He and Claire had a really tough time five years ago—they'd come incredibly close to ending things, and Staś and Cary were old enough to know what was going on. Sometimes Jim was afraid that Staś only saw the worst in him, and he'd spend the rest of his life making decisions based on doing the opposite of what he imagined Jim would do. It was reassuring to know all was not lost. That he hadn't completely failed at this.

"I think we're close to finding out who killed that girl," Jim says after a while.

"Really? Who?"

"Just between you and me?"

"Of course."

Jim tells him a little about the recent developments in the case, trying to make a "teachable moment" (as they say) about looking for the little details, about not picking the low-hanging fruit, about sticking with your gut. But he's also bragging a little. Showing off for his kid, who wants to be like him when he grows up. And for a minute, Jim feels good about himself and what he does, feels that he doesn't have to explain or justify it to Staś. The boy gets it. Maybe he would make a good cop after all.

"Dad."

"Yeah?"

"Is that him?"

Jim looks.

And shit, yeah, it's him.

Terrill Lee Stanton. Out in front of Mugsy's Tavern. His head no longer hangs low. He's feeling confident. He's made up his mind about what he's going to do. And he's going to do it soon.

"Stay here," Jim tells his son.

"I can help you."

Jim turns to lock eyes with Staś. "I mean it. No matter what you do, do not leave this car. Not until I come back."

Staś doesn't like it, but what choice does he have but to agree?

Jim moves without consciously controlling his body, it seems. All at once he's out of the car and he's got his revolver in his hands and he's moving across Frankford Avenue and reality slows to a languid crawl as Stanton straightens his shoulders, then reaches for the door handle...

"Stop!"

Maybe it's the presence of Staś across the street, but things play out much different than Jim would have imagined. For one: he tucks away his gun and reaches out and grabs Stanton's arm before he can open the bar door.

"Hey—what's going on? Who the fuck are you?"

"I'm the guy telling you to get against the wall, that's who I am," Jim says.

Stanton's face is slammed up against brick, arm twisted up behind him, while Jim pats him down. Inside the bar are the sounds of laughter and piano chord changes and off-key singing.

"What are you doing? You a cop or something?"

"Shut up, asshole."

Jim finds Stanton's wallet tucked away in the left front pocket of his fleece jacket—hah, so no one will rob you, is that it? He flips it open, sees his state ID card, confirms his identity. Not that he had any doubt.

It's surreal to be touching him. The skin of Jim's right hand, touching the skin of Stanton's right hand, the hand he used to hold the gun and squeeze the trigger thirty years ago. Though cells grow and die, don't they? Every seven years, as Jim read once? So this collection of cells wasn't there when his father and Officer Wildey were killed. They're the great-great-grandsons of those cells, even if the man who wore them is the same.

"Please, man, I don't have anything."

"I don't want your money. I've been watching you."

"What?"

"Last night. This morning. Now. This bar. What are you going to do? Rob it? Just like you used to in the old days!"

But as Jim continues to pat down his suspect, there's nothing in the way of weapons. Not even a comb. If he intends to stick up the bar, he's either going to do it with an index finger poking the inner lining of his jacket pocket, or with no small amount of sheer balls.

"No way! I've never robbed a bar in my life, I swear!"

Jim decides to let that one go. For the moment.

"So what are you doing here, felon? You're a long way from the halfway house."

The situation is still tense as fuck, but Jim can feel Stanton's back muscles relax a little. "So you a cop after all."

"Yeah, I'm a cop."

"Can I see your badge, *Officer?*"

"Shut the fuck up and answer my question. What are you doing here?"

"I'm here to see someone."

"Who?"

"My kid. My boy. He works inside."

This wasn't something Jim expected. This fuckhead has children? Jim would ordinarily chide himself for not knowing this, but he didn't even think about the possibility. Monsters don't *have* kids. Monsters eat kids. Ruin lives.

Jim sighs, then orders Stanton to sit on the sidewalk, hands behind his back, back against the wall.

"What's his name?"

"Who? My son? It's Roger. Roger Howarth. His mama named him."

"So if I go in there and ask this Roger Howarth who his daddy is, he's going to say Terrill Lee Stanton."

Stanton shakes his head. "He doesn't know me. We never met. My girl was pregnant went I got sent away. So he wouldn't know who the hell you're talking about."

"Convenient."

"It's why I was up here last night and this morning," Stanton says. "Trying to work up the nerve to talk to him. I must have walked up and down that block a million times. But somebody told me he works at this bar, so I had to try, you know? You got kids, man?"

"Yeah," Jim says. "And I used to have a daddy, too."

Confusion breaks over Terrill Lee Stanton's face. "What? What do you mean?"

"Don't give me that bullshit about never robbing bars. Why else were you put away for thirty years?"

"Look, man, I've said it too many times to expect anybody to believe me, but I didn't do it. I didn't kill those police officers. I was trying to *help* them."

Right now, in this moment, Jim would very much like to grab Terrill Lee Stanton's ears and bash his head back against the brick wall of this bar, over and over, over and over, BAM, BAM, BAM, until the back of his skull was nothing but smashed fruit, so he could watch the lights of his lying eyes slowly flicker away to nothing.

Oh, that would be so nice.

But Staś is in the car, watching him closely, so all Jim can do is whisper *you fucking liar,* then tell Stanton to get going back to Erie Avenue before he reports him.

When Jim finally climbs back into the car and Staś asks what happened, he tells him,

"It was the wrong guy."

GO HOME, AUDREY

May 10, 2015

As they drive away from the Woods, Audrey steals glances at her father. The Captain looks troubled. Not his usual grim, nor his usual gruff—the man is truly *bothered,* as if he's eaten something that has disagreed with him. Like a baby goat.

"What is it?" Audrey says. "Trying to phrase the right way to say *I told you so?*"

"No, that's not it. I'm thinking about the story Taney told us. The drugs, Wildey, Stanton, the whole thing."

"What about it?"

"The story he told me forty-five years ago was very different."

They drive in silence, headed back down Frankford Avenue toward home. Audrey resists the urge to gloat. Guess Little Miss Forensics Expert has a point, now doesn't she? But it's no fun to gloat when your target looks like he's had his dick knocked in the dirt.

"How different?"

The Captain says nothing as he keeps the car moving at a steady thirty-five miles per hour down Frankford Avenue. Audrey looks out of her window. There are campaign signs all in the storefronts. Up here, mostly the white mayoral candidates. KENNEY. DEHAVEN. Once in a while you see a lone WILLIAMS, but not too often. Not that it matters to Audrey. Whoever runs this fucked-up city is in the hands of the super-rich anyway. She's not going to be here long enough to hear the results. She needs to finish this project and get home to Bryant.

"Dad?"

Nothing.

"*Dad.*"

"What, Aud, what?"

"Can I please, please, *please* take a look at the stupid murder book already?"

The Captain doesn't have the actual murder book, of course—just his version of it, which he started gathering as a teenager obsessed with solving his father's murder. Most kids Jimmy Walczak's age collected baseball cards; he collected clippings of crime stories and photographs of the crime scene and his own typed notes on index cards. All of these were pasted into a scrapbook meant for dead flowers or whatever. He picks it up from his desk in the basement and underhand-tosses it to Audrey. She catches it.

"You were probably a scream at parties," she says.

"What do you mean?"

"Never mind."

She flips through the pages, which are mostly newspaper clippings and photos and random notes in neat Catholic-school penmanship— the notes of a kid who wore a plaid tie to school. The final pages in the scrapbook, however, consist of a young Jim Walczak copying as much of the real murder book as he could. Including outlines of the bodies, with little red X marks showing the entry wounds.

"How did you get a look at this?"

"Taney checked it out for me. Gave me an hour with it, then took it back. I wrote as fast as I could and then spent the next few hours trying to write down every detail I could recall."

"Taney. Our drunk, racist source. Did you ever check out the murder book again? I mean, yourself, when you were a police officer?"

"Didn't think I needed to. I'd already copied everything important, and by that time, Stanton was in jail."

He taps the scrapbook of murder. "I didn't even look at this thing until years later, when Stanton got paroled in ninety-five."

"Well, we can't trust anything that came from Taney. I don't like him."

"Liking him has nothing to do with it. Are you saying he showed me phony notes? Why would he do that?"

"I'm saying let's go down to the Roundhouse or wherever and check out the actual murder book."

So of course the murder book is missing. Along with any record of who may have checked it out last.

First they go to the Roundhouse, where they navigate crowds of back slaps and jokes as the Captain makes his way through the building. Hey, Boss, back so soon? Look who missed us! Whatsamatter, getting tired of *Wheel of Fortune*? That takes forever and an hour. The Captain disappears for stretches, to gab with this one or that one, leaving Audrey to wait in metal chairs with passing cops eyefucking her as if she's some kind of perp. It's her tats, she knows it, along with her wrinkled jeans and ratty faux-vintage N.W.A. T-shirt. She wishes she had a sticker that read DON'T SHOOT! CAPTAIN'S DAUGHTER or something.

Turns out, after all that...all homicide records prior to 1980 were shipped over to the massive city archives near Thirty-First and Market, on the fringes of Drexel University. The archivist is polite, but the search takes forever and *two* hours and yields jack shit.

"Things get misfiled," he explains. "I'm really sorry. I can make a note to contact you if it turns up."

The Captain nods and thanks him. Audrey wants to frog-march him into the archives and force him to keep looking, but the Captain shakes his head. As if he didn't expect to find it all along.

Which of course gets the wheels in Audrey's head spinning.

What if Taney's not the source of bad information? What if it's her dad?

By the time they leave, it's close to dinnertime. They stop at a pub inside Thirtieth Street Station. The Captain orders himself a Caesar salad and a beer, buys his daughter a cheeseburger deluxe and a beer. He refuses to spring for a Bloody. She pouts a little. He ignores her.

They watch busy commuters rush up and down the halls. Better to wait here anyway. The Schuylkill Expressway will be a parking lot this time of day.

"So," the Captain says, "do you have everything you need?"

"Hardly," she says around a mouthful of meat, onions, pickles, and brioche bun. She power-chews, swallows. "You're kidding, right?"

"Listen," the Captain says. "I know you're proud of what you found on that bar, but do you know how old it is? How many shoes and knees and umbrellas and god knows what have chipped away at that thing over the last century?"

"I can tell a bullet path from a dent, Dad," she says. "You're paying good money for me to learn this shit."

"You," he says, "are assuming there were no other bullets fired in that bar at any other point in time."

"Unlikely," Audrey replies. "The coloration was consistent. I'd be willing to testify in court that those bullets were fired at the same time."

The Captain sighs. "I just don't know what you're hoping to find."

"Gee, I don't know, Dad...the truth? Why do I have to explain this to you? This is what you did for a living!"

"You want me to reopen a fifty-year-old case just because you found some bumps and scratches on a bar?"

The Captain stabs at his Caesar salad like it's personal. Audrey drains her beer, nods at the bartender for another, and, when he approaches, bats her eyes and quietly asks for a Bloody Mary, please? Bartender nods. Dad just shakes his head.

Whatever, dude. Benefits of not being able to drive.

"Let me turn this around for a minute," the Captain finally says. "Let me tell you what I've found out about you."

"Me?"

"The number that keeps calling. It was unlisted, so I had someone run it."

Down at the Roundhouse, while she was waiting forever...oh man, so diabolically crafty, Cap. The man is old, but he still has some moves.

"Congratulations," Audrey says. "Or you could have saved us five hours and just, oh, I don't know, asked me."

"Tried that. You told me it was Sister None of My Business. I disagreed. You live in my house, it becomes my business."

"You're kidding, right? I've been living in your house for a grand total of three hours!"

Other boozing commuters turn to look at them. The Captain doesn't care. He leans in closer.

"Who are Mr. and Mrs. Jamie Tennellson?"

"You're such an asshole."

"I'm an asshole for asking questions? You told me you had two roommates. You didn't tell me they were a black married couple in their late fifties."

"What does it matter that they're African-American?"

"It doesn't, Audrey," he says. "But it matters that you're not telling me the truth. I assume the money for rent I send you goes to the Tennellsons, correct?"

No, not correct, Audrey thinks. But screw him. This kind of shit is exactly why she's kept her life—her real life—quiet for the past two years.

"You want me to keep going, or do you want to tell me the story?"

"I want you to go fuck yourself," Audrey says, and leaves.

Once again Audrey finds herself on the Market-Frankford Elevated, rumbling down the tracks, listening to a computerized voice tick down the old familiar stations. Erie-Torresdale. Church. Margaret-Orthodox.

The El is turning out to be remarkably handy whenever she has a blowout with one of her parents. A ride straight back to the Northeast, all for only two bucks and change. Not counting bus transfer.

Which she needs, because she's not in the mood to walk from Bridge and Pratt all the way up to her father's house in Mayfair.

As she rides the 66, she realizes she doesn't have a key. But that's okay. She knows a way or two to sneak back into the ol' family manse. Mainly through the basement.

Where her father keeps his scrapbook o' murder.

Okay, she's willing to admit that she's furious, and inclined to think the worst of her father at this particular moment. But c'mon. It was awfully strange for him to be so uninterested in his father's murder, no? Especially after she told him what she'd found?

He wouldn't let her look at the scrapbook. Only flipped through it fast. Explaining it to her.

She needs that book.

Well, no, what she really needs is the original murder book. If she tries to cite her father's scrapbook as a primary source, her professor will pretty much laugh until she cries blood.

What if *the Captain* is the one who checked it out all those years ago, and it's packed somewhere in the basement?

Come on, Audrey Kornbluth-Walczak, come out with it. Admit what you're really thinking.

That your own father killed the man he *believed* murdered his father. Right then, in November 1995, just days after he was released from prison.

She thinks about her own childhood, tries to pin down when it all went wrong. Hmmm, that would be 1995, the year Terrill Lee Stanton was released on parole. The same year her parents split up. You remember the awful, drunken Thanksgiving. The Christmas your dad wasn't around. Valentine's Day 1996, when Claire sat you down and explained to your five-year-old self that Daddy wasn't going to be living here much longer.

What would cause Dad to go off the deep end?

A homicide detective who planned and executed the perfect murder. That might do it.

Why would he agree to help her, then?

Because that's what homicide cops do. They let you do all the talking, all the storytelling. They hold your hand until they reach the end of the story and boom, you're in handcuffs waiting for Ol' Sparky.

She roots through her father's basement possessions looking for the real murder book, but somehow she knows she's not going to find it down here. If her suspicions are correct, he probably burned it. Hell, maybe he burned it during the barbecue they had on the thirtieth anniversary of Grandpop Stan's murder.

Here you go, kids, a little extra seasoning for the kielbasa.

No; that couldn't be right. That was May 1995; Terrill Lee Stanton wasn't released until August. She needs to find out when he died, exactly how he died, somehow trace her father's movements around the same time...

Wait.

As usual, she's missing the real question.

The real question is...*Did Terrill Lee Stanton do it?*

Based on her rough examination of the bar, the answer has to be no. Unless he held two guns and fired both at the same time, all gangsta style, at strange angles. *Maybe* he was one of the shooters — but if so, he had a friend. Her father's explanation that he had an accomplice doesn't make much sense, either. Why wouldn't Stanton offer up this mysterious second shooter in exchange for a lighter sentence? Hell, offer up a cop killer and he could probably have cut his sentence in half.

Nope. Doesn't make sense.

God, is she really going to do this? Follow this whole thing through to its natural conclusion — which might end with her father in handcuffs?

Audrey's cheap-ass cell goes off. It's a local number she doesn't recognize. Which means it could be anybody within the city of Philadelphia, since she purged her contacts a year ago while drunk and angry one night.

It's a gamble: what are the chances this is someone she'd actually want to talk to?

Her call log is already full of a Houston area code she doesn't want to deal with right now.

Against her better judgment, she swipes the screen. "Impress me."

"Aud, it's me."

"Me who."

"It's *Cary*."

Her brother. His name is only two syllables, but both are packed with sheer panic. He sounds like he's drunk and he's been crying.

Audrey's internal alarm goes off: *Oh God, Dad*. Something happened to Dad. And here I am rummaging through his papers while he's somewhere out there clutching his chest and falling to his knees and...

"Spit it out, Care! Is something wrong with Dad?"

"No... it's Staś. He's gone."

STUBBORN STAN

February 6, 1965

"Stan—come the fuck on already!"

This is it. Finally. Stan knows it as sure as he knows how to spell his last name: this is the night his partner is going to get him killed.

"Go go go go!" Wildey whisper-screams. But Stan can barely hear him as he opens the front door and takes a step inside the chilly building while Wildey climbs up the fire escape.

After weeks of false leads, their snitch, Terrill Lee, said it was happening tonight. Big heroin deal on the top floor of a four-story apartment building at Twenty-Second and Diamond. Wildey got all excited. Here we come, white wolves. Let's finally see your faces.

Stan's not so sure. What reason do they have for heading up to this apartment building anyway? The word of a self-described agitator who says he likes to see stuff burn? Could be a trap waiting for them up on the fourth floor, for all he knows. Stuff the pigs, two-for-one special.

But despite his internal grousing, Stan huffs it up the stairs— there's no elevator in this place. Wildey proposed a two-front attack, to make sure nobody goes scurrying out the back door. Said his cop daddy John Quincy raided more speakeasies during Prohibition than anyone else on the force, and he learned one important lesson: cover all exits, always. Stan didn't say it out loud, but he's sure his own father would have something to say about that.

The stairs seem to go on forever. The paint on the walls is dirty and chipped, the rug worn down to a thin ghost of itself. He's sure nobody's bothered with maintenance in this place since the 1940s, when the neighborhood started going black. The halls smell like grease—foreign cooking full of exotic ingredients.

Finally Stan reaches the fourth floor, finds the apartment—4B. He pulls his service revolver, then puts his ear up against the door. Male voices, murmuring. Some sharp laughter, *hah hah hah.* You're not going to be laughing in a second. As he takes a step back, Stan tastes copper in his mouth. His own blood. This can't be a good sign. He steels himself for the job ahead. Just boot the door, point your gun, tell everyone to stick up their hands. You know, the kind of stuff Jimmy thinks you do all the time. Hero cop stuff.

Then comes a loud crash—glass breaking.

And a battle cry:

"Freeze, motherfuckers!"

Oh shit, Stan thinks. What the hell—Wildey agreed that Stan would take lead, catch 'em off guard, then Wildey would open a window and come in.

As Stan leans back, putting his weight on his back leg, ready to take down the door—

It opens.

Two white guys in dark suits holding guns stand in the open doorway, both just as surprised to see Stan as he is to see them.

"Well, shit," one of the white guys says. He has a buzz cut, thick eyebrows, and beady eyes. "This is an awkward situation."

Stan walks them back into the room at gunpoint. They've already lowered their weapons, telling him to take it easy. Stan ignores them, calls out to his partner. "Wildey, you all right?"

Wildey, meanwhile, has his revolver pointed at three Negro men dressed like they're headed out for a night on the town. One of them, a thick-necked bulldog of a man, has a shotgun pointed back at Wildey.

"You said you had this under control," the bulldog says.

"Shut up, Sam," says one of his colleagues. "Not another word!"

Wildey looks the bulldog in the eye. "How about it, Bey-Bey? You want to put down that gun, or do you want to do something stupid?"

Bey-Bey squints as he cocks his head slightly. "I know you?"

Stan doesn't like this at all. That bulldog's shotgun could cut Wildey in half and send both pieces of him flying back out the way he came.

"Yeah, I know you, Bey-Bey," Wildey says. "How many times did I pinch you for robbing craps games back in West Philly? Surprised to see you uptown."

"Wildey," he says with a tone of recognition.

"Now why don't you put down that gun and let's talk about what we're gonna do next."

But what Samuel "Bey-Bey" Baynes is going to do next is rack his shotgun with a loud *KA-CHAK*. His two partners tense up. Holy shit, is he really gonna kill this cop right here in this apartment?

Stan forgets about the white guys and turns his revolver on Bey-Bey. "Don't do it, motherfucker," he says.

"We're okay, Stan!" Wildey says. "Bey-Bey isn't stupid."

Bey-Bey is not stupid. But he's also not about to go down for this. There's a ton of heroin in this apartment and he knows it's enough to sink him. Which is why he suddenly aims his shotgun at the ceiling and pulls the trigger. *KA-BLAM*.

The plaster above their heads explodes—white shit rains down on their heads. Wildey recoils from the blast, which is what Bey-Bey wanted, because now he's charging forward, using his shotgun as a battering ram.

Stan is about to squeeze the trigger when the two white guys seize the opportunity to tackle him, knocking him off his feet.

The length of Bey-Bey's shotgun smashes into Wildey's forearms and forces his body back through the shattered windows and onto the fire escape.

Stan doesn't see what happens next because the two white guys are punching and kicking the crap out of him. It feels like he's tumbling around in a clothes dryer along with a couple of bricks—there's no way to anticipate where the next painful blow will land. Yet Stan holds tight to his gun. You never, ever let go of your gun. The punches and kicks he can take. But if one of these bastards picks up one of their own guns, he's going to have to defend himself. And he doesn't want to have to shoot somebody tonight—not if he can help it.

After a few blows, however, it becomes clear that the white guys are more interested in hightailing it out of here. One of them scrambles out of the doorway, headed for the stairs. "Come on!" he shouts to his partner, Buzz-Cut Guy.

Oh no you don't. Stan reaches out and grabs a fistful of pant cuff, which is enough to catch Buzz-Cut off guard and bring the man down hard. He scratches against the worn carpet with his fingernails, trying to claw his way up to a standing position, but Stan's already climbing up the guy's legs, his revolver still in his right hand. If he can reach the guy's head, he can give him a good wallop and take the fight out of him.

But Buzz-Cut turns and swings a fist across the top of Stan's head. Which hurts. A lot. He tastes blood in his mouth again. Buzz-Cut wriggles loose, his knees and elbows knocking on the floor as he tries to get up.

"Let go, you stupid asshole!"

Then he's free. Stan, though, catches him again at the top of the stairs, grabbing his pant cuffs, but both of them go tumbling down, limbs flailing around in a mutual effort to slow their descent. The blows seem to come from all angles. After a while it's hard to tell what's a step and what's a fist or an elbow.

Stan, however, maintains a viselike grip on his revolver.

And by the time they both reach bottom, Buzz-Cut is twisted up in a ball with Stan pointing his weapon at him, telling him he's under arrest.

By the time Stan has Buzz-Cut in cuffs and is back on the ground floor, other red cars from the Twenty-Second have shown up—neighbors must have heard the shotgun blast and called it in. Stan pushes Buzz-Cut toward a pair of uniforms, then runs around the side of the building, yelling for his partner.

Wildey, though, is already on the ground, dragging an unconscious Bey-Bey along the alley floor, away from the fire escape. Wildey's shirt is untucked and his face and arms are bleeding but he's smiling anyway.

"That was fun," he says. "Let's do it again."

SORRY JIM

When Jim opens his eyes Sunday morning he's fully prepared for it to hurt. He knows this one's going to be especially bad because he doesn't clearly remember going to bed last night—not putting his glass in the sink, not undressing, not slipping under the covers, none of it. After a certain point, it's a complete blank, and it takes a ridiculous amount of booze for Jim to get there.

The last things Jim remembers are returning home with Staś, hands shaking with rage, praying nobody will notice. Claire telling him Michael Sarkissian of *Metropolitan* magazine left a message. ("Are they writing something about you?" she asked. "I hope not," he replied.) And calling Sarkissian back.

Sarkissian giving him grief about meeting on a Sunday, but Jim insisting—telling him there's something important about Kelly Anne that he needs to run by him.

Sarkissian joking, asking, "Do I need a lawyer?"

Jim, enjoying the few seconds of panicked silence on the line while he hesitates before replying. "No, I don't think so. Just want to do a little fact-checking."

And then going to his basement office to read through his murder scrapbook and fantasize about what he'll say to Terrill Lee Stanton face to face the next time they meet up. Because there will *absolutely* be a next time.

You fucking coward.
  You didn't even tell him your name.
  "Detective Jim Walczak, fuckhead—you murdered my father."

Well, no more pussyfooting around. You've been keeping this cold little ball of hate in your guts for thirty years now. Time to let some of it out. Murdering son of a bitch owes you that much, at least. The courtesy of an explanation. An apology.

Something.

Jim remembers pouring vodka over ice and reading through the clippings, the familiar headlines all over again. TWO COPS SLAIN IN FAIRMOUNT BAR. And NO ANSWERS IN DOUBLE COP MURDER MYSTERY. Jim put on the Rolling Stones and poured another vodka rocks—the first one seemed to have simply vanished—and traveled back to that Friday in May 1965 all over again. What would his twelve-year-old self tell him to do, now that he knows his father's killer is just a few miles away?

You know the answer, you coward. It's what you've wanted all along. To pull the revolver out of its holster and kick in the front door and stick the barrel in his mouth and make him beg for his life and in exchange for his life you're going to make him tell you what happened.

The only person on this earth who knows what happened in that bar that day is only a couple of miles away. You missed your chance this morning and this evening. Tomorrow morning, you do it right.

But a few vodka rocks later the same voice says *why not do it now.*

Jim remembers walking around the sleeping form of his oldest son on the couch, the house being quiet when he steps outside, climbing behind the wheel, putting it in reverse, dinging the car parked behind him, cursing. And after that...

No fucking idea.

"Can we keep this off the record?"

This is the first time Jim's heard a *journalist* speak these words. Noon Sunday at *Metropolitan* magazine and the offices are deserted.

Lights out. Desks unmanned. Except for Sarkissian's desk, of course. He's dressed in Sunday casual—a long-sleeved polo shirt, khakis, and sneakers. Just a family guy who had to dart back to the office to pick up some notes he forgot. At least, that's what he probably told his wife back in Narberth.

"This is a murder investigation," Jim says.

"This is also my marriage."

"That's between you and your wife," Jim says. "'I'm here for Kelly Anne Farrace. So tell me, how long did you two have a relationship?"

Sarkissian leans back in his chair, exasperated.

"And like I said, can this please stay off the record?"

Jim spreads his hands as if to indicate his agreement. But things like *on and off the record* matter to journalists, not cops. "I just want the truth."

Michael Sarkissian is thirty-nine, handsome, a Penn grad, and happens to hold the keys to Kelly Anne Farrace's career.

"We started out as a mentor-and-mentee thing, you understand? She wanted to break into writing for the magazine, and I oversee the department and feature wells. She would pitch me stories, and I'd tell her how to improve them, turn them around to make them surprising . . . that sort of thing."

Jim nods. Sure. His head has stopped throbbing, but he could easily vomit at any moment. He keeps both feet flat on the floor and his movements to a minimum. Sarkissian probably reads this as Jim being Stern Cop.

"We became friends, and . . . well, after a while, we lapsed into something else. Something I regret now, looking back on it."

"Lapsed?"

"I didn't mean for it to happen. Neither of us did."

Outer Jim nods like he understands, projecting total empathy. Inner Jim knows better. Come the fuck off it. *You didn't lapse. You wanted to know what it would feel like to stick your cock in her mouth. Or up her ass.*

"We weren't exclusive," he adds.

"Well, sure. You're married."

"No, I mean, she dated other guys."

"I don't suppose," Jim says, "she told you any names? Because I'm trying to put together a list of people who were closest to Kelly Anne."

"No, she never mentioned names—just that she saw other people. She didn't want there to be any misunderstandings."

"Were there?"

Sarkissian shakes his head and squints. Of course not.

"Did you have sex with Kelly Anne the night before her death?"

Horrified look. "No."

Jim knows he's lying. Tells all over his face. Was it a quickie in the coat room at Circa, or was it back at her place?

"Well, someone did," Jim says, then proceeds to share with the editor the findings of the coroner. Jim hates himself for enjoying the conflicted expression that washes over the editor's face.

Is this on or off the record, Mr. Sarkissian?

Jim drives back home because Claire wants him home. No, not wants; she pretty much *demanded* it. Despite the fact that he's got to bring Aisha up to speed, and he's eager to run with this Sarkissian thing, and he'd really love to see how Terrill Lee Stanton is enjoying the Lord's Day . . .

(Don't you remember, Jimbo?)

Sundays, however, are sacred to Claire. "You're Jewish," he once joked. "Shouldn't it be Saturday?" But Claire didn't think that was very funny. Bad enough he had to go downtown to interview the editor at noon. And yes, she understands that homicide cops work around the clock. The job is never really over. But Claire made him promise that whenever possible—if such a thing was in his power— he'd leave Sundays open.

"One day you're going to wake up and this house will be empty. And you'll be sorry for all you missed."

It's not that he doesn't want to be home. It's just that he doesn't know how to just *be* at home, with nothing else tugging at his brain.

Audrey wants to play Sorry! and happily sets up the game pieces on the dining room table. Jim takes a seat next to her, his stomach still roiling. Claire smiles at them as she passes, headed for the kitchen. She loves seeing her husband and children play.

The pawns move around the board and Audrey takes peculiar delight in sending Jim's pieces all the way back to the beginning. "Sor-RY, Daddy!"

Most board games drive Jim insane. He doesn't see the point. You're just going through the motions. This one especially. But Audrey loves it so he shuts up and plays. He considers this his penance for the heavy boozing of the night before.

He wishes he could ask his father how he did it. The whole family thing. Granted, his pop was a career patrolman. He wasn't obsessing over homicides. But even toward the end of his career, when they assigned him to the worst district in the city, Stan Walczak was there. He was present. Drinking tomato juice and laughing with Jim before school in the morning. Waking up before he got home from school to fix him a snack. Taking his boy to Phillies games. (*When was the last time you took your kids to a ball game?*) His pop never talked about cases. Somehow, he left it all in the squad car.

"Your turn, Dad," Audrey says.

Jim flips the next card. The whole time, he's only half-paying attention, which is probably why she's kicking his ass. But he can't help it. He tries to dig up the shattered memories of the night before but it's painful, difficult.

He's starting to wonder if he did something horrible like go outside and climb behind the wheel of his car and then drive to the halfway house on Erie Avenue.

(You made him beg, didn't you, Jimbo?)

The phone rings once and boom—Audrey darts away from the dining room table and runs to the wall to pick up the receiver. She loves being the first to answer the phone. Or push an elevator button. Or reach the front door. She'll elbow you in the face to get there before you.

"Daddy, it's some lady for you."

Jim tries hard not to smile. "Is it Detective Mothers, sugarpop?"

Audrey shrugs. How is she supposed to know? It's just some lady.

"Thanks, Aud." Jim puts the phone to his ear. "Detective Walczak."

"I can't believe you. *This* is your suspect?"

Jim's guts turn cold as he recognizes the voice.

"Hi, Sonya."

Claire raises an eyebrow, swirls the spoon in her coffee impatiently. Jim mouths the word *work*.

"Why are you hassling Mike Sarkissian?" Sonya is saying. "Do you really want those two scumbags who raped and murdered Kelly Anne to go free? And are you prepared for *Metropolitan* to crucify you in their feature well?"

Jim supposes the mayor has assigned Sonya to this case full-time now. Round-the-clock care and feeding of the homicide unit on the weekend before Election Day. Hound every movement, question every decision.

"Is Sarkissian a friend of yours?"

Staś is pretending to play with the last of his spaghetti, but he's listening, too. Jim realizes he probably should be taking this call in another room.

"Please," Sonya says. "He's a spoiled little brat. Believe me, if he had *anything* to do with this murder, I'd be doing naked cartwheels in Rittenhouse Square. But he didn't. You're wasting your time. And pissing off someone who can give us a lot of grief."

Outer Jim's been patient so far. The mayor can be an important ally. God knows Jim's superiors would want him to play along like a good little soldier. But clearly, Outer Jim isn't working with Sonya. So it's time to give her a little Inner Jim. He takes the cordless phone and walks into the kitchen with it, out of his family's earshot.

"Sonya," Jim says in the sternest whisper he can manage, "I need you to back off."

She doesn't fuss or protest. Jim gets the sense that she likes this. She just made him flinch.

Deep breath now. You let Inner Jim show his face for a second, but that's okay. Tuck him back in bed and let Outer Jim handle it from here. "Sarkissian was with Kelly Anne eight hours before she died," Jim says. "Far as we know, he's the last person to see her alive. I can't ignore that."

Sonya sighs. "You really know how to fuck a girl up the ass, don't you, Detective Walczak." Interesting choice of words, there. "Look, I know Mike—he had nothing to do with this. He isn't the type. Only reason he didn't step forward is because he didn't want to become the news and wreck his marriage."

"I'm not investigating his marriage. I'm trying to find out what happened to Kelly Anne."

"Can I give you a piece of advice, then?"

"What's that?"

"Tread lightly."

"What do you mean?"

"I mean there was someone else I know who was in close proximity to Ms. Farrace eight hours before she died. By chance, did you ask Michael where he took his fact-checker for drinks? It's a really popular spot in town right now—perhaps you've gone there yourself recently. Say, Wednesday night?"

And then all of a sudden Jim understands what this phone call is really about.

LOST AUDREY

May 10, 2015

Audrey has no choice but to take the 66 and the El back down to Center City, to Eighth and Spruce, to Pennsylvania Hospital. Dad is probably already there, and she has no car. Nobody can pick her up. *Stop thinking about yourself for once, Audrey,* Jean tells her, kids screaming in the background. *Look, I gotta go.* Yeah, sure, bye, Jean.

None of this makes sense.

On the bus, Audrey reads the news on her phone—short mobile update from a local TV website.

Police Officer Staś Walczak, the son of retired captain James Walczak, found dead in a Center City hotel room, reportedly from a self-inflicted gunshot wound. He was 37 years old.

They mispronounce both names, making it sound like a guy named Stass Wall-Zack killed himself instead of her brother.

The 66 takes forever, crawling up and down Frankford Avenue, wheezing diesel as if unsure if it can make this one...last...trip. Audrey tries Cary again to see if he's learned more but he's not picking up. Hesitates, then tries her dad. No answer there, either.

But back on the Web, a blogger has put together the coincidence that occurred to Audrey right away: two Philly cops named Walczak, killed almost exactly fifty years apart.

Audrey cuts through the throng of reporters and TV cameras outside. The uniform stationed at the door stops her, but she explains that she's family. Uniform doesn't believe her. Audrey pulls out her Houston driver's license, except it says AUDREY KORNBLUTH. Exasperated, she tells the uniform that her brother is dying in there. "You want to stop me? Fucking shoot me." Audrey pushes past him. The doors swish open for her.

Unfortunately, a TV camera catches this exchange.

Fucking wonderful, she thinks.

Everyone's in the main hospital lobby, even though there's nothing they can do except wait.

The first person she sees is Cary, who is a red-faced teary wreck. He won't even look at Audrey. Jean comes over and halfheartedly apologizes for being short on the phone, but everyone is so shocked, and they wanted to get here right away. See, when he was rushed here he was still alive, and the doctors tried to save him, but—

Audrey interrupts. "He's dead."

Jean nods.

No no no. This doesn't make any sense.

"Is what they're saying true? That he—"

Jean leans in close and whisper-barks at her. "Don't say that. We don't know what happened, okay?"

Audrey doesn't need her shit right now. She needs to find out what really happened.

Will has his arm around Claire, who won't look at Audrey, either.

"Hey, Mom. I'm so sorry."

Will nods. "Thank you, Audrey."

Wasn't talking to you, asshat.

"Mom?"

But Claire just shakes her head. Buries her face in Will's overcoat. Apparently she can't deal with Audrey right now. Never mind that maybe Audrey could use a fucking hug or something.

Bethanne is somewhere else—maybe in the room with Staś. Audrey has never been her biggest fan, but she wouldn't wish this kind of suffering on anyone. Jesus, their kids. Their bratty little kids...

And the Captain is in the corner, talking to a pair of detectives in suits. He does turn to look at Audrey, just once, just for a second, but it's enough. It's an eye-burst of rage and betrayal and hurt. Audrey's the one who flinches first.

She should march over there and demand some answers. She's his baby sister, after all. Not some grubby stranger who wandered in off Eighth Street.

Of course now her brain is flooded with memories of Staś when he wasn't a complete dick. Holding her arm to guide her the first time she wore roller skates. Picking her up and carrying her inside the first time she fell and bloodied both knees. Covering her ears when loud sirens blasted down the street. Staring down jerks on the block who made fun of her.

What has happened in the time since their last conversation — which, all things considered, was about as chummy as they ever got?

Audrey scans the waiting room again, looking for an opening from anybody (besides Jean) who might want to talk to her. None comes, so she bites the bullet and walks over to her father.

The detectives notice her first, give her the up-and-down. The Captain extends a hand in her general direction. Not for her to hold. He's merely pointing her out.

"This is my daughter, Audrey."

Mumbled *sorry for your loss*es tumble out of their mouths, and then they resume their conversation.

"Sorry to interrupt," Audrey says, and all three give her dead cold cop looks. "But I don't even know what happened."

The Captain dismisses her with a curt shake of his head. "Later."

"No, Dad, how about now?"

One of the detectives runs interference. "Miss Walczak, I'm sorry, but we really need to speak to your father right now. You understand."

Not a question, but a statement of fact. *Of course you understand.*
But she doesn't.

None of this.

She pushes her way past the reporters and makes her way onto Eighth Street. Have a field day, fourth and fifth estates. Let me know what you find out.

An hour later Audrey is blowing her last twenty dollars on a Bloody at McGillin's. She leaves a fat tip and uses the remainder to purchase sexually suggestive seventies jukebox tunes—much to the dismay of most patrons. The Sweet's "Little Willy." Slade's "Cum on Feel the Noize." The Addrisi Brothers' "We've Got to Get It On Again." The Raspberries' "Go All the Way." And yes, of course, Starland Vocal Band's "Afternoon Delight." Audrey is convinced she was born thirty years too late. She should have been a slutty little teen in the seventies, rocking out to this shit.

She's no raving beauty, she knows that. But she can attract attention when she wants from a certain type of man. Especially with one hand on the juke, her hips rocking side to side, sucking down her drink. It's not long before a bunch of middle-aged business guys in ties are surrounding her, totally amazed she knows these songs, offering up dollar bills ("you pick 'em, sweetie") and, soon enough, drinks. Vodka drinks.

Skyrockets in flight...

She should never have come home.

Should have stayed in her fucked-up situation back in Texas, where at least she was ignored and belittled for a completely different set of reasons.

Where she didn't have to deal with all this death.

As Mac Davis croons "Baby Don't Get Hooked on Me" and Audrey's coming out of the ladies' room, one of the business guys is waiting for her. *How clever of you.* He puts on his serious moves, suggests they go to his Infiniti G35, which is parked in a garage just across the street. *I'll take you wherever you need to go.* Audrey wants to ask, *How about all the way to Houston? I travel light.*

When she tries to push past him, he gets pushy in return. Grabs her hips, tries to shove his tongue down her throat. He misses by a wide margin and ends up licking her jaw. Which...ew.

She twists away. *You know, if my brother were here, my cop brother, he'd kick your ass on the street outside. That is, if he weren't dead.*

Guy *really* insists now, embarrassed, probably. Trying to save face. He puts a hand around her throat, pushes her against the wall. Nobody's around; restrooms are on the second floor, and it's late.

She feels fingers dance around her lower belly, feeling for her waistline, looking for passage south.

Yeah, he's going for the magic button that he thinks—in his drunken judgment—will make her change her mind.

She actually hoped this would happen.

Because she feels no guilt whatsoever when she punches his Adam's apple hard and fast, then follows up with a shot to his liver, which drops him to his knees.

She hears footsteps coming up the staircase so she crouches down, too.

"He had a little too much."

Guy coming up the stairs—a friend of rapey business guy here—nods and smiles, heads into the john.

Audrey feels around the guy's ass for his wallet. Plucks it out. Takes the cash inside. "You even *look* at me again and I'll *annihilate* you," she whispers hot and heavy in his ear. Then she tucks the money in her pants.

Now she can get on to some proper drinking at some other watering hole.

Annihilate it all.

A little after midnight, just as he's locking up for the night, the man Audrey knows as Pizza Counter Guy spots a young woman passed out in the narrow alley next to the restaurant. Hooker? Maybe. If so, she's new to this neighborhood.

The alley is the width of a small closet. Extend your elbows and you're bumping into brick even before you clear a few inches. So it's probably more like she tilted a few inches in one direction, found the gentle embrace of a wall, then slid down it until her ass hit the ground, knees popped up, boots scraping across the cement until her toes bumped against the opposite wall. Maybe she thought it was a safe place.

Pizza Counter Guy puts down the boxes he's carrying and makes his way up the alley to her. He crouches down, feels her wrist for a pulse. Finds one. He can't see her face because her long dark hair is fanned across most of it. Just as he brushes some of it aside to see if she's bleeding or hurt, her eyes pop open like a horror movie vampire's.

"Don't," she says.

He tells her to relax, everything will be okay. And it will, because now he recognizes her. This is the young woman who tore up his counter a few days ago. Repairs of which came out of his salary. (The owner was not happy about the slapdash way the panels were reattached to the former bar.)

"My whole family's cops. Don't even think about it."

Pizza Counter Guy assures her he is not thinking about anything.

"It's me," he says. "You know, from the pizza shop?"

Audrey locks eyes with him. "Right. Pizza Counter Guy. Heh. Funny running into you here."

"Uh, I work here. I think you know that."

"Baby, I don't know a god-*damned* thing."

Again Pizza Counter Guy admires the ornate tattoos, full sleeves, that cover both of her bare arms. Crows and thorns and roses and something that resembles the flesh of a serpent. Where is her coat? What is she doing out here alone? She exhales and he can smell the stink of booze. Ah, so that's what she's been doing.

"Can you stand?" he asks her.

"Baby, I can't stand anything anymore."

So this is how it's going to be.

She rolls to one side in an attempt to rise, ping-ponging her way up the walls. Her whole body is shaking. He puts his hands up as if touching her aura, ready to catch her if she suddenly tumbles forward or backward. Slowly, though, she steadies herself. She looks at Pizza Counter Guy. Then she turns away and vomits on the wall. Not a girly kind of vomit, either.

He digs inside his bag until he finds a pack of tissues, pulls one out, holds it out to her. She ignores it, staggers a few steps away, clears her throat, spits a few times, moans, curses. After a small eternity she turns and asks,

"You don't happen to have a car, do you?"

"Yeah. Just lemme grab these pizzas, okay?"

The pizzas are still waiting on the sidewalk—five white, green, and red boxes, stacked neatly, held together with bungee cords.

"Wow, you really do take your work home with you," Audrey says.

As he tucks her into the passenger seat, Pizza Counter Guy explains that he made a deal with the owner of the shop. Instead of chucking the leftover food into the rusty green Dumpster out back, he boxes up whatever's left and brings it to the clusters of homeless folks around town on his way home. Usually it's a bunch of assorted slices, a little congealed with cheese and grease, but still okay. Sometimes rolls a few days old go in there, and sometimes he even sneaks in a bunch of fresh hoagies.

"What are you going for, the Last Decent Man in Philadelphia Award?"

Pizza Counter Guy shakes his head, closes his door, flips the ignition. "There are a lot of good people here. You just have to open your heart and your eyes a little."

"Oh Christ. You're religious, aren't you?"

"Well, yeah, I'm a deacon," he says.

"How divine."

Pizza Counter Guy insists on driving her home first, but Audrey says no way—people are waiting for their food.

So PCG steers his ancient-yet-spotless Civic (well over 130K on the odometer) and takes off for the Parkway. He explains there's an unofficial rule: police won't bother you between the hours of 10 p.m. and 7 a.m. as long as you pick up your boxes or mattresses or whatever and move along before the tourists arrive.

"Are you one of those people who walks around saving prostitutes, telling them about Jesus?"

"I talk to anybody who looks like they need it," Pizza Counter Guy says.

"Captain Save-a-Ho, to the rescue!"

"Uh-huh."

"Tell me—when a hooker passes out, do you call it a Ho-Down?"

"You weren't looking too good back there yourself, Little Miss Thing."

Audrey considers this. "You thought I was a junkie, didn't you?"

He smiles. "Well, for a second there...I thought you were a hooker."

She laughs and it sounds like a bark.

Audrey doesn't know what it is about him — maybe his kind face and easy manners. Maybe it's all that divinity schooling. Maybe it's because she doesn't even know his name. But after the purge of her guts, she begins a purge of her mind. They drive up the Parkway, then to the dark corners beneath I-95, then finally up to Mayfair, but along the way she ends up giving Pizza Counter Guy her life story.

How she's been living in Houston the past three years to get back on the straight and narrow but has only ended up fucking up her life even more.

How she had an affair with an older married musician guy and ended up getting pregnant and thought she'd just get rid of it — boom, done, move on. But couldn't bring herself to do it, couldn't even tell her parents about it, not right away anyway, because they'd just want to swoop in and try to "fix" things and control everything, and she didn't need that shit at that particular moment.

She tells him how her only lifeline — in a weird M. Night Shyamalan twist — was the parents of her baby daddy, a retired black couple who took her in and helped take care of Bryant while she worked and attended classes. Who are watching Bryant right now, back in Houston, while she's getting shit-faced and puking on the side of the building where her grandfather was shot and killed fifty years ago.

"Wait — how does that work? With the guy's wife and all, seeing that they're her in-laws?"

"Badly," Audrey says.

So no, married guy's wife doesn't know. Her own friggin' in-laws and she has *no idea*. She thinks the Tennellsons are just kindly old people helping some chubby white girl in trouble with a biracial baby get back on her feet.

"What's really weird is when the baby daddy comes over and pays extra-special attention to Bryant, right in front of her, and he gets this weepy look in his eyes, because you see, I guess the wife's tubes are tied, and they're never gonna have kids."

"Oh, that's not going to end well," Pizza Counter Guy says.

Even the homeless people tucking into the cold pizza look at her like, *Boy, and I thought my life was fucked up.*

The Tennellsons aren't even all that nice to her. They adore their secret grandson, of course, and as far as they're concerned, the less Audrey's around, the better. She feels less like a mother and more like the babysitter who squeezes in a little kid time between work (bartending at a seafood joint) and studying (CSI school). So when she told them she had to fly back to Philly to attend her grandfather's memorial service, they were overjoyed. Told her to take her time. Don't hurry back now, you hear?

The more she surrenders control to the Tennellsons, the more tenuous her connection with her son.

But it's a war she feels ill prepared to fight, with no one on her side. She rebels, they kick her out—and probably fight for custody.

"You need to get out of that situation," Deacon Pizza Counter Guy says.

"What I need," Audrey says, "is to finish this independent project, finish my degree, get a job, then get my own place, my own phone, my own utilities. Preferably in thirty days or less."

"What about your parents? I've got to think they'd want to help."

"Yeah, you would think, wouldn't you? I'm used to doing it on my own. I've been on my own since I was a kid."

By 1 a.m. the food is gone and the Deacon drives her up to Mayfair.

"So . . . if it's not too personal . . . what were you doing out by the shop tonight?"

After all that purging, however, Audrey can't bring herself to tell Deacon Pizza here the truth. That her cop brother killed himself this afternoon. (She doesn't want to accept it as real. Not yet.)

And that all this drama in her life and screwed-up family began at that corner of Seventeenth and Fairmount, in a dive bar. And maybe she's holding on to this foolish dream that if she can figure out what happened back then, she can try to understand what the fuck is happening to them now.

STAN SITS AND FREEZES

March 10, 1965

Every night and every morning they sit in their big red machine and watch a house on Queen Street down in Southwark.

Southwark is *way* out of their bailiwick. They could land in serious shit for being here. And they've been doing this for a week now. Wildey calls it "applying pressure." Stan doesn't care what he calls it—he doesn't like being down here. Too many bad memories.

Southwark is where Stan grew up, and he would rather be patrolling the Jungle than sitting here right now. A lot of Poles came to the Washington Avenue port just a few blocks away when they immigrated to this country. The ones with enough money hopped the trains to destinations north and west—some as far as Chicago and Milwaukee. Those with no money ended up stuck here, competing for space in dirty, overcrowded rowhomes and scrambling for work along the docks with everyone else.

If you could find work that the Irish, the Italians, and the *murzyns* hadn't picked up for themselves.

Still, the Poles called this area *Stanisławo,* meaning "the neighborhood around St. Stanislaus Church," which was the center of their social life. To the peasants back home, the word conjured paradise and a promise of better times.

The reality was much different—unless you knew someone with money or connections.

Stan has never been one of those people, even though he was named for this goddamned place. *Stanisław*. He would have liked to ask his father why.

The place looks more or less the same, though cleaner. They're tearing down the slums of Society Hill to the north and blasting through some of the old blocks along the riverfront to build I-95. Tons of construction work to be had now—if you know the right people.

Same as always.

Of course Stan can tell Wildey none of this. Because none of this matters to the business at hand. All Stan can do is protest on the grounds that this is very stupid for their careers.

The first night Stan sat there in the cold machine, looking around, terrified to be recognized by someone.

"We're going to get recognized," he said.

To which Wildey replied,

"That's the idea, partner."

Wildey has followed up on their big bust from the previous month. Seems the black buyer—Bey-Bey—is still facing serious narcotics charges. But the white dealer has been let go, case dismissed, get out of jail free. How is that even possible?

"Maybe he had a better lawyer," Stan offered.

"No, you're not understanding me. He was let go. All traces of the arrest—gone. At least, the white half."

Now, the narco unit is small, Wildey explained. Only ten guys under one commander. But the city claims the problem is equally small. According to the US Department of Health, there are only 557 known addicts within city limits. ("Shit," Wildey said. "I think I know five hundred and fifty-seven addicts personally.") To dismiss these guys caught with *that* much dope makes *no sense* whatsoever.

Soon as he found out, Wildey went to their lieutenant for answers. The loot had nothing to give them, except that it was narco business, implying that the white guys were undercover cops.

"I know a little something about undercover narco work," Wildey told Stan. "Usually, the job doesn't involve bringing the shit. Undercover cops are the ones *buying* the shit, then making their arrests."

"You were narco?" Stan asked.

"Lifetime ago."

"So what do we got?"

What they had were two names—the two dealers they arrested at Twenty-Second and Diamond. Samuel "Bey-Bey" Baynes was the bulldog with the shotgun. Buzz-Cut turned out to be Sherman "Bud" Van Meter.

"I know Bey-Bey's deal," Wildey said. "He doesn't interest me. Van Meter, though, is of supreme interest."

"Maybe he's undercover narco after all," Stan says that first night on stakeout detail.

"If he's narco, he'll give us the professional courtesy to tell us to fuck off. But I don't think we'll be seeing Bud."

"Then what are we sitting out here in the cold for?"

"To see who else shows up."

That knowing smile of his, like he's figured out the clue in a crossword puzzle long before anyone else. Drives Stan nuts.

"Sometimes I don't understand half the shit you say."

"Look, I'm kind of hoping he *is* narco," Wildey said. "Because if he's not, then Terrill Lee's crazy-ass stories have the ring of truth to them. And that, my friend, means we're living in a much scarier place."

Yeah, there goes Wildey on his crazy conspiracy flights. The whole world's against him and his people. Well, guess what—the whole world's against everybody. But Stan doesn't say any of this, because it'll just get Wildey excited all over again. Tonight, though, day seven of this, he's tired and cranky and can't resist.

"Tell me again why we're doing this?" Stan asks.

"Because we're good cops."

Stan has to admit, that rocks him on his heels a bit. *Because we're good cops.* He's long since stopped thinking about the job in terms of good and bad. There's the job, you do it, and your goal is to come home alive.

"Sometimes I wonder why you go looking for trouble. Don't you want to come home to Junior every night?"

"Sure," Wildey says. "But don't you want Jimmy growing up in a better city than this?"

So they sit on Queen Street, day in, day out, with nobody approaching. Their red police car isn't exactly inconspicuous. Then they start sneaking down from the Jungle to cruise the area at odd times, checking out 226 Queen Street—Van Meter's given address—at random times. Still nothing.

But now, tonight, the seventh night of this, someone does show up.

And it's not "Bud" Van Meter.

They park themselves on Front Street, right next to the construction site that will someday be I-95. Stan remembers the houses along here. Tight, cramped little immigrant homes that were Polish in his day but Irish a generation before that and German and Swedish generations before that, before there was even a country here.

From his angle on Front, though, they can keep an eye down Queen, see who's coming and going.

A sedan with bright lights crosses Front, moving the wrong way up the street. Soon they're headlight to headlight.

"Here we go," Wildey says. "Good things come to those who wait."

"This looks like the opposite of a good thing," Stan says, moving his hand to his revolver.

"Uh-uh. If I'm right, you're not gonna need that. Just follow my lead."

Two stocky men in suits come out of the car, walk up to their machine on either side. Their coats are parted and Stan can see their sidearms. They're not exactly reaching for them. More letting them know that they're keeping the option open.

"You fellas lost?" the one on the right asks.

Wildey sticks his head out of the passenger side. "Evening, Inspectors. No, we're not lost. Just following up on a suspect."

The guys trade looks. How the hell can Wildey see that these guys are inspectors? The other one, more heavyset, is coming up on Stan's side. He makes a show of checking out the numbers on the side of their machine.

"You're a long way from the Jungle."

"Yeah, well, sometimes the inhabitants, they do sneak out," Wildey says.

The one on Stan's side says, "This one is Walczak." Pronounces it right: *wall-CHAK*.

"And we got Officer Wildey over here." Another correct pronunciation.

(Later, Wildey will say this was the moment he knew—that nobody gets their names right on the first try. Again, Stan doesn't understand what he's talking about.)

"You go on back to the Jungle, boys. Leave Southwark to us."

Wildey nods as if he agrees. And then he slams open his passenger side door, nailing the guy in his knees. Guy drops to the ground before he has the chance to reach for his revolver. Wildey slams the door into him again, metal crushing his nose, spurting blood down the side of their machine.

The other inspector is cursing and starting to draw his weapon. Stan knows his own speed. By the time he climbs out from behind the wheel, this guy could draw his weapon and open fire at them through the windshield. So there's really only one option. Stan lunges out with his left arm, grabs up a fistful of the guy's shirt and tie, and yanks him forward with all his strength. Guy's forehead slams into the top of their machine, busting it open. He's still struggling, though, so Stan gives it to him again, feels the fight go away, then drops him.

"Drive, drive drive!" Wildey is shouting at him.

"Did we just assault two inspectors?"

"No," Wildey says, "we most certainly did not."

JIM TREADS LIGHTLY

November 5, 1995

Tread lightly.

Good advice, despite the source.

As much as Jim would like to nail Sarkissian for this, he knows it doesn't fit. Sarkissian has an alibi for the rest of the night and morning—home with his family in Narberth. Doesn't mean he's in the clear, but nothing about it feels right.

So Jim goes back to his timeline of Kelly Anne Farrace's last twenty-four hours alive and again considers the mysterious JDH. Those initials match no one at the magazine, nor anyone in Kelly Anne's circle of friends. He realizes he has to go back to Circa. See if anybody can remember Kelly Anne leaving. And if so—was she alone?

But now the hard part: selling this to Claire.

"You're just upset that Audrey kicked your Sorry! ass."

"It's true. I lose one more time to my five-year-old daughter, I won't be able to show my face around town."

A wounded expression shows on Claire's face for an instant before she smiles. Jim reviews what he said, trying to figure out what upset her.

"You sure this is about the girl's murder," she says. "Or would you rather not be here?"

"I want to be here," Jim says. "You know that."

Claire doesn't answer, which is her way of disagreeing with her husband. She claims she's over what happened five years ago, but the old suspicions emerge now and again. Especially when the job takes him away from home more hours than usual.

"Go," she finally says. "Otherwise you're going to mope around here like a bear with a sore butt."

"I'm sorry," he says, and kisses her forehead.

At Circa Jim orders a tonic and lime, starts chatting up the waitstaff. He recognizes a few faces from Wednesday night. But no one remembers Kelly Anne, let alone her leaving. A check of Wednesday's receipts reveals nothing—apparently, Sarkissian bought all her drinks. Halfway through the pile Jim sees his own card receipt there. Somehow he spent $89. He thought he'd popped in here for one drink, then moved on. How had he spent that much?

(Because one doesn't do it for you anymore, Jimmy. You know that. Takes at least three to make a dent in that armor of yours. Or turn you into a real killer...)

Briefly he considers taking his receipt, pocketing it, so that no one will know he was ever here. Some defense attorney could have a lot of fun with this. *Ladies and gentlemen of the jury, do you know who else had a drink in the same bar as Kelly Anne Farrace the night she died...*

No. He's not that kind of cop. The receipt stays.

Jim steps outside Circa into the cold November night. Walnut Street is sleepy. Not many pedestrians.

Help me out here, Kelly Anne.

You stepped outside—were you with someone, or were you alone?

We're only a few blocks from your apartment. Did you go home, get lonely, then call someone over?

Or did you in fact just go to bed so you could rise early the next morning for a jog before work?

Jim stands on Walnut Street, watching kids leave the bar. Some in pairs or triplets, some alone. So carefree. They're all so impossibly young, and they have no idea what's out there in this city.

Wait wait.

"Thirty Under Thirty." The last piece Kelly Anne was reporting. Working alongside her mentor, Sarkissian. She wasn't out here socializing. She was out working. Nine p.m., the family man has to go home, but the young aspiring writer is still on the beat. Maybe she met up with an interview subject.

Jim hurries over to Kelly Anne's apartment, flashes his badge at the super, gains access. CSU has been and gone, but that doesn't matter. He searches through her cluttered little desk until he finds the file folder containing the legal pad he was hoping to find. Her notes on the "Thirty Under Thirty" package. She was the kind of girl who brought her work home with her. This job was her life.

He spins through the names of candidates, looking for his match:

Max Kennedy. Carolyn Odell. Lisa Jablonski. Eric Lindros. Jeff Steen. Traci Lynn Burton. Jeffrey Gaines. Jim's just north of forty and he has no clue who any of these people are. Well, Lindros, sure—he's a Flyer. (Though hockey's not Jim's thing.) But come on, where's the Mysterious Mr. JDH?

And then, scribbled on the legal pad:

John DeHaven.

The name fits.

But who the hell is John DeHaven?

Kelly Anne's notes don't shed much light on it.

pol

Politician?

fundraising genius

Young guy from money, then. The smartest fundraisers always seem to be people born into loads of the stuff.

If you're such an up-and-comer, Mr. DeHaven, why didn't you up and come forward when Kelly Anne turned up dead in a stairwell?

easy on the eyes

So an attractive rich guy—and possibly the last man to see Kelly Anne Farrace alive.

AUDREY GOES TO CHURCH

May 14, 2015

Staś may be the second Walczak to die wearing the badge, but he won't be counted among the heroic fallen. His name will never be etched onto a skinny brass plate and mounted in City Hall's courtyard memorial.

Because her brother's death is ruled a suicide.

The past three days have been horrible. Arrangements were made quickly, but nobody knew what else to do except avoid the media. Dad's house in Mayfair ended up being the unofficial family way station. Cary would drift in and out, just to check on Dad, but ended up lingering to drink the beer in the fridge and do shots of the vodka when he thought nobody else was looking. Even Claire stopped by once, without Will for a change, though she didn't say much. She didn't speak to Audrey about anything other than the basics. *The funeral will be Thursday. Make sure you wear that dress with the sleeves. The limo will pick you up here at eight.*

Audrey bit the bullet and called the Tennellsons to explain what had happened. They were suspicious until they looked it up on the Internet— as if she'd lie about something like this? They put Bryant on the phone. He said "Dada." They were teaching him *Dada.* Wonderful.

How about Mama? Mama could use a little love right about now.

Usually a fallen officer receives a massive civic turnout, from the mayor on down. But today St. Matt's is half empty.

Audrey is surprised Staś could have a funeral mass at all. She assumed the church denied them to suicides. And it's not as if they can fudge this with the priest; it's all over the papers and on the Internet. The church, however, is more understanding and compassionate these days. As the priest explained at the wake last night, none of us know what's going through an individual's mind, or what is troubling their soul, in their greatest moment of weakness.

But still, Staś—what the hell *were* you thinking the moment you checked into that room and put the gun in your mouth?

Three days later and Audrey still has no clue. By all accounts he and Bethanne were happy. He wasn't the best cop in the world, but he had no complaints or scandals dogging him, either. He was a hard worker, loyal, and a loving father.

This, of course, was all according to the media. Audrey and her older brother were not close at all. Staś basically cut her off when she was fifteen and he found her standing on the fringe of Pennypack Park with her asshole friends, drunk on Natural Light. She'll never forget the pinching of the steel cuffs around her wrists, his face lit up with the headlights of the prowl cars, eyes narrowed. *What the fuck is wrong with you, Aud?*

Fuck you, Stosh!

Only ten years ago but it feels like a lifetime.

The Captain looks like a black mountain in his suit. He stands in the front left pew, grasping the wooden rail in front of him, white-knuckling it. Chin up. Eyes locked on the altar. Not once does he glance over at the casket. At Mom. At any of them. Claire is across the aisle, on the right. The body of their older son lies between them like an accusation.

A half dozen beefy cops, the last few buddies the Captain has left, are scattered in the pews behind him. But there is no family at his side other than Grandma Rose, at his left, trembling a little. Meanwhile, on the other side of the aisle, Cary, Jean, Bethanne, and the kids cluster around Claire.

Audrey stands in the vestibule, not sure where to sit. She typically sides with Claire in these matters. When her parents divorced, her older brothers sided with their mother instantly—Audrey was young and just kind of got swept up in all that. But she's been living with her father for much of the past week. Either side seems like a slap in the face to the other.

So she chooses a seat halfway back from the altar, along with the rest of the strangers. No idea who they are—probably just lookiloos. Or reporters. Or parishioners who go to church every day, no matter what's playing.

One older lady, though, looks familiar and keeps staring over at Audrey, smiling politely. Yeah, hi, good to see you, too, whoever you are.

Then it hits her. Right right—she's the daughter of the ancient bigwig union guy who spoke at the memorial service last week. Lucky her, she gets to attend all the Walczak death services.

Audrey waves back, totally conscious of how much she's sweating in this goddamned long-sleeved dress. She's already worn it three times since she's been home and hand-washed it once—but obviously she didn't do that good of a job. Stale perfume and tomato juice seem to rise up from the cloth in cartoon stink lines.

Ugh.

"Eternal rest give to them, O Lord; and let perpetual light shine upon them," the priest is saying. The incense makes her gag. She doesn't know how much more of this she can take.

"Hey, Audrey," a soft voice says to her. "I'm so sorry. Only found out this morning."

Holy crap, it's Pizza Counter Guy, who's slid in next to her! He's wearing a suit and everything, looking suave and cool and perfect despite the heat. And here's Audrey, a hot mess and a half.

"Thanks," she says, and turns her attention back to the end of the funeral. Oh God why. I mean, it's nice he came and all, but...

Audrey stares up at the gilded cross mounted over the altar and thinks: *If you* do *exist, you're both a sadist and one wily deity.*

After the funeral mass the casket is carried out by Cary, a cousin on Claire's side, and four of Staś's cop friends. The casket rolls into the back of the hearse. Bethanne and kids are tucked away in a limo. Audrey stands on the sidewalk in front of the church, waiting for the inevitable next step. She wishes she were home. No; she wishes she were in a bar.

But there's still the cemetery and then a small thing at Staś's house.

And then, she supposes, the inevitable. Home to Houston to face the sad music of her hopelessly messed-up life. She gave her professor the best excuse in the world—cop brother killed himself—but it won't put her off forever. She's going to have to come up with something else or fail.

She watches her father greet the few attendees on their way out, thank them for coming. Union Boss Daughter Lady approaches him but he won't look her in the eye. He actually turns away, marching down the marble steps away from her. What's that about?

The rest of Audrey's family pile into the waiting limos. Red-eyed Cary stops before he climbs in, gives her a wave. C'mon, we're waiting for you. But Audrey ignores him and gives her escort an elbow in the arm.

"Hey, Pizza Counter Guy."

"Yeah?" he says.

"Any chance you can give me a ride to the cemetery?"

"Don't you have your family right there waiting for you?"

"Eh," she says. "I'm not a limo kind of girl."

Pizza Counter Guy smiles. Shows her the way to his old but pristine Civic. Cary watches them leave, perplexed.

"You didn't have to come," she says as they pull away.

"Well, I had to give you grief in person for not telling me about what happened to your brother. I wish you'd talked to me."

"You're probably the only Protestant deacon in the world who would come to a Catholic funeral mass to *give* someone grief."

They pull away and follow the funeral procession. Someone's helpfully stuck one of those magnetic flags on the hood. They fall in line. Audrey eases back into the seat, flips the AC on full blast. She'll enjoy it while she can. Pizza Counter Guy says nothing.

"Okay, okay, what's your name? I can't go introducing you to my family as Pizza Counter Guy."

"Lord, at last. I thought you'd never ask."

"Shut up already and tell me."

"It's Barry."

"Really? It's *Barry?* Barry as in the president?"

"Yeah. Well, no, not like the president. It's short for a longer name that I ain't gonna tell you. But for the record, my last name is K——"

"No," she says, putting a finger to his lips. "No last names. I don't want to get too personal."

They follow the hearse up to the national cemetery over in New Jersey. Grandpop Stan is there alone, as he's been since 1965. Now, a half century later, he'll finally have company—a grandchild he never met. *Hey, you look sort of familiar. Who the hell are you again?*

The grave has already been opened up. Her father, the Captain, poises himself on the edge, as if he's about to fling himself into it.

The crowd is much smaller than at the mass. Looks like just her family, along with some of Grandma Rose's relatives who drove or flew in for the burial and some of Staś's colleagues. Audrey stands in the back, as if just a spectator. Barry stands by her side, head bowed, one hand covering the other. The sun is bright and hot. So much for the cliché of a stormy funeral where the skies open up just as the final prayers are uttered.

After the brief service they put Staś down into the ground above Grandpop. Some people cry. The Captain stares down into the open grave, saying nothing.

Audrey wants to go up and hug him, or something. But she's afraid he'll turn around with a puzzled look on his face.

Eventually they drift away. Jesus, Audrey thinks. Did all this just happen?

She lingers at the grave. Down there is the casket containing the ninety-one-year-old body of Stanisław Walczak, forever paused at the age of forty-one. Open the casket, Audrey thinks, and there would be the face of my grandfather. With the six feet of dirt removed, this is the closest Audrey will ever be to him.

And this is the awful thought she has—God strike her dead for this. This is not the time, she tells herself; her stupid independent project is dead.

But if you were to open that coffin and examine his fifty-year-old corpse, would you discover the two bullet holes in the back of his skull, which is the official story? Or would his bones tell you something completely different?

What do you say, Grandpop?

STAN AND SONNY

March 30, 1965

Stan's dead asleep when he hears the knocking on the front door. It's too early for his shift, isn't it? Where's Rosie? He rolls over.

There's more knocking, though. Insistent now. Goddammit. If this is his partner with another "development" he's going to be pissed.

He pulls on his pants, shuffles down the hallway. Jimmy is in his bedroom, listening to loud music when he should be doing homework. It's an argument Stan doesn't need right now. The songs are so loud they bleed through the headphones. That Bob Dylan guy. Stan honestly doesn't know how his boy can stand listening to him. Singers used to have to be able to sing on pitch. But now all the old crooners are considered lame. If you can scream into a microphone, you've got a career.

Or maybe Stan's just cranky because he was woken up prematurely.

Down the stairs, to the front door, shuffling in bare feet. Stan opens the storm door and sees a face through the screen he hasn't seen in a long time.

Jimmy's headphones are on while he's doing math problems, which to his mind, is the only reasonable way to do math problems on a boring Tuesday afternoon. He's listening to the new Dylan, which he's just discovered and is loving. The bombast of "Maggie's Farm" gives way to "Love Minus Zero/No Limit" and for a second there he swears he hears his own name in the mix.

No, it's not on the album. It's coming from downstairs. His pop, shouting up the stairs at him.

"Jimmy, for Christ's sake!"

He slips off his headphones.

"Sorry, Pop! Coming!"

And he starts to rise but Pop says, "Stay there. Tell your mom I'll be back in a few. Do your homework!"

Jimmy sits back down, confused. Dylan croons through the headphones. Where is Pop going? It's not time for his shift yet. Downstairs, the front door slams shut. After a moment's hesitation Jimmy pushes aside the math homework and runs to his parents' bedroom and pulls the curtain aside just in time to see his father walking next to some guy, roughly the same height and build, wearing a hat cocked to one side. Dad's in his trousers and T-shirt.

All parents have ESP, Jimmy believes, and his pop is no exception. Pop turns back to look up at the window and gives Jimmy a wave. Not to say hello, but to urge him back to his math problems. The guy in the hat turns to look, too. His face is familiar to Jimmy, but he can't place it. Then they're out of view, heading up Bridge toward Jackson. Who *was* that guy?

Jimmy stares at his math problems for a while before realizing — wait, I don't have to do this. He closes the book and picks up his guitar. He's still trying to figure out the lick to the Stones' "The Last Time." There's a twang he can't quite get right. His pop is tired of hearing it and has pretty much banned him from playing it. So he saves it for when Pop's working. Or for times like now, when he steps out of the house and Jimmy doesn't feel like doing his stupid homework anymore.

Stan and Sonny walk one long block down to the taproom at the corner of Bridge and Jackson Streets. Stan stops when he reaches the corner, shoves his hands in his pockets because he doesn't know what else to do with them.

"What are you doing here, Sonny?"

"Boy's really getting big. Love to meet him one of these days."

"You know that's never gonna happen."

Sonny nods his head like, *yeah maybe, maybe.* He looks around the neighborhood, taking it all in. This isn't his neighborhood. Wouldn't live here if you paid him. He's from Port Richmond, the Polish enclave nestled near the waterfront. Sonny still can't figure why Stan would move to a place like this.

"Come on. Lemme go back and at least say hi to the kid. You just tell him I'm an old war buddy."

"No."

"Doesn't seem right, seeing who's he named for and all."

Now Stan can't keep his fists in his pockets anymore. The right one comes out and whizzes through the air and slams into Sonny's face so hard his fedora goes flying off the top of his head.

Sonny staggers back a step, shakes his head, tightens his own fists, wondering if they're really going to do this. Yeah. They're really going to do this. Stan is already at him again with a left. *Bam.* With a right. *Pap.*

Sonny recovers enough to charge forward and tackle Stan in his midsection. There's enough weight and muscle behind Sonny to slam Stan backward into the side of a brick wall. It hurts, but also breaks his fall. Stan comes out swinging again, probably faster than Sonny realized, because he lands a few good shots in his ribs, but Sonny starts defending himself.

They used to fight in their youth, no-holds-barred brawls that would only end when one of them would stoop low enough to take a shot at the balls or the lower belly. They've fought before as adults, too, but pulled back before taking it too far. When you're a kid you think you can recover from anything. When you're older it's a different story.

And Sonny's heart isn't in this—he's throwing back punches to save face, but there's no anger there. So Stan loses heart, too. What does he think he's doing?

They break away and huff and puff and examine their knuckles for cuts, feel their ribs to make sure there's nothing more than bruises.

"That was a cheap shot," Sonny says bitterly.

"What do you want, Sonny?"

Sonny spies the bar across the street. "I want to talk to you about something. Come on. Let's discuss it over a drink."

Inside, Stan orders his usual glass of Schmidt's while Sonny orders a Scotch and Drambuie with a lemon twist on the rocks. Look at the fancy guy. Almost nobody's in the bar, since it's 4 p.m. on a Tuesday. After Rohm and Haas lets out, the place will start to fill up.

"You see what happened in Alabama last week?" Sonny asks. "Murzyns walking right up to the cops, telling them off. All because Martin Luther Coon comes down and tells them to! Unbelievable."

Stan picks up his beer but doesn't drink. "I don't think that's what happened."

"Oh, did your *partner* tell you all about that?"

"I read the papers."

"Keep reading those papers. And keep your eyes open. You got a housing project just a few blocks from here. Just wait. One day you'll be chasing coons in the Jungle and some loudmouth will give the order and they'll all come spilling out, breaking into houses and setting them on fire. Can't think you'd want that for Rosie and Jimmy."

Goddamned Sonny, always looking for an angle on his family. Stan can't let him anywhere near them. Sonny Kaminski belongs in the past, not his present. He wishes the man no ill will, but he can't let worlds collide. For a while there, a decade ago, Stan thought he could do it; he learned otherwise.

"You gonna tell me what you want? I've got to get back home."

"I don't want anything, Stanisław. I'm here to give you something."

"What's that?"

"Some good advice. Get the hell out of the Jungle, any way you can. And stay away from your *murzyn* partner. He's got a past you want no part of."

"Don't we all?"

Sonny shakes his head. "That's how you see it, huh. What a shame. What a fucking waste."

"I've gotta go," Stan says as he rises from his stool. He's not worried about the tab. Sonny Kaminski's got plenty to throw around town.

But Sonny reaches up, grabs Stan's upper arm, squeezes it tight. "Listen to me, dammit. Just give me a few more minutes of your precious time. You owe me a little time, at the very least."

This is not the place for another fistfight. Stan allows Sonny to steer him back to his seat.

"I know you've been down in the old neighborhood, hanging out on Front Street. I don't know what he told you, but you're stepping in a world of shit."

"We were chasing a suspect."

"Don't give me that horseshit, Stan. You don't know what the hell you're doing. It's all him, isn't it? Following his lead, listening to his wild stories?"

Stan picks up his beer, takes a long swallow, finishing it. Signals for another, which the bartender gives him quickly before retreating to the opposite end of the bar. He must recognize Sonny from the papers and doesn't want to get caught up in any of this.

"George Wildey is bad news," Sonny continues. "No better than those *murzyns* you lock up every night. Only difference is, he somehow got himself a badge and a gun."

"What are you talking about?"

"He's not in it for the job. He's in it for revenge. Did that *murzyn* ever tell you about his father? He was a cop, back in the twenties and thirties," Sonny says. "Worked down on the waterfront. Guarding liquor warehouses. Any of this ring a bell?"

Stan's guts turn to ice. He doesn't want to hear this. None of this.

"Ambitious guy, John Quincy Wildey. Clearly he had something to prove. And boy, did he like locking up white folks. This was a murzyn with a big chip on his shoulder and something to prove. Just like his kid."

"I've gotta go," Stan says. "Rose is expecting me."

"Sooner or later you're going to realize that we can't mix with those people, that shit between our species will never be right. I can help you. I've always been here to help you. I know Rose would want that."

Stan shoves a finger in Sonny's face. "Stay away from my wife. And don't ever come back here again."

Sonny flashes that patrician smile of his that he turns on for all the newspaper photographers. "All I'm saying is be careful. Don't let some *murzyn* do your thinking for you."

Never mind about my murzyn, Stan thinks as he walks back home. Rosie isn't home from work yet. He closes the door and hears that awful guitar lick come to an abrupt halt. Jimmy comes running down the stairs. Stan's had a beer and a half but he could use another two or three right now.

"Who was that, Pop?"

Stan is tempted to just tell him the truth already. He's going to find out someday, might as well be now.

But instead Stan says,

"He's a gangster."

JIM AND JOHN

November 5, 1995

John DeHaven is not only listed, but he's just a few blocks away in a well-kept trinity on Delancey Place. Great starter pad in an excellent neighborhood for an aspiring whatever he is.

Jim hears loud machine-gun fire from a computer game. He pushes the door buzzer for three full seconds. The gunfire dies. Jim pushes the buzzer again, three full seconds, and hears someone running down the steps from the third floor.

The young man who answers is, indeed, easy on the eyes. He's got the regal look of someone who often says, *Yeah, I did some modeling for a while, but what really excites me is urban politics.*

"John DeHaven?" Jim says, showing him the badge. "Detective Jim Walczak, Philadelphia Police. Can I talk to you for a moment?"

"Of course, Detective, come on in."

DeHaven leads him into the house, which is small, like all trinities. Three floors: kitchen and modest living room area on the first, master bedroom and bath on the second, and office on the top floor, which is where they talk.

"We've actually met before," DeHaven says. "Can I get you a beer?"

"Yeah? Sorry, I see a lot of faces. And no thanks—I'm on the job." Jim looks around at DeHaven's desk, his books, his computer, the art on his walls. All neatly arranged and hip. "Where did we meet?"

"At Penn. You spoke in a journalism class once. About what the media gets wrong about homicide investigation."

"You're a Penn grad," Jim says, nodding. "And you're what, twenty-four?"

"Twenty-five."

"And already considered an up-and-comer. One of the top thirty Philadelphians under thirty."

DeHaven nods. "I thought you might be stopping by because of that. You're probably working your way down the list."

Jim shakes his head. "No, just you."

If DeHaven hears this, he pretends like he doesn't understand the significance. "I still can't believe what happened to her. We met only once, but she seemed like such a strong young woman."

"You met her twice," Jim corrects.

"No," DeHaven says, then lets a confused smile bloom on his face. "Fairly certain it was just the once. I keep track of all my appointments."

"You know, that's funny. Because so did Kelly Anne Farrace."

Of course now John DeHaven excuses himself on the pretense of checking his appointment book, even though his desk is up here, on the third floor. Kid going to get a gun? Jim doubts it. He's the kind of Alpha Chi thickneck who picks on girls, not grown men. Kid going to run for it? Jim thinks, let him. We'll have fun chasing him down and wrapping this thing up.

For the first time since he caught this thing, Jim likes somebody for this crime.

Up from the stairwell comes murmuring—DeHaven on the phone. If he's smart, he's calling his lawyer.

Their next exchange will be crucial. Jim knows he's bluffing and running on instinct here—all he has, really, are three initials in a weekly minder. The defense attorney in his imagination would have a field day with that, coming up with thousands of other names that fit those letters, including *Jim Da Homicide cop*. ("So you admit, Detective, that you were drunk and prowling for pussy the night before Kelly Anne Farrace's murder?")

So Jim has to let DeHaven think he knows everything—then sit back and let him confirm it.

"Sorry to keep you waiting," DeHaven says. "Thought my appointment book was home, but I called my assistant and it turns out it's back at the office. I'm happy to have a copy sent over first thing in the morning."

"We'll get back to that," Jim says. "What I want to talk about is this past Wednesday night. So I understand you met Kelly Anne at Circa..."

"I didn't see Ms. Farrace Wednesday."

Jim spreads his hands. "Don't misunderstand me. I'm just here to fill in some gaps in her schedule. The more dots I can connect between Kelly Anne leaving the bar and her body being dumped on Pine Street, the sooner I can catch who did it."

"Like I said, I didn't see her Wednesday. Otherwise, I would have come to you guys to tell you what I know."

They go round and round on this for a while, but DeHaven's either smart or he's been expertly trained. Admits nothing, sticks to his story. Jim will bet he has a titanium-clad alibi for all his movements the Wednesday night through Thursday morning.

Still, though—he likes this guy for it.

Something about his face, his eyes, his demeanor, is extremely familiar to Jim. This is because Jim has sat across from dozens of killers before, and after a while, they all begin to share certain characteristics. A family resemblance. The clan of Cain.

And this smug bastard is one of the tribe.

But Jim knows he's reached a brick wall tonight. He'll pick it up first thing in the a.m. with Aisha, attack DeHaven's alibi with everything they've got, then haul in this son of a bitch officially and crack him.

"Have a good night," Jim says.

"You, too, Detective," DeHaven says. "I'll walk you out."

As Jim makes his way down the stairs, he notices again how clean and orderly everything is. Maybe it happened here. Did he lead you back to his lair, Kelly Anne, for an off-the-record session? Did you not give him what he wanted? Did the spoiled brat punish you for that, then have Mommy and Daddy pay for a cleaning service to wipe all traces of you away?

On the ground floor DeHaven rushes around Jim to reach for the door. Jim tenses for a second, waiting for some kind of attack—but the kid's just opening the door.

And standing there on the sidewalk is Sonya Kaminski, with a combination of fury and disgust on her face.

So this is who DeHaven called. His family has pull with the mayor's office, too.

"You know John here?"

"Know him?" Sonya says. "I gave birth to him."

AUDREY AND BARRY

May 14, 2015

There is no luncheon after the funeral; instead the family gathers back at Staś's house in Jenkintown, a small suburb just outside the city limits.

While there's no law that prohibits cops from living outside Philly, most of them choose to live in the city they police. Staś was one of the exceptions. Bethanne is from upstate and hates the city with a passion. Jenkintown was the compromise. Good schools and a reasonable commute for Staś.

Barry, to his credit, seems perfectly at ease with the Walczak clan, even as Cary gives him the crazy eyes. "This is Barry," Audrey says by way of introduction, and adds nothing further. It's probably driving all of them crazy. Barry? Where did this Barry come from?

Audrey excuses herself to go pee. But really it's just an excuse to go snooping around upstairs.

The house is bigger than she thought and also shabbier. Guess they were taking the remodel-one-room-at-a-time approach. The second-floor bathroom is bright and clean and sleek...and all in stark contrast to the three disaster areas that are the kids' bedrooms. Clothes and toys scattered around like an accident site, scuffs and marker streaks on the walls, unidentifiable stains on the ancient wall-to-wall carpet that might have been shag once. It is strangely familiar to Audrey.

Hah hah, Staś, you were cursed with three slobs just like me for kids.

Staś always resented that (a) Audrey got her own bedroom and (b) it was a complete and utter wreck at all times.

The third floor features an unfinished, stripped-down-to-the-plaster bathroom (guess that was next on Staś's to-fix list), Staś and Bethanne's pristine master bedroom, and a small bedroom off to the right.

The bedroom.

Audrey twists the knob; it's unlocked. Inside, it looks like an office. Exactly what she hoped to find.

Staś wasn't much of a reader. Most of the office is high school sports trophies, CDs, and cardboard banker's boxes full of files. There are empties in the trash can. A set of Sony headphones draped over a boom box at least fifteen years old. Now Audrey understands the purpose of this room. This was Stan's refuge from the rest of the house, just like the Captain's basement lair.

And it looks like Staś brought some of his work home with him. On a small dresser there are a notebook and a couple of files on top of a blue binder.

Blue fucking binder. Wait wait...

Audrey flips the files aside and holy shit there it is. The missing murder book. The Philadelphia Police Department uses the same blue binders for all their homicides. In a city like this, with hundreds of bodies dropping ever year, they most likely purchase them in bulk.

What was *Staś* doing with this one?

She's not proud about the horrible thoughts flooding her brain. That Staś is somehow involved in a family cover-up, that nobody wants Audrey to figure out the truth, because the truth would be too awful. That her dad knows, too, and...

But when she opens the cover she realizes it's not the murder book she thought.

This is the one about the jogger who was raped and strangled twenty years ago—Kelly Anne Farrace. Audrey has dim memories of this case. She was only five years old at the time but remembers her dad was out of the house a lot for this one. And every few years, someone would do an anniversary piece on the killing, asking the same question: "The Pine Street Slaying: Is Anywhere Truly Safe?"

Staś, why were you looking at Dad's old case?

You weren't homicide. Always suspected you didn't have the stomach for it.

She flips through the pages, speeding through the case. The way she remembers it, two scuzzbags were charged with the murder. But when it came to trial, the whole thing collapsed. DNA didn't match. Or something like that. The real killer apparently got away—though most people went on assuming the scuzzbags did it and got lucky.

What were you doing, Staś? Trying to one-up Dad?

As if echoing her very thoughts, an angry voice startles Audrey.

"What are you *doing?*"

It's Bethanne, in the doorway, hands on her hips, eyes puffy, mouth twisted up in rage. A million comebacks spring to mind but Audrey checks herself. The woman just lost her husband. Even Audrey's not low enough to give her attitude now.

She can also choose to lie, or come up with some ridiculous excuse about looking for a tissue or a piece of loose-leaf here in Staś's office. But again, Bethanne doesn't deserve subterfuge. Audrey uses her feet to pivot the chair so she's facing her sister-in-law.

"I don't think Staś killed himself. I want to find out what happened."

Audrey steels herself for Bethanne to go nuclear. Instead she takes the seat across from Audrey. She's so close their knees almost touch.

"I *know* he didn't kill himself. But nobody wants to listen to me. Especially your father."

"Don't take it personally. That's just his way. Grim and cryptic."

"He wasn't always that way."

"No, I know."

Bethanne leans forward and crosses her arms. Either she's cold or she's trying to stop herself from shaking.

"So what did you two talk about last week? I know you had drinks with him. He came home all tipsy. Which wasn't him."

"I was planning on doing a project about Grandpop Stan's murder. Staś stopped by to talk me out of it. He thought the Captain's heart couldn't take it. That me asking questions would push him over the edge."

"Did you stop working on the project?"

"What do *you* think?"

Bethanne allows herself a small smile. She's known Audrey since she was five years old, even babysitting from time to time. The surest way to get Audrey to do something was to tell her *no, you can't.*

"I came up here to see if Staś was working on anything."

"The department already sent people to look through his things. They told me nothing looked out of place."

"What about this?" Audrey says, picking up the Kelly Anne Farrace murder book. "This was one of my father's cases. Why does Staś have this?"

Bethanne nods. "He always told me that was the case that made him want to become a cop just like his father—but it was also the case that *broke* his father. Don't you remember? I guess you were too young. Staś and I had only been dating a few months back then."

"That's the year my mom and dad split up," Audrey says.

"It was the next year, but yeah, that's when things started going wrong. Staś would stay over my house whenever he could. He just couldn't deal with being home."

"Lucky him," Audrey says, and looks down at the binder in her hands and notes the date range on the cover: 11/1/95 to 3/17/97. Early November 1995, she realizes. Holy shit. This was the case her father was investigating when Terrill Lee Stanton died of a drug overdose in a halfway house near the Frankford El.

DUPEK

April 17, 1965

George gets it first and worst.

He's making his way home first thing in the morning, headed up Washington Lane to his quiet little house, when he hears the scream of tires and rustle of bodies. He grew up in a shitty neighborhood; his street radar is fine-tuned. He knows the sounds that indicate he's about to get jumped.

And these assholes should know better than to mug a goddamned cop on the way home from his shift.

But these are no ordinary assholes. They're a precision strike team. They move faster than anticipated. George's hand is barely on the grip of his service revolver before he feels his knuckles explode in white-hot agony before going mercifully numb. Then more whipcrack strikes on his upper arms and knees, which is when he feels his body drop to the ground.

Far as he can make out, there are three of them—all with hard-wood nightsticks.

George feels a stick around his throat. Hands and knees on his body, pinning him to the concrete. A masked face up close in his, telling him:

"Back off, nigger."

"Who the—"

Someone snaps a cheap punch into his mouth. The lower half of his face explodes. He drinks his own blood.

"Or you'll be next."

George tells Stan about this the next day—not like he can hide the bruises. But he waits until they're in the car, away from other ears. They sit there in their big red machine, not pulling away, their bagged lunches on the console between them.

"You want to tell me what happened?" Stan finally asks.

"We're pissing somebody off," George says. "That's what happened."

"Yeah," Stan says in a faraway voice that makes his partner turn around and really give him a close look.

"Holy shit. They get to you, too?"

Last night was Tuesday night—trash night.

Stan is hauling the dented silver can down the alleyway to put it out on Ditman Street. He's just cleared the building on his right—the back end of a corner grocery store—when a hunk of steel taps the left side of his skull. Stan bites the inside of his cheek and sees stars.

"Don't move, *dupek*."

Stan doesn't move, still holding the trash can, because he knows that's a revolver to his head.

"I don't have anything on me," Stan says, which is the truth. He's wearing his undershirt, slacks, and slippers, for Christ's sake, because he was just taking the trash out. No keys, no wallet, certainly not his piece.

"Don't want your money," the voice says, and jabs the gun against Stan's head again to emphasize the point.

"Look, I'm a cop, all right? Don't do anything stupid."

"Yeah, we know you're a cop. We also know your wife and kid are back in your house, defenseless. Any idea what could be happening to them right now?"

All the muscles in his body go tense. Rage floods his bloodstream instantly, powerfully. He wants nothing more than to tear this man apart for just uttering the words *wife* and *kid*.

"Don't," the man with the gun says, now pushing the business end of the revolver into Stan's head with enough power to force his head against the wall. His ear scrapes the rough brick. He's still holding on to the trash can. Not out of fear. If it comes to it, Stan has no objection to beating the hell out of this guy with the can. That is, if he's not shot in the side of the head first.

"They'll do her first, so your son can hear. And maybe if you're lucky we'll drag you back there, give you the chance to beg for your kid's life."

"What do you want?" Stan says through gritted teeth.

"Get your *murzyn* to mind his own business."

"Rosie and the kid?" George asks quickly.

"They're fine, it was just a bluff," Stan says as he drives up Broad Street.

"Huh," George says. "You get a bluff. I get the goddamned black beat off me."

"I'd rather a beating than for anything to happen to my family."

"Yeah, I see your point. Guess they don't know about me and . . . hang on hang on."

"What?"

"They don't know about me and Carla getting back together, because according to my file, we're still separated."

"Your file? What, at headquarters? What does that have to do with anything?"

"Come on, Stan. They knew our home addresses. They knew we were cops. They knew exactly how to threaten you. They knew they had to beat the shit out of me to make their point. That's because they're fucking cops, man. We've been chasing cops this whole time."

They drive in silence for a few minutes, both processing.

"This is messed up for real," George finally says.

"Doesn't have to be police, you know. Just someone with access to our files."

"Which makes it the same thing as the police, if you think about it."

As Stan drives he can feel his heart racing even before he's consciously aware *why*. He's been sitting on this for a while. If he doesn't bring it up now, he never will.

"Do you know a guy named Sonny Kaminski?" Stan says.

George turns to look at him. "Well, that's a question out of fucking nowhere."

"Well, do ya or not?"

"Not personally, no. Don't want to. We have what you might euphemistically call some, uh, family history."

God no. Please, God, don't let him say the words.

"How's that?"

"I never told you this, because I didn't want you to think you were jinxed or something, ridin' around with me. You know my daddy was a cop, but I never told you the whole story. John Quincy Wildey was one of the few black men on Smedley Butler's squads of Prohibition raiders. Got himself a commendation by ol' Gimlet Eye himself. And after they booted Smedley out of the city, my daddy kept on fighting. He hated liquor, and hated those who peddled it. No offense to your beer and all. Guess it was the Southern Baptist in him."

"What happened to him?"

George exhales slowly. "One night he got a tip—somebody was ripping off a government liquor warehouse down on the waterfront. He and his partner went to check it out, partner took the front, my daddy took the back. Sure enough, yeah, there was a whole gang of them, truck waiting and everything."

God no, Stan thinks. Please stop now.

But Wildey continues.

"Now, my daddy—who I've gotta say was a fairly clever man—knows that it's like, six heisters versus the two of them. They're outnumbered, outgunned. Not as if they can call for backup in the middle of all this. So my daddy goes to their getaway truck, knocks out the driver, opens the hood, and messes with the engine some. Heisters come out, see their driver missing, and freak out. Say something about him chickening out. A plan's a plan, though. They load the beer and after they're finished one of them gets behind the wheel to start the truck. It won't start. Which really pisses him off."

It's surreal, hearing an oft-told tale from the other point of view.

"My daddy comes out, *Freeze, police!* Gun out, got the drop on these stupid bastards. His partner got them covered from the other side. Nowhere to go. They're exhausted, and two cops have them in their sights."

The guy behind the wheel is named Jan Kaminski.

"So the guy behind the wheel, he's madder than any of them. He takes one look at my daddy, revolver in his hand, and says . . . now, this is according to my father's partner . . . he says, 'Goddamn you, nigger, making me do all that work for nothing!'"

Actually the way Stan heard it was *You goddamned* murzyn, *making me do all that work for nothin'!*

"And then he shot my daddy."

And then Jan Kaminski pulled the trigger *and shot that black bastard dead.*

"Killed him right there."

And then all Jan Kaminski's pals would laugh, because the execution was the punch line.

"They all ran, leaving the beer behind."

That black bastard still owes me for a night's work!

Haw haw haw . . .

"My daddy died at the scene. I had no idea until the next morning. I was only, shit, four years old. But that morning I knew everything would be different from then on. And you want to know the truly messed-up thing?"

"What's that?"

"A year later President Roosevelt made beer legal. A year later, it would have been like my daddy died stopping a bunch of assholes for stealing soda pop."

They share a moment of silence for John Quincy Wildey, killed in the line of duty, December 1932.

"They ever catch the guy?" Stan says, knowing the answer already.

"No," George says. "But that's what I was getting at. They never caught the gang, but a few months later someone else arrests this band of bootleggers. Word is, their leader always bragged about killing some black cop. His name was Jan Kaminski, father of the guy you asked me about. So how do you know him?"

At this point they're almost at Broad and Columbia but Stan can't hold it in any longer. He pulls their Falcon to the side of the street, leaps out of the seat, runs to the corner, and pukes on the side of a building.

ORPHAN WITH A GUN

November 5, 1995

"This is a courtesy, Sonya," Jim says. "Nothing more. I just want to let you know we're going after him for this."

"Hear me out. Five minutes is all I need."

It's almost closing time at the Palm. Sonya wanted to go somewhere private, but Jim purposefully chose a public place, just to make sure things remained civil. Once they arrived Sonya insisted on ordering drinks, even though alcohol is the last thing Jim wants worming through his bloodstream. He needs to be more clearheaded than he's been in his entire life. Christ, what was he thinking? He shouldn't even be here with Sonya. He should be rousing Aisha from sleep and preparing to take this raping, murdering motherfucker down.

"Two Stoli martinis, very dry, three olives," she tells the bartender.

"One martini for her," Jim says. "I want a tonic and lime."

"Is this Jim Walczak, turning down a free drink from the City of Philadelphia?"

She's trying to keep it light, like it's all no big deal, *hah hah* won't you look silly in the morning. But her eyes tell a different story. They're predator eyes. She wants to sink her teeth into Jim and give it a snap and a jerk.

"The only thing I'm going to suggest," Jim says, "is that you contact your attorney. For both of you."

She moves in close. "I need to explain something to you."

"Just tell me one thing, Sonya. Does the mayor know?"

She ignores the question. "Johnny had nothing to do with this.

The only thing I'm guilty of is protecting a young man's future. When that girl turned up dead, Johnny told me everything. That he was talking to her in the club that night. He wanted to turn himself in for questioning!"

"He should have. You should have told him to talk to me."

"And have his name all over the fucking papers? Nuking his future? No, I don't think so. You know how this works, Jim. It's like chewing gum stuck to the bottom of your shoe. It sticks to you all day long."

Jim shakes his head. "This is a *murder,* Sonya. You can't go playing around with this like it's some bond issue or whatever the hell it is you people do."

Sonya's martini arrives and she takes a healthy swallow. Jim watches her carefully. Here is a mother whose son is about to be accused of one of the most horrific crimes in recent memory. Yet she's out here, sipping her Stoli like there's nothing to worry about. He'd love to see one little tremor, one tiny tell. Her cool resolve worries him. This were him, with Staś or Cary in this kind of hot water? Jim would be jumping out of his own skin.

"You knew all along," Jim says. "The mayor didn't send you. You asked for the assignment. To protect your kid!"

"*Mea culpa,* Jim. And don't pretend you wouldn't do the same. But that's not all."

"What do you mean?"

"Ever wonder how *you* caught this case? You weren't next on the rotation, were you? Hmmm."

"Are you saying you got me on this case?"

"Well, no, I don't have that kind of power. But when the horrible news broke, I immediately thought of you—my favorite homicide detective. And I made a simple suggestion to the mayor."

"After you spent a long night cleaning up after your son."

Sonya frowns. "You'd better watch what you say, Detective. You're tap-dancing with a slander lawsuit."

Jim rests his head in his hand, elbow on the bar. "Look, Sonya, it doesn't matter what you say, I'm going after him for this."

She locks eyes with him. "I'd offer to blow you in exchange for your courtesy, Detective, but that would be a little creepy. Even for me."

"What are you talking about?"

"You still haven't figured it out, have you? I guess that makes sense. You were only twelve when my uncle died. Suppose your mom never told you."

"Your uncle? Who the fuck is your uncle?"

"His name was Stan Walczak. He was a Philadelphia police officer, killed in the line of duty."

She's either drunk or insane. Most likely insane. Bringing his father into this, trying to save her own son.

"John is your nephew," she continues. "You bring him in, you're destroying your own family."

"Jesus Christ, Sonya, this is a new low, even for you," Jim snarls. "I know my family. *You're* not my fuckin' family."

"Jim, for a smart man, there's so much you don't know. I'll bet you never even thought about where your name came from."

"What?"

Was she honestly suggesting that he was named after "Sonny Jim" Kaminski? That the union boss and his father were siblings? No, sorry, can't be. Though something tugs at his memory. One afternoon, a few months before his father was killed—a man stopped by the house. A guy in a fedora, nice clothes. He and Jim's pop went for a walk. Pop came back angry. When Jim asked about the guy, his pop snarled and said he was nobody. *A gangster.*

Sonya leans into Jim now, her lips to his ear. "I don't care what you believe, *cousin*," she says. "But if you bring in my son, *your nephew*, I will destroy you."

Jim takes this moment to suck in some air, clear his thoughts for a moment. *Don't let her taunt you, Inner Jim. You're leading the most important homicide investigation of your life—Outer Jim needs to be in charge here.* But it's hard to keep his composure. The entire world seems to be spinning a little faster now. He feels a strange lightness in his head. Like he's been in an accident and the shock is preventing him from remembering what the hell just happened.

"Go right ahead," he finally says. "You've got nothing on me."

"Really? Then tell me what you've been doing visiting a certain halfway house on Erie Avenue for the last three days in a row."

A cold little ball forms in Jim's stomach.

"Don't make me do this, Jim. For your family's sake."

"Do what, Sonya?" he says robotically, because he already knows what she's going to say. She's been orchestrating this from the beginning. Probably before the body was even discovered in that stairwell. Arranging the pieces on the board so her son would come out the winner no matter what. Asking for Jim—secret cousin Jim—to be assigned to the case. Dogging it every step of the way. Ears in the department and eyes on the street. Watching Jim's every move, so that if he got close to John DeHaven she'd be ready. Only, the people watching Jim saw something else, didn't they.

"I have photographs," she says quietly. "Friday morning, Friday night, Saturday morning. Saturday night... Do you want to take the stand and explain why you were visiting a parolee's halfway house all weekend long?"

Jim stares at her.

"Especially considering that parolee is now dead?"

BABY BLUE

May 14, 2015

The funeral dinner at Staś's house comes to its slow, awkward end. Nobody wants to be here, but nobody seems to be in a hurry to separate, either.

Cary is absolutely and embarrassingly shitfaced. Jean makes excuses as she tries to pry him away from the small table serving as the bar, which excuses do nothing to disguise that he's calling her a harpy and a controlling cunt. The Captain sits in the corner, either lost in his own reveries or astral-projecting his body to another place. Will seems all twitchy about being away from his expensive toys in his downtown lair, so Claire says her goodbyes and heads back to Center City.

Which means it's Audrey's turn to go.

She asks Barry if he minds giving her and her grandma Rose a ride back to her place, explaining that she wants to stay with her grandmother for a while, make sure she's okay. Barry's cool with that—which half-stuns Audrey. Usually when a guy puts up with an all-day family event he's looking for a little reward for his labors. Barry, though, just rolls with it. Kind smile on his face, too.

Good on you, Captain Save-a-Ho.

The ride from Jenkintown doesn't take very long. Just down Route 73 to the Boulevard to Harbison, then right on Torresdale and up one block to Bridge. Grandma Rose sits in the back, nervously, peering over Barry's shoulder to make sure he's going the right way. Audrey chokes down a couple of *Driving Miss Daisy*

263

jokes. (Again, not the time, not the place.) Barry pulls to the side while Audrey helps Rose out of the car and across the street. Audrey runs back to kiss Barry on the cheek, tells him she'll call later.

"Wow, a kiss," Barry says. "You'd better watch out. You're getting personal."

"Kiss my ass," she says with a sly smile.

Back inside, Audrey helps Grandma settle on the couch. She's not grief-stricken. She's not trembling anymore. She just seems weary. Audrey can understand. It's been an exhausting day.

"You okay, Grandma?"

"I'm fine, I'm fine."

Audrey excuses herself to go pee—for real this time. But she's a little spooked when she pauses halfway up the staircase to glance at the framed portraits on the wall. Grandpop Stan. Her father. Staś. Two down, one to go. If you're a policeman on this wall and your name happens to be some derivative of *Stanisław*, well then, you're shit out of luck.

Only, Staś wouldn't kill himself. She *knows* this. Bethanne knows it, too. If someone killed him…who? And why? And who were those strangers at the funeral? Once she's back downstairs, Audrey sits down next to the only source she has left. Her grandmother— the only person she knows with useful memories.

"Grandma, do you remember the lady Dad was talking to after the funeral?"

"Who, sweetie?"

"Tall, dark-haired cougar, Christian Louboutin pumps, about my mom's age. Do you know who she is?"

"Oh, you should talk to your father."

"Well, I tried, Grandma, and he's not exactly gushing with information. So I'm asking you."

Grandma Rose sighs. She looks at Audrey to see if there's any chance. "She's your father's cousin."

"How come I've never seen her before?"

"No, no. On his father's side."

Now, Audrey is no genealogy expert, but for her father to have a cousin, Grandpop Stan would have needed a sibling. And that would be impossible, because Grandpop Stan was an orphan. No siblings, an immigrant mom who died giving birth to him, and an alcoholic father who died eight years later.

Grandma Rose catches Audrey staring off into space, trying to do the ancestral math.

She laughs. "Don't believe everything you read in the papers, kid."

Then she rises, touches her thighs as if steadying herself, then walks to the stairs. "I've got something to show you. Wait here."

After the first five minutes, Audrey thinks maybe Grandma went upstairs to use the bathroom. You know, with a book. After five minutes more, Audrey begins to suspect that Grandma forgot whatever it was she went upstairs to fetch, then lay down and fell asleep. And by the quarter-hour mark, Audrey begins to fear the worst. That the strain of burying her firstborn grandson was too much for her big Italian heart.

But no, here she comes back down the stairs, carrying a scrapbook Audrey's never seen before.

"Your grandfather would have a fit if he knew I kept this," Grandma says. "It's the only picture I have of the two of them."

Audrey leans over her grandma's shoulder as she flips through the pages. The old cellophane crackles with each turn. At first, Audrey can't parse what the hell she's looking at. Yellowed newspaper advertisements, black-and-white burlesque photos. Then she stops on a raven-haired dancer with a bosom like twin torpedoes.

"Can you believe that?"

Those eyes. That smile.

Holy crap.

"That's not... that's not you, is it?"

"Time's a bitch, isn't it?"

"And you give me shit about my tattoos?" Audrey asks.

"Tattoos are hideous. Men don't want to see tattoos. They want to see your skin."

"So wait wait. You were a stripper?"

Grandma recoils as if she's been slapped. "Audrey! I was what they call an *exotic dancer*. No one saw anything else except your grandfather."

"Where the hell is this? Looks pretty swank, Grandma."

"Midtown. That's where all the hot clubs were after the war."

Audrey reaches over and flips back a page or two to look at the addresses on the clippings. Yeah, sure enough—Twelfth Street, Thirteenth Street, Spruce, Pine, Camac, the heart of what is now called the Gayborhood. Pretty much right where Will and Claire chose to shack up. She wishes Staś were alive right now for many reasons, but mostly so she could tell him that just a few short blocks away from McGillin's, Grandma Rose used to shake her moneymaker.

"Jesus."

"And here's what I wanted to show you."

A five-by-seven black-and-white, showing a bar. Classy joint, from the looks of it. Loads of liquor along the mirrored bar. Brass foot rail. Girls in fancy-ass vintage dresses (though, duh, Audrey thinks, they weren't vintage back then) and swells in suits.

"What year was this?"

"Nineteen fifty-one," Grandma says as she taps one of the guys in the suits. "There's your grandfather."

Hello, Stan Walczak, you suave son of a gun you.

She taps another swell.

"And that's James. His brother. You should ask *him* what happened to your grandfather."

WALK THE LINE

May 1, 1965

On the first of May Stan Walczak and George Wildey find themselves back where they started—the scene of a riot waiting to happen.

"Yeah, let's go to the top brass, let's report it," Stan mocks. "Wonderful idea."

"Hey," George says, "at least they let us keep the leather jackets."

Crazy thing is, their meeting with the chief inspector two weeks ago seemed like an unqualified success. The CI listened to their stories, with George taking the lead and Stan chiming in with corroborating observations. There seemed to be a team of white heroin pushers selling huge amounts all over North Philadelphia. Worse still, this team seemed to have access to police files. They knew where to make the deals without worry about police involvement. If they weren't rogue cops themselves, then they appeared to have help from someone within the department.

The CI was by turns horrified and intrigued. Stan and George were especially pleased when he assured the officers that he'd look into this personally.

A week later they were bumped from the special post-riot squad and rotated back into street patrol, no explanation given. "Orders from on high." Either there was a conspiracy, or they'd breached some kind of departmental etiquette and needed to be taught a lesson.

The last day of April they receive new orders: report to Girard College at 4 a.m. the very next morning—a Saturday. Police informants claim that Cecil B. Moore plans to lead a gang of protestors over the ten-foot wall that rings the college, so Commissioner Leary dispatches one thousand cops to guard every inch of that wall. Undeterred, Moore changes his mind and leads a roving band of picketers to march nonstop along the wall, singing "We Shall Overcome."

Standing around in the hot sun in his leather jacket, Stan sees that the police outnumber the protestors pretty much twenty to one. "This is a load of shit," he tells Wildey, who has to agree with him. Nothing but cops, spread out around the campus perimeter wall. Moore, a former marine with a fondness for cigars and silk suits, keeps the protestors in lockstep like a military unit. Nobody on either side is gonna step out of line, not in front of the TV cameras or newspaper guys, anyway. Wildey, meanwhile, keeps an eye out for Dr. Martin Luther King, Jr., who's in Philadelphia for the next few days. Maybe he'll stop by the wall. "Would be pretty cool to see him."

Day two, Sunday, is more of the same. Endless marching, singing, chanting. Wildey hears that at night, when the reporters go home, cops will chant back in response to "We Shall Overcome"—"oh no you fucking won't"—and smack their batons on the metal barricades in front of the main campus gates. There's no sign of Dr. King, much to Wildey's disappointment.

Day three, Monday, still no Dr. King. Stan's feet are killing him, an ache that seems to shoot up his legs and spine. What makes the pain worse is that all this standing around seems to be for nothing. And just when Stan thought he was finally adjusting to the last-out shift, here he is working days. When he comes home at night, he's too tired to play with Jimmy or talk to Rose for long. He forces down supper, tries to sleep, can't, has a few beers, tries again to sleep, can't, and before long it's time to report back to work.

Day four is more of the same. Stan begs for a day off—but request denied. Moore's marchers continue their endless loops around the campus. Stan begins to think he's going to spend the rest of his career guarding this stupid wall. The cops and the protestors are locked into an angry stalemate. Nobody can leave until the protestors go home, and the protestors won't go home until Girard College opens its gates to black kids.

Day six, though, Wildey surprises him. "I've been doing some digging this week and I think I've hit the mother lode."

"What are you talking about? Digging what?"

"I've been doing some investigating on my own and I think I've got another source who'll talk to us."

Stan's about to ask him *source for what* when he realizes that Jesus Christ, Wildey's still after the Jungle Wolves.

"We're gonna meet him tomorrow—he's over at Eastern State."

"Your source is a con? And we're supposed to just trust him?"

"We can at least hear him out?"

"When are we supposed to do this?"

"Noon. Our badges will get us access. I've already called the prison."

"We'll be here tomorrow."

"No we won't," Wildey says with a grin. "Because we'll be playing hooky."

That night Rosie makes *gołąbki,* stuffed cabbage rolls in red sauce, one of Stan's favorite meals and one that Jimmy loathes. The name refers to a Polish word for pigeon, which to Jimmy's mind makes it all the more disgusting. He sticks to the side dish of mashed potatoes and only pretends to eat the *gołąbki* by cutting open the cabbage and chopping into the ground beef and rice mixture a little. He asks to be excused, which is fine with Stan because he wants to talk to Rosie alone.

"I'm taking off work tomorrow," Stan says. "But I'm still going to work. George and I have to check on something."

He's told her nothing about chasing white drug dealers and murderers through the Jungle. He's never brought his work home before, and he's not going to start now. She's made it clear that all she wants is for him to come home safe from his shift; the details don't matter. But he's got to tell her something, since he'll be leaving the house in his civilian clothes.

"Check on what?" Rosie asks.

Stan doesn't want to lie to her, either. The one time he did almost ended them ten years ago, and he doesn't want to be in that position ever again.

"We've got a snitch who might be able to tell us about a bunch of crimes we're trying to solve."

Rosie nods, cuts some cabbage with the flat of her fork. "Why do you have to take off work to talk to this man?"

"He's over at Eastern State Penitentiary. We want to look like we're just old friends visiting so the other prisoners don't assume he's a rat. You understand?"

She does, and they finish their meal without another word. Stan drains the rest of his beer, pitches the empty can into the garbage, then plucks another one from the fridge and takes it to his recliner, where his *Evening Bulletin* is waiting. Upstairs, Jimmy picks at his guitar strings, the same riff over and over again. Ordinarily Stan would yell up and tell him to close his goddamned door, but he's too tired to get into it right now. He sips his beer, leans back and tells himself he's just going to close his eyes for a minute.

CHOKE DOWN THE RAGE

November 6, 1995

Jim doesn't go home until very late Sunday night. He just drives, aimlessly, blindly, only returning at dawn to shower and change his clothes before heading back to the Roundhouse. Claire says nothing, not wanting to start a fight. He's grateful. On his way out Audrey runs up to him and clamps her entire body onto his lower leg like a deadweight, begging him not to go to work today. "I have to, sweetie," he says. "Daddy has to go."

Aisha tells him he looks like shit. Jim thanks her for that observation. They go through the timeline again, and the list of possible boyfriends, and she brings up the *JDH* initials again and Jim stares at her and says he has nothing. Then they go back through it again and Aisha says this isn't going anywhere — maybe it's those two knuckleheads after all. Jim says yeah, maybe. Let's press 'em, see what we got.

And with those words, Jim knows that this is the beginning of the end.

Later that day word leaks to the media that the police have two "persons of interest" in custody and that they're on the verge of confessing.

This is not true. The deliverymen maintain their innocence. Aisha pushes harder, even when the DNA comes back and it's not a match.

Jim says nothing.

He tries to convince himself he's doing nothing wrong. Kelly Anne was a fact-checker. Let's examine the facts. Does he know for a fact that John DeHaven raped and murdered Kelly Anne Farrace, used her own keys to break into her apartment, changed her into jogging clothes, then dumped her body in a stairwell on Pine Street? Maybe if he had a forensic trial establishing all this. But he doesn't. So there's no way to be sure. Because John DeHaven is not a person of interest.

In this city, killers go free all the time.

Just look at Terrill Lee Stanton.

That evening Jim drives over to 2046 Bridge Street and tells his mother they have to talk. She offers him some leftovers, coffee, tea, maybe some sweets—but Jim doesn't want any of that right now. He just wants the truth.

"Yes, your father had a brother," she says quietly.

"Sonny Kaminski."

His mother nods.

"Jesus Christ, Ma, why didn't you tell me?"

"Your father didn't want anyone to know. He never even told me. I only found out because Sonny told me after your father died."

Now Jim remembers. Of course. He was there at his father's funeral. Lots of guys in suits were there, paying their respects to Pop, but until this moment he didn't remember that "Sonny Jim" Kaminski was one of them, putting his hands on Jim's shoulders, squeezing them, almost massaging them, telling him everything was going to be okay, which of course Jim knew was a lie.

"You're named after him, you know. Your father didn't want anything to do with his old family but he couldn't resist."

The old family—the Kaminskis, his mother explains. Stan ran away from home when he was just a boy, leaving his younger brother behind. He was always torn up about that, but how could he bring his brother along? Stan was just a kid himself; staying alive on the streets would be difficult enough. He changed his last name to the name of a lodger they once had: Walczak. He always said he became a cop because his father was a bad man and he wanted to make up for it.

Beyond that, he never liked to talk about the job much. Being a policeman just became a way to make ends meet.

"Your father didn't want you to know," Rose says. "I always hoped that when you got older, he would change his mind. But then he—"

"I have an uncle," Jim says. "I have an entire family I didn't know about."

Something occurs to his mother. "How did you find out? Who told you?"

Jim says, "I was working on a case with his daughter."

FIGHT THE FUTURE

May 15, 2015

As Audrey walks down Front Street she rehearses the words in her head, but there's no way it doesn't sound funny.

Hi, uh, Mr. Kaminski, it looks like I'm your great-niece and I think you might know who killed my grandfather and his partner back in 1965.

Sonny Jim Kaminski lives on Kenilworth, just two blocks below South Street. It's a surprisingly beautiful block just beyond the edge of downtown. Back in the day—"the day" being the summer of 2005 or so—Audrey and her asshole friends in high school used to troll South Street and its tattoo and piercing parlors, its bars, its sex shops. Everyone told them South Street was over, but fuck you, man. It's over for you because you're old.

Kenilworth is just two blocks from that circus and yet worlds away. Who knew the ancestral family home was so close to Zipperhead?

It's the day after Staś's funeral. Audrey called Sonya Kaminski's office (or is that Great-Aunt Sonya's office?) this morning to arrange this little awkward meet-and-greet. Sonya herself is supposed to meet her at 106 Kenilworth, even though she's busy running her son's quixotic campaign for mayor.

Yeah. Democratic mayoral hopeful John DeHaven: totally Audrey's cousin, too.

Or something like that.

Being the adoptee, Audrey always felt like the poor relation growing up. Turns out she's the poor relation in a family that is itself a poor relation to the ultrapowerful Kaminskis. Kind of makes a girl feel like a photocopy of a photocopy. She should be out busking in front of the condom store, not knocking on this door.

Still, she knocks.

Waits.

The door opens to Great-Aunt Sonya, who smiles at her.

"Hello, Audrey. I'm so glad you called. Come on in."

The interior is all expensive wood and plush carpet and interesting art.

"Sorry we didn't have the chance to speak more at the funeral. But it's primary season, and my son John, as you probably know, has pretty much every minute of every day scheduled for him."

"Gotta be tough."

Cousin John running for mayor. Guess it would be a faux pas to slip Sonya here a resume, ask her to pass it along to her cuz.

"Anyway, my father is expecting you. Just up the stairs to the bedroom—he has a hard time with the stairs. Can I get you anything to drink before I leave?"

Probably poor form to ask for a Bloody Mary, so instead Audrey says no, thank you.

"Hope you find what you're looking for," Sonya says, then leaves.

Ho boy.

Up the stairs she goes to the second floor. The walls have all been knocked down, making two smallish bedrooms into one decent-sized room. In the middle of all this space is a large-boned man in a wheelchair.

"Hello, Audrey," says a quiet voice. "I've wanted to meet you for a long time now. So glad you called."

Oh, there's definitely a resemblance to her grandfather Stan. Same deep-set eyes, almost like a pair of shiners. Wispy gray hair. Strong jaw—the kind that can take a punch, even if it's part of a weak old man now.

"Glad you invited me," she says.

"This is your ancestral home, believe it or not," Sonny says. "You don't know the delight I felt when I heard this house had gone on the market. Snapped it up at a good price, too—though I would have paid double or even triple to get it back."

Audrey looks around. "Nice place. A little small. Don't you big shots go for urban mansions?"

"Would you believe that a hundred years ago there were nineteen people crammed into this place? Not even the same family. Your great-grandfather Jan Kaminski rented a room for himself and his wife. Later, we boys came along. I don't remember a single private moment."

"Must be nice, having this all to yourself now."

"To be honest, it's lonely."

"Awww."

Sonny's not sure how to take that. "Did you really come here to mock me?"

"No, I came here to talk about my grandpop Stan. Seems you might know who killed him and haven't said a word for fifty years."

"So Rosie told you." The old man grimaces. "Up until now you've been perfectly fine with being completely ignorant of your own history. Kids like you...you think life began when you opened your eyes and cried for your mama, no idea of what came before."

"I know my history," Audrey says. "For instance, I know that the Liberty Bell cracked one day when Ben Franklin lost a bet and he kicked it. But then Rocky put it back together again, so it was okay."

"My grandson is going to be the next mayor of the city, and he's going to get it back on track. You know how much we've lost over the past sixty years? James Tate started it, stupid prick handing over power to the Negroes. How are they supposed to handle power? They can't even handle their own lives."

"Can we not do the whole racist thing right now? I'm not here about your grandson. I want to know who killed my grandfather and George Wildey."

Sonny Jim closes his eyes and smiles, as if relishing a private memory. For a moment, Audrey worries that the tough old buzzard has fallen asleep on her (wouldn't be the first time). Or worse—that he's died, before she's had the chance to hear the truth. But no, he opens his eyes and fixes them on Audrey like laser pointers.

"You're different from your brothers," Sonny says. "What is it about you?"

"I have tits?"

Sonny guffaws and shakes his head. "Yeah, I suppose you *are* one of us, aren't you? Sonya had a mouth on her, too, when she was your age. Quite the hell-raiser."

Audrey thinks: *No fucking way am I like you people.*

"I don't know if anyone told you," Audrey says, "but I'm adopted."

"Is that what they told you?"

She has no clue what he means by that—hell, she only just found out the Walczaks and Kaminskis are related.

"Can we stick to the topic at hand?"

Old Sonny Kaminski's face drops, all traces of levity gone. He shifts his body in his wheelchair as if to seem taller.

"You want to know who killed my brother? His stupid black partner, that's who."

"I don't have my degree yet, but I'm pretty sure George Wildey didn't pull the trigger."

"You ever hear that word they use—*brother?* Hey, brother, what's happening, brother. They have no idea what that word means. So when my own flesh-and-blood brother partnered up with a *murzyn...*"

"You should seriously stop using that word," Audrey says.

The old man leers and nods his head. "Right, right, I almost forgot. You screw *murzyns,* don't you. In fact, one of them is the father of your child. Little half-breed Bryant, back in Houston."

Audrey feels the breath rush out of her lungs, her skin go frying-pan hot. She doesn't know how this old man knows all this (hell, her own father doesn't know). She doesn't care.

"If you ever say that about my kid again I swear to God I'll pull you out of that chair and kick the living shit out of you."

"Big words for the daughter of a whore."

"Big words for a racist prick in a wheelchair."

The creepy old man smiles like a dog—all teeth, wild eyes. "You fucking people. Pointing fingers at me. Clawing at me, all the time. Seems like every generation I have to deal with one of you Walczaks."

"So what—did you *deal* with my grandpop Stan, too?"

Audrey means, of course, that rich ol' Sonny Jim here didn't want to deal with his blue-collar cop brother making trouble for him. But Sonny gives her a cold, dead stare for a moment before his eyes go wandering.

"I didn't mean to do it," he says quietly. "It was an accident."

SHOTS FIRED

May 7, 1965

Inside the taproom at the corner of Seventeenth and Fairmount, a
novelty polka is playing:

Someone stole the keeshka
Someone stole the keeshka
Someone stole the keeshka
From the butcher's shop

First time Stan played it for George on New Year's Day, his partner
couldn't stop laughing. It was the most absurd song George had ever
heard. What made it even funnier was when Stan told them the performers were local boys, the Matys Brothers, from down in Chester,
and they'd recorded the song at Broad and Columbia, in the heart of
North Philly. Stan said it with such pride, which just made George
laugh even harder.

"Hey, barkeep," George calls out over the song, "get my Polish boy
here another Schmidt's. Who stole the kishka, man. Heh heh heh."

The world-weary bartender looks up, wondering why a black cop
would play a polka on the jukebox, shuffles over to the taps.

Sunlight streams into the bar. Another gust of hot air.

Both Stan and George turn to look, half-expecting to see the construction worker again, as if he changed his mind.

But it's not the construction worker.

It's a man with a gun.

Specifically, a revolver.

The winos stand up, revolvers in their hands, too.

Both Stan and George instinctively reach for their sidearms. Both remember—at pretty much the same moment—that they're in civilian clothes. No guns. No nightsticks.

No nothing.

"Fuck *meeee*," George says, already on the move.

Stan couldn't agree more.

As the winos lift their guns Stan and George do the only thing they can: heave themselves over the bar, knocking the old, petrified bartender down on his ass in the process.

And over their heads—

BLAM BLAM.

A chamber spins twice—

Two quick finger squeezes, double-action.

A mug on the bartop explodes.

BLAM.

Another chamber spins—

Finger squeezes, double-action—

BLAM.

A chunk of wood sprays off the bar.

Someone yells,

"Stop that shit! Stop it!"

Down below, Stan and George crouch down and scan the back bar for weapons. There are none. The trembling bartender looks at Stan, then at George, his eyes lit up with *what-the-fuck-is-going-on?* This old man has been wiping away beer rings since FDR made it legal to do so. He pegged them as cops from the beginning. He did not, however, count on somebody deciding to open fire on said cops.

"You got a piece back here?" Stan asks. "A scatter gun? Something?"

Bartender shakes his head no, no, no.

Stan grunts, looks around, considers a bottle, but—what's a bottle going to do against a couple of guns?

George says, "Sometimes you ever think the whole fucking city's against us?"

"Yeah, I'm starting to believe that," Stan says.

The polka ends, and on comes George Wildey's final selection. It's a tune he thought Stan might appreciate because of his boy and that lick he was always playing around the house. It's the Staple Singers' original version of "This May Be the Last Time," a gospel-infused wail that now fills the bar. Eerie. Funereal. Otherworldly.

Right about now George is regretting the selection. He'd give anything for that goofy-ass polka to come on right about now.

"You two!" a voice shouts. "Come on out from behind there. Hands in the air."

Stan and George look at each other, their noses just a few inches apart.

"Don't think we have a choice, man," George says finally.

They come out from behind the bar.

"Okay, now strip."

"What?" George asks.

"Do it! All your clothes, down to your skivvies!"

Stan recognizes the winos, now that their chins are up and eyes fully open. They're the fake police "inspectors" they dealt with a few months ago. This isn't going to be a friendly warning. The fact that they want them to strip can't be a good thing.

What choice do they have?

So Stan and George remove their civilian clothes, all the way down to their white undershirts and boxers. They're told to kneel in front of the bar, hands behind their backs. George complains about the broken glass on the floor. Their captors don't give a shit. The bartender, meanwhile, is told to stay the fuck down, facing the floor, like he was told.

The winos hold guns to the backs of their heads.

"May I inquire as to what this is about?" George says.

"Shaddap," one of the winos says. Deep neighborhood accent. If George had to peg it, he'd have to say Whitetown, one of the river wards.

"I just want to know if you're gonna kill us or not. My knees are getting all cut up and shit."

Stan shoots George a look.

"Stop giving them ideas."

The bartender, still facedown behind the bar, cries out, "Just go! I don't want any trouble in here!" His voice is muffled by the tile floor.

"Shut the fuck up and keep your face on the floor like you were told!"

George looks over at Stan. Once again, he has no idea what's going through that thick-necked Pole's damn fool mind.

"You know, when we partnered up nine months ago," George says, "I should have known we'd end up like this."

That gets a grim smile out of Stan.

The door opens and with it comes light. Another gust of hot air blows through the room. Then the door slams shut and someone whispers.

"Hey," Stan calls out.

More whispering and murmuring. Like the fact that they've got two cops in civilian clothes kneeling on the floor of this taproom, on broken glass, doesn't matter in the slightest.

"Hey, look, can you hurry it up? I've got tickets to the Phils tonight and don't want to be late."

Then a voice says, "You're a stubborn *schnudak,* you know that?"

Stan's face relaxes when he hears the voice. "You've gotta be kidding me..."

George's eyes dart toward Stan. "Who is it? Please tell me you know what's going on, Stanny boy."

But Stan ignores his partner.

"So this is all about you putting the scare into us," Stan says. "Isn't that right?"

"No, Stanisław. We're a little far beyond that now."

Then he hears the click of a revolver and then he feels the cold steel against the back of his head and knows this is it.

"You know whose gun this is? Think hard. It'll come back to you. You used to sneak it out of the shoe box and look at it."

"Stan," George says, eyes wide, "come on, man, what the hell is going on?"

"The old man kept it. Like a trophy. And when he died, he passed it on to me. Never thought I'd be able to use it like this. I think the old man would be happy we were still getting some good use out of it."

"You son of a bitch."

"I have to admit, I thought you were playing a sick joke on me. You, partnering with *him*. Thought you asked for him specifically, just to prove some kind of point."

Stan realizes what his brother is saying. Jesus, is that what all this is about? No, he didn't know George Wildey from any other person until they were partnered at the riots. Just like Jim to think it was all about him.

"I didn't know," Stan says. "*He* doesn't know!"

George says, "Stan...know what?"

Sonny Jim Kaminski pulls the gun from his brother's head and taps it against George Wildey's head. The force rocks George on his knees a little.

"Ouch."

"Does this gun feel familiar? Huh, *murzyn?*"

The winos with the guns laugh and change their positions. If something's going down, they want their piece of the fun, too.

Stan squirms on his knees. *Please don't do this. Don't be this stupid.*

"Yeah, I know you didn't know, Stan," Sonny Jim says. "Which makes me wonder about fate and life and all that. This is a small city, but not that small. I like to think that fate has brought us to this moment here, where there is an important choice to be made."

The next thing Stan knows, he's being lifted off his knees. Legs have gone numb, so the winos continue to hold him up as he regains his footing.

His brother smiles as he holds up the revolver. Stan knows which one it is. Of course it would be. The old man was always proud of that .38 Special. Carried it like he was an Old West gunslinger. Considered himself a Polish outlaw. Other thugs around Southwark shared a single pistol. Not Big Jan Kaminski. No, he had to have one of his very own. Spent their money on a gun instead of putting food on their table. His logic, of course, was that the gun would put food on the table.

Sonny Jim holds it to his brother, grip out.

"Go on. Take it. Fully loaded with the stuff you're used to. Winchester–Western Metal Piercing Super-X. Am I right? Cocksucker won't feel a thing."

"No."

"You can end this right now. We don't want to have to worry about you anymore. You take your boy to that ball game tonight. Hell, I'll even spring for the hot dogs and beer."

"Fuck you, *Sonny Jim.*"

"Hey, you're among friends here. They just want to know you can be trusted to do the right thing. Make sure you remember whose side you're really on. There's too much at stake."

George, on his knees, both understands what they're saying—the life-and-death shit—and at the same time has absolutely no idea what they're talking about. *Which* side?

"Uh, Stan? Really would love to know what the hell is going on. If this is some elaborate practical joke, it's really not fuckin' funny."

But Stan can't hear his partner because he's thinking of his sweet Rose, about how mad she'll be when she hears what happened. Mostly, though, he thinks of his boy, Jimmy, and how disappointed he'll be to miss the Phillies game tonight.

"Go home to Southwark, Sonny. Leave us alone."

"You don't understand. Southwark's your home, too. You got yourself all confused playing around in the Jungle. Family's family. After all this time, I'm willing to welcome you back with open arms, all forgiven. You just gotta do one little favor for me."

"Let us go. We stick to the old arrangement. You stick to your side of the city, I stick to mine. I don't know why it has to change now."

"Thought you'd be smarter than that. Rose thought so, too. She was counting on you to save her. Guess I'll have to."

Now Stan is ready to explode—how many times has he warned his brother about even thinking about Rosie? But Sonny's arm is already moving. The revolver in his hand is pointed at the back of George's head. His thumb cocks the hammer back with a metallic click. Finger ready to squeeze.

No.

Stan lunges forward, slams into Sonny's knees. Knocks him off balance.

The revolver goes off—

BLAM.

Bullet WHACKS into the front of the bar—six more inches to the right and it would have buried itself inside George's skull.

"You stupid son of a bitch!"

Stan responds with a jackhammer punch right to his brother's nuts. The impact is so hard it lifts him off his feet. Sonny falls on his ass.

George senses his chance—

He scrambles to the bar, turns around.

The winos lift their guns.

Pointed right at him.

Cock their hammers.

Stan leaps up into the air just as they—

Open fire.

BLAM.

BLAM.

BLAM.

The first bullet is like a punch to the shoulder and spins him around. The second slices through his back and emerges from the front of his belly. The third misses, buries itself in the bar. The shots feel like punches. His whole body goes cold.

Sonny Jim roars in horror, screams *NOOOO*. Starts pounding on the wino next to him, beating him with the butt of his revolver. The wino stumbles backward, drops his own revolver. It clatters on the tile floor. "YOU STUPID MOTHERFUCKER!" Sonny Jim is screaming. The other shooter is paralyzed with fear. Christ—they shot the boss's cop brother!

Stan looks over at George, who's all wide-eyed, his face splattered with blood. *My own,* Stan thinks. Oh Christ, Rosie is going to be upset.

"Go," Stan tells his partner.

George scrambles across the tile floor, toward Sonny Kaminski. George heard the piece drop. He's gotta get it.

"HEY HEY HEY!" someone shouts.

But before he can reach it, someone kicks him in the stomach. George doubles up and slowly flips over. "Let me at him," Sonny snarls as he staggers over to George. He crouches down now, even though it hurts, and places the barrel of the revolver against George's forehead.

"As I was saying, I'll bet some part of this gun feels familiar. Maybe the ghost of your daddy is crying out right now, oh no, not again. You want to cry now, too? Beg for your life, just like your daddy begged for his?"

George just stares at him. The face of pure hate. There's no talking to a man like this, no reasoning. With someone like Sonny Jim Kaminski, you can only speak the truth.

"I don't have to cry for my daddy," George says, "because my partner's got my back."

And indeed he does.

Stan Walczak rises from the tile floor just high enough to reach the revolver in one of the winos' hands and force his finger to squeeze the trigger and pull off a sloppy shot. BLAM. Sonny Jim twists and screams out—he'll never walk again. But he pulls the trigger on the way down, BLAM. The side of George's head disappears. The other wino turns and fires at Stan, repeatedly, BLAM BLAM BLAM. But he's a stubborn Pole, and it takes the other one to join in the effort, unloading their weapons at him before he finally falls. Some of their shots miss, embedding those Super-X bullets in the front of the wooden bar, all while the bartender cowers on the other side, praying to God they're not strong enough to punch all the way through.

ANOTHER SHOT

November 7, 1995 (Election Day)

Jim wakes up around 4 a.m. with a full-blown panic attack. He can't do this. He *knows* he can't do this. Might as well put the gun in his own mouth and pull the trigger. He barely makes it to the bathroom before he vomits up his mostly liquid dinner. He tries hard not to choke or cry out—doesn't want to wake Claire or the kids. But he hears the voices in his head—

Am I really about to let a killer go free?

Objection, Your Honor, the detective presumes to prejudge my client?

Objection sustained, Sonya. Your first cousin should rephrase.

Thank you, Your Honor.

Mr. Walczak, let me remind you that in this city, killers go free all the time.

The mayor is reelected in a landslide. Sonya Kaminski, along with union boss "Sonny Jim" Kaminski, shares the stage with him at the Bellevue during the postelection party, streamers and confetti and balloons everywhere. Part of the team that's going to lead Philadelphia into the twenty-first century. Not too long ago workers would flee downtown before night fell, and muggers and rapists and scumbags would control the city streets. But the mayor turned things around. Locked everything down tight. Reclaimed Center City, which comprised the original Philadelphia city limits back during the Revolutionary War. This had been a battle, too. They were only getting started.

Sonya Kaminski tells a reporter she'll help with the transition into the new term but plans on returning to work with her father.

However, her son, John DeHaven, Sonya tells the reporter, is someone to watch. He's already done so much at such a young age.

Jim drives along Erie Avenue. He doesn't even have to think about the address. Before he knows it he's pulling up outside the halfway house and climbing out of the car and staggering a little because he's had more than a few drinks and reaches for his gun and is relieved that it's still there.

Inside, he flashes his badge at the landlord, asks to be taken to Terrill Lee Stanton. The landlord sighs and says he hasn't seen Stanton in days—didn't his parole office tell him? What is he talking about—Stanton's missing? Yeah, the landlord tells him. Looks like he did a runner. Been gone since Sunday night, according to the PO.

Jim asks for the key to Stanton's room. Landlord gives it to him, no questions asked. He walks the four floors up to Stanton's room—4B. Tumbles the lock, opens the door, steps inside. Once he sees the sad bed with the paper-thin mattress and lumpy pillow, the banged-up dresser, the threadbare carpet that may have started out as brown but has faded to a sickly gray . . . he remembers.

Late Saturday night.

Nobody knows he's here.

Just Jim . . .

. . . and his father's killer.

"Don't do this, son. You're making a big mistake."

"I'm not your fucking son!"

Jim Walczak has his father's killer at gunpoint. To complete the circle he should force the man to strip and kneel down on the dirty threadbare carpet. He should tap the barrel of his revolver against the man's skull, let him think about the last few seconds of his life. Then pull the trigger.

But shooting him would be a mistake. Ballistics too easily traced. He's murder police. He knows how detectives will read this scene. It's important to present an airtight narrative.

Jim tosses Stanton a small leather bag. The man catches it by reflex. Looks down at it. He knows a works bag when he sees one. And he knows what Jim wants him to do.

"This ain't gonna give you peace."

"Shut the fuck up and take the needle out of the bag."

"I knew your father. He was a good man. He wouldn't want you doing this."

At first Stanton pretended not to know his father. But then he sighed, shrugged his shoulders, and admitted the truth. Yeah, he knew Jim's father. Yeah, he was their snitch a couple of times. But he didn't kill them! Why would he do such a thing? He needed them, and when they got killed, Stanton said, he knew he needed to lam out of North Philly for a while. The big bad wolves had come for them.

Wolves? Jim had no idea what he was talking about, wolves.

"There are things you don't understand, my son," he said. "The wolves have taken over. They *won*."

Now Jim looks down at Terrill Lee Stanton's lifeless body, needle hanging out of his arm. The stink has stayed confined to this room. Another day or two and his hall mates would have started complaining.

Did Jim force this man to stick the needle in his vein at gunpoint? Did Jim really kill this man?

No.

The "parole officer."

If Jim had killed him Saturday night, the PO would have found his body the next night—when he told the landlord Stanton had pulled a runner. A real PO would have called the cops, the EMT. But a fake PO would have looked at the body, wiped down fingerprints, and left the way he came, telling the landlord that Stanton was missing, not dead. Probably told him to leave the room alone for a while, too. A PO who was not a PO. But in the employ of the Kaminski family.

Jim didn't do this. He was drunk and stupid Saturday night but he was not a killer.

Killers—they were on the other side of his family.

THE FINAL SHOTS

May 15, 2015

Audrey takes the El back toward Unruh Avenue in a kind of daze. So much to process and none of it even remotely what she expected. It's all just so goddamned Cain and Abel.

The only thing that's clear is that she needs to speak with her father. Like, right away. But he hasn't been answering his cell. Which leaves her no choice but to take the El and the 66 home to Mayfair and wait for him there. Maybe pour him a double vodka on the rocks, because he's going to need it.

Your secret uncle killed your father. Or ordered him killed. Or at least ordered his partner killed, and Grandpop Stan put himself in the way.

The El speeds down the tracks. There are no seats, since it's rush hour, so Audrey stands and holds the slightly slimy pole to keep her balance. She feels eyes on her. She turns to look. Nobody. Paranoia's a funny thing, isn't it? Doesn't take much, really, to tip your whole world on its axis. She remembers the day Claire sat down and explained that she was adopted. They wanted to wait until she was old enough to understand, but before that happened Claire and her father had split up. She was six years old and probably not ready to hear this kind of news. She'd look at all the parents picking up their kids in the schoolyard thinking—wow, all those moms and dads actually wanted their kids. Not mine. They gave me away for someone else to deal with. It fucked her mind up for a very long time.

Audrey snaps out of her reverie and turns. Whoa whoa whoa. Someone is *definitely* looking at her. She can feel the *eyes* on her, she swears. She believes in extrasensory perception because how many times have you just thought someone was looking at you and you turn and boom—someone's looking at you?

The Bridge Street terminal—last stop on the El—can't come fast enough. She blends into the crowd and walks with them down the long concrete stairs toward the terminal proper, which is fairly busy for the middle of the morning. She's a cop's daughter; she knows what to do. Stay with a crowd. She pulls her crappy cell from her bag and tries her father one more time. Maybe he can pick her up.

It rings six times, then nothing. No Dad. Where the hell are you?

She's thinking about trying again when someone punches her *hard* on the shoulder.

She spins, drops the cell, which cracks on the ground. The entire terminal is echoing with this giant boom.

People around her begin to scatter. She wants to reach for her phone—she can't leave it here in the Bridge Street Terminal, for Christ's sake—

And then—

BOOM.

Another punch.

Audrey's on the ground before she even realizes she's fallen. She feels cold all over. There's someone in a hoodie looking down at her, and it's only when she sees the gun in his hand does she realize, holy fuck, I've been shot.

We're basically bags of water, a professor once said.

And someone just shot her bag at least twice.

She's a living—for now—chunk of ballistic gelatin.

The guy in the hoodie is aiming the gun, a revolver, at her face now, and she's pretty much toast and too weak to do anything about it.

Audrey thinks about that old song about how you can't get to heaven on the Frankford El.

Au contraire, mon frère.

But then something spooks him—the rush of footsteps and the loud cries of grown men. The man in the hoodie disappears. She tries to be a good policeman's daughter and remember the details of that face for a sketch artist later. Later. How optimistic of you. You, of all people, should know what a bullet can do to a human body. You watched all those shows. You studied it in class. All to prepare you for this moment, when you're shot and bleeding out below the Frankford El.

She reaches out her hand. *Daddy, pick me up. Please.* Her body is so damn cold—she doesn't even feel the pain of the bullet wounds. Her hand is the only thing warm. That's because someone's holding it. Squeezing it.

It's a man's hand—rough skin, strong, somehow familiar.

The same man tells her to *hold on, hold on, hold on.*

It's a nice thought, but at this point the decision is kind of out of her hands.

STAN

May 7, 1965

Stanisław Walczak stays alive for a surprisingly long time, considering a portion of his brain has been obliterated. Must be the stubborn Polack in him.

He reaches out toward his partner across the tiled floor but George looks like he's already moved on. Mouth open, eyes open, staring up at the ceiling. Face splattered in blood.

Your quarter's run out on that jukebox, George. Why don't you go play us another three songs. Surprise me.

George says nothing. There might be a hint of a smile on his face, though.

This was not part of the Plan, was it, George?

Heh heh heh.

Someone's screaming. There are sirens. Stan tries to focus on his breathing. If you're still breathing your heart is still pumping. Heart still pumps, you're still alive. Fuck you, Sonny Jim. I'm going to live. I've got to take my boy to a ball game. With that thought, Stan passes out for a moment.

When he wakes up there is someone touching his hand. Squeezing it. A female hand.

Telling him to *hold on, hold on, hold on...*

Funny thing is, now that he's awake again, he thinks maybe it's the other way around. That he's holding some pretty girl's hand and telling her it'll be okay. She is everything. She is salvation. She is the future. He opens his eyes and he's the one crouching down, and she's the one on the floor. Dark hair,

296

full lips, bright eyes. She looks just like Rosie did when they first met.

And then it hits him with the bright wattage of a thousand stadium lights who she is, what she's doing.

Stanisław Walczak has never seen anyone so beautiful in all his life.

JIM

November 7, 1995

Jim drives home to Unruh Avenue. Audrey runs up to him and squeezes him tight. Wife Claire is in the kitchen, preparing supper. She'll be pleased to know that he's home for a family meal for once. Too bad he can't eat. His stomach is a black pit.

He's made the anonymous phone call, tipping them off to room 4B on Erie Avenue. The rest is up to God. He pours himself a vodka rocks, eases himself into his recliner, and waits to see if someone will show up to arrest him.

He feels the first chest pains several hours later. He stumbles out of bed, still drunk, thinking he's having a heart attack. As he's standing in front of the bathroom mirror, his vision goes blurry and his fingers feel numb and there's a choking sensation around his neck. He slams a fist into his chest as if he can shock his heart back into a regular rhythm. *Please God,* he says, *don't let me die like this. Not at this sorry point in my life.*

The next day a cardiologist at Pennsylvania Hospital says the EKG shows nothing—most likely an anxiety attack. Which is not surprising, considering his line of work.

But his life and career slip out of their groove. Any joy he once found in the job is gone, robbed by the knowledge that he's betrayed his badge. Where he used to fantasize about killing Terrill Lee Stanton, now he thinks about working up the courage to arrest John DeHaven, consequences be damned.

But he doesn't have that luxury. The consequences wouldn't just fall on him. An organization willing to kill a man and frame a cop wouldn't hesitate to go after that cop's family.

AUDREY

May 16, 2015

The good news: she's not dead.

The bad news: she's pretty fucked up.

Claire repeatedly tells her: don't worry, your father is on his way. She wishes she could talk but she can't, not with this tube down her throat. She can't move her arms. She could blink Morse code—but of course that would require her knowing Morse code.

Captain, I solved it, you'll never guess who did it!

No, seriously, you'd better sit down.

She's had plenty of time to fit the rest of the pieces together. Oh, the independent study in her head is the most brilliant thing ever. Not that she'll ever live to write it.

She tries to tell Claire with her eyes: Mom, I really need to see Dad. Where the hell is he? Why hasn't he been around to visit me?

More good news: doctors say her "extra padding" probably saved her. Which is better than saying that being fat saved her life.

Three cheers for postnatal weight gain.

More bad news: she really needs a kidney. Two, actually, but one is needed immediately, otherwise it's renal failure city. This is a problem when you're adopted. Usually, a kidney is something you hit up a sibling for. Claire is in the room when the doctors tell her the news.

"So I'm boned," Audrey says. Her throat still burns like hell even with the tube out of it.

299

"No, you're not *boned,* daughter," Claire says. "Your brother is going to give you one of his."

"Cary? The same Cary who cries when he cuts his finger?"

"Your brother loves you."

"How do they even know he's a match? Don't they have to do tests and stuff?"

Claire is looking at her funny. Like she's ready to burst out into tears or laughter or maybe both.

"He's a match," Claire says, "because he's your brother."

After Claire explains the full story, Audrey wants the doctor to come back into her room to request a brain transplant, too, because her mind has just been blown.

James Walczak and his wife, Claire, married young. Had two sons in short order, the way young married couples do. They had no clue what they were getting into. Their life was chaotic.

By 1989, roughly the fourteen-year mark of their union, Jim and Claire grew apart. Both strayed, made stupid decisions. Acted on impulses without thinking through the ramifications. Fortunately, they came to their senses in time to save the marriage, realizing that their will to be together was far stronger than the little weaknesses that conspired to drive them apart. Claire was able to break off her affair cleanly.

Jim, not so much.

The woman he was seeing was pregnant. She was single, lonely, and broke and saw Jim as her financial lifeline. She lied about her pills. When Jim broke it off, she threatened to tell Claire about the baby. Instead, Jim told Claire about the baby. Claire was gutted but held her ground. She was not going to surrender her marriage to some money-chasing whore from South Philly.

The mother then told Jim she was going to abort the child so she could move on with her life. This hit Jim hard. He was all for women's rights, but he was also raised Catholic. That was half his child in there, he believed. He begged her to reconsider. She toyed with him for weeks before finally agreeing to have the child and surrender custody to Jim and Claire... *if* they paid her medical and other living expenses. The number she had in mind went far beyond any rational medical and/or living expenses, but Jim was making good money as a homicide cop in those days. They were flush and saving up to buy a home in the near burbs outright, cash on the barrelhead.

Instead they brought Jim's baby girl home, explaining to the boys that they had decided to adopt. Claire named her after her favorite actress: Audrey Hepburn.

Audrey wishes her father would show up. There's so much she wants to tell him. But mostly, she just wants to feel his arms around her again. Her *real* daddy. Something she never thought she'd have.

But now the anesthesiologist is here, and they've wrapped her in a warm blanket, and they're giving the shot, and they're telling her to count backward from a hundred...

STANISŁAW KAMINSKI

1933-1951

Your daddy has to go on a trip, his drunk uncle tells him one morning.

But Stanisław knows what his father's done. He heard everybody talking downstairs when they thought he was asleep.

His daddy has shot someone. A police officer, and now he has to hide.

Stanisław watches as he packs fast, packs light. Daddy uses an old T-shirt to wrap the .38 Special he bought from some gangster over near Ninth and Christian. He packs two boxes of ammunition, too—WESTERN .38 SPECIAL SUPER POLICE LOAD, the box reads, 200-GRAIN. The gangster who sold him the ammo told Jan this is what cops use all over the country. If you're going to get into a gunfight with a cop, you want to have the same stopping power.

And then he's gone without a word, leaving Stanisław and his younger brother, Jimmy, with an uncle who's hardly ever around and a loose collection of rough men and women all in the same business— bootlegging.

The cops come around and ask questions but not for too long. His uncle jokes that it's a *murzyn* cop so they're not taking it all that seriously. Hell, Jan could have stayed home!

There's no school for Stanisław. He's needed at home to take care of the cooking (whenever someone wants to eat) and general tidying up. But most of his time is taken up with the house project— digging out a subbasement where his uncle figures they can hide booze or weapons or even a person for a while. Stanisław digs and Jimmy holds the buckets steady. They don't want anyone to know what they're up to, so every time two buckets are full, Stanisław has to carry them out the back, down the street, past the sugar refinery to an empty lot down by Delaware Avenue. He dumps the buckets, comes back for more. The dirt is wet and heavy and hard and smells like mold. *It's probably shit from fifty years ago,* he thinks. The metal handles dig into his palms so hard that the lines never go away.

Nobody stops him or questions him—he's just a stupid little Polack playing with a couple of buckets of dirt.

His uncle says he wants this pit dug out by Christmas, and that means at least fifty runs and ten buckets per day. His uncle "supervises." His uncle drinks a lot. His uncle is impatient. His uncle yells a lot when he's drunk. One night he yells so loud it startles Stanisław and he drops one of the dirt buckets onto the kitchen floor. His uncle calls Stanisław a stupid *schnudak* and kicks him down the stairs. He tumbles down with the half-empty bucket. Stanisław's nose is bloodied and his lip is split and his ankle screams.

Jimmy cries when he sees his older brother, which makes Stanisław furious. He dumps the rest of the foul dirt out of one bucket and marches up the steps with it. His uncle is taking a pull from his bottle when Stanisław swings the bucket and smashes the bastard upside the head with it. The bottle shatters on his face, which is now a half-mask of blood. The uncle roars. Stanisław drops the bucket and runs out the back door and into the city.

He doesn't intend to stay away forever. Just until his daddy gets home a few months from now. He picks the farthest place he knows in the city—Frankford—and hops the El there, ducking the fare. He doesn't know anyone in that neighborhood but his daddy took him and Jimmy there once to see a movie at a gigantic theater near Orthodox Street. It seemed nice.

Now it seems alien, frightening. He ducks into the nearest place with an open door—a café with live entertainment. He tells the bartender he's waiting for his daddy (technically not a lie). The whole place shakes whenever the El comes roaring past, temporarily drowning out the piano player set up in the corner. Stanisław is starving so he asks for a sandwich. Bartender puts in the order, no questions asked. The piano player catches his eye, smiles, and bangs out a song Stanisław actually recognizes—"Baby Face." A joke on him, he guesses. Bartender holds the sandwich and asks Stanisław if he's sure his daddy will have the money to pay for it. He lies and says yes and quickly devours the sandwich.

Of course after an hour or so with no father, the bartender realizes what's up. He threatens to call the police but Stanisław begs him not to—can't he work it off instead? The piano player takes up his defense, telling the bartender to cut Little Man a break.

The bartender doesn't want to call the cops, of course—he's selling liquor in teacups and doesn't want the bluecoats to use a visit as an excuse to shake him down for another payment.

So the bartender cuts the nine-year-old a break. He'll work at this café for the next eight years—cleaning dishes, then lugging boxes, eventually even learning a little piano and filling in on the keys once in a while. The El constantly roars over their heads, and during that first year Stanisław thinks about going back home to see Jimmy, just to make sure he's okay.

But he doesn't dare. His uncle is most likely still fuming.

On July 22, 1934, John Dillinger is gunned down outside a movie theater in Chicago and everybody in the café is talking about it. Stanisław picks up the *Ledger* and reads the story, excited to learn how they finally caught Public Enemy Number One. He likes cop and crime stories.

But below the fold on the front page is a short piece about an attempted jewelry store heist.

Shot dead was the alleged ringleader, Big Jan Kaminski, forty-two, of the city's Southwark neighborhood.

When he joins the US Army in '43 he enlists as Stan Walczak—the name he's been using since leaving home. He lifted the last name from a poker-playing lodger who was once kind to him, taught him some magic tricks.

A bunch of years later, while working at a nightclub near Kensington and Allegheny, he meets Rosie Avallone, a short funny girl with an amazing bust. His pals warn him to back off—she's dating some young gangster type. But Stan is back from the war and feeling like he's ready for anything. He asks her out. He shows her his service photo. She says she likes how he looks in a uniform. Stanisław tells her good—because he's joining the police academy. No gangster would mess with a cop.

At first, the decision is all bravado—and a lack of other options. Piano playing is fun but doesn't pay nearly enough to start a family. A cop can make $2,400 a year with potential for advancement. Decent, steady money in 1951.

But it's not just about that. He realizes he wants to bury Jan Kaminski for good. And replace the police officer he killed.

And besides—Rosie likes how he looks in a uniform.

Before long the gangster catches wind of this big Polack Rosie is seeing. Stan's pals try to warn him. He's got a violent streak and is fond of his .38 Special.

Then one day he walks into the club when Stan is in the middle of a tune and comes right up to the piano and bangs on the top and says, *Goddammit, I can't believe it's you!*

The gangster is his younger brother, of course—Little Jimmy

Kaminski all grown up. People around town call him Sonny. They don't let on to anybody else. Not even Rosie. In private, though, his younger brother tells him he's lucky.

"If it were anybody else," Sonny Jim says, "I would've had you killed."

CAPTAIN JAMES WALCZAK (RET.)

1995-2015

Homicide Detective James Walczak is headed for a divorce.

In early January Philadelphia is hit with a winter storm of historic proportions—thirty inches of snow. The city can barely keep up with plowing the roads. Jim and Claire and the kids are trapped inside their small house on Unruh Avenue for three days. Fighting is constant. Audrey cries a lot. Jim drinks too much. The roof of their deck, overloaded with snow, collapses.

Claire leaves the following summer, in the sweltering heat of August 1996. She can't deal with his moods, his depression, his drinking. She wants a better life for their boys, she says. He notices she doesn't include Audrey in that. Despite all her promises, there's still that painful division. *Your kid, not my kid.* She suspects he's been cheating again and that he's wracked with guilt, hence the drinking. Let her think that. Better than the truth. Maybe it's better that they go away. Safer for them all.

That fall, Staś goes off to the police academy in spite of his father. On graduation day Rose hangs his photo on the wall near her staircase.

Homicide Detective Jim Walczak watches his highest-profile murder case unravel in the courtroom.

In February 1997, Timothy Hoober and Bobby Haas are tried for the murder of Kelly Anne Farrace. They claim they were beaten and forced to sign blank pieces of paper that would later hold a typed confession. After a monthlong trial, both men are acquitted. There's simply not enough physical evidence to convict. Jurors also don't find the prosecution's case compelling. The murder of Kelly Anne Farrace is considered unsolved.

Captain James Walczak retires from the Philadelphia Police Department after thirty years of service. There is a small retirement party but none of his children (nor his ex-wife) choose to attend. He visits his father's grave and begs for forgiveness for his sins. He takes care of his mother, Rose, bringing her groceries and doing small repairs on the house on Bridge Street.

Within a few months of retirement, however, he finds himself growing restless, drinking way more than he should. He enters a program and emerges forty pounds lighter. He begins to consult on cases for the department from time to time. He also reinvestigates his own cold cases, hoping to make up for some earlier career missteps, though he'll never admit this to anyone else. To those who ask, he simply explains that he's keeping his mind busy. There's one case, however, that he refuses to touch, despite reporters calling him every year, on the anniversary of the murder. The most he'll give is a mostly subvocal *no comment* before hanging up the phone.

Retired police captain James Walczak receives a letter informing him that his father, Stanisław Walczak, will be honored with a plaque recognizing his service to the city of Philadelphia on the fiftieth anniversary of his death—May 7, 2015. It's both an honor and a terror. James gets very drunk that night, listening to the 45 on repeat until he can't stand it anymore and pulls it off the record player and snaps it in half.

In the cold sober light of morning he calls each one of his kids, asking them to attend. Not for him. But for the memory of their grandfather. And their grandmother Rose.

He's pleasantly surprised when they all agree. Even Audrey, who will fly back from Houston to attend the event.

He misses her more than words can convey.

Retired police captain James Walczak hears the news about his daughter, Audrey, and collapses. He is rushed to the same hospital — but no one tells Audrey, since she's fighting her own battle.

The prognosis for Jim is not good. The heart disease is too advanced. Surgery would be a gamble that even in the best-case situation would result in only half a year, a year tops.

Jim, however, refuses to go out like this.

He asks Cary to go to the house on Unruh Avenue and bring back files from the Kelly Anne Farrace murder. If Cary knows one thing, it's police paperwork. Then he summons a lawyer and Lauren Feldman, the former editorial assistant who is now city editor of the *Philadelphia Daily News*.

As they gather around his bedside, Jim tells them he believes mayoral candidate John DeHaven murdered Kelly Anne Farrace twenty years ago, disguising her rape and strangulation as the result of a random street attack. DeHaven's mother, mayoral advisor Sonya Kaminski, abused her position at City Hall to cover up her son's involvement. Furthermore, he believes that his police officer son, Staś, and daughter, Audrey, were attacked by those close to the Kaminski family in an effort to keep this quiet.

Lauren Feldman can't rush back to the newsroom at Eighth and Market fast enough.

The story breaks the next day — a Saturday, typically the worst day in the news cycle. But the word of the retired police captain is more than enough to sink the campaign. And for the DA to assemble a grand jury to investigate the Kaminski family's criminal ties going back to the 1960s. Jim's lawyer cautions him that he'll be crucified for this. "I'll bring the hammer and nails," Jim replies.

But before the grand jury can be assembled, Jim's condition worsens. He tells Claire, Cary, and a recovering Audrey he wishes to be buried next to his father and his son over in the national cemetery in Beverly, New Jersey.

Audrey tells him, "You're not going to die, old man." Clasping his hand tight, even though there's an IV line running into it. "We've got too many bad guys to catch. Father-and-daughter detective shit."

"The family business," Jim says, smiling.

"You know I love you, you grizzled old bastard?"

Jim knows. And on June 10, 2015, he gets his wish.

P/O AUDREY WALCZAK

May 7, 2016

Audrey crouches down to pick the cigarette butts and chewing gum wrappers and other unidentifiable urban detritus from her grandfather's memorial plaque. "Sorry, gentlemen," she says. "But I've been away for a little while."

Bryant tries to help, too, dropping down to his knees and rubbing his great-grandfather's name with the lollipop he's been sucking on. Only through quick reflexes does Audrey prevent him from returning the lolly to his mouth.

The plaques are in good shape, one year later. Barry kept up with the cleaning of the plaques as long as he could, but quit the pizza joint by summer's end to attend grad school in . . . wait for it . . . *Houston*. Very romantic, and quite a surprise. But nobody was more surprised than Barry when Audrey revealed she was taking Bryant and moving back to Philadelphia as soon as possible.

She never finished her independent project; she dropped out of CSI school. However, none of the professors gave her the gas face since they all knew what had happened to her family in August. Her mentor even suggested that she write about her experiences and submit that as her independent project. But Audrey doesn't see the point. She has other plans.

Barry likes that she's a cop and he's a deacon. She can plug 'em, he can plant 'em.

Ben Wildey claims he can make Audrey a decent shot in one hour.

They're at the range early this morning—her request. Ben was

311

thrilled to hear the news—especially after all the bad stuff that seemed to haunt the family this past year. Of course, it didn't hurt that Audrey flattered him by saying she wanted to learn from the best.

"Most cops think they can outshoot anybody," Wildey says now. "Let me tell you something: the average cop can't shoot. Maybe fifteen percent can. And listen—it's all hype that cops are outgunned by drug dealers. They don't need more bullets. They need to be better trained."

All it takes to be a decent shot, Ben explains, is good eyesight and two and a half pounds of pressure to pull the trigger. "No size or strength requirements, male or female. Anybody can shoot a gun."

Sounds good. Ben sits her down in his office and places the two different types of handguns on the table in front of her: a revolver and a semiautomatic. Audrey is more interested in the revolver, of course. Official department weapons are Glocks, but Audrey likes the idea of carrying something extra. Something a little more personal.

Ben asks Audrey if she's left- or right-handed. She tells him left, but that she bats right. "Why?"

Ben explains that when left-handers shoot semiautos, the ejected shell invariably hits them in the head.

"Really hard?" she asks.

"Yup," he says. "Enough to put your eye out."

Audrey decides to become a right-handed shooter. Ben continues his safety lesson on semiauto shell ejection. "Just be careful with certain kinds of shirts. Hot ejected shells can land in funny places."

"How about we stick with the revolver."

"Good idea."

Ben points to the revolver, a .38 Special, not too dissimilar to the gun used to kill their grandfathers, and explains that a revolver draws bullets from a cylinder, as opposed to a semiautomatic, which draws from a magazine.

"Pick it up," he says, and she does, marveling at how heavy it is. He shows her how to open the cylinder—thumb, middle, and ring fingers around the cylinder, index and pinky splayed on top—and load the bullets. Her hand position resembles a deviant peace sign.

The next step—and most crucial—is learning how to fire both single-action and double-action. The names are misleading. Single-action involves two actions: You cock the hammer, then pull the trigger. Double-action is really a single, continuous action: you pull the trigger back until it cocks itself and then squeeze off the shot.

After donning protective eyewear and headset (and buttoning the top of her shirt—just to be safe), she stands at the range table. Ben staples a bull's-eye target sheet to the cardboard backing.

"Okay, single-action. Aim for six o'clock on the bull's-eye." Cupping her left hand under her right, Audrey raises the .357 to eye level. She uses her left thumb to pull back the hammer and then places her right index on the grooves of the trigger. She closes her left eye and adjusts her position until the two rear sights and front sight form a W beneath the target.

"Go ahead," Ben says.

She fires.

Suddenly there is white smoke everywhere, as if someone has set off a firecracker directly in front of her.

"Good shot," Ben says. "You're just an inch below target." Good shot, indeed—considering a second ago she couldn't even see the damned thing.

"Go again," Audrey says, smirking.

The trick, according to Ben, is lining up your shot. Once you know how, you never lose it—no matter if the target is twenty-five, thirty, or a hundred feet away. Ben guides her through forty-nine more shots, varying between single- and double-action, finally giving Audrey a human silhouette to shoot at.

Out of twenty shots at thirty-five and fifty feet away, she manages to put fifteen slugs in Mr. Silhouette's "kill zone," plus two decent shots in his left arm.

Ben Wildey doesn't lie. An hour later, Audrey can shoot better than most guys on the force.

She's lost thirty pounds since last year and has to admit—she looks pretty fucking good in a uniform.

ACKNOWLEDGMENTS

The idea for *Revolver* was seeded in my previous novel, *Canary,* in what was basically a throwaway line. (My subconscious mind likes to play games with me, I swear.) And it blossomed into life on March 24, 2014, when I read a *Philadelphia Inquirer* piece by Barbara Boyer about the 1963 murders of two police officers in Lodi, New Jersey. The bitter anger of their families, even after all these years, was palpable. It brought to mind a murder in my own extended family—that of a Philly beat cop named Joseph T. Swierczynski, who was gunned down by a gangster outside a bar at Ninth and Christian on March 20, 1919. And while the shooting of Michael Brown in Ferguson, Missouri, wouldn't happen until I was deep into the writing of this novel, cops and race were very much on my mind from the very beginning.

I've dabbled in historical fiction before—my first novel, *Secret Dead Men,* was set in a 1976 I barely remember, and *Expiration Date* is about time travel to the early 1970s. And I've spent seven (plus) years researching a novel set in Prohibition-era Philly that I'm hoping to finish before I die. But now came an opportunity to write some historical fiction and show its visceral impact on the present. I'm a big fan of William Faulkner's line from *Requiem for a Nun:* "The past is never dead. It's not even past."

To re-create that past, I had some homework to do. I'm hugely grateful to Michael J. Chitwood, Joseph R. Daughen, Steven Swier-czynski, and Frank Wallace for spending time and sharing memories with me. Their firsthand accounts helped enormously.

I also devoured heaps of newspaper and website articles and books in researching *Revolver,* but especially useful were *Case Study of a Riot: The Philadelphia Story* by Lenora E. Berson, "That Long Hot Summer of Rage" by Will Bunch, *The Peoples of Philadelphia* by Allen F. Davis and Mark H. Haller, *Black Brothers, Inc.* by Sean Patrick Griffin, *Tough Cop: Mike Chitwood vs. the "Scumbags"* by Harold I. Gullan, and Civil Rights in a Northern City: Philadelphia, which is Temple University's amazing digital archive about the civil rights movement in Philly (northerncity.library.temple.edu).

Feedback and advice from my early readers—Lou Boxer, Robb Cadigan, Joe Gangemi, Allan Guthrie, and Robert Kulb—was very much appreciated.

That lovely map at the front of this book comes to you courtesy of Mark Adams and Jason Killinger, a.k.a. Eyes Habit. My writing area is adorned with their maps, which are a constant source of inspiration. (I'm a map nerd.) Take a peek for yourself at eyeshabit.com.

Huge thanks to my editors, Joshua Kendall and Wes Miller, who not only saw the early promise of the idea, but also helped me find my way throughout the writing process. High-fives to the rest of the team at Mulholland Books as well as Inkwell Management and the Gotham Group.

All of my love to my home team—Meredith, Parker, and Sarah—who have to put up with me when I'm staring at a corkboard littered with index cards or walking around the house, mumbling to myself. I couldn't do this without them.

ACKNOWLEDGMENTS

The idea for this novel came literally the day after we adopted Sherlock, our Aussie shepherd–border collie mix. I plotted quite a bit of this book while walking him. He offered no special insights into the novel or its themes, but definitely thought I should include dead squirrels, if possible.

February 21, 2016

ABOUT THE AUTHOR

Duane Swierczynski is the Edgar-nominated author of nine novels, including *Canary, Severance Package,* and the Shamus Award–winning Charlie Hardie series (*Fun and Games, Hell and Gone, Point and Shoot*). He's written over 250 comics for Marvel, DC, Dark Horse, Valiant, and IDW, and most recently wrote *The Black Hood,* the first comic for Archie's new Dark Circle imprint. Duane has also collaborated with *CSI* creator Anthony E. Zuiker on the bestselling Level 26 series. Duane lives in Philadelphia with his wife and children.

MULHOLLAND BOOKS

You won't be able to put down these Mulholland Books.